Dana Thomas Weber

THE
<u>TALLEST TIMBERS</u>

*A story of finding one's true self in a chaotic and
distracting world.*

Christine – thank you for you're hospitality! It was a pleasure to have met you!

Dana

Holland Press
United States of America

ISBN 978-0-9965498-1-3
Ebook ISBN 978-0-9965498-0-6

This is a work of fiction. Names, characters, businesses, places, events and incidents are either the products of the author's imagination or used in a fictitious manner. Any resemblance to actual persons, living or dead, or actual events is purely coincidental.

Printed in the United States of America on acid-free paper.

Holland Press
www.HollandPress.co

www.DanaThomasWeber.com

To Branden Colby Weber

"be yourself- not your idea of what you think somebody else's idea of yourself should be."

— Henry David Thoreau

CONTENTS

PART THREE : Clarity

PART FOUR : Found

PART ONE : LOST

CHAPTER ONE
A Lost Soul Among Us

SHE HAD CREPT CLOSER to gain a better view of a lifeless body that turned out to be her own. Confusion and shock set in before noticing the other driver fleeing the scene by foot. Swiftly, she followed. Despite a final glance over his shoulder with a battered and bloodied face, he ignored her screams.

Returning to the wreckage, her calls and questions continued to fall on deaf ears and, bewildered, she rambled backward toward the dense evergreens that lined the winding road while the medics and police carried on at a frantic pace. They were seemingly unaware of her presence that night and nothing was the same since.

As she recalled that fateful night, Julia now found shelter among a different patch of hemlocks. They were, in contrast, deeply familiar. On this late August afternoon their soft needles caught the frosty strands of her hair as she gazed blankly toward the single-story white clapboard house with dingy paint and a ragged roof cluttered with moss. The house, once tidy, safe and happy, was now unsettling to her.

Regardless, she had sensed a presence in the dwelling and

returned to investigate. The late afternoon sun cast long shadows around her and she moved deftly among them with electric anticipation as the blue fabric of her dress skimmed the overgrown grass. The changing leaves suggested that colder temperatures would be here soon, but she wasn't concerned. She no longer felt the cold. She was immune to the elements and the forest was her hiding place.

To no avail, the woods presently tried its best to summon her return with its deafening rustling leaves. She continued on with the crooked back porch steps never leaving her sight. This once-plucky adolescent was channeling her former self as she advanced. Finally, the first of the aged wooden steps was below her feet. The sight of the warped floorboards conjured memories of her mother's coffee breaks while she had watched the deer graze. What would she think of her daughter who now found shelter among the descendants of those very same stag and doe?

With all the strength and courage she could muster, she rapped her dainty fist against the wooden edge of the screen door. The clattering sounds echoed into the quiet air. Nothing. She tried again with the outcome much the same. Exhausted and weak, she banged against the rickety door until she sensed the vibrations of footfall. Hope filled her petite frame and she peered through the door glass with her wide green eyes. The kitchen window suddenly darkened before the interior door was harshly opened and a muffled sound came from a strange face outlined with shoulder-length, coarse hair. With a prominent mustache and beard, it was clear this man was not her dad. Who was he? Why was he in her family's house?

Frightened, she fled the dwelling as she willed herself to remain undiscovered. Refuge was swift among the timbers and hope turned to guilt as memories started down the same dizzying path. Leaning back against a sturdy pine, she looked up at the rosy sky through the swaying treetops as she tried to grasp new meaning from the torrid recollections.

She blamed herself for the accident. She should never

have asked her parents to take her to that inconvenient dress shop. It was too expensive by her family's standards, anyway. Over time, desperation to find her family had turned into constant restlessness. She wanted to be at peace. She wondered if her brothers still cared about her.

CHAPTER TWO
Aren't We All a Little Lost?

"LIFE DOESN'T HAVE TO be that hard," the old man grumbled as he patiently peered over his round, tortoise-rimmed glasses. The sweltering heat of the day had caused his spectacles to slide down past the bridge of his long, thin nose.

The impatient woman he addressed appeared to be in her mid-forties. She offered a snide kind of smile with pursed lips and placed her credit card back into her designer bag. Expertly holding her phone between shoulder and ear, she grabbed the brown paper bag from the man's weathered and wrinkled hand while peering down at him with disapproval. Her high heel caught in the soft ground for a second before she straightened her posture and turned to leave the popular Tuesday afternoon farmers market stand.

People watching anywhere in the city never disappointed and a motley crew of individuals had shown up to stroll the lush park. Snippets of personalities provided snapshots of a thousand different ways to live a life.

Lacey Williams witnessed the odd and tense exchange from a few spots back in the line and was not entirely sure of what happened. The mood lifted when the gentleman next in queue stepped forward to pay for his goods. He had smiled at the irritated woman when she departed. She had snarled a string of concerns into her phone. Something to the effect of needing various children picked up from various events, a dog still at doggie day care and a work meeting that would make her late on Thursday. Apparently her car had an appointment, too. Lacey couldn't help but take in the events that unfolded in front of her and quickly disregarded most of it. It was none of her business. Goodness knows she had her own troubles to contend with day in and day out.

Placing three teetering apples on the worn and splintered wooden table, the old man stared at the customer who was more youthful than he. The younger, sandy-haired man fished a few crumpled dollars from his crisp khakis and placed the money on the table as the palm of his suntanned hand playfully slapped the wooden surface. The thud hung in the still and humid air caught beneath the majestic oaks.

"Keep the change, Jimmy. I know you need it," he said in a cocky tone. His tilted smile was playful and eluded to a level of familiarity with the elder. He crossed his arms and waited for the farmer's response.

"Ha. Sammy Boy, I need your lousy change like I need a fly to swat. I suppose you want a bag with this measly purchase? Lord knows how I supported a family with cheapskates like you buying three gosh darn apples from me every week. Some big shot attorney you are, huh?"

The elder's eyes twinkled despite the frown he displayed. In no time both men were laughing like old friends.

"I'll tell you what, Jim. If times are that hard, you keep your precious paper bags. I brought my own this time," the younger man retorted.

"Yeah? Okay then. Be on your way and stop holding up my good customers who actually keep me in business," the old-timer stated as he glanced at Lacey with an old Hollywood smile and a wink.

The handsome regular gave a hearty laugh and a shake of his head before waving the old man off.

"See you next week, Jim," he called out as he left. There was a bounce in his step as he passed Lacey with a flirtatious grin. A sailor's tan highlighted his slightly rugged good looks. Tucking her shoulder-length, auburn hair behind one ear, her cheeks reddened as she returned his glance.

As the farmer leaned his small frame and dry knuckles against the table, he lifted one arm to resituate his glasses with the back of his wrist. He retrieved a handkerchief from his back pocket and straightened up before removing the glasses altogether to wipe the sweat from his face and forehead.

"Hello, young lady. What can I get for you today?" he asked as he cleaned his glasses with the handkerchief before returning the cloth into the back pocket of his blue jeans.

"Hi. Just a half dozen ears of corn, please. Oh, and a cantaloupe and a pint of green beans."

Lacey wondered if she should add something to her order. As ridiculous as it was, she didn't want to be chided for not buying enough. It all looked delicious anyway and she was hungry having not eaten since a bagel with cream cheese that morning.

"A pint of blueberries, too, please?" she added.

"Sure thing! This corn is real good. You can't beat sweet corn in late August. Need butter and salt, though. Always need lots of butter and some salt ..." his voice trailed off as he efficiently snapped open one of his trademark paper bags and began filling her order.

A wisp of grey hair slipped down to his forehead and he once again pushed his misbehaving eyeglasses back into place with his forearm without skipping a beat. In seconds her bag was neatly filled with fresh-from-the-farm produce and he neatly folded the top of the bag closed before presenting it with the 'Miller Farm' logo proudly showing. She silently wondered how many harvests of corn, peaches and blueberries he had seen come and go. He always worked alone at his stand. What did he do in the winter for income? Annapolis is too cold in the winter for fruits and vegetables.

She noticed the edges of the well-used table were rubbed dark and smooth from where his hands now came to rest. His gnarled fingers splayed away from him and a thin gold band adorned his ring finger. His watery, sea green eyes gave her every bit of his attention at that moment.

"You cookin' up a good summer meal tonight for your

family? The cold will be here before you know it. Enjoy this summer food while you can, how 'bout it?"

His question and comment snapped her overworked mind back to the present task at hand and she placed a crisp twenty-dollar bill in front of him as she pulled her purchases toward her.

"Just me, so, this will last the rest of the week. You're right – it's delicious when in season."

She smiled demurely and thanked him as she meekly collected the bit of change he had ready for her and placed it back into her wallet. Snapping the change purse closed and folding the Italian leather wallet, she deposited it into the matching purse before slinging it over her right shoulder. She quickly smoothed her short-sleeved vanilla blouse then did the same for the matching skirt. Bending her knees slightly, she adjusted her tall stature to carefully lift and cradle the full bag in her right arm. He watched her delicate mannerisms with amusement as she prepared to leave his stand.

"Alrighty, then. You have a good evening and if you need some dinner company, you just give me a call," the farmer said gruffly. "The guys today must be more pathetic than I thought if a pretty girl like you is still available."

His easy wink and hearty laugh elicited a chuckle from her. Lacey nodded a good-bye as he started filling another customer's order with the same edgy comments that only a character like he could get away with nowadays.

As her modest heels sounded along the winding concrete sidewalk, she made her way back through the city park and toward the main street where she had parked her car. The robins hopped in the grass and the squirrels flitted here and there. A nearby fountain shot a short stream of water into the air before it cascaded down into a crisp, clear pool. Lacey looked longingly at the tranquil feature and her feet begged to splash around in the cool liquid, unaware that such an action would be frowned upon in this gentile setting.

A quick stop at the organic food chain store for more odds-and-ends and she would be heading back home for the evening. As a real estate agent, she had planned her last appointment of the day to be a showing at the house across from the city park entrance. Once in a while, her well-laid plans worked out and she was now glad to see her gleaming Lexus sedan waiting nearby.

A long day was coming to an end and she had only tender and swollen feet to show for it. Rushing toward the car during a break in oncoming traffic, she clicked the remote to lift the trunk and situated her purchases in no-spill positions. She opened the driver's side door and slid into the car's hot interior. Without so much of a second thought, she had the key in ignition and air-conditioning on full blast. The cold air raised her thick hair away from her neck while pushing the humidity away.

Now that her appointments were done for the day, she twisted her hair up casually with the hair clip she had left in the middle console and glanced down at her BlackBerry that was tucked unusually away from her in the cavernous compartment. Sighing, she reached for it. Her thumb scrolled and clicked the worn roller to read through the notices of five missed calls, three voicemails, six new emails, and a text. Every last correspondence was from a client or colleague.

"Well, that will teach me to leave you for twenty minutes," she silently scolded as she placed the phone in the hands-free cradle.

Finding mind-numbing relief from the blast of unnaturally cold air, Lacey unconsciously stared at a blue minivan parked in front of her while her body tingled from its first moments of quiet respite all day. A suit-clad mother approached the van from the nearby day care building. She balanced the handle of a car seat carrier containing her baby on her left arm and held onto a curious and wanting-to-wander toddler with her free hand while all the while ushering them into the back seat. Lacey looked to her phone to listen to the messages before the stranger could notice her watching for no apparent reason.

The non-urgent messages played and a nearby receipt from

her morning coffee and bagel now found a second life as a note pad. She hastily jotted down the numbers and reminders before deleting the recordings. Her glossy red nails tapped the steering wheel then waved a thank-you to the driver of the BMW who allowed her to pull from her spot and into the stream of oncoming traffic.

Fifteen minutes later, and after dealing with the city's mounting traffic, she was pulling into the nearly full parking lot in front of the organic-themed grocery store. Keeping her phone close this time, she dropped it into her purse and walked confidently toward the main entrance. A stream of customers filed in and out around her. Faces were scrunched as they passed the sun's brilliant, low lying rays and overly tired children occasionally cried out from the carts that were precariously laden with paper and reusable bags adorned with pineapple tops and fresh-cut flowers. Lacey trudged on as she pulled a cart toward her then ventured inside.

The store aisles were crowded and she second-guessed her decision to shop for groceries at the five o'clock hour. Apparently a good portion of the population had the same idea. Excusing herself multiple times, and sometimes even having courtesy bestowed upon her, she reached the dairy section. Greek yogurt, organic skim milk, and eggs were placed in the cart before arriving at the cheese displays.

"What are we looking for today, miss?" the cheese monger pressed as he brushed his hands on his white apron.

"Nothing specific, just browsing," Lacey answered.

"Here, if I might make a suggestion, this Roquefort just came in and is incredible. Just unbelievable."

The knowledgeable lad adjusted his white hat and reached for the selection as he tried to be accommodating to his customers' usual expectations. Lacey glanced at the price after he handed the tiny and wrapped wedge to her for inspection.

"Thanks, but I think I'll keep looking," she answered while trying to sound polite. He was already walking away.

"*The thirty-five bucks a pound is unbelievable, too,*" she thought and walked to the more generic section to pluck a half pound of ordinary Swiss from the shelf.

Behind her she could hear a couple musing loudly over the expensive cheese selection and she glanced their way.

"Babe, we should pick up something nice to accompany that Bordeaux for tonight. I worked too hard today and that bottle is calling me," the male announced loudly to his mate.

"Hmmm. That sounds good," his female companion agreed in a soprano voice as she adjusted her blinding diamond ring.

The cheese monger returned to rave about the Roquefort and easily won them over. They were baby-faced and in their twenties.

"*So much for creating a financial nest egg,*" Lacey silently mused before heading to grab a few bagels on her way to checkout.

Using the cart for support to take pressure off her pinched toes, she approached the front of the store, all the while feeling her mood deteriorating in spite of herself. Her abused feet filled half of her mind and the atrociously long lines filled the other half. She thought about leaving her cart and walking out. That was not her nature, though, and she really had nothing against the store or her own purchases. All the same, her temperament was unusually foul and the people around her were simply making it worse. Their conversations rang out obnoxiously.

"Is this gluten-free? I thought it said gluten-free? The label is not clear. You should bring that up at your next meeting," a morbidly obese woman barked at the poor cashier.

"Have you tried the vegan chocolate cake from that new bakery on Capitol Street? We bought it for Josie's birthday and she lu-*ov*ed it," a pale, skinny thirty-something in gym clothes raved to her friend. "Worth every penny of the seventy-dollar price tag, I must say. You only turn two once, right?" Her laughed was piercing.

"Do you mind using six rubber bands on that container? Three one-way and three the other way should keep it closed, I think. Here, let me. Like this," a short guy with wire-rimmed glasses instructed as he reached to take the plastic container of dinner he had assembled from the hot buffet.

Lacey huffed a sound of exasperation as she looked around to see if she was the only one taking note of these outward displays of unbalanced personalities. A few others in line were patiently flipping through magazines or staring ahead with calm expressions plastered on their faces. She made a mental note that she should learn from their more composed examples and began to place her groceries onto the conveyor belt. In the end, the cashier announced a total charge that, like always, was more than expected. Anymore, this was true of any shopping experience regardless of the establishment. Lacey swallowed her surprise as she always did and paid the bill before moving on with her life amidst the masses.

Arriving home by six, she was grateful to pull into the gravel parking spot at the duplex she owned on Cathedral Street with the thought of unwinding the rest of the evening. The tree-lined street was always welcoming and her lovingly renovated property instantly reminded her what her strong work ethic, financial discipline and dedication to her clients had earned her at thirty-five years young. Juggling the grocery bags, she remotely locked the vehicle with her work tote and purse hanging from her forearm. The car assured her it was secure by sounding the obligatory beeps and she tenderly stepped up to the porch. She closed the double doors to the vestibule behind her and entered the foyer as she immediately kicked off her polished black heels. Soon, the creamy interior of the foyer enveloped her and the dark wood staircase gleamed.

She walked gingerly along the narrow Victorian hallway as she carried her bags into the remodeled kitchen. As she started to boil water for dinner and put groceries away in the cherry cabinets and stainless steel refrigerator, her phone buzzed from where it lie on the sandy granite countertop. The oversized floor tiles felt cool and refreshing to her bare feet and her grumbling stomach reminded her that a home cooked meal was what she needed to prioritize at the moment. She resisted the urge to reach for the beckoning smartphone. With no appointments scheduled for the next day, she reasoned she would be able to attend to any matters then. There was no need to let work interrupt a quiet evening at home after a brutally long day on the run. She clicked on the Lena Horne Pandora station on her laptop to get her mind off work, poured a glass of icy cold Sauvignon Blanc to try even harder to get her mind off work, and started to husk the corn to prepare it for the pot. The action reminded her of preparing dinner with her grandmother years ago. Mouth watering, she tasted the imaginary sweet corn they used to pick from the garden and how it dripped with real melted butter. She continued to focus on the menial task at hand in an attempt to resist the call of the smartphone that was ringing again. Her attempts were futile and she was reaching for it within seconds after cleaning only two ears of corn.

Two minutes later, she was calling a first-time buyer back to alleviate his irrational fears about a few minor property inspection findings. Fifteen minutes later she was moving on to quickly address some questions posed in recently received emails. Before she moved on to the texted request to show one of her listings, she was mindlessly eating from a box of Wheat Thins she had grabbed from a nearby cupboard. She had abandoned any thought of preparing a home cooked meal while she reviewed a troubling appraisal that threatened to derail an upcoming closing. She turned off the stove and reached for the block of Swiss cheese as she topped off her glass of wine.

"Life doesn't have to be that hard." The farmer's no-nonsense words entered Lacey's thoughts.

The words were full of optimistic hope. While they may very well be true, Lacey Williams struggled more and more with finding her own form of contentment.

CHAPTER THREE
Partners In Grind

THE ALARM CLOCK SOUNDED its usual six o'clock morning wake-up. Lacey uncharacteristically hit snooze more than once. Lying in bed not wanting to face the day, she decided she would entice herself with a sweet espresso concoction and a bagel from City Dock Coffee after a morning run. Her files were waiting for her at the office and she had a list of tasks a mile long. Still, dark skies and pelting rain on windowpanes begged her to sleep in. How nice it would be to turn on some mindless television and waste the day away, she thought as if that was something she would ever consider doing.

Lacey jumped out of bed before she could entertain that appealing thought and dressed for a rainy morning jog. Descending the stairway and reaching the front door, her mind immediately began to run through the tasks on deck for the day as she stepped out onto the front porch. She started a pre-run stretch to delay the cold rain shower that waited for her. Upcoming closings, scheduling conflicts, nervous buyers and sellers, and mortgage hassles were just a few of the everyday issues she needed to cater to in order to find continued success in the world of real estate. Lost in these thoughts, Lacey didn't notice her tenant sitting on the adjacent porch.

"Don't even tell me you are going out in this pea soup of a mess." Bryce Gathers called out over the rain to her friend and landlord.

"Hi, Bryce. I most certainly am. How long are you home for?"

Lacey walked over to the low wall that divided the old porches.

"Two weeks starting today. That running outfit is way too cute to get wet. Get over here for some coffee and proper porch talk. I'll grab another cuppa for ya," the always-energetic flight attendant insisted.

"I really need to …" Lacey started. Bryce was already inside her half of the stately property and within seconds she was back with a steaming cup of coffee made exactly the way Lacey liked it. Lacey stepped over the wall to join her neighbor.

"Ah-huh. I knew you couldn't resist. You need a break. Sit," Bryce ordered while moving her over-sized wicker chair to face the empty one in the set.

Taking a seat on the cushion accented with a pastel herringbone design, Lacey sank down into the comfortable chair and took in the caffeinated, rainy morning aroma prior to indulging in a hot sip.

"How do you know I need a break, anyway? Mmm, this coffee is excellent. What is it?"

"Girl, you always need a break. I never see you without talking in that damn phone. The coffee's authentic Jamaican Blue Mountain. I'm hooked."

"I can see why. My eyes are open now. Thanks. So, what's new with you?" Lacey got comfy and cradled the steaming cup as she waited for her friend and neighbor to fill her in on her exciting life.

"Well, I got home yesterday around three after a marathon of flights and crashed immediately. Woke up at four this morning and figured I might as well come out here and enjoy this soothing rain. I think my sleep pattern will get back in check right about the time I start back to work, you know?"

"I bet. What fantastic destinations did you travel to and what interesting people did you meet?"

"Montego Bay, hence the coffee selection. I met a very sweet British gent there during some rare downtime, too. I'll save that story for cocktail hour, though."

Lacey laughed at Bryce's hint of a juicy story.

"I can't wait to hear that one," she said as she took a sip of coffee.

"How 'bout you? What've you been up to while I've been gone?"

"Not much," Lacey shrugged and tilted her head and her long ponytail swayed.

Bryce looked at her with one perfectly plucked eyebrow raised. Her black bob of a haircut was stylish and presentable even at this early hour and was in contrast to the pink and blue striped pajama bottoms, stretched grey NAVY sweatshirt and fuzzy pink slippers she donned.

"What?" Lacey asked dryly.

"What did we talk about before I left?"

"Less work and more fun."

"Right. And?"

"I failed to accomplish that, " Lacey said with a wince and a bite of her lower lip as she waited to be berated.

"Lacey, I'm serious. I'm all for working hard, but really. I'll hold my tongue. It's early," Bryce started before giving a stern look and returning to her coffee.

"Thanks for that. I know. It'll slow down soon, though. I can't just ignore the business that's there for me. I won't have any money in January and February if I slack off in the spring and fall."

"It's not fall yet and if I know you, you have plenty of money in the bank. Regardless, these people can wait a few hours for a call back in most cases. If not, let them go."

"It's just the nature of the job and if I slack off, there's another agent to take my place. I am getting a little tired of the pace. I'll admit it."

"Well, I just worry about you. You shouldn't be alone with your work, or just your clients, so much. It's not healthy." Bryce stated kindly with a smile to let Lacey know she had only the best of intentions.

"I'm not alone. I have you!" Lacey stated enthusiastically and sarcastically at the same time. Bryce choosing to move into the other half of the duplex had been the best thing to happen to Lacey since she bought and renovated the run-down property ten years ago. Not only did Bryce turn out to be a reliable and respectable tenant, she had turned into one of Lacey's closest confidants. They were similar in age and their personalities complimented one another. Lacey adored Bryce's spirit and sense of humor about life.

"Yep, you got me alright," Bryce laughed. "Lucky you! And I'm not giving up on you, dear. I enjoy your company too much to let you become someone you're not. Anyway, how's about a little wine and cheese on the deck this evening so long as this rain lets up? Think you'll be able to make a little bit of time for little 'ol me?"

"I wish. I have to take some new buyers out tonight. If you're up for a nightcap, I'll join you when I get back?"

"As long as I don't pass out from exhaustion. I'll try for a nap today to help me rally."

"So, then," Lacey exclaimed as she sat her empty cup on the table and stood to leave. "Thanks again for the coffee and I'm glad you'll be home for a while. I think I'm going to fit that quick run in before I head to the office."

"Good for you. Hope to see you later and be safe out there today."

"Will do.

Bounding down the steps, Lacey found the chilled droplets invigorating. She dodged the uneven bumps in the century-old brick sidewalk and splashed in a few puddles just for the fun of it. The misty air smelled of salty seawater as she ran past the moored sailboats that applauded her efforts with clanging riggings. A few sea gulls undeterred by the rain coasted by and glided to their respective perches. She continued on while her normally racing mind focused only on her steps. Constantly in motion, two miles were efficiently covered. Soaking wet, she rounded the corner to arrive back on Cathedral Street with only a hot shower in mind and a sense of accomplishment. She would still be in her office by nine.

The small real estate office was housed in an old brick row home on West Street. The original shutters were painted glossy black and held back by decorative iron bars and the stone steps leading to the front door were trodden in the centers from a hundred years of shoes. Treading on these same steps with bright red pumps, Lacey reached the entrance and pushed open the swollen wooden door.

The slash and hum of the remote office printer and fax provided evidence of those hard at work already in the sterile atmosphere comprised of ink, paper, and electric office machinery.

"Oh, hey Lacey. I thought you might be my nine o'clock appointment showing up early," the middle-aged woman said from her seat at the reception desk.

"Good Morning, Jane. No, just me," Lacey greeted as she walked over to the coat closet to stash her wet umbrella out of the way. "Good luck with your appointment," she cheerfully called as she ambled back towards the open space workroom filled with fifteen cubicle-style desks. At one point the two rooms that had been joined together to make this work area would have been a family's living and dining room and Lacey was constantly struck by the notion of what the original homeowners would think of the way their private living space was now being used. That exact thought crossed her mind with the sight of the fireplace mantle behind her desk. Flanked by framed publicity clippings, it was no longer a cozy source of family gatherings with its dry-walled hearth and real estate reference books positioned atop

Placing her work tote on her desk, she pulled out her laptop and phone and, along with a few manila files from her desk drawer, placed everything on her neat workspace while stashing the red leather bag under her cubicle-space desk. Engaging the thin, silver MacBook Air, she heard the synthesizer-like chime that let her know her partner in the everyday grind was powering on. Never to waste any time, she leaned back in her office chair and started to scroll through her BlackBerry. Soon however, her train of thought was broken by the sound of her colleague, Connie.

"Well you're here early. I haven't seen you here in ages. Look at that beautiful blue blouse. You are always dressed so nice," Connie said in her raspy smoker's voice with a tone that wasn't as complimentary as the words implied. Connie was a staple in the office, although, she never seemed to produce much in the way of sales.

"Hi, Connie. Well, this business does require you to be out of the office occasionally. How are you?"

Lacey chose to leave out the fact that when she did come in, she tended to show up early in the morning or late in the evening when there weren't a lot of, well, distractions.

"Oh, fine. People are crazy aren't they?"

Lacey nodded her agreement in more ways than one. Connie continued without pause.

"I have three doozies of deals and they are all falling apart. I have the buyers and none of them are being reasonable. I feel so bad for the sellers. I just hope they close. I need the money. This market is horrible."

Lacey nodded again in a weak attempt to show sympathy. This year has been her personal best and the market, in her opinion, was strong. She glanced back to her phone to feign interest in something imaginary. Connie wasn't getting the hint and continued on her miserable rant.

"I mean, these buyers and sellers today are nuts, aren't they? Too much HGTV- watching and Google makes them all experts. Don't even get me started on the banks," Connie said with an exasperated sigh as she waved hello to a fellow incoming agent. He politely smiled and made a beeline for his desk with a knowing glance to Lacey whose normally patient demeanor was eroding more and more by the day. She began to click away at her laptop as she answered a mortgage officer's email. Looking up and seeing that Connie was not heading back to her desk anytime soon, Lacey had no choice but to engage her.

"Maybe you just need to have a sincere talk with the buyers. It might help to alleviate any irrational fears."

"Who knows? They don't listen to me," Connie said and changed the subject. It was obvious she just wanted to complain.

"Yeah? Well, good luck. I hope they close."

Lacey gave a pleading glance to the broker-in-charge that ran the boutique office and who was now walking their way.

"Lacey! Connie! How are we doing on this rainy morning?"

Richard Lyndhurst had been in the Annapolis real estate scene as long as anyone could remember. A robust salesman who lived alone and was married to his career, he had seen it all, for sure. He was always pleasant to be around and Lacey enjoyed working in his office. The energy he exuded was contagious.

"Nice to see you, Lacey. You ended August with some incredible numbers. It's been an incredible year for you, for that matter. Everything going well?" he exclaimed more than questioned as he looked over the faxes that had come in overnight on the printer near Lacey's desk.

"Hi, Rich. Thanks. Yes, all is well for the moment."

" 'For the moment' is right. Hope everything continues to go smoothly. Let me know if you hit any bumps in the road you need a hand with."

"I certainly will," Lacey agreed, as she looked down at her laptop in another attempt to dissuade any further interaction with Connie who was, as always, full of doom and gloom. Connie turned her attention to the business owner.

"Good morning, Richard," she called out as she moved on to her next victim. "I really need to talk to you. I have these buyers …"

The dapper and portly broker looked up at Connie and gave a wave for her to follow him to his office where they could discuss her issues of the day. In response, she exclaimed the need for a quick smoke break first. Lacey could hear the amusement in his voice when he declared he would be waiting.

Finally undisturbed, Lacey took a mind cleansing breath and got to work. She glanced at the time on her laptop. A good portion of the morning was gone and she hadn't accomplished a thing other than a little conversation with Bryce and a run. Hungry emptiness reminded her she had even failed to honor her breakfast treat promise. Sitting up straight to stretch her tense back and neck muscles, she read her next email. Something about paying a monthly fee for some service she did not need. Delete.

Lacey worked without interruption for the next few hours and quickly made up for any lost time. She was efficient to a fault and had a knack for prioritization and perfect timing. Necessary settlement paperwork was emailed to attorneys and calls were returned to loan officers. She emailed listings worth consideration to a handful of buyers and provided showing updates to sellers. She extensively worked the files along until each had been drained of needed attention.

"*Lunchtime,*" she thought.

It was a little after one and she had covered most of the items on her to-do list on her calendar. It felt good to have the nagging and time-sensitive chores off her mind. She decided it was a good time to break for lunch and maybe work from home until her evening appointments. Everything was under control and she was even a little ahead of the curve on all of her transactions. It was a rare day when no unexpected problems arose. She had been hunched over her laptop and phone for hours and now, her eyes were tired. Looking out the window across the room, she zoned out for a few seconds and let her mind and eyes take a break. The clouds had been swept away and the day had tuned sunny. She felt the need to get outside and enjoy the rest of her day.

A shiny, black Volvo SUV pulled into view in the adjacent parking lot. A tall, slender man in his forties stepped out of the drivers' seat wearing sunglasses to shield his eyes from the dazzling light reflecting from paperwork he reviewed in motion. As he walked toward the sidewalk, he was all business, although, his pressed blue and white gingham shirt suggested he had personality. She noticed he was strikingly handsome as well as familiar. As he walked out of view, Lacey came back to reality and started to pack up her belongings.

CHAPTER FOUR

We Meet Again

THE FIRST DAY OF September proved to be a perfect afternoon for a late outdoor lunch now that the rain clouds had passed. Lacey sipped a Pellegrino with lime from her table at the nautical-themed restaurant along the Annapolis City Dock and watched the sun reflect upon the agitated water. The gulls were out in force after the stormy morning and their shrill chatter blended with the sounds of the thuds of the boat hulls bobbing in their tethered stations in port. Placing her bubbly glass of mineral water back onto the restaurant coaster, she picked up the laminated menu.

A waiter arrived at her table and seemed carefree and happy now that the lunch rush was over and his pockets were full of tips. He and the other servers had been jovial together and were resetting the tables when Lacey arrived. She had taken a seat among the straggling lunch diners who were soaking in every last bit of summer.

"Have we decided?" he inquired as he took a playful long step toward Lacey's table before standing straight with clasped hands placed in front of his apron.

"I think I have," she slowly said while taking one last look at the menu. "Crab cake salad and a side of sweet potato fries?"

"No problem and good choice. May I bring you another mineral water with your meal?"

"Yes, please, and how about that warm apple cider

special?" Lacey handed over the menu with an appreciative smile.

Looking back out to the water, she eased into the curved iron seatback and ingested the salty sea breeze while taking in her surroundings. She noticed someone. Standing on the rocking and rolling docks below stood the man in the gingham shirt. Again, there was something familiar about him and Lacey leaned forward to get a better look. He glanced up in her direction and she sheepishly looked away before pulling a Realtor magazine from her tote.

Moments later her waiter brought out the mug of cider complete with two cinnamon sticks and updated her that her lunch would be out in a few minutes. She picked up the warmed mug with both hands and brought it to her lips.

The aroma recalled autumn and her childhood spent trekking through the fallen leaves at her grandparents' cabin in upstate New York. She had not visited the rustic property in fifteen years or so, however, could still feel the iron front door handle in her palm and sensed the mustiness the woodsy cottage inherently possessed. She thought about those days and how free she was. Roaming those forested eight acres represented her most cherished childhood memories. A piney perfume infused with moss, bark and fern had been ever present and somehow remained with her after all these years. The times had been simple and comfortable and for a spell she was a ten year-old forest explorer rather than the grown-up, over-worked version of that girl.

"How do I know you?" A voice shot out from in front of her.

"Excuse me? Um, hi," Lacey cleared her throat and looked up at the man from the docks now standing in front of her.

He laughed before continuing.

"Sorry. Didn't mean to startle you. You just look so familiar. I didn't want to be rude by not saying hello. How do we know each other?" he softly asked.

Lacey leaned in toward her table and set her mug in front of her. Her thick hair was wavy from the rainy morning and the locks fell past her shoulder as she pulled her sunglasses up onto her head.

"Uh, I'm not sure. You look familiar to me, too," she offered with a casual grin.

"Hmm," he crossed his tan arms in front of his chest and stood straight with feet apart as he looked directly at her for a moment.

Lacey felt her face redden as she tried to come up with an answer.

"Well, it'll come to me of it the second I sit down. I'm Sam. Nice to meet you." He extended his right arm in greeting.

"Lacey," she answered as she stood slightly to return his firm but friendly handshake. It lasted a few seconds longer than it should have. Releasing his hold, he pushed away an errant piece of summer-highlighted hair and crossed his arms again while keeping a wide stance. He appeared to be preparing to interrogate her as he tried to solve the nagging question in his mind. He had a youthful surfer quality to him reminiscent of the 1950's film genre that made young girls swoon. A strong jawline and slightly crooked nose gave his looks a little more depth and Lacey was intrigued. His confidence was pleasing and there was an aura of self-made success about this man that any woman would find alluring thanks to visceral human nature.

"Lacey," Sam repeated with a smile as he mulled the situation over. They shared a moment in silence before he began to retreat backward. "Well, Lacey," he warned with a pointed finger in her direction, "I will remember where I know you from and I do hope to see you real soon."

With a wink and a dashing smile, Sam pivoted on the heel of a polished loafer and walked toward a table already circled by supposed friends. The waiter arrived and placed her lunch before her with a porcelain thump while Lacey caught a glimpse of Sam. He pulled out a chair next to a longhaired blonde who was sipping a glass of white wine. She offered her cheek as he placed his hand to her back with a quick kiss then greeted the other men with friendly handshakes. They seemed like a jovial group and Lacey felt lonely for the first time in long time. She placed her napkin across her lap and took a bite of a seasoned French fry.

Watching the little group off in the distance reminded her of how isolated she had become. She had always made friends easily and enjoyed the company of others despite her independent spirit.

Ever since graduating from college, however, she focused on career goals and making sure she saved enough money to get through the slow times of the year. Bryce was right. She did have more than enough money in the bank and most of her material assets were either paid off or had considerable equity. Having been raised by a Navy Officer, she was no stranger to self-discipline and it had served her well in many ways. The roots of her career established quickly, but it now branched into every corner of her existence. The long-term friendships she did retain were on life support via emails, Facebook and occasional token dinners. The realization was unnerving before the buzzing of her vibrating phone reminded her why she never had time to feel lonely.

"Hello, this is Lacey," she greeted as she brushed the crumbs from her fingertips with the dark green linen napkin.

"Hi, Lacey. Brenda here. Slight problem to discuss with you if you have a second," the loan officer stated briskly.

Lacey's nerves perked up and her fingers tingled as she held the phone to her ear. Brenda Timmons was fearlessly handling the loan of Lacey's most no-nonsense and powerful clients, Stuart Benson. An attorney with Benson and Benson, he was the son of the firm's founding partner and the second half of the office nameplate. Plainly put, he would be infuriated if his closing, scheduled in exactly fourteen days, should be delayed. Richard Lyndhurst had referred him to Lacey and she had excitedly accepted the referral knowing the affluent price point the client would come with. It had quickly become apparent that Richard was not up to the task of dealing with the rich and spoiled son of Mr. Stuart Benson and quietly handed him off to her with the excuse that he would be out of town too often this summer to provide the top-notch service Stuart deserved.

Now, Lacey searched deep inside for the courage to competently deal with the matter at hand as she inquired on the update.

"Okay. So, underwriting has red flagged something on this transaction on their end and I'm working on finding out what we need to do to make this problem go away. It looks like the condo association of the building Stuart is buying into is currently involved in a lawsuit that no one was made aware of. Did you know about this litigation?"

"No. No, I had no knowledge of a lawsuit. That building is one of the most sought-after buildings in Annapolis. Condos there sell in minutes when they do come on the market."

"Well, according to underwriting, the association recently filed suit against the contractor who constructed the building. While that is bad enough in underwritings' eye, the fact that the lawsuit involves a faulty structural beam is even more alarming to them and they are threatening to deny the loan."

Lacey felt her blood run cold and she pushed her plate away from her as she sank back in her seat. She was already wondering how she would break this news to Stuart who would see any problems with the deal as being her fault.

Brenda continued in her no-nonsense and to-the-point tone a professional like Lacey appreciated.

"It's not the first time I have seen something like this and I'm thinking we'll be able to work through it, but I expect there to be a delay with this closing. I wanted to let you know immediately."

"Alright. So, what do you need from me? I cannot let this deal fall apart and Stuart is not a reasonable person to deal with. Saying he will be angry would be quite an understatement."

Lacey was short of breath just starting to think about how this scenario might continue to play out.

"I understand. I would suggest giving me twenty-four

hours to sift through the facts and to make some calls before you talk to Stuart. You know how these things go. Maybe we'll get lucky and it will work itself out by tomorrow and there may be no need to alarm him. For now, here is what I need from you ..."

Grabbing a pen from her tote, she began to jot down the loan officer's instructions on the magazine now lying closed upon the table.

"Alright," Lacey quietly repeated. "I am getting in touch with the homeowner's association right now. I'll call you back as soon as I know more."

"Perfect. Talk to you then."

Brenda disconnected the call and Lacey felt the blood drain from her face. It pained her when any deal went south, but it was much better to work with clients who worked with her on a solution rather than against her, as Stuart Benson surely would.

Motioning for the waiter, Lacey gathered her materials to head to the condominium building's main office. She had every intention of righting this wayward deal before having to make a dreaded call to Stuart.

She met the waiter halfway and reviewed her bill. Handing him enough to cover the tab with a generous tip and receiving a to-go box in return, she returned to her table to box up her mostly uneaten meal. As she turned to leave in a rush, she ran straight into Sam.

"Whoa," he steadied her with his hands on her arms and she looked up into his surprised face. Situating her sliding work tote handle back up onto her shoulder and gently flipping her hair back out of her face, she returned a surprised expression before stepping back. His arms slid back to his sides.

"I'm sorry, Lacey. I didn't expect you to turn to leave so quickly. I was just coming by to tell you I figured out how I know you. You were at the farmers market on Tuesday, right? In line at Farmer Jim's?"

Sam's upbeat spirit was still in tact, but he could see that

Lacey was now distracted.

"Farmer Jim? Um, yes. Okay. He is the older man that has had a stand there for years, right?" Lacey stammered. She was making an effort to focus on Sam rather than the upsetting news she had just received. She collected herself and tried to relax. She liked what little interaction she had had with Sam so far and didn't want to come off as rude.

"That's the man. He is a character. Always giving me a hard time. Anyway, sorry to hold you up. I just realized you were in line behind me that day and had to tell you I solved the mystery," he declared while gesturing with open arms. His crooked smile was endearing. He pulled his Ray Bans up onto his head and revealed the deepest blue eyes. Situating his hands on his hips, he took another look at her. She just knew he could tell she was preoccupied and she instantly felt remorseful about that for some reason. She knew nothing about this guy except that he had a tendency to purchase a few apples at the farmer's market on a regular basis. There was no denying there was some deeper connection between them, though.

"Oh, yeah. I remember now. You bought apples," she recalled as her face warmed to the same shade of the fruit she mentioned. Her dim attempt at conversation sounded hollow to her and she was slightly embarrassed to admit she had noticed him as well.

Sam handed her the Realtor magazine she left on the table.

"Looks like you were about to forget this."

She took the trade publication from him and smiled wearily before tucking it away.

"You enjoy the rest of your day, Lacey, you hear?" he added thoughtfully.

She agreed with a nod and a wave and started to head toward the steps that led back down to the street where she had parked. Sam was still standing where she had left him when she turned a glance in his direction. He turned his gaze from the water to her when he heard her voice.

"Maybe I'll see you next week?" she called out.

"I'm quite sure I'll need to refresh my apple supply by then."

Lost in his charming aura, Lacey forgot her troubles for a second or two and the feeling was blissful. She was thankful for the bright spot that was brought on by Sam. She waved a quick goodbye and dashed down the steps to the sidewalk leading to her car. As she started for the Crestwood Condominium building, the work stress of the day certainly occupied her mind, but she was acutely and pleasantly aware of the spark left by Sam.

CHAPTER FIVE
Samuel Francis Hinkley

"ALRIGHT. ALL RIGHT. Trust me. I really do have this under control. I understand your concerns. Give me twenty-four hours to talk to the rest of them."

Slamming the phone down after an obligatory good-bye, Samuel Francis Hinkley leaned back in his high-back office chair and clasped his hands atop his head. Palms to face, he yelled a little muted frustration into his hands. Work was not going so well today. Leaning forward and collecting himself, he called for one of his better young lawyers via the intercom system.

"You rang," Brian answered wryly as he opened the frosted glass door of Sam's office. His crisp white shirt showed a flash of paisley on the inside cuffs and collar as he peeked in to see what the partner-in-charge needed. Always ready to oblige, he looked to move up quickly within the ranks of the fledgling firm.

"Yeah. Sorry about that. Didn't want to get caught up in the water cooler talk with the Chatty Cathy's," Sam explained as he leaned back again and propped his heels on the edge of the mahogany executive desk. "Have a second?" he added while motioning to one of the leather occasional chairs.

"Sure. Good decision. Brad is giving a dissertation to Allison and Rob on how reality television is rotting the minds of the young and asking from input from anyone in earshot," Brian said as he made himself comfortable and pulled the chair in closer to the desk.

"Hmmm. Well, can't say I disagree with him, but my own reality is rotting my mind at the moment. On that note, Philip Ellis just called and reamed me out again. There is no pleasing that guy. He seems to think another firm will meet his demands better. Part of me wants to release him so that he can see about that. The sensible side of me knows we have too many billable hours wrapped up in his case. In addition, we need that win and I know we will come out on top on this one. He may own the largest construction firm in the city and have a black heart, but I do believe he is hands-on with every job and I find it hard to believe he was negligent. He cares too much about his business," Sam rambled.

"Agreed. A win in this case would earn us some fantastic exposure. We'd be competing in the big leagues then," Brian interjected.

Bringing his fingertips together, Sam nodded and rested his chin on his index fingers. Focusing his attention back on his most eager-to-succeed colleague, he continued.

"That's right. That's right. What I need from you is to hit the streets today with these leads," Sam slid a piece of yellow legal pad paper across the desk. Various names and addresses were scrawled on it.

Brian quickly leaned forward to catch the yellow sheet as it slipped off of the edge of the desk.

"That paper has a partial list of subcontractors that worked on the job in this case and some who have worked with Ellis Contracting in the past. Get a feel for them and build rapport. Don't scare them off. We'll be calling some up as witnesses. Let me know which ones we should focus on to help our case and which seem particularly eager to help us. We need to get to them before the other side tries to manhandle or bribe them or whatever those slime balls do to win case after case."

"Got it. I'll head out now."

Brian rushed out. Sam glanced at his smartphone to see who had been calling. Tara. Three missed calls in ten minutes. Her flurry of calls suggested something urgent. Despite wanting to distance himself from her, he called her back. She answered on the second ring.

"Hello, handsome."

"Hi, Tara. What's up?" he asked hastily.

"Well, don't sound so eager," she sighed. "I'll be all alone tonight. Care to keep me company?"

Sam fiddled with a paperclip on his desk and tried to think of what to say.

"What's Len up to?"

"Guys night at the club."

"Why don't you call up the other wives?" he suggested trying to sound impartial.

"You don't want to see me?" she cooed.

"You know I do. This is just, well, kind of sleazy. You and I both know it. I'm working a big case anyway and will be tied up with it for awhile."

"Why don't you let me take your mind off of it for awhile?"

Sam bit his lip for strength.

"You're killing me, you know. C'mon, Tara. I'm trying to do the right thing here. For you, for me and for Len. I'm done. Let's just pretend it never happened?"

To his surprise, she caved.

"I've been thinking the same," she sighed. "You're right. Okay. Never happened. Still friends?"

"Still friends," he said cautiously while wondering what her idea of a friend was.

Hanging up the phone, he wondered what the hell was wrong with him until his thoughts turned to Lacey Williams once more. He had a million things to do at that moment, but all he wanted was to see her. He felt a connection when they spoke briefly at lunch the week before. The Realtor magazine gave away her profession and he had been able to locate her online easily.

Turned out her office was a block from his law firm and he had made it a point to walk past her building every chance he got. There was no denying she was creeping into his thoughts more and more and he needed to do something about that. Tomorrow was Tuesday and he held out hope he would see her at Farmer Jim's stand.

"Okay. Back to work slacker," Sam muttered to himself. Picking up the Ellis file, he started to review his notes and think about the best approach.

Ellis Contracting had a firm grip on most of the big jobs around the city. It was a third generation company. Philip didn't have the soul of his father or grandfather, but he knew what he was doing and didn't fool around. He had a reputation for going the extra mile and getting the job done right the first time. This was until the Crestwood Condo fiasco. One small crack in a big-time cement beam combined with conflicting structural engineer reports, and the integrity of his eighty-four year old company was comprised. Sam didn't blame Philip for being on edge. Sam had the case under control, however, and was starting to Sam's little firm had the opportunity to win the biggest case yet and the pressure was enormous.

While Brian was out talking to the long list of subcontractors, Sam had his own list of people he needed to check out. At the top of that list was Lacey Williams, that is, if his usual walk past Lyndhurst Realty ended in a chance encounter.

Pulling his grey suit jacket from the antique mahogany coat hanger next to his office door, he dropped his keys into the jacket pocket and flopped the jacket over his forearm. Taking his slim briefcase from the floor, he walked into the main work area of the office.

"You all have a fine evening and keep doing what you're doing," he called out to the two paralegals typing away on his way out the front door. Sam waved a signature farewell into the air in response to their unison send-offs and hopped down the front steps onto the sidewalk.

He slowed his pace as he walked past Lyndhurst Real Estate and even more as he strolled into the parking lot. Pulling the keys from his pocket, he took his time getting into the SUV. Casually scanning the vicinity, it was clear Lacey was nowhere in sight. He started the car and pulled out of the lot. Making a left and heading off to the first address on his list, he felt the disappointment set in. He wondered what it was about this woman that interested him so. Other than the development of his career, nothing had piqued his interest this way. Not that he had a problem with that. To focus on his livelihood without distractions was the manner in which Sam Hinkley preferred to live his life.

CHAPTER SIX
Something Stronger

SITTING AT HER DESK on hold, Lacey fidgeted with a paperclip until it broke in two. Time slowed to a crawl while waiting for her call to be answered by Stuart Benson and the five minutes that had passed so far felt more like five hours. She looked out the window to calm her nerves while drinking lukewarm coffee out of habit. Stuart would not be amiable with this.

"Stuart Benson."

Lacey was caught mid-sip and choked from the interruption.

"Hello? Who is this?" he demanded.

Finally able to take a breath, she greeted him before going into a planned version of her side of the dialogue.

"Hi, Stuart. Lacey Williams."

Silence.

"I am calling to give you an update if you have a few minutes," she continued.

After a couple seconds he replied curtly, "Well, go ahead."

"I've received a call from your loan officer. Underwriting has flagged this file and there will most likely be a delay in your closing."

Lacey could hear his irritated sigh. She went on to briefly explain the areas of concern.

"People move into that building everyday. I have a colleague who settled on a unit there last week. Why is this a problem, Lacey? I need to close on time and you to make that happen. It's your job. Start doing it."

His ignorant and rude words represented a punch to the gut. She felt her blood pressure rise.

"From the lender's standpoint, they simply need to protect their investment and verify this issue is being handled properly. I am frustrated by this as well and I assure you I am doing everything I can in order to close on time or as soon as …"

"On time is the only acceptable answer," Stuart interjected. "So what exactly are you doing about this foolishness?"

She was ready to answer that question point blank and went on to do so. Once Lacey reported the events aloud and ticked off what she had done to expedite manners, it was clear to her that she certainly did nothing wrong and, if anything, is the reason they would most likely settle the deal near their scheduled date. Stuart would not be satisfied, though.

"Email a copy of that letter to me for my file," he asserted. "We are to close next Friday. I see no reason why that can't happen."

"In this case, there will probably be a delay so that the checks and balances process can occur. That is just how the mortgage industry operates. The good news is, I fully expect this loan to close and we will only need to push the closing back by a week. I will keep the heat on, but I want to be up front with you and set realistic expectations."

"Well, maybe I need to talk to some other lenders."

He was intelligent enough to know that proposal made no sense. She felt the urge to put him in his place and was tired of working for unreasonable clients like Stuart Benson who showed little to no respect for others.

"Regardless of the lender you work with, they are all going to ask for the same thing. You would have the same concerns if you were lending a considerable amount of money to someone for personal use. Many of the more recent closings in this building have been closed as cash deals, though. That would solve the problem of a closing delay. Would you prefer to pay cash?" Lacey asked sweetly.

"Uh…no. I would prefer to keep my money invested where it is at the time being. Keep me posted on this matter, Lacey."

"That's what I thought," Lacey mused. They closed the call on more polite terms and Lacey felt a sense of relief that the conversation was over. There was still a slight chance that the underwriters could come back with a loan denial, however, that was very unlikely. Lacey chose to not worry about that scenario for now.

Placing the office phone back on its cradle, Lacey sat back in her chair and stretched her arms to the ceiling. She needed some fresh air and was worn out from a long day under florescent lights. Looking out the window at the trees bordering the parking lot, a sight caught her eye and, to her surprise, gave her spirits a little jolt.

Sam. She thought it strange that their paths kept crossing. He was a sight for sore eyes and she found herself watching his every move. His sandy hair was tousled from the early autumnal breezes and he seemed a little preoccupied. He was squinting in the afternoon sun and glancing back to the sidewalk as he reached into his suit jacket for his keys

Without hesitation, she gave hasty goodbyes to her officemates and rushed out the front door. She felt like a schoolgirl.

Calmly, she walked out onto the sidewalk only to see the taillights of Sam's car. A missed opportunity, for sure, but the farmers market would be tomorrow and she planned on arriving at the same time as last week with hopes of seeing her new friend. A premature thought entered her mind when she realized how be nice it would be to have a companion to share her less than stellar days with. Once again, it became painfully obvious that she had isolated herself with work being the reason, or excuse.

As she strode the short distance to her own car, she thought about this. Her days were full of tiny battles from morning till night. She rarely slept without waking to work-related thoughts or tasks. The harder she worked, the more the problems multiplied. It was all exhausting and unfulfilling. Inviting friends back in her life regularly might just be the distraction she needed.

Situating herself in the smooth leather car interior, she fastened the seatbelt and placed her work tote and purse in the back seat. Noticing she had voicemails waiting, she slipped her Blackberry into the hands-free unit on the dash and listened.

"Hi, Lacey. This is Ron Roberts with Attorney Simon's office. Just wanted to let you know I received your emails. We have everything we need to close next week on the Taylor Street property and I'll pencil it in. Let me know what time the buyers and sellers want to close and where. Thanks."

"Ms. Williams? Hi. I noticed a house you have listed on Capital Avenue. Can you call me back to give me some more information? My number is ..." Lacey punched the number two to save the second message.

"Hello, Lacey. Thank you for the paperwork you forwarded. It was a big help. My underwriter called back after reviewing it. A fourteen-day delay is definite for the Crestwood closing. Can you let Stuart Benson know? Call me when you get a moment."

She felt her stomach flip. This would be good news to anyone but Stuart. She decided to wait until she was back in her home office to call him and listened to the last two messages.

"Hi, Lacey. This is Bill. Thanks for talking to me the other night about my inspection concerns. The more I think about it all, though, the more I realize I don't want to move forward. I think I need to buy something newer. Can you call me when can? I figure I need to sign some papers or something to get out of the deal? I'm sorry. Let me know. Okay. Bye."

"Lacey. John Drummons here. The appraisal came back on the Fisk Street property and it is lower than the sale price. This deal is dead unless the sellers will agree to take about seven thousand less than they originally agreed to. Call me."

As she disconnected the phone, she pulled into the gravel

drive. Turning the car off, she went numb until the tears began to flow. It was all becoming too much to deal with day in and day out. Dressed in her impressive suit, she sat in her impressive car parked in the drive of her impressive home on the impressive street alone with tears of frustration and disappointment wetting her cheeks. As if nature was mocking her, a rain shower moved in again and water cascaded down the windshield.

She hadn't known how long she sat there, but was startled all the same with the knocking on the driver's door window. Bryce stood there with her huge umbrella and a concerned look. Lacey lowered the window a bit.

"Hi, I'm just getting off the phone. Meet you on the porch," she fibbed as she concealed her tears.

Bryce walked around the front of the silver car and, in an instant, slipped into the passenger seat. There was no fooling her. She was used to comforting people in uncomfortable and awkward settings. Without words, she pulled lip-gloss from her jeans' pocket, pulled the shade mirror down and casually applied the make-up.

"Do you need some?" she nonchalantly asked with the lip balm pointed toward Lacey.

"I think I need something stronger," she answered as she wiped the remaining wetness from her face.

"You never followed-up on that night-cap. Care for an early Happy Hour?"

"Do I ever. Mike's?"

"I'm just along for the ride. Put this baby in reverse and let's get the hell outta here."

―――――――

Mike's Crab House sat along the seawater and was a Chesapeake Bay staple for Maryland Blue Crabs and beer with friends. The bar was a favorite of local professionals and old salts and its unpretentious vibe was just what Lacey and Bryce were looking for. They huddled under Bryce's gigantic umbrella as they dodged the puddles in the rocky parking lot and ran for the shelter of the wooden crab shack.

By now it was well after lunch and way before dinner and, other than a few dart players, they had the bar to themselves. Bryce headed to the bar and Lacey told her she would meet her after freshening up.

In the small restroom, Lacey was relieved to find it empty and she leaned against the porcelain sink to look into the mirror. Her face was splotchy and her hair a wreck. She had bloodshot eyes with dark circles. She barely recognized herself. Pulling a section of brown paper towel from the dispenser, she wetted it with cold water. The cool dampness awakened her skin while smelling like wet cardboard. Her purse contained a brush and enough make-up to make her feel better about re-entering the world after the tiny breakdown and she used the powder, blush, and red lipstick to thoroughly hide any signs of previous weakness.

Back at the bar, Bryce was chatting it up with the bartender who had already prepared her order. Her short stature left her crossed ankles dangling far above the brass rail and Lacey could hear her bubbly voice lifting the atmosphere as she relayed some random story about a recent travel.

"Hey. There she is," Bryce announced while Lacey took her seat next to her.

"Alive and well again. What do we have here?"

"A sure-fire cure for whatever is ailing you. Tequila and an icy draft."

"Cheers," Lacey gestured with a raised shot glass.

"So, you look more human now. Nice recovery."

Lacey kept from choking on her beer as she stifled a laugh and used a cocktail napkin to blot her lips.

"Thanks. I am so embarrassed. I really have no idea what came over me," she said sheepishly while shaking her head.

"As long as you're feeling better now?"

"Yes. So, sorry I didn't call you about that drink the other night. I got home later than expected. The buyers surprised me by wanting to put an offer in on one of the places we looked at. First night out. They knew what they wanted, though."

"Yeah? Good for them. So what else is new?"

"Not much. What did you do today?" Lacey asked tentatively. She suddenly sensed a tension between them.

"I was on my way out to get my nails done until I saw my good friend crying in her car."

Lacey shifted in her seat. She was suddenly annoyed by Bryce's tone.

"I appreciate your concern, but you didn't have to stop. Like I said, I'm not sure what came over me."

The college-age bartender walked back to them and removed the empty shot glasses. The two stalled their conversation until they had a little more privacy again. Bryce turned to Lacey.

"Of course I would stop to check on you and I don't care about the nail appointment. I'll go tomorrow. I do know what came over you, though."

"What?" Lacey took a drink and defensively crossed her legs and arms.

"You are totally unbalanced and don't get angry with me," she added when she saw Lacey start to object. "I've been there. I've tried to take on one too many shifts in the past and wiped myself out. It's draining and depressing and you start to lose control of your emotions. Thankfully, I get a long break after I do that to myself and I know better before doing it again. You don't get that break. I know. But …"

Lacey's phone started to ring as if trying to stop Bryce's meddling. She reached for it and looked at Bryce as she silenced the ringer.

"There," Lacey announced proudly. "Now let's talk about something else. Like the guy you met in Jamaica?"

Bryce sympathetically agreed to drop it and went on to tell Lacey all about the British Airlines pilot she met during a layover. The bartender leaned at the far end of the bar and talked sports with one of the waiters and a couple walked in to the adjacent restaurant. The mounted televisions delivered the news and weather and the whole scene was easily distracting to anyone except Lacey Williams. All she could think about was the call she just ignored and how she would handle the voicemails she had checked before breaking into tears earlier. As Bryce signaled for another beer and Lacey smiled her false interest in the story, it was clearer than ever to her that she just might be shoulder-deep in career that was sucking the life out of her.

"What if I'm not cut out to be a real estate agent?" Lacey blurted out in the middle of Bryce's description of the pilot she was supposedly falling in love with.

Bryce set her freshly poured beer down on the cocktail napkin immediately and deliberately.

"Wait a second," she said pointedly at Lacey. "I didn't mean to make you doubt yourself. You are fantastic at your job. I just think you need to step back from it for an hour or so or a weekend now and then."

"I can't. That's the problem."

"Sure you can. Turn of the darn phone and go do something that takes your mind off work. Easy." Bryce pushed her seat back from the bar and held her glass with one arm crossed as she delivered her prescription for a life of balance.

"Not easy. Not for me. That's my point. I know colleagues who can do that and I wish I could. I've tried. I am more miserable trying to ignore work than I am when I never take a break. On top of that, every time I try to take time off, I get bad news and I get depressed over it. I get too emotionally involved and want to make everyone happy. It's just my personality and I don't think I can change who I am. I don't know what to do and I know I can't keep living like this forever. I want more out of life."

"I see what you're saying. It's probably what makes you so good at it, really. So, you *have* thought about all this before. I was really starting to feel bad about bringing it up more and more and actually started thinking that maybe you were just happy being busy with other people's problems twenty-four-seven," Bryce admitted with relief. She was not one to interfere in another's life, but no one else saw Lacey as much and on such a consistent basis.

In silence they watched the television screen dole out one bad news story after another. Lacey ordered another beer and the national news correspondent worked to sober them with stories of tragic fires, childhood traumas, shootings, and vehicle accidents. The bartender served her the draft with a genuine smile and it warmed her heart a little. She pulled a hair clip from her purse, twisted her long mane atop her crown and fastened it in place. Removing her black Tahari suit jacket and placing on the seat backrest, she swiveled the bar stool toward Bryce with an unexplainable sense of determination and hope.

"I just want to be happy again," she said with a grin. "Why shouldn't I be, right?"

"That's right. So, just be happy. More tequila?"

"I think I'm good in that department," Lacey said with a smile. "I jumped into this career when I was nineteen with a part-time job and I moved forward full-steam. What the hell did I know about myself then? I need a fresh start."

There was a light in Lacey's eyes for the first time in years.

Bryce leaned her elbow onto the bar. "What are you going to do? You should be a flight attendant with me! Maybe we could do some of the same flights eventually!"

"Not a bad idea," Lacey mused. "I don't know, though. It is nice working for myself. I just don't know," she shrugged with a crazed giggle.

"Sounds like we need to have dinner and start brainstorming your escape from your current reality."

Bryce rubbed her hands together like a mad scientist would. "You are just terrific. Yes. Dinner and a margarita?"

"Now you're talking, sister. David," she called to the bartender, "Can we get a table?"

PART TWO: DISCOVERING

CHAPTER SEVEN

Help From a Loved One

WHEN JULIA FINALLY FOUND her brother, she had not even realized it. In her search for her siblings, she had returned to their home time and time again only to find it empty or full of strangers. Prior to that, she had visited her grandparents' house only to find it uninhabited. She could not endure the disappointment any longer and a force of nature compelled her to move on to the Williams' cabin and then down the path to the river. She remembered that her brothers were always fond of playing along the riverbank. They taught her how to skip stones and she liked to read under the shade of a mighty maple while they fished. It made sense that they would settle along the water. She no longer stumbled over stones as her feet glided effortlessly along the river's edge. Now and then, she even walked into the current to avoid shrubbery and fallen trees and not even that force could hold her back. Forging on and on, she eventually came to an old building. She vaguely remembered it. Painted cobalt blue and a hub of activity, it gave the impression of being a good place where happy people gathered. She watched all sorts of patrons come and go for days on end before noticing one constant presence.

Helpful and kind, he also possessed a strong and tough

quality that hadn't been part of his nature years ago. In addition, he was sad. This she intuitively knew.

She didn't know him yet, but she was curious and without him knowing, began to keep him company day after day. He regularly ventured to the river's edge to begin and end each day. By the eddy he drank from a familiar mug. He came and went in an old brown Ford that she recognized. At the end of each workday he worked tirelessly as he retuned pieces of gear to rightful spots. Sensing his loneliness, she decided to help one afternoon. Moving in to stand next to him, she helped lift and arrange.

As she worked alongside this gentle soul, her concentration had failed her and she suddenly dropped her side of the heavy lifting. He twisted to recover control of the now wobbling canoe and his face met hers. She recognized him instantly. It was Chase, her beloved brother. His dimples gave him away while he struggled with the awkward weight of the gear and his muscular arms and facial stubble had hid the boy she had known him to be. Julia reached for him and he walked away. She called out to him and he, like everyone else she encountered, ignored her. She needed to communicate with him. With deliberate concentration, her energy caused his favorite mug to smash to the floor of the garage. Her ploy worked, but she immediately regretted her actions. Hopelessly and helplessly standing before her big brother she silently begged for his attention. In response, his face was ashen and contorted in a painful expression.

Kneeling, he gingerly collected the pieces of broken ceramic and quietly wept as he cradled a large piece of the mug in his hand. It had been their mother's, she now realized, and had been a Mother's Day gift from this youngest son. She knelt next to him and placed her arm around his shoulders to try to comfort him.

He was in such pain and she wanted to make it go away. She had to make him feel better. She knew he was a good person and deserved a good life. Her strong connection to her brother allowed her to see he was full of hurt and regret.

It became clear to the little sister that peace would not come her way until her brother found a little of it for himself.

CHAPTER EIGHT

James Eustice Miller

FOR SIXTY YEARS HE had been selling produce in and around the Annapolis area. One would be hard-pressed to find an individual today who had logged that much time in the same livelihood. As a newly married man back in 1954, he remembered how proud he was with his ability to support his lovely wife, Esther, and then the three sons she bore. Doing this with his hands on land they owned elicited even more pride. Of course, as a farmer's wife, Esther certainly did her part to help bring in the bacon, literally. To say being a farmer has changed in that sixty years is an understatement. He could not fathom being able to afford farmable land in this era never mind the equipment, feed and other necessary supplies. Then again, he often mused, the public was not paying six dollars for a dozen ears of corn back then like they do in this city market he now sat and reminisced in.

"Six dollars," he thought and shook his head.

The amount of money people paid for life's provisions was mind boggling to an eighty year old man like him. Over time he had come to notice many things among those he regularly served. High-end vehicles, expensive tech gadgets, and brand new homes appeared to be the norm nowadays. From what he knew from his sons, the phones he saw everyone carrying cost more than the truck he bought decades ago. That Chevy served him well and was even the same vehicle he drove to market that day. To James it was gratifying to care for practical belongings that boldly withstood the test of time. To others, material commodities had to be new, shiny, and expensive to garner pride from today's society. Their over-priced and often meager possessions were displayed like badges of honor.

None of it was honorable in his modest opinion. As far as he could tell, the majority of his patrons were surely slaves to the creditors and banks. Not James. The loan he took out to buy a newer tractor twenty years ago was enough to send him to an early grave. He chuckled as he thought back to that day and smiled even more when he thought back to the day the loan was paid off early.

He disliked owing anyone anything. The independent man had spent a lifetime enjoying the fruits of his labor with his family around a proper dinner table. Restorative sleep came easily to him and his family every night. He could not have asked for more.

The day that found James reflecting on the past was a slow day at the market. It had been drizzling off and on and the threat of more rain seemed to be keeping the crowds away. It was fine by him. He sat back in his folding chair under the oversized pop-up tent and propped his tired feet up on a closed box of potatoes. A slow day at market happens, of course, and James wasn't about to fret. He accepted what each day brought. Being the son of a son of a long line of farmers had taught him to roll with the punches. He didn't expect the world, or the weather, to cater to him. Accept life, don't fight it, was the sentiment he was taught by his own father. So, he leaned back and took a rest as the workday came to an end.

As his thoughts began to slow, James, or Farmer Jim as his regulars called him, took a sip of coffee while taking in the sights. He watched the interactions of the strangers around him. He appreciated the business that the Annapolis Farmers Market brought and the people were typically good to him.

However, he couldn't help but to notice how rushed and anxious everyone seemed to be these days.

Goodness knows life is challenging, there is no denying that fact, but, James thought that today's families made it harder on themselves and wholeheartedly believed that family was the most precious possession and more fragile than anyone wants to admit. The cost of living was astronomical in his experienced eyes and he figured it was no wonder recent generations strained and strived to achieve a different kind of life than he was accustomed to. On that note, salaries earned today were astronomical compared to what he was used to living on.

He contemplated. Was society creating a mad world, or, simply responding to a world gone mad? Whatever the answer was, he gave thanks to have been able to raise his family during a simpler time. Still, he was convinced a simpler life does exist for those who want it. Maybe the more folks stay in motion, the less they had time to think about it all.

James was scanning the small crowd from his post when he noticed Sam still wandering around the grounds. He chuckled at himself for pondering the current state of affairs of America's families and stopped his philosophizing long enough to become curious as to what Sam was up to. It wasn't like him to be aimlessly meandering the market.

"Ahem. Hi," James looked up to see where the female voice came from. He noticed the young lady from last week standing in front of him under her yellow umbrella.

"Hey, little lady. Nice to see you. You caught me slacking off. What can I get for you?" James slowly got up from his chair and smiled.

"Hello. May I have a pint of tomatoes and some leaf lettuce, please?"

"Why you sure can. How was that corn you bought last week? I guess you made it without me?"

Lacey didn't have the heart to tell him she had not even cooked it yet. She hoped it was still good. She made a mental note to make it for dinner that night.

"It was delicious. All of your produce is so good." Lacey felt her cheeks blush. "Well, you didn't give me your number so I couldn't call you, of course," she added with a smile.

"Okay. I guess I'll let you off the hook," James answered with a hearty laugh.

He started bagging her order when he looked up to see another customer approaching his table. He laughed out loud when he saw who it was.

"Hey, ho! Look who's back. Well, well, well," James teased. Starting to grasp with situation at hand, he decided to take it easy on his friend.

"So, I forgot something. Sue me why don't you? Do you want my business or not?"

Sam stepped forward with his black golf umbrella overlapping Lacey's smaller one and glanced sideways at her. She offered a shy smile.

"Of course I want your business, Sammy. You just need to wait your turn while I finish up with this lovely lady," he retorted in an ultra-polite manner and with his trademark wink. James slowly placed the crisp paper bag of items on the table for Lacey.

He tossed in a couple of apples as he did so.

"This guy can't get enough of these apples I grow, so, I thought I would give you few to sample."

"Hey, why does she get free apples?" Sam asked with mock annoyance.

"Because she is a lady and she is pretty and I like to give gifts to all the pretty ladies," James laughed as he collected the money from Lacey.

"Why, thank you! I am sure I will enjoy them very much. You are too kind."

"Geesh. This guy lays it on thick, that's for sure," Sam said with an eye roll.

"Anything else sweetheart?" James took his time finishing up just to irk Sam and to get a grip on the scenario that was revealed to him. He loved a good love story and there appeared to be one unfolding in front of his eyes.

"That's all. Thank you." Lacey wasn't sure what to do next. It was obvious Sam came back to see her, and she was happy about that, but she didn't want to seem eager. She turned to leave. Sam gave what appeared to be a frantic look to James. James stood back and crossed his arms. He was enjoying seeing Sam squirm, but decided to help out.

"Uh, just a second, Miss....?" James said as he started to fish for the important details Sam needed to know but hadn't the opportunity to find out yet.

CHAPTER NINE
A First Date

"AFTER YOU," SAM OPENED the door to the Severn Cafe wide and bowed his head as he motioned for Lacey to enter before him.

"Why, thank you," she said playfully as she stepped from the wet deck into the warm and dry marina restaurant and deli.

On Farmer Jim's suggestion, they decided to meet for a cup of coffee and Sam quickly suggested this place he was familiar with that was within close proximity to the park. Evening was starting to settle in and the casual eatery overlooked the sailboats in port. Many had their interior lights on suggesting their captains were moored for the night. It was a cozy, misty setting.

As they approached the counter, Sam took his wallet from his back pocket and insisted on paying.

"If Jim finds out I let you pay for your own coffee, I will never hear the end of it," he reasoned. Lacey had to agree with him. Politely asking for a decaf with a splash of cream, she took a seat at one of the many empty tables by a window. Removing her trench coat, she smoothed her suit and hair. Still dressed from work, she had rushed to the market thinking she may have missed her chance to run into Sam. She had felt her heart skip a beat when he had made his appearance. After her heart-to-heart talk with Bryce last night, she was ready to start enjoying life a little more and willed herself to at least put her job in a healthier perspective for now.

Regardless, sitting at the table alone, she reached for her phone out of habit. The battery was about to die. Looking under the table for an outlet, Sam arrived with their coffees.

"Did you loose something down there?"

"Oh, hi. Uh, no. My phone is about to die and I was looking for an outlet."

"Ah. I see. Doesn't look like there is one down there," he bent down to help her look. "Do you want to switch tables?"

Lacey felt silly. It was going on six and she had put in a long day. An hour or so of a break would do no harm. This is exactly what Bryce meant with her recent tirades and Lacey increasingly detested the power this thing had over her.

"No. A dead battery would be a relief."

"I know what you mean. Mine keeps a tight grip on my mind as well. It's hard to find balance with it. I struggled with that love hate relationship for a long time. Still do, actually. Tell you what, as far as I'm concerned, my phone is dead, too."

And with that, Sam took his own phone out of the pocket of his suit jacket and confirmed the phone powered down before returning it to it's hiding spot. After removing his jacket and folding it neatly over the empty chair at their table, he loosened his dark blue tie and unbuttoned the top button of his crisp, blue shirt. Leaning back and resting his bent elbow on the back of the adjacent chair, he gave Lacey his full attention. She was under the spell of his charisma. Trying hard to appear less interested, she looked back at her coffee and took a sip with her freshly painted pink nails reflecting the warm lights from the nearby wall sconce. Before he had a chance, she started the conversation.

"The world won't come to an end if we take a break for an evening, right? Well, I don't know what you do, but I can say that's the case for me. I need to do it more often," she said with conviction.

"By the tone of most of my clients, you would think I *was* handling the world's affairs. I take my work seriously, but, yeah. I'm with you. Here's to a much-needed break."

He lifted his cup to second that motion. She glanced up from her cup mid-sip to see his eyes still on hers.

"So, Sam, what *do* you do?"

"I'm a lawyer. Probably shouldn't admit that, though. I try to represent the good people of the world only, you should know. And, I'm going out on a limb here, but, I'll guess you are a real estate agent."

His assured grin told her he had done his research.

"Why yes I am. How did ..."

"At Dockside when we met at lunch. I noticed you had a Realtor magazine."

"Oh. Very observant," she laughed. "Not sure if I should admit my profession, either. Although I give my heart and soul to it, not everyone has a good experience with their agent. I'd like to think I do a good job."

"I'm sure you do, sure you do," he trailed off in his quirky, but, poised way before continuing. "Hey, we're all just trying to survive in this crazy world, right? Are you from Annapolis?"

"Not originally. I grew up in upstate New York. My father is with the Navy. We moved here when I was in high school when he became an Officer and we've been here since then. They have a property outside of the city, but I've lived here in town since college."

"How did you get into real estate?" Sam rolled up his sleeves and leaned in with arms crossed, forearms resting on the table. His blue eyes were mesmerizing and his summer bronze tint made them stand out even more.

"While I was in college, I took a part-time job assisting a successful agent and I was hooked. To earn more money and help with showings and open houses, I got my license at nineteen and by the time I was out of school, I had a few of my own clients. It just kept snowballing from there."

"Where are you from?" she asked as she blotted her lips with a napkin. She was feeling a little insecure with the way Sam listened to her so intently.

He ran one hand over his head and his blonde locks quickly repositioned themselves.

"Born and bred right here. My parents sent me to Georgetown Prep before I headed off to American University."

"Impressive. I'm not so sure my Frostburg State degree in business and my small town high school diploma can compete. So do you live and work in town?

"You know as well as I do the real education comes after the diploma. I am still in town, to answer your question. My firm is on West Street and I can actually see my home from this very seat."

He motioned out the window with a nod.

"You can? Where?" Lacey was a bit confused She peered out at sailor's sky setting in over the calm harbor.

Sam relished her confusion and leaned in with elbows on table. With a look that must persuade one jury after another, he revealed his little secret.

"I do, in fact, live out there, Miss Lacey. You see, I live on my sailboat that is moored just a few steps from here."

He adjusted his seat so that he, too, was now gazing at the horizon.

"On your boat? Doesn't it get cold in the winter?"

"No. It is a small space and heats up nicely. Not much storage and I do keep a vacant apartment in a rental building for when the weather acts up too much. Anyway, any home I have tends to be for sleep only."

"Very interesting," Lacey nodded. "So how did you end up living on the water?"

"About five years ago when I was approaching forty and re-evaluating my life. I started my own firm and needed capital. My house was more upkeep than I had time for. Something had to go. I knew I could go without the house before I could rid myself of the boat. Plus, the house had a lot more equity. So, I moved aboard."

He changed the subject back to Lacey.

"The daughter of a Naval officer, huh? How 'bout that." Sam let out a low whistle.

"I've never known anything else. He's a good man and my mother has just as big a heart. I've had a good upbringing. Can't complain," She respectfully and truthfully said. Out of respect, she left out the fact that she knew her upbringing was different from that of her friends. Her bed was always made with military precision and she had impeccable manners by the time she was four.

"Brothers or sisters?" Sam asked as he peered over his clasped hands.

"No. Just me. How about you? Are your parents living in town?" He took another swallow of coffee before pushing his chair away from the table a little to allow him to stretch his legs.

"I do have a big sister. She's in politics, God help her," he added with a shake of his head and a chuckle. "My parents moved to Florida awhile back. Couldn't take the cold weather anymore, they claimed. I'm thinking of sailing the Intracoastal next year as a way to meet up with them. You should come along."

Lacey laughed at his half-serious request.

"Yeah. All right. We'll see about that. What would you do about work?"

"That's why we have all this technology, right? That's how I see it. What's the use of being tethered to these laptops and smart phones if we sit in the office all day?" Sam seemed to be trying to convince himself of his words more than anyone else.

"I agree with you. Well, keep me posted on the trip. I could use a little bit of adventure in my life."

"Hey, I see my neighbor is on the dock checking his lines. Check out that sunset," Sam pointed out as he nodded toward the west. Lacey turned around and was floored by the red streaks that were now the brightest crimson shades.

"Gorgeous," she declared.

Sam noticed the red tones in his companion's tresses matched the blazing sky. He agreed with her assessment.

"You care to take a walk? Just out to the dock. I can introduce you to my neighbor, Gus. He's always good for some interesting conversation."

Lacey began to decline his offer then thought of her conversation with Bryce the night before.

"Why not?" she concurred aloud.

Sam folded his jacket over his forearm and waited for her at the door with one hand in his pocket.

"G'night, Mandy," he called to the high-school age cashier who was pouring over a textbook behind the counter. She mumbled a moody response as she continued on with her studies. He held the door open for Lacey.

They walked quietly together as their dress shoes clicked and clopped along the outdoor deck of the café and then the all weather docks. Lacey fell in line behind him as they passed the various sailboats that all looked the same to Lacey's untrained eye.

"Gus, my man. How goes it?" Sam casually called out to the middle-aged man kneeling on the dock before them. He looked up from where he had been adjusting the lines that kept his vessel in place. His round face was friendly and his gray hair thick. Rosy, round cheeks punctuated his broad smile.

"Hi, Sam. Nice night, huh?" Gus stood and brushed his hands on his khaki shorts and began to shuffle toward them in worn Sperry's.

"Sure is. Red sky at night, " Sam trailed off. "I wanted to introduce you to my friend, here. Lacey Williams, Gus Stover."

The new acquaintance gave a hearty handshake welcome and rushed into various conversation starters with Sam. None actually developed into a proper conversation.

"Gus, who are you bothering?" A woman with shaggy, blonde hair shouted out from the sailboat that Lacey assumed belonged to Gus.

"Just Sam."

"Oh, go right on ahead then!" Her laugh was infectious and she disappeared below deck.

"You two get on up here for a drink. Verna made dinner, too. She always makes enough for company. She knows I tend to bring home strays."

Gus started walking toward his boat with a slight limp. Sam shrugged at Lacey who found herself following along like a lost puppy. On deck, Sam and Lacey took a seat on the built-in teak bench as Gus brought rum and Cokes with limes for all.

"Hope this is okay for you, Lacey? "

"Yes, thank you, Gus."

"Aren't you going to ask if I'm okay with it?" Sam bristled.

"Don't really care what you think, Sammy."

Lacey laughed at Gus who plopped down across from them.

"Tell her she's staying for dinner!" Verna yelled from the galley.

"I can't tell her what to do, Vern!" Gus yelled back to her as he shook his head and rolled his eyes dramatically then added, "You'll have to tell her if you can't stay, hon. I can't win with that woman."

Lacey chuckled at the hosts and nodded. She was not sure how the night would go and reminded herself to simply enjoy the moment.

"Gus is a Navy man," Sam said to Lacey. "Lacey's father is a Naval Officer," he added leaning his elbows atop his knees with *The Verna Mae'* tumbler between his fingers.

"That so? Who is you father?"

"George Williams."

"You don't say? Hey, Verna," Gus shouted over his shoulder. "George Williams' daughter is dining with us tonight! I know your father very well, Lacey. I suffered an injury that forced me into the office. Your dad and I worked closely on a few details. He is one heck of a man. You tell him Gus Stover says 'Hello'. Bring him by sometime, you hear?"

"What a small world. I can't wait to tell him I met you," Lacey offered sincerely. She was enjoying time with Gus more and more.

The lively conversation continued until Verna stepped up on deck to call them down to eat. Lacey could not imagine trying to turn down their gracious offer and wanted to stay anyway.

"Let me grab a bottle of wine, Verna," Sam insisted as they stood. "Lacey, you can pick the wine. Come with me for a second."

Lacey glanced at Verna instinctively and Verna nodded her motherly approval.

"That's fine, Samuel. We have plenty of wine here, though. Hurry back."

Gus retreated to assist Verna and Lacey followed Sam over to his boat with the midnight blue hull and white accent stripes. It was beautiful on the outside and she found it even more impressive once on board. Her heels still off and lying on the deck of the Stovers' boat, she nimbly stepped into the cockpit while Sam held her hand to steady her.

"You seem to have your sea legs," he noted.

"Living in Annapolis and having a father in the Navy will acquaint you with your share of boats. It's been awhile, I hate to admit. It is nice to be back on water even if we're docked."

She followed him down into the main salon and was in awe of the details. An intricate nautical star was imbedded in the glossy wood floor and the interior recessed lighting was dimmed to perfection. The galley details were nicer than those in her own kitchen. Elegant ivory hued upholstery surrounded them and tasteful nautical accent pillows were placed precisely at the right angles to encourage one to lounge awhile.

"Not that I've ever been invited aboard a vessel like this one. I don't blame you for selling your house for this beauty."

"Yeah, I kind of went overboard when I decided this

would be my home. Not the wisest financial decision. I threw caution to the wind and glad I did. Here's the wine cabinet."

Sam opened a lower cabinet door to reveal a dozen or so racks of wine that were securely stowed. They decided on a Pinot Noir and a Sauvignon Blanc together.

On the way back out, Lacey noticed a few nautical charts scattered on a small couch that was tucked away in the corner. With such immaculate surroundings, the misplaced maps were obvious.

"Are you planning a trip?" she asked nodding toward the papers.

Sam shook his head and looked down at his feet as he held on to stair railing with one hand and clutched both bottles of wine in his other.

"You could say that. I love looking at the charts and planning voyages. Like the trip to Florida I mentioned. Actually casting off is another story. One of these days I'll make the time for that."

"I can relate," she confided. "You should go for it. Take a break once in a while."

"You're right. I have a feeling you rarely take your own advice, Miss Williams?"

"Guilty as charged."

Sam helped Lacey from the schooner and continued to hold on to her hand during the short walk to the neighboring sailboat. The nightfall air was chilled and Lacey was thankful for the warm cabin of the Stovers' boat. Dinner was festive and Verna and Gus proved to be the ultimate hosts. Lacey was thoroughly entertained and Sam proved enchanting even in the offbeat humor of the night. Eventually, dinner came to an end and they lingered over mineral waters and coffee as stories were provoked and embellished before Lacey bid them all good night and gave sincere thanks for a wonderful evening. Sam walked her to her car.

"So much for a quick cup of coffee. What a great night. Gus and Verna are marvelous and I had the best time with you, Sam."

Whether it was the wine or hearty laughs, Lacey was not sure. Regardless, it was one of the best evenings she had had in years.

"Me, too. It's been *real* nice."

Sam nodded slowly as he said the words and took a long look at Lacey. As they stood next to her car, Sam politely kissed her cheek.

"Mind if I give you a call for a real dinner date sometime soon? I'll leave my boisterous neighbors at the dock. I promise."

Sam posed the question with self-assuredness and sweetness at the same time.

"That would be nice," she answered while still holding his hand. "Although, I would welcome their company anytime. They are too much fun."

"You'd change that tune if you lived next to them," he laughed. "Make no mistake, I mean that lovingly. They are quite a pair. You drive safely. I'll talk to you soon, Lacey."

Walking backwards and keeping his eyes on her all the while, he let her hand go and she settled in to the driver's seat. With a wave, she headed home. Sam stood with his hands in his pockets and watched her head off into the night.

She made it a record two blocks before checking her phone at a red light. Time with Sam Hinkley was becoming time away from the mental demands of work and it was divine. In light of the perfect evening, Lacey purposely refrained from reviewing her emails and voicemails and instead called her college roommate, Ashley. She was feeling the need to reconnect with old friends and work toward finding her true self again.

CHAPTER TEN
Business First

IN THE LOBBY OF the Crestwood Condo building, Sam tensely sat on the plush leather sofa awaiting his meeting with the lawyer for the Home Owners Association. Supposedly there had been some problems with a few of the banks closing on loans for the building's prospective new tenants and the current residents were not happy. Sam wasn't sure what he was supposed to do about it, but here he was all the same.

"Sam. Thank you for meeting with me today," John Dartmouth came breezing in through the main entrance and came to a stop as the men exchanged handshakes.

"Sure. No problem. I don't have much time, though."

Sam followed John to a nearby meeting room.

"Me neither," John stated as he held open the door for the fellow attorney. Sam stepped into the drab room that smelled of mildew and wondered how such a building, which commanded such high prices and demanded such high fees, could not afford to update their common areas. John motioned for Sam to take a seat at the large table.

Sitting across from one another, both men pulled a legal pad and pen from their briefcases. John began the discussions.

"So the HOA is eager to settle this matter."

"As is my client, I can assure you," Sam replied.

"I'm just going to play it straight with you, Sam. Some of the banks' underwriters are having a problem with this suit hanging over our heads and current and prospective residents are voicing their frustration that too many units are not selling as buyers look to other buildings while this plays out. The more units that are empty causes the over all values to go down while the fees go up. I am going to put this out there point blank to save us all time and money. Would your client be willing to settle out of court?"

Sam paused as he hid his surprise. He was not expecting this. The trial was looming and, frankly, Sam was feeling fairly upbeat about their chances. The more he learned, the more convinced he was that Philip Ellis was not negligent in the least. A trial avoidance would not necessarily be a bad thing, however.

"I'm not so sure about that, John. It is looking pretty good for us I have to admit. Under what conditions?"

"My client is willing to settle for five million."

"The structural report I have in my office says that no repairs are needed. This issue is cosmetic and the result of natural settling. I'll do my job and take this to my client, but don't hold your breath, John. I'm thinking we will just let this go to trial."

"Are you sure you want to do that, Sam? A start-up firm like yours might not rebound from a less-than-desirable ruling."

John sat a little straighter in his chair, which Sam noticed had been elevated in order for his colleague to look down upon him. John worked for one of the largest firms in town and that was all he had going for him.

"Ah. Thanks for looking out for me, John."

Annoyed, Sam stood and calmly pushed his chair back in place.

"Like I said, I'll take this to my client and get back to you," Sam stated briskly as he placed his pen and paper back into his worn briefcase and started for the door. John followed and stood in the doorway as Sam exited the room.

"Think about it Sam. Don't lead your client astray. Let's all avoid getting dragged through the mud, huh?"

The defendant's lawyer looked back to see John's lanky frame leaning in the doorway with arms and ankles crossed. Ignoring the comment, he faced forward again and headed toward the same door that a female was entering from the opposite direction. It was only a matter of seconds before he realized that the woman who had just entered the main doors to the lobby was none other than Lacey Williams.

It had been over a week since they had coffee and dinner at the dock. He should have called her already and he meant to call her a dozen times. Something had always gotten in the way.

"Oh, hi, Sam," she said in a surprised voice.

"Lacey. Hey. I have been meaning to call you. Work has been really hectic," he said guiltily as he nervously ran his fingers through his hair.

"Oh, yeah. I know how that goes. Don't give it a second thought. Really."

Still standing in the lobby, Sam could hear John on his cell phone talking to his paralegal about another case. He wanted to talk to Lacey more, however, this was not the right time. Not with John Dartmouth in earshot. The conversation was awkward to say the least.

"So, do you have a showing here?" Sam asked.

"No. I have a client looking to close on a unit here and we've been delayed. I'm here to pick up something for the underwriters. It's been a little rough."

Lacey sighed as she pulled her hair back behind her shoulders and crossed her arms as she waited for Sam to continue the bland conversation.

Sam wasn't sure what to say. He assumed Lacey's frustration was due to the lawsuit he was handling. Not that he could talk about it anyway, but he certainly could not with the snide plaintiff attorney in the vicinity. That man could not be trusted and Sam could not risk having his words twisted.

"Well, I'll let you get on your way, then. I really am glad I ran into you. Are you free this Friday? Want to grab a drink with me?" Sam hoped he sounded sincere.

"I can't this Friday. Another time, though?"

"Absolutely. I'll give you a call, okay?"

"Sure. That would be nice."

"All right then. We'll talk soon and get something set up. Good luck with your deal."

"Thanks, Sam."

Lacey stood straight as an arrow as she waltzed by him, her clicking heels echoing throughout the marble and glass lobby. He stole a quick glance her way as she entered the main office. She seemed prepared for battle in the same way he and John were. Different battles, same war.

Leaving the building, Sam was feeling badly about how the conversation went with Lacey and was kicking himself for not getting in touch with her sooner. They both had demanding careers, but he wondered if she was busy on Friday or if her words were made-up. He made silent pledge to call her tomorrow and set up a proper dinner date.

For now, it was back to his office and back to the important matters at hand. Unless his client surprised him, this case would still go to trial and he was ready to get down to business. His mind churned with the facts of the case he would focus on as well as what a winning outcome would bring to him and his business and the spring in his step returned.

CHAPTER ELEVEN
Chase Robbins

CHASE SLID DOWN SLOWLY with his back against the damp block wall until his body was crumpled and slouched upon the cold concrete floor. The flashbacks returned. A time in his life that was full of moments he desperately wanted to forget. He was sorely mindful that those moments had re-sculpted him. So much had been taken from him. His hand still held pieces of the broken mug he had bought for his mother one Mother's Day long ago. He wiped his cheek with a fist that sluggishly became unclenched while telling himself it was just a mug. A mass-produced ceramic mug that claimed his mom was number one. Now it was in pieces on the floor much like his life.

Positioning himself away from the wall and resting on the soles of his feet, he looked down at the fragments of white stoneware in his palm. His mother's face flashed into his mind and was immediately followed by the angelic face of his little sister. He eternally envisioned her as the spunky little girl with untamed long hair who was forever tagging along and feigning to be as capable as her unruly older brothers.

In reality, they had always known she needed protected and failed her in the end. Tears overwhelmed him once more and he became angry for letting his emotions take hold.

His palms tightly encircled the shards of cheap white ceramic until drops of blood escaped the confinements of his uncomfortable skin. The effects were nothing compared to the pain he held tightly in his gut. Sitting there alone he was surprised by his raw reaction to the broken tactile memory. He thought he was beyond that point now that he had managed to put some years behind him.

Walking to the trash bin, he let the pieces of the mug slip from his hand and into the garbage bag before taking a broom and dustpan over to the shattered pieces still on the floor. Methodically, he swept up the mess and deposited the fragments into the trash. It was getting harder and harder to hold onto any tokens of the past and Chase realized they were just sad reminders. They never provided the deep comfort he expected of the objects. He walked over to the rows of kayaks and made sure the gear from the day's trip was stored properly before turning out the lights He would be guiding a group of fishermen at dawn tomorrow and knew he had better retreat up the rickety steps to his apartment home and call it an early night.

Home. The word was still strange to Chase. He had not felt a sense of home in over a decade. A touch of anxiety set in as he realized that he might never experience family or home again.

Dusk fell and the geese gathered. He watched them flap their wings and listened to their frantic calls as they instinctively readied the flock for the trip south. Nature's organized chaos. Taking in a deep breath of the musky late summer air he was drawn to the river before turning in for the night. Nights and evenings were hard. As a river guide, he kept busy during the day with the pleasant company of his group and the charge of keeping them safe. Once they left and the gear was placed back in the storage garage, he always felt the sting of a lonely life. He told himself he liked the calmness his solitary life brought him, but in reality he knew the right company would be a welcome comfort.

He kept a painted Adirondack chair high on the bank nestled among a patch of wild shrubbery. He slouched into the deep seat of the chair and watched the water flow by him. It never stopped and reminded him that he needed to emulate that force if he wanted to be whole again.

He walked slowly back to the former mill along the stony drive. Without warning, a familiar scent wafted along a breeze and it brought a sense of unusual comfort. He tried to place it. A familiar perfume maybe? It was gone as quickly as it came. Passing his truck, he noticed the glove compartment door was ajar and opened the passenger side door to close it. A few of the contents had spilled out onto the floor and he attributed it to the loose clasp on the compartment door. Slamming it shut a few times, it finally caught. As he did, something on the bench seat caught his eye.

A gold herringbone chain caught the setting sunlight. He immediately recognized it as a Christmas gift to his little sister. She had rarely taken it off. As he held the tiny, delicate bracelet in his rough hands, he envisioned her sitting in this truck that had belonged to their father. She loved accompanying their dad to the local hardware store on the weekends and singing along to the country 8-tracks he always played. Blinking and forcing back the last of his tears, Chase was grateful for finding the bracelet and tucked it safely in his shirt pocket. A location that was purposely as close to his heart as he could manage.

CHAPTER TWELVE
Calm Before the Storm

LACEY HADN'T BEEN OUT on a Friday night in months, so, she was looking forward to meeting a few old college friends for dinner at one of her favorite restaurants, Severn Inn. A martini or two, a view of the water and some laughs was just what she needed. She had worked from her tiny home office that was tucked away in the attic. The cozy space was hidden from the outside world with the exception of the grand sycamore branches that stretched to peek in through the dormer window. The sight of them made Lacey feel as though she was escaping to a private tree house in the middle of the city.

With no real office distractions, she worked through her agenda quickly and followed-up with her clients. All were in good spirits and appreciative of the work she was doing for them. Even Stuart Benson was glad to hear his closing was scheduled and the paperwork Lacey had worked tirelessly to retrieve from the association alleviated any qualms the bank's underwriters had had. She set a time to meet him the following Friday at the condo for the final walk-thru prior to the closing.

She gazed out the window at the leaves that dripped from the mottled limbs before her ringing cell phone caught her attention and she peered at the digits of the incoming call. The number was slightly familiar, but she wasn't quite sure that she should answer it. She was intent on actually making it to dinner on time, possibly early. As the phone rang a fourth time, it dawned on her. The number was Sam's. Letting the call go to voicemail, she headed to the spiral staircase that led to the second floor landing to start getting ready.

Walking into her bedroom, she opened the door to the small closet and plucked a pair of black skinny jeans and a sheer black blouse. She also thought about Sam and their last encounter. She had no expectations of a next day call, but had thought their date went well. When a week went by without hearing from him, she figured he wasn't interested. Their awkward meeting at the Crestwood did not do much to change her view of the situation. She would try to play it cool with him for now, she told herself, and listen to his message later.

Putting music on to fill the quiet atmosphere of her townhouse, she took her time getting ready while sipping on a glass of wine. By six o'clock she was showered and dressed, with her hair dried and slightly curled. Choosing a few key pieces of jewelry, spritzing her favorite perfume, and pulling her tall black boots from the closet shelf, she was relaxed and ready to go. She returned to her office to fetch her phone and gave in to the impulse to listen to Sam's message as she hopped back down the narrow staircase.

"Hey, Lacey. It's Sam. Just calling to see if you want to grab some dinner with me next week. Give me a call when you can. Talk to you later."

Lacey placed the phone in her shiny black clutch purse and decided she would call Sam over the weekend or maybe even wait until Monday. She didn't like to play games, but he certainly didn't seem eager to see her again and she didn't want him to think she was waiting for his call. She considered the thought that she was possibly being overly sensitive. At any rate, she was officially ready for a stiff drink and to put these last couple of weeks behind her.

Walking out into the warm evening air, Lacey left the porch light on and navigated the uneven brick sidewalk. She noticed Bryce had left a light on inside and her porch light on as well. It was comforting and thoughtful of her and Lacey looked forward to seeing her in a week or so upon her return. Once in the car, she put on her favorite shade of rouge lipstick and backed out onto the street with a Dave Matthews Band song playing on her iPod. It took her back to her carefree and fun-filled college days that she missed terribly. The friends she would be seeing that evening were from that time in her life and they had a special bond as a result. Too much time has passed. It had been two years since the last time they all got together.

As she drove the short distance to the restaurant, she thought about her life. She had been doing that a lot lately. The crying-in-the-car episode, drinks and dinner with Bryce, and then the night on the boat with Sam had all changed her a little bit. She had a lot to be proud of, however, the recent events showed her something was missing. Nothing material or tactile and she couldn't put her finger on it. Lacey had been on edge for some time now and just didn't feel like herself. Sure, it would be nice to meet someone special and start a life together. That goes without saying, but it was more than that.

She needed to find herself again and be happy with herself before she could manage to build any kind of deep relationship. Her steady work was slowly turning her into someone she didn't recognize anymore. Others found her to be impressive while she tolerated herself for the sake of doing what she was supposed to.

Turning up the playlist, she sat at the red light as the drawbridge was raised. She thought about Sam living on his boat as she watched a line of sailboats head out of port for an evening cruise. Their captains no doubt wanted to take advantage of this unexpected warm day. With that though, she decided she would call Sam back over the weekend and give him the benefit of the doubt. Maybe he really did get sidetracked with work. She of all people should understand that. The bridge returned to its position and the light turned green. The sound of the horn signaled it was time for her to move on.

CHAPTER THIRTEEN
The Straw That Broke Her

AFTER HANDING THE VALET her keys, Lacey walked into the buzzing restaurant and headed to the bar to meet her friends. She was a little early, so, she took a seat in the upscale lounge to wait. She ordered a Grey Goose martini on the rocks with a twist and pulled out her phone to see if she had any texts from those she was to meet. Nothing from anyone. No emails, no texts, no Facebook messages. While some might be disappointed, this lack of communication from her ever-present smart phone elated her and, along with the first sip of her icy martini, she was anxiety free. She put the phone down on the bar and took another sip of her cocktail. Her seat had a view of the harbor and she sat back and soaked it all in. Life was good.

"Hey there, Lacey," a friendly voice called from close range. Lacey turned to see it was one of her college roommates, Rebecca.

"Rebecca! You look fantastic. It is so great to see you," Lacey stood and gave her brunette friend a long hug. "You cut your hair! I love it."

"Thanks," Rebecca sincerely replied as she took a seat next to Lacey and ordered a Chardonnay. "After the twins were born, I needed a pick-me-up and was tired of having a ponytail twenty-four-seven. So how've you been?

Rebecca nodded a thank you to the bartended and didn't hesitate to take a gulp to start the night off right.

"Good, good. Can't complain. I work a lot, but I'm afraid

of turning anything down. You never know what the market will bring." Lacey noticed that she was justifying her actions without outward reason.

"I see your name in the Real Estate section of the paper for stuff like 'most sales ever' all the time."

"I don't think I have been bestowed with that exact honor, but, thanks all the same. So, how about you? Twins? Wow. Their pics on Facebook are so adorable. I can't wait to meet them in person. Are they doing well?"

"Yes. They are incredible. A lot of work, but worth it two hundred percent. Kevin and I are very thankful," she took a sip of her Chardonnay and added, "*and* I very thankful that he was able to be with them tonight so that mommy could get out of the house."

"Me, too! Cheers to Kevin!"

The friends giggled together and clinked their glasses once more.

"Hey, can I join this party?" The smiley blonde called out from the door. Her full, natural ringlets completely accented her personality.

"Oh, no. Now the trouble starts!" Rebecca teased their friend and stood to welcome her. Lacey pulled a seat over to them to give Ashley a seat at the bar with them.

Once she was settled, she ordered a Blue Moon from the bartender and the three friends were talking and laughing non-stop as if they were still back at college.

"It's like meeting back at Al's," Ashley declared paying homage to the dive bar they frequented back in the day.

"Yeah, uh, this place looks *just* like it." Rebecca said sarcastically as she looked at her swanky surroundings.

"I think the drinks were a wee bit cheaper there, too," Lacey added as she joined in with the joke.

"Just a little. Didn't they have drafts for, like, twenty-five cents?" Ashley reminisced.

"Ah, the good old days," Rebecca looked off into the distance as if daydreaming.

The three friends talked endlessly and frantically as they

caught up on their respective lives. Eventually, they made their way to the maître de and took their seats at a table by the window with a shimmering view of the water and the boats docked in the restaurant's marina. In no time another round of drinks were served along with a feast of appetizers. The conversation was non-stop and they were blissfully unaware of life outside of their round table.

"Excuse me," Lacey said as she stood and placed her linen napkin next to her plate and picking up her purse. "Ladies' room break."

Lacey was happy. The night reminded her that she needed to make an effort to create more balance in her life. Her spirit had dulled over the years and she wanted to hold on to the light-hearted side of herself.

Before heading back to the table, she stopped in the sitting area of the restroom to add a little lipstick and check her hair. She noticed her phone was lit up in her clutch and noticed she had one missed call. She picked up the phone and listened to the message as she reddened her lips. In no time, her flushed cheeks matched the shade of the lipstick as the voicemail played.

"Lacey. Stuart Benson here. I have been doing some thinking. I no longer wish to purchase the condo. Please email me a release by the morning and I will sign it and email it back you by Monday. Call me to confirm you received this message. Thank you."

Lacey sunk into the leather chair next to her. She was sick to her stomach. She had spent so much time showing properties to Stuart and then countless hours making sure the deal stayed on track. Why would he choose to walk away now when he knew the red tape had been cleared? She felt tears welling up in her eyes due to the sheer shock of the message.

Despite the hurdles in the end, this was not a transaction that she thought was in jeopardy of falling through and she was counting on that closing to get her through the slower winter months. She had referred two other buyers to other agents in her office due to not being able to give proper time to their home searches because of her current workload. Stuart Benson had taken the most time with the coddling he demanded on top of the deal itself and now it was all for nothing.

She suddenly feared walking back out into back out into society. She couldn't stay in the restroom all night, but dreaded the festive atmosphere that awaited her. Anymore, her tears were always just below the surface and she was too downhearted to even try to hide her mood. Ten-dollar cocktails and a twenty-six dollar dinner were suddenly not in the budget since a large portion of her anticipated income just walked away. Maybe he would change his mind? She analyzed the possibilities as a coping mechanism. A bad day at work led to a rash decision? Overthinking the lawsuit the condo association was involved with? By morning, this could all be back on track again. She felt a little better. It wasn't the first time a buyer or seller called her off the cuff and said something they had no real intentions of following through with. Taking a deep breath and patting her eyes and face with a cold paper towel in a form of deja vu, she headed back out to join her friends.

"Hey, we thought you fell in. Everything okay? We waited for you to start dinner. Dig in," Rebecca said as she took a bite of her seafood pasta.

"Lacey, you alright? You look flushed," Ashley looked at Lacey with concern.

Afraid she would burst into tears, Lacey put on a brave face and took a sip of ice water.

"I'm fine. Sorry. You didn't have to wait for me! I made the mistake of checking a message on my phone and a work issue popped up. It will probably work itself out by tomorrow. I don't want it to spoil my night. I'm having too much fun," Lacey declared as she cut into the perfectly seared scallops.

"Don't worry about it," Ashley replied. "If it makes any difference, I had one of the worst days at work ever and I think it took me the whole drive here just to start to feel a little bit better. You two made me forget about it in milliseconds and now we will do that for you."

"That's right," Rebecca chimed in. "We can't let anything spoil this evening for us. No more work talk, no more baby talk, no more real world talk. Remember that time we skipped class to head to Towson Lake? I always think about that day when life is making me a little crazy."

"That was the best day!" Lacey exclaimed. "It was that first really warm day of the year and I can still feel the sun on my skin and the distinct smell of spring."

"And the water on my toes. I don't remember us doing anything but sitting on that dock and watching the water and talking. Perfectly simple," Ashley recalled as she reached for a piece of bread as the waitress refilled their water glasses.

"The thing is," Rebecca said between bites, "we had no money, crappy part-time jobs, boyfriend problems, and lived in a cinder block cell of a dorm that we are, at least I am, still paying for. Regardless, it was still one of the best times of my life. This life after college is wonderful to me, don't get me wrong, but it can quickly take on a life of it's own. Anytime that starts to happen and things get a little too intense, I think of that peaceful day and remember that we don't need much to be truly happy. It gets me back on track."

A reflective quiet came over the table in the first time all night.

"That is so true, Rebecca. I really needed to hear that." Lacey couldn't believe how her friend's words could start to erase the feelings she had just brought to the table. Rebecca was right. Lacey would be fine with or without Stuart Benson and his drama. In fact, moving forward without him might be the best thing.

"No problem. That will be five cents," Rebecca joked as she referred to Lucy's therapy session cost from the Peanuts. The threesome laughed once again and Lacey felt cautiously better.

Endless coffee and some sinful desserts later, the night was winding down and the chatter in the restaurant started to wane. Rebecca declared it was way past her bedtime and she needed to return to help her husband with their darling babies.

"I'm not worried about the girls," she said as she gave one last hug to Lacey then Ashley. "I just hope my husband is still standing. Lord knows I can't do this without him!"

"Text us when you get home, okay?" Lacey asked. "And thanks again for cheering me up. I hope I didn't bring everyone down too much with my buzz kill work talk."

"Not at all, Lacey! Stop it. The night was perfect. See you all soon!" Rebecca passed out warm hugs and blew a kiss as she headed home to the muddled comfort of her little family.

Ashley and Lacey sat back down to pay their bills and get ready to leave, too.

"Work sucks, doesn't it?" Ashley said out of the blue.

"It sure can. A necessary evil. I think I just need to be better about keeping it in its place and not letting it consume every part of my life."

"I didn't want to bring it up earlier, but, I lost a patient today and it was pretty rough. It put things in perspective, though. Rebecca was right and we all need that reminder from time to time."

Lacey looked at Ashley as she placed her credit card in the holder for the waitress to pick up. Ashley was an ER nurse and Lacey could only imagine the scenarios that play out daily in her line of work.

"Oh, Ash. I'm so sorry. I can only imagine," she said sympathetically while waiting to see if Ashley wanted to talk about it.

"Not to sound insensitive, but, it happens, you know?" she said as she smiled a little at Lacey to let her know she was okay. "This just hit a little close to home, is all. I'm fine, really, but, like I said, it put things in perspective."

"I'm sure it does. For what it's worth, I can't imagine a better nurse to be at someone's side."

"That's kind and means a lot. Really," Ashley offered with all her heart as she shook the troubling thoughts from her mind and distractedly patted the table.

Lacey and Ashley signed their receipts before walking toward the exit. They stepped out into the night air and a cool sea breeze had kicked up while they waited for their cars to be brought around. Saying goodnight and wishing each other safe travels, each was on her way home in a matter of minutes and back to the lives they had fell into. Lacey quickly remembered the task Stuart Benson demanded once she was driving home and the joy of the evening started to fade as a sinking feeling in her stomach replaced it. While she had much to be thankful for and her life was not one she should complain about, she also knew that something needed to change. Her work life seeped into every event and overshadowed every joyous moment. Her modest level of self-made success was breeding resentment.

CHAPTER FOURTEEN
A Step In a New Direction

IT WAS SUNDAY MORNING. Lacey had always envisioned Sunday mornings being typically lazy. The paper, fresh coffee, and a stroll with a dog she didn't have. Sunday mornings for Lacey, like any other morning, was just another workday. Usually she was preparing for an open house and sometimes squeezing in a showing for a client beforehand. So, this being a rare Sunday without any appointments scheduled, she had been looking forward to it all week. In typical fashion, however, something had come up to ruin the chance of a day off.

Stuart Benson seemed to have been rejecting her calls and his contact method now boiled down to abbreviated texts that had even the mechanical fonts shouting at her. She had left him a few messages since his dreadful call on Friday in hopes of actually speaking to him in order to better understand his position and help him; even if that meant starting the process all over to find the right home for him.

"Upon receipt, I shall immediately email the release back to you so that you may process the return of my deposit. Thank you," was his only emailed reply with any substance. It was as if she was communicating with a robot.

She gave up on expecting to talk about this as two professional humans and had emailed the release on Saturday night.

Sitting in bed with her laptop, she now noticed that a new email had been delivered. The executed release was attached and the deal was off. The scanned image was burning a hole in the screen along with her retinas. She felt sick. Rolling out of her billowy bed, she pulled on a pair of old, tasteless sweats to weakly prepare for a quick dash to the office. She hoped she was early enough to avoid anyone being there. She would turn in the file and, once the seller signed the release, her office would mail a check to Stuart and she could move on. That thought gave her a wave of relief.

An hour later, the deed was done and Lacey was sitting on her back deck with a block quilt made by her grandmother, cup of coffee, the Sunday paper and a bagel. She did what she needed to do well within the timeframe that required of her and was intent on salvaging this day. Desperation fuelled her desire to turn this experience into something better. Fall was beginning to show on the trees surrounding her city yard and the morning nip evaporated.

She watched a bird at the birdfeeder at the edge of the fenced, green space. It unwound her so she kept that focus. How nice it would be to soar freely in an inherent, uncluttered way of life while the human race continued complicating their lives below. The bright red cardinal chirped at her and flew away only to return seconds later to dine again on the black sunflower seeds he couldn't resist. Remembering times she had neglected to maintain the food supply she had willingly offered made her a tad ashamed.

She picked up the paper as her house phone rang and she went into the kitchen to answer it.

"Hello," she greeted.

"Hi, Lacey. I was just thinking of you and figured I would give you a call before you headed off for the day," Lacey's mother's comforting voice said. She stepped out onto the back deck once more with the wireless phone to enjoy a talk with her loving mother.

"Hi, mom. Glad you called. I'm just sitting here having breakfast and reading the paper. And watching birds at the birdfeeder."

"Well, that sounds like a lovely morning. I usually don't

hear anything of the sort from you. Do you have an open house today?"

"Actually, no. So, I have the day free. What are you doing?"

"Dad and I are going to visit grandma. You should meet us there."

Lacey's grandmother was an energetic octogenarian who had recently moved to the area to be closer to her son and daughter-in-law after Lacey's grandfather had passed away.

"That sounds nice. I'll think about it, but I don't think I would make very good company today. I had sort of a bad weekend. I might just enjoy the day at home with no plans to shake off my bad mood."

With her mother's prompting, Lacey went on to divulge the events of the weekend. Her mother listened patiently.

"You know, it sounds like you just need a little break. You could come stay with us for a weekend or maybe make some plans with the friends you saw on Friday?"

"That's not a bad idea. It would have to be somewhere without cell reception, though," Lacey joked half-heartedly. "I'd throw this thing in the garbage if I knew my life wouldn't go right along with it."

"How about the cabin? Unless they have added a tower in the vicinity, a cell phone never works there. Call your friends to see if they want to join you and we'll get the key from grandma. Your uncle was there last week and said it is still a perfect getaway and he cut extra firewood while he was there."

Lacey's mind immediately turned to the unpainted and perfectly weathered cabin that sat among the hemlocks. She envisioned herself there wholeheartedly. She was struck by the notion that a peaceful place like that exists year round and she never thinks of going there. Her pulse slowed.

"That's a really good idea. I bet Ashley and Bryce would join me in a second. Rebecca probably couldn't leave the twins for the weekend. Ashley and Bryce would love it, though. Do you think it would be okay to call them now before you talked to Grandma?"

"Do it. Grandma wants people to use it. She hates that she can't get there as much and feels better knowing it is being checked on and aired out regularly. Call Ashley now and let me know when you girls want to go."

"I will! I'm so glad you called. I feel better already thinking about an escape."

"Good. You enjoy your day and don't let that lunatic of a man bother you. He is obviously troubled. Just be happy you are able to function as a reasonable adult. I'll talk to you soon."

Lacey cleared off her outdoor patio table then ran upstairs to her bedroom and jumped into bed with her laptop. She sent an email to a colleague who often covers for her when she needs help and asked if he would be willing to monitor her business for a weekend in an upcoming week. Then she called Ashley and Bryce. Their phones went to voicemail and Lacey left a detailed messages. It was then that she did the unthinkable. Without thinking about how best to spend her time, she curled up under the down comforter and turned on the flat screen TV that was positioned on the wall in front of her queen sleigh bed. She was taking a day off.

A bag of bar-b-que chips, a Hershey's chocolate bar, and a can of ginger ale later, Lacey was feeling devilishly good. Her discipline kept her from pouring a glass of wine so early in the day, but she was getting close to staging a coup against her own personal regime. She needed this lazy day more than she realized. Her only goal was to numb her mind to see what territory it has a tendency to go to when she allowed it to wander. She watched endless comedies and romances on Netflix then caught up on the shows she had DVR'd to the system's capacity. She began to feel restful as her meaningful inaction eroded the day.

Her laptop dinged, she still couldn't part with her gadgets, and she read the new email. Terrance Walker was free the second week in October and he would be happy to cover for her.

"Well, that was easy," Lacey thought. *"Why don't I do this more*

often?"

She burrowed back into the comfort of her own little nest and mindlessly changed channels to find something else to watch. Sunday marathons of so-called reality TV was prominent and was killing her better mood so she clicked off the TV and headed to the bath to luxuriate in a hot bubble bath in her deep claw foot tub. As the steaming water expanded the lavender-smelling bubbles, she took a deep breath in and left the room to pick her most comfortable loungewear. Hearing her cell phone, she begrudgingly tore herself away to answer it. She would never be able to relax if she left the call go.

"Lacey, you are a genius. I've always wanted to go this cabin you have speak of so often and I need a break too. In the past twenty-four hours, I have been vomited on by a drunk teen, told I don't know what I'm talking about and arm slapped by an immature thirty-something woman who *doesn't want a shot*," she finished with a mock baby voice. "When can we go? Now?"

Lacey chuckled. That all sounded much worse than her current hassles.

"Not now, unfortunately! How about the second week in October? I'm so glad you want to go."

"Done. Putting in my time-off request now. Got to go, but we are on for the week of October 10."

Ashley abruptly ended the call. While her spirits were lifted, she called Sam before she could think of a reason not to. After a few rings, his phone, too, skipped to voicemail and she left a message before turning off her phone for the next few hours. It would only be a matter of time before a client or two called with an urgent request to see a property that she wouldn't be able to schedule on late notice anyway. It all could wait until Monday. Stepping into the hot water, she let her body and mind slip into a baptismal state. She strangely felt like a new person.

CHAPTER FIFTEEN
Mountain Air

THE LOOSE GRAVEL POPPED and crunched under the weight of the car as Lacey pulled into the short driveway of her family's rustic property in the outskirts of the Adirondack Mountains. Everything seemed a little different since the last time she was here. Of course, she was much younger then. The cabin seemed closer to the road than she remembered and smaller. Strange how the mind tends to exaggerate matter in one's youth. Unless, fond memories just become bigger and brighter as our lives become increasingly mundane. Still, the road was quiet and the property semi-private. Putting the car in park, she wrapped her scarf around her neck and pulled on her fleece gloves as she exited the warm car.

The October temperature was dropping dramatically now that the sun was going down and the higher altitude was not helping matters. Fall was not only in the air; it was also tinged with winter. It was distinctively different than early October just south of the Mason-Dixon. Lacey crossed her arms in front of her for extra warmth and took in the nostalgic scenery.

Everything seemed to be well maintained and in order. The surrounding forest was carpeted with ferns and still lush with hemlocks that were also bigger than she remembered. They very well may have been the loftiest trees she had ever laid eyes on. She gave a silent prayer that none should fall on the two-room cabin as she peered up at the swaying treetops. The exterior wood on the cabin was so grey it was almost white in some spots. Tangles of rosebushes with mostly bare vines did their best to embrace the aging property. Straggling pink cushion roses decayed proudly here and there. Both were beyond their prime, but utterly charming in their own way.

She pulled her phone out of the pocket of her fleece pullover to see if Ashley had texted her. No signal.

"Finally," she thought as she turned the power off and returned it to her pocket. As Lacey had been preparing to leave the house to pick up her friend, Ashley had called to report she was still at the hospital from her shift the day before. A charter bus crash had sent throngs of patients to the ER and Ashley wasn't able to leave yet. She promised to try to meet up with Lacey in New York, but had no idea when the ER would slow enough for her to leave. She had also received a voicemail from Bryce alerting that she was on a delayed flight and wouldn't be home in time. While disappointed, Lacey understood her friends' positions and, on a whim, headed up to her family's property alone. She now second-guessed that decision, as she stood alone in the eerie quiet of evening. A crow cawed in the distance and the forest exuded a wispy and hollow greeting. She had become accustomed to a certain level of connectedness and daily purpose. Being here now seemed a little ridiculous.

Slinging her overnight bag over her shoulder as she picked up the cooler of rations she had prepared, she started toward the front door of the cabin and assured herself she would feel better once she settled inside. Stepping up to the porch, she was transported back in time. The rustic branch railings still revealed the same twisted knots and protrusions she remembered as a little girl. The Adirondack chairs were faded, however, still coated in the shade of red she remembered. She could not wait to sit on those same seats she had spent hours in reading, writing and sketching so long ago. She grasped the iron door handle and it just felt right. Opening the door, the stale smell of the pine-paneled interior wrapped her like a warm wool blanket.

In a sense, she was home. The same brass lamp with an olive green shade sat to the right of the door. She clicked on the light source and relief washed over her to find the light bulb worked and the cabin's power was on. Yellow glow illuminated the green, brown and beige barkcloth curtains and matching sofa slipcover. Lacey ran her fingertips over the coarse curtain material and held it in a fist.

The toile scenes depicted men in an old time pastoral settings plowing fields by hand and women dressed in billowing dresses collecting baskets of flowers. She set her bag on the steamer trunk-turned-coffee table where a small pile of well-read Reader's Digest magazines sat piled on top of a lace doily and it made Lacey miss her family and the person she once was. Making sure the door was locked behind her, this citified country girl continued her trip down memory lane as she turned on any and every light she could find before walking into the adjacent and open kitchen area where she deposited her cooler on the stained and faded Formica countertop covered with silver boomerangs. She took a seat on one of the two barstools as though she sat there every day. So many memories rushed into her mind that she couldn't keep track.

It was a bittersweet feeling to be here without anyone to share it with. The cast iron sink had yellowed from decades of use and faded pictures of her extended family were unceremoniously tacked to the vintage sea foam green refrigerator with utilitarian black magnets. Not able to sit still yet, she slid the barstool back under the L-shaped countertop, retrieved her leather duffel and walked back to the bedroom to continue settling in for the night. The queen-sized pine bed and mismatched dresser dominated the small room. The top of the dresser displayed Nancy Drew and Hardy Boys mystery novels, among other outdated titles, and a small Carnival Glass lamp with an antique white ruffled shade was straight from 1950.

The air from increasingly cold nights was trapped in the cabin making it at least ten degrees colder than the current temperature outside. Lacey's mother had arranged for the chimney to be cleaned and had let it be known that cured firewood was ample. A few space heaters were tucked away in closets, but this evening called for a more traditional heat source. She readied the hearth and her fingers numbed while crumpling old newspapers and making a kindling teepee. Once added, the split logs caught quickly with robust crackles.

Kneeling before the orange glow, she was hypnotized by flaming fingers caressing the dry cherry wood. After standing by the fire to warm her fingers and toes for a bit, she decided to unpack her cooler and fix a plate of food. First things first, she pulled a water glass from one of the pine cabinets and treated herself to a heavy pour of Merlot. A paper plate of cheese, crackers, and grapes substituted for a hearty dinner. She added two logs to the fire and plopped down on the sofa to soak up the heat. The flames were mesmerizing. Besides adding another log, she must have sat staring at the red, yellow, and blue flickering hues for an hour before her eyelids soon sagged.

With a start, she jerked her head upright as she woke from the same position hours later. The fire was burning low. A great horned owl hooted loudly and Lacey wondered if that was what woke her from her deep, albeit uncomfortable, slumber. She placed two more logs on the fire with the intent to keep it burning all night for warmth and an irrational sense of protection. Walking from room to room, she extinguished only half the lights.

It was now unnerving to suddenly be in this once familiar place after all these years. The setting was drastically different than the life that she had become accustomed to in Annapolis. Poking the fire back into a small blaze, she walked to the nearby window to take a peek outside. A full moon cast shadows over the forest's edge and the shapes of the looming trees were etched on the ground covered with a light frost. Movement caught her eye and she nudged the blind to the right to get a better look.

Lacey gasped as she clearly saw the silhouette of a petite figure with light blonde hair at the edge of the woods. Although it was hard to tell in the night, and as ludicrous as it were, it appeared to be a young girl in a dress. She cupped her hands against the glass to shade her eyes from the interior firelight for a better look. A light fog could be seen swimming around the figure and the mist made the vision that much clearer. Not believing what she was seeing, she widened then shut her eyes tightly while moving any errant hairs away from her view. Again, she peered wide-eyed into the misty night. She was afraid to breathe. Suddenly, a deer sauntered into view. Faced with a completely natural sight, Lacey emptied her lungs of shaky air while spying the group of four deer foraging for food.

Fear morphed into amusement. She reminded herself that this is a safe place full of comforts and she returned to the couch after double-checking that the front door was indeed locked. As her tired eyes watched the flames dance, she felt somewhat dejected that this beautiful setting was borderline frightening to her now. Maybe she had changed even more than she realized. Maybe her work-consumed life in the city wasn't such a bad thing, she thought. A multi-colored afghan was draped behind her. The soft blanket had been crocheted with her grandmother's unwrinkled hands many years ago while Lacey had sat by her side and flipped through a teen-marketed magazine. The memory and fuzzy yarn brought a little consolation to an unsettled Lacey. She pulled it tightly around her shoulders and, like a lunatic, yearned for what she was trying to escape from.

Suddenly, she missed the phone actively signaling a constant stream of client requests and thought about her busy schedule that kept her from being scared in the night. She was not as lonely in that life as she had thought and this little trip was exactly what she needed in order to help her gain appreciation. Still clad in the knotted yarn blanket that now served as a cape, she walked back to the bedroom to grab a few more blankets and some pillows. Lacey set up a makeshift bed on the sofa before going to the kitchen to make a cup of tea with milk and sugar like her grandmother always used to do in the evening then clicked on the under-cabinet radio just like her grandfather always did.

Only one or two stations came in and soon the quiet twang of Classic Country songs hung in the night air. She returned to her post. Resting her back against the arm of the sofa, she put her feet up and adjusted the blankets over her legs and wool-covered toes. The stack of Reader's Digests along with the tea and quiet music ironically helped to get her mind off of the loneliness and desolate solitude she had come for. The fire was going strong and it was cozy and Lacey wished she could enjoy it more. In the end, she told herself she would make it through the night and head home in the morning.

Soon enough, sunlight streamed through the frayed edges of the worn blinds in the cabin. The magazine she had been reading when she drifted back to sleep was splayed across her blanketed chest and the fire was reduced to glowing embers and charred pieces of firewood.

Amazingly, she did feel rested and restored. Easing up and onto her feet, she snapped open the rolled blind at the window next to the front door. Gazing past the front porch to the yard, the forest was barely visible through the thick mist that surrounded the place. No signs of people in the fog. She derided herself for thinking such absurd notions. The car windows were shrouded in condensation and everything was as it was when she arrived as though time had stopped when she walked through the door. Lacey was delighted when she saw the seemingly same handful of deer grazing again at the edge of the mowed lawn. She sat down at the small wooden table at the window and watched the gentle creatures bob their heads up and back in the gray morning as they enjoyed their breakfast.

Breakfast. With that thought, Lacey realized how hungry she was and how much she needed a strong cup of coffee. In a few short minutes, she was digging the coffee pot from an organized lower cabinet. She plugged it in and readied the brew and the smell of coffee began to overtake the aroma of the charred firewood and together, the scent was sweet and reassuring. Adding some paper and kindling, she stoked the fire to take the chill off the morning and headed to the little back bedroom to dress for the ride back to her city home later that morning.

With a plate of fruit and a toasted bagel with cream cheese, she was back at her table watching the wildlife from the comfort of the warm cottage. She took a sip of hot coffee and enjoyed the peaceful company of the deer. With the now roaring-again fire in her sight along with the heavy morning fog blanketing the pines outside, she was giddy with the simplistic beauty of it all. She wondered how she had stayed away from this place for so long and felt her soul being stirred.

Soon the deer leaped and scattered into the thickets and the quiet was interrupted by a banging knock on the loose screen door. Lacey jumped with a start

CHAPTER SIXTEEN
Uninvited Guest

ASSUMING THE KNOCK MUST have been from Ashley, Lacey brushed the crumbs from her sweatshirt and walked toward the door. She felt bad that Ashley drove all this way while Lacey planned on leaving for home. She would, of course, now have to stay another night and her mind prematurely churned with that idea.

Tugging the sticking wooden door open, Lacey was startled to find a man about the same age as she standing where she expected to find her female friend. Talking through the screen door and keeping a firm hold on the inside door, she hesitantly greeted the stranger. He was taller than she and his rugged appearance suggested a durable and capable nature. He was different than the white-collar guys she normally encountered. His chiseled face with strong jawline was slightly hidden under unshaven stubble and a knit cap with a visor. She nervously waited for him to explain his visit.

He seemed just as taken aback at the unexpected sight of her.

"Uh, hi. Sorry to bother you. Is Tim here?" He said in a slightly gruff tone.

"No. No, he's not," she offered and immediately regretted giving any indication that she was here alone. What else could she say, though?

"Oh, man. I am so sorry. I … I thought that was his car out there. Well, uh, I'll be out of here in a second. I was just dropping off this canoe for him. He knows about it," he awkwardly stammered. "Think it's okay if I just put it on that side of the cabin?"

His expression softened with a nod to the right. He was clearly uncomfortable.

Lacey's tension eased. Her Uncle Tim did have the same car as she. His was newer and a better model, but looked much the same.

"Oh, sure. I don't see any harm in that. I'll let him know you brought it by."

Regaining her posture, she swiftly deduced that her answer indicated Tim would be there soon, just in case this guy was not what he seemed.

He muttered his thanks and his shy smile revealed dimples that were a direct divergence to his broad shoulders and muscular physique. Lacey noticed the worn Ritter's River Landing t-shirt showing under his unbuttoned red flannel before he turned away. She was familiar with the establishment as it was a landmark business located a few miles from the cabin. Saying thank you and goodbye, she shut the door and instinctively locked it. From the shadows, she watched him walk to his late 1970's two-toned brown and tan Ford pick-up truck and effortlessly dragged the green canoe from the bed of the truck. Hoisting it to shoulder level, he precariously balanced it with two hands before quickly walking it to the side of the cabin.

He looked up as he walked past the window and Lacey was embarrassed to think he might have noticed her watching him. After she heard the thud of the canoe being put in place, she opened the door to appear less odd.

"Hey, thanks, again. I was going to see if you needed any help, but apparently not."

"Nah. I lift these things in my sleep. Once you get it balanced, they aren't too bad to move around; at least not these smaller ones."

He stopped in the grass and Lacey stepped out onto the porch.

"I'm not so sure about that, but I'll let my uncle know you

brought it by."

Lacey crossed her arms in front of her for warmth. The misty morning air was chilly.

"Tim's your uncle? Then you know Jamie and Chris well?"

Jamie and Chris were Lacey's cousins and the three of them were about the same age. Back when they were in grade school, they would accompany their grandparents to the cabin a few times each summer for a week or a long weekend.

"Sure do. They're my cousins."

Lacey blushed when she realized the stupidity of her obvious answer.

The canoe deliverer rocked back on his heels and put his hands in the pocket of his jeans as he smiled up at her. Dimples flashing, he nodded.

"Yeah. I guess they would be. I grew up in one of the houses down the street. We lived here year-round and I hung out with Jamie and Chris and their ... cousin," he slowly recalled and he pointed at Lacey with slit eyes. "That wouldn't be ... ?"

"Wait a second! Chase?" she said a little more loudly that she had intended with her hands on her hips.

"The one and only," he answered with arms held out to his sides.

"I can't believe it. Those were the best times!"

"Yeah they were. Do you remember when we used to walk the trestle to wade in the creek?"

"Yes. I didn't walk it, though. I crawled. It terrified me. Why did we have to walk across it anyway? We could have just stayed on this side of the creek bed," she pointed out incredulously.

Chase laughed and shook his head.

"Nah, no fun that way. You know, I still walk over that trestle from time to time and it's crazy. It's like it shrunk and the water is nothing. It was so much more when I was twelve."

"I was scared to death of it and I do recall raging rapids beneath. Too funny."

They laughed and reminisced together for a bit before Chase said he had to leave.

"It was great seeing you and thinking of all those good times. Maybe I'll run into you again," Lacey kindly said.

"Same here."

Chase took a few steps toward his truck before abruptly stopping and turning to Lacey who had a hand on the door. She stopped when she heard him add, "You should stop by the Penn Tavern tomorrow night. They have some good specials."

"Aw, thanks. I'm leaving today, though. I'll keep that in mind for next time," she said in a friendly voice.

"Too bad. Well, it was great seeing you. Talk to you later, Lacey."

Getting back into the truck, Chase backed out of the drive and it was quiet once more. Lacey stepped back inside as the heat from the fire cancelled out the cool outside air trying to take over.

"Now what?" she thought.

She made her way to the open kitchen area to start to clean up and get ready to head back home. Turning on the archaic under-cabinet radio, she grinned and shook her head as she remembered one of only a couple stations to come in clearly was still tuned in on the dial. The Hound was a radio staple around there. On Saturday nights, it played country classics by the likes of Hank Williams and Patsy Cline. Lacey recalled playing cards or reading with the muffled slide guitars coming from the same radio decades ago. Her tastes in music had changed over the years, but hearing that station now was soothing. She hummed along to the tunes she vaguely knew as she busied herself with putting the cabin back in order and re-packing her bag and cooler for the drive home.

In an hour or so she was ready to leave and bid a silent farewell to the little cottage filled with so many memories. She promised herself she would return again and would stay more than one night. Locking the door behind her, she walked to her car and breathed in a good measure of fresh mountain air to last the long drive home.

Sliding into the shiny and clean vehicle, she realized her car felt comforting, too, though. She had thought this trip would put everything in perspective and it had only confused her. An example of some kind of split personality, Lacey seemed to be unsuited for any particular world at the moment. She plugged her phone and charger in and placed it on the dash holder to power back up.

Once back on to the interstate, she listened to her messages. The first message was from a past client reaching out to her to advise they were looking to sell over the next year with a new baby on the way and wanted her to meet with them when she got back in town. The next was another first time buyer who was distressed out about an inspection. The third was the same buyer saying to disregard his first message as he spoke with Terrance about everything. The fourth was from Ashley and the fifth was from Samuel Hinkley.

"La-cey," Ashley started off with a singsong voice, *"I know you are in Timbuktu with no signal, but, I REALLY hope you get this. I am finally home after working non-stop for the past forty-eight hours and good news.... I was still able to take the rest of the week off. PLEASE tell me I can escape my insane life and meet up with you. Call Me."*

"Lacey, Lacey, Lacey," Sam started with his usual way of understated fanfare. *"We are playing phone tag. You're it. Call me. I want to take you out for that dinner if you'll still let me. Guess I'll just wait to hear back from you. Later."*

His mention of a second date stirred Lacey's emotions. She would naturally agree to his invitation.

Passing a rest stop, Lacey pulled in to return the calls and immediately called her clients back to arrange a time to meet. Leaving a message, she let them know she would be happy to meet with them and offered her congratulations on their growing family. Next, she phoned her buyer to let him know she received his message. He was in good spirits now and apologized for jumping to conclusions. He appreciated her callback. Lastly, she focused on the calls to Ashley and Sam.

"I am so glad you called. I NEED to get out of here. I'm afraid my car will automatically take me back to work. How's the cabin?" Ashley said breathlessly as she claimed to have run to her phone from the second floor of her townhouse.

"Well, I'm actually in my car and on my way back. Want to meet for dinner tomorrow instead?"

"What? Are you serious?" she cried. "What's wrong? Why so soon?"

"In all honesty? It's a little scary up here at night," Lacey meekly confessed.

"Oh, wow. You little chicken. Listen, we need a proper vacation. Turn your car around and go back. I can seriously leave here in twenty minutes. It's early enough that I won't hit any traffic and I'll be there before dark. I promise to bring copious amounts of wine to get us through the night."

"I don't know. I just spent the whole morning cleaning the place and closing it up again."

Lacey was hesitant to agree to stay. In her mind, she was already in the comfort of her home waiting for Bryce to return for coffee on the porch and getting ready for a date with Sam.

"Oh, please. You haven't even given this vacation a chance. C'mon. Please say yes."

Ashley was a hard friend to say no to. Lacey considered her request for a few seconds before agreeing.

"Yes. There, I said it. Now get here before dark, but drive carefully."

"Good girl. I will see you before the sun sets. Bye."

Before leaving the rest stop, Lacey called Sam.

"Why hello, stranger. How nice to hear from you," Sam obviously recognized her number.

"Hello to you. For two people who never turn their phones off, we have been hard to reach."

"You said it. So, what do you say to dinner this week with me?"

"I would love to, although, I am out of town."

"What? Where are you and when are you coming back?"

"At my family's cabin in New York. I plan on being back before the weekend."

"Oh, yeah? I'm envious that you got out of Dodge. Happy for you, too, of course. Want to call me when you get back and we'll go from there?"

"Sure. Looking forward to it."

"Me, too. You be careful up in the big, bad woods, all right? Watch out for bears."

Amused at his offbeat humor, she returned the send-off with well wishes for him in his home out on the water and confirmed she would be back in cell phone range by Saturday.

CHAPTER SEVENTEEN
Learning to Relax

THE NEXT MORNING, ASHLEY and Lacey realized they had put quite a dent in the case of wine Ashley had brought with her from Annapolis. Ashley had arrived later than expected, but early enough for the two friends to catch up before they both admitted they were exhausted. The wine, and company, did the trick to rid any fears of the dark. Shortly after midnight, Lacey happily called out an inebriated goodnight from her bed to a snoring Ashley already asleep on the sleeper sofa in the living room. The following morning, they nursed their headaches with water, Tylenol, and coffee as they tried to get a start on the day.

"I'm heading out to the porch," Ashley declared.

"Why? It's freezing out there."

"I'll bundle up. The fresh air will get rid of my headache. Care to join me?"

"Sure. It's worth a try," Lacey mumbled as she rubbed her temple with her free hand. The other cradled a cup of steaming coffee.

They opened the door and each wrapped her respective blanket around herself for more protection from the cool air.

"It's actually not too bad out here," Lacey mused as she sat down in the Adirondack chair furthest from the door.

Ashley took a seat in the matching chair and they sat in silence as they looked out onto the yard and woods in the distance.

"Do they have a McDonald's around here? I need some

grease," Ashley asked.

"No. That does sound good, though. What the hell were we thinking? Red wine is the worst headache."

"I have no idea. We have no tolerance because we work too damn much and normally fall asleep before the bottom of that second glass. Still, you'd think we would know better."

"We really *are* out of practice. Let's vow to go out one night a week, or at least host a weekly get-together, after we get back."

"Deal," Ashley said. "Maybe if we work some more fun into our boring lives we wouldn't act like fools as soon as we have time off."

"Or, here's a crazy idea. What if we actually knew what to do with ourselves when we do have time off?" Lacey pondered as she allowed the steam from the mug to caress her cheeks as she stared off into the distance.

"Like what?"

"I don't know. Some kind of activity besides drinking to excess?"

"So you think we need a hobby?"

"I guess. The problem is, at least as far as I am concerned, I don't think I know *what* to do with myself when I have any time off. It's easier to just keep working."

"Okay, I hear you. You're right. Like yoga or something."

Ashley was putting some obvious consideration into the question

Lacey busted up at the thought of Ashley excelling at yoga. She just couldn't imagine her boisterous friend partaking in anything so passive.

"What the hell is so funny?" Ashley asked incredulously as she leaned back to give Lacey a look.

"You *do* need to do some yoga," Lacey shot back. "Nothing, nothing at all! I just can't see you doing it, that's all."

"Yeah, I really don't think I have the patience for it. I would be one angry yogi." Ashley settled back into her chair and took a sip of warm coffee.

"That's what I mean, though. I don't think we have ever sat still long enough to really know ourselves. We just work and go out to restaurants when we have the time. We never find out what truly makes us happy."

Ashley silently placed her mug on the armrest and pulled her knees close to her before glancing over to Lacey.

"*Are* you happy?"

Lacey leaned her head against her fist and returned Ashley's glance.

"No. I guess I'm not," she answered with a heavy sigh. "Shouldn't I be, though? I have so much. I have a lot to be happy for. Are you happy? Your life is kind of like mine."

"Well, I guess I'm not either. That kind of sucks to admit, doesn't it?"

"Yes. It really does! I mean, I don't expect to start every day laughing and doing cartwheels out the door or anything, but well, I'd like to be more ... content. It's a bit of a relief to realize what the problem is."

"I hear doctors say that all the time with patients. Once you know what the problem is, you can fix it. We have some life-fixing to do, don't we?"

"I suppose we do. My neighbor, Bryce and I had the same discussion the other night. She's been harping on me for months to find more balance. You and I, I think, are both guilty of working too much, don't you agree? I've been even thinking of getting out of real estate and sales completely. I don't know what I'd do with myself, though."

"I can't see you doing anything else, honestly."

"Me neither. I have no idea what I should be doing. I think I'm having a young life crisis."

Ashley looked at her long-time friend's dejected face and started to laugh.

"This is serious, Ash. I don't want to live like this the rest of my life and I have no idea what to do about it."

Looking at Ashley, who was still laughing, Lacey found comedic relief, too, while repeating how serious of an issue her dilemma was. Ashley started to subdue her laughter to speak again.

"Lace, you're not dying. People change jobs and lifestyles all the time. This is really not a big deal." Ashley stood and reached for Lacey's mug to refill it.

"You're right. I am over-reacting, huh?" Lacey realized.

"Yes. I'll get us some more coffee and we can start dreaming up your new life. I have some ideas I'm sure you'll go for," Ashley giggled.

A good dose of liquids, aspirin, laughter and conversation peppered with many *what-if*'s later, Lacey and Ashley came back to life. It was almost noon. They returned inside to get ready for whatever the rest of the day might hold. Lacey was very appreciative of the updated plumbing that was added a few years ago as she took a steaming hot shower. Her throbbing headache had subsided. Ashley gave the same report once she had a chance to freshen up and they sat on the couch wondering what to do.

"What time is it?" Ashley asked.

"One-thirty," Lacey answered as she glanced at the clock.

"What? Time moves so slowly here. I seriously thought it was closer to three or four."

"Nope."

The conversation continued at this boring pace for a quite some time until the two decided to play cards.

"How about a Bloody Mary?" Lacey asked. She had noticed the sparse liquor collection in the cabinet above the refrigerator had enough vodka and Bloody Mary mix to make at least two cocktails and she had picked up a bag of ice and some other provisions on her way back to the cabin yesterday.

"Spoken like a true alcoholic with no hobbies," Ashley teased. "Speaking of which, what the heck *do* you all do up here? It is beautiful and all, but it sure is remote."

"It depends. Hike, sightsee, read. I don't know. I haven't been here for so long. When I was little we played non-stop all day and were exhausted by the time we came inside. I'm sure we fell asleep pretty early. I just remember my parents and grandparent's playing cards and reading. My grandpa would have a couple beers and make a small bonfire. Stuff like that."

"Humph. Right. Like you brought up earlier, how sad is it that we don't know what to do other than drink to excess and stare blankly into the horizon when we have absolutely nothing to keep us busy?"

Lacey agreed with her as she set two spicy Bloody Mary's on coasters on the old wooden table. Ashley finished shuffling and asked what they should play. They decided on Rummy and she dealt the cards. The fireplace was ablaze and they took turns adding logs as they played game after game.

"I need a break and you're killing me at this game, anyway. The sun's out in full force. It's a shame to stay inside," Ashley said as she pushed her chair out from the table and stretched her arms up over her head while arching her stiff back.

"Sounds good. Let's go."

The air was unseasonably warm as the sun highlighted the portion of orange and yellow leaves that were left on the trees. The cottage was surrounded by half an acre of yard and which extended to a forest dense with tall hemlocks. A modest trail was visible at the edge of the forest.

"Where does that lead?" Ashley asked as she pointed out the trail.

"It is a small path worn from walking down to the stream then river below. It meets up with a deer path. Come on, I'll show you."

They started down the path and the smell of dirt, pine and sap floated on the air around them. Soon, the gurgling of the stream could be heard and Ashley was charmed. Goldenrod and ferns extended along the trail's edge creating a border so perfect in nature.

"Now *this* is nice," she exclaimed excitedly. "I never realized how little time I've spent in nature. Look at these yellow flowers. They are prettier than any I've ever spent money on." Ashley said. Admittedly, did spend most of her time indoors when she wasn't working. A city kid all her life, a vast forest setting such as this was not something she was familiar with. City parks were about as close to nature as she got and even then, it was only the fringe she experienced.

"Aren't they? That's Goldenrod and most people detest it as a weed. As a child I would always pick bunches of it and put it in a glass as a table centerpiece. I spent so much time here as a kid with my cousins throwing rocks and looking for crayfish. It makes me glad to see it is just as pretty as I remember it."

The next hour was spent skipping rocks in the wider and deeper parts of the creek as they continued along the trail. The fern tips softly brushed their shins and squirrels darted from limb to limb above. Filtered sunlight highlighted the evergreen branches all around. They reminisced about their fun times in college together and complained about their respective work challenges to a degree. For the most part, though, the conversation was light and easy as they walked and walked until the turned to follow the trail back to the cabin. Nature gave them mellow and serene dispositions.

"So what time is it now? We should go grab some dinner somewhere," said Ashley.

"Not sure. I'm starving, though."

Back inside the cottage, the clock on the wall showed four o'clock. Lacey and Ashley were flabbergasted by how slowly time crept along. It seemed to be part of an otherworldly time zone.

"Maybe we can get some senior citizen's discounts if we head out for dinner now," Lacey joked.

"Yes, then we can also be asleep by eight. Man, are we losers or what?"

"It's supposed to be a relaxing vacation, remember. There *is* a little town about four miles from here that has a really cute main street. If it is how I remember it, there should be a decent restaurant or two there. Want to check it out?"

"Absolutely. Mind if I change for our big night on the town?" Ashley asked.

"I think we have time. I'll put the fire out and freshen up, too. We probably reek like campfire."

An hour later they were in Lacey's car with a feel-good set of music playing from the iPod. Freshly changed into jeans, boots and sweaters; a tan V-neck for Lacey and red turtleneck for Ashley. They were getting their second wind. Regardless, they both declared they saw no red wine for the duration of the evening.

Entering the small town of Kline, they were pleasantly surprised to find a number of options. They opted for the aptly named Bistro On Main and were soon shown to a booth. The restaurant was quiet and dated, but clean. The faint smell of Pine Sol mixed with old wood and vinyl settled in the air around them and, on a more-savory note, the smell of fresh tomato sauce and basil wafted from the kitchen. A Victorian-era bar remained on the far side of the dining room and a bartender stood behind his station polishing glasses then cutting lemons. Lacey wondered if he expected a crowd for a Tuesday. It was early yet, she reminded herself.

A waitress soon arrived.

"Anything to drink, hon?" she greeted as she looked at Ashley over her bifocals.

"A water and a Sam Adams, please."

"Draft okay?" she asked curtly.

Ashley agreed and Lacey ordered the same. They put in an order for breaded zucchini as well, per waitress's suggestion.

"What are you thinking of getting?" Lacey asked.

"Besides everything? I don't know. I could go for pizza or pasta, but I might fall asleep right here after dinner if I do that."

They decided on the cheeseburger and fries the menu deemed famous. The waitress refilled their waters and asked if they needed anything else before retreating to the bar to chat it up with the bartender. Soon, a bell chimed and she stood back up to meet a couple at the door. A steady flow of patrons began to arrive and the restaurant livened up a bit.

"So, I've probably said this a million times last night, but, I'll say it again now that I'm sober. I am so glad you got here and convinced me to stay. Cheers," Lacey toasted her friend.

"Well, I am so happy to be here. You are really lucky to be able to come to a place like this whenever you want. I think I would be here all the time despite the fact that every hour spent here equals three in the real world."

"I guess that's the point, right? I should use it more often."

Lacey went on to tell her about her first night spent in the cottage alone and how uneasy she was. She mentioned how startled she was, initially, by Chase's visit.

"Wait, wait, wait. Back it up. Who is this Chase character you speak of?"

"Just an old friend. He lived up the street from the cabin and he would always come around when my cousins and I were visiting with my grandparents. We were all about the same age and just ran around the woods, goofing off a lot. We had a club."

"A club?"

"Yeah. The Falcons or Eagles or something." Lacey laughed at the memory of the innocent rituals they made up and how they would build lean-tos in the woods.

"So, this Chase guy walks back into your life after how many years and you just say 'Nice seeing you'? Is he cute?"

"Sure, I guess. Depends what your type is, right?"

"Uh-uh," Ashley nodded while leaning back in her booth with arms crossed and peered at her friend. Lacey started to blush while her friend proceeded to interrogate her. "He must be pretty darn handsome because you, my friend, are as red as a beet."

"That would be because you are staring at me, you weirdo."

Lacey put her fork down to stare back at Ashley. She could feel her face get warmer and warmer so she looked away and took a sip of water.

"So does he still live nearby?"

"I have no idea, Ashley. I talked to the guy for, like, five minutes."

"And what did you talk about?"

"You know, you're really very nosy and should work on

your social skills. Nothing, really. Like I said, he dropped off some canoe he picked up for my Uncle Tim and let me know he was going to put it on the side of the cabin. I said I would let my uncle know. Then we realized we knew each other so we got a kick out of that. That's that."

Ashley knew there had to be more to this story and used silence to get her friend to talk more.

"He also suggested I make a point to stop by the Penn Tavern and said he would be there."

"And that would be ... ?"

With arms still crossed, Ashley made a motion with her wrist to continue.

"Tonight."

CHAPTER EIGHTEEN
Good Old Days

ONCE ASHLEY HEARD THE full story of the encounter from Lacey and, of course, the part about tonight's very casual invitation, she was practically signaling for the check to make her exit. She had somehow gotten the idea that Lacey and Chase's happenstance was more than it really was. At any rate, they had found the place only after Ashley obtained detailed directions from the waitress at Bistro on Main. Despite the directions being based on old oak trees, forks in the road, and nondescript dilapidated buildings, they had somehow found their destination.

The Penn Tavern appeared to be a colonial inn or roadhouse in its former life. The stone structure sat just a few feet from the now paved road and horse hitching posts still lined gravel lot to the left. The front door was painted dark red and a lighted wooden nameplate hung above the door with the establishment's logo highlighted in gold. It gave the impression that the old tavern was not as forlorn as the location and exterior suggested. As Lacey and Ashley pulled into the lot, the car's headlights cast a glow on the dozen or so vehicles already in the lot.

Most were pick-up trucks and Lacey noticed Chase's old truck immediately. She didn't dare mentioned this to Ashley since she seemed to already be planning the pair's nuptials.

They used the side door from the parking lot and the sound of Johnny Cash and an abundance of intoxicated male laughter entered the stale night air. The interior wasn't too shabby, although only a few steps up from a dive bar. Surprisingly, it wasn't smoky, a delicious aroma of food hung in the air and it was not a place that caused every local at the bar to turn and stare at the newcomers. So, it was better than expected.

The only concern was that they were the only females in the place. Against their better judgment, they walked up to the bar and took a seat before they could stand out any more. Lacey was ready to suggest they leave. Coming to an unfamiliar bar full of unfamiliar men in the middle of nowhere might not have been the brightest thing they had ever done. Before she could say anything, though, Ashley was ordering a drink.

"And for you?" the burly, bearded bartender asked as he squinted at Lacey from his towering vantage point.

"Miller Lite drafts are a buck fifty," Ashley hissed.

"Miller Lite, please," Lacey requested.

He brought two draft glasses foaming over the brim and slid them in front of the friends.

"Starting a tab? If so, I need a credit card," he said in a baritone voice.

"Sure, here you go," Lacey passed him a card to hold.

"Thanks," he said in a forced manner.

Lacey and Ashley exchanged glances before taking a sip of frothy ale.

"A dollar fifty? This is insane. I'd barely have to work if I lived here. Between the decent meal we had and the prices at this place, you could live on pennies," Ashley pointed out in disbelief.

"I'm not sure where you would work if you lived here, so, you'd have only pennies to spend. This place isn't too bad. I was going to suggest we leave. Have you noticed we're the only girls here?"

"We'll just have a couple then hit the road. As long as we stick together and stay somewhat sober, I'm sure we'll be fine," Ashley considered aloud.

Lacey could tell that Ashley was having second thoughts as

well.

"I thought you were heading home today," a sturdy male voice said from close range.

Lacey looked toward the voice and found Chase standing behind Ashley. Ashley turned toward him and immediately looked back to Lacey with the widest-eye expression Lacey had ever seen. As if that was not enough, she began quietly kicking Lacey in the shin. It was all she could do to keep a straight face as she looked at Chase's inviting expression. His light brown hair was cut close and visible now that he no longer donned a hat. He presented an approachable vibe and was dressed similar to when she last saw him. Even with his unpretentious and overly casual look, he could have been on the cover of an Eddie Bauer catalogue. Lacey could easily envision it. Chase kneeling next to a canoe with a yellow Labrador Retriever somewhere along the rocky Maine coast. The trite brought a smile to her lips.

"Chase! So nice to see you," she said in a more friendly way than she had intended. The sight of his familiar face brought relief. "This is my friend, Ashley."

Ashley mouthed an "*oh my*" before turning to say hello.

"Hey, Ashley. Nice to meet you."

Chase shook Ashley's hand. Lacey thought Ashley just might fall off her barstool from leaning too far toward him.

"So you decided to stay a little longer I see?" he continued with his right elbow on the bar and bent in close to be heard over the music.

"Yes, well, it turns out Ashley was able to make it up here after all, so, I extended my trip. This place seems pretty cool…the drink prices are unbelievable. Thanks for the tip."

"That's nothing. The food is what makes the place. The owner moved here from NYC where he was a chef. He bought this place dirt-cheap and churns out the best food you can find around here. Maybe anywhere."

A brief, but slightly awkward silence came over them until he continued.

"Do you two, uh, want to join our table? We have plenty of

room," Chase asked hesitantly while he looked behind him at a table situated in a far corner. Two other guys were devouring steak dinners.

Ashley shrugged with a nod at Lacey.

"Sure. Thanks, Chase," she answered.

They picked up their purses and drinks while following Chase toward the table where introductions were made.

"So, that's Rodney," Chase pointed to a heavyset friend who quickly set his fork and knife down mid-bite and quickly used a napkin before nodding hello to them. "Rodney, take a breath and meet my friends, Lacey and Ashley."

Chase shook his head and laughed quietly. His dimples were on full display and Lacey could tell Ashley was smitten.

"Hi. Sorry. I didn't even see you there," Rodney self-consciously offered with a friendly grin. "Nice to meet you both," he added with a little wave.

"And, that there is my big brother, Gregory," he announced as he motioned toward the equally handsome male seated to the right of Rodney. The brothers appeared to be close in age. Whereas Chase was now clean-shaven with closely cropped brown hair, his brother sported a slightly scruffy face and short, untamed dark hair. Their similar facial features made the fact that they were related undeniable.

"He was too cool to hang out with us when I knew you way back when, Lacey. You probably don't remember him."

Chase put his hands on Gregory's firm shoulders and gave his brother a playful slap on the back and he moved behind to take his seat.

Lacey and Ashley took two of the three empty seats at the round table.

"Maybe you were too much of a loser back then, did you ever think of that?" Gregory fired back good-naturedly at his brother.

"What? Please. I think it was the other way around. So, guys, Lacey here is Tim's niece. She grew up going to the Williams' cabin and we hung out together when we were probably, what, Lacey, nine, ten, eleven years old?"

Chase moved his empty plate out of the way of the group and crossed his forearms on the table. He was noticeably more relaxed and less nervous than he had been at their first encounter. It was Lacey who was now a little timid. Chase leaned in slightly toward her from his seat across from her. He waited for her answer.

"That sounds about right. I was about ten or eleven when I remember hanging out with you. Those were the good old days, huh?"

He nodded in agreement and Lacey could feel her cheeks heat up with his eyes on hers. She nervously took a sip of beer to break the exchange. They all focused on the older brother as he joined the conversation.

"Wait a second. Lacey, did he drag you into that obnoxious group that one summer with that stupid club?" Gregory boomed with a hearty laugh.

Lacey and Chase looked at each other as they tried to stifle a laugh before recalling the exclusive group they had formed.

"The Buzzards!" Lacey and Chase yelled out in unison.

Lacey gently gave the table a slap broke into in an all out laugh. She looked at Ashley.

"That was the name I was trying to think of earlier, Ashley!"

"Who names themselves 'buzzards'?" Gregory asked while he continued to make fun of them with his hazy recollections of his little brother's antics. The way he portrayed it all made it sound even more hilarious to the tablemates who were carrying on like old friends now.

"Sorry, Lace. That is a pretty sad name for a group, or club, or whatever it was," Ashley said as she raised an eyebrow.

"Buzzards rule, you all drool!" Lacey and Chase sang out in unison again. By now they were wiping tears of laughter from their eyes.

Gregory, Ashley, and Rodney rolled their eyes as they regained their composure.

"Hate to say it, but, I must hit the road," Rodney stated as he stood and grabbed his jacket from the back of his chair.

"The wifey told me to be home early and I must oblige if I want to live to see another day. It was nice meeting you two. Long live the Buzzards, Chase. I think your brother's just jealous he wasn't a part of the gang. See you guys later."

"So, do you two live somewhere in New York?" Gregory asked as he signaled for another round.

"No, we both live in Annapolis," Ashley answered for them.

"I moved there in tenth grade with my parents," Lacey added.

"That's why I never saw much of you after those few good summers," Chase said and Lacey noticed he was wistful. "So when did you get here, Lacey?"

"Sunday."

"It was Monday morning when you said you were leaving," he recalled thoughtfully. "That's a long drive for a one night stay."

"She got scared of the dark," Ashley divulged loudly with a slight choke on her drink. She stifled her cough and snickered at her friend's expense. Gregory found the humor in the situation along with Ashley.

Lacey shot Ashley a stern look before rolling her eyes to start the explanation.

"It was great until something woke me up in the middle of the night. Then, yeah, it was a little, well, I don't know. I'm just not used to being in the woods alone. You all would have felt the same," she justified.

Leaning back, Chase gave Lacey a considerate smile before uttering a chuckle himself. He leaned one elbow over the backrest and drained the rest of his beer before looking back at her. Their eyes caught hold and held a brief, friendly gaze as Gregory and Ashley continued to make fun.

"So, can we change the subject?" Lacey suggested in good humor and thanked the bartender for the freshly poured draft placed in front of her. "Do you two still live with mommy and daddy down the street?"

Seeing their expression, she hoped that they didn't. She

regretted her callous words.

The brothers exchanged a glance.

"So what if we do?" Chase said.

Lacey could feel Ashley staring at her while she looked at the brothers with a blank expression.

"Oh, no. I really didn't mean anything by it. That came out wrong."

Forget red. Lacey's face was purple.

Chase and his brother leaned back on their respective chairs with the same elbows propped on the backrest. It would have been comical if Lacey was not so embarrassed.

After letting her squirm, they relaxed and burst into laughter once again.

"That was pretty good, little bro," Gregory chuckled. "No, Lacey. We're just pulling your leg. We have graduated to the real world and do not still live at home."

Chase was trying to catch his breath and rubbed his face while gaining composure.

"Sorry. I couldn't resist," Chase apologized to Lacey as she threw a balled up napkin at him. "Please forgive me. Anyway, I live in an apartment above Ritter's River Landing in Kline. Gregory has a place about a mile from there."

"My brother is one of the best river guides money can buy, I'll have you know," Gregory looked proudly at his brother as he gave him a slap on the back. Chase shook his head and looked down at the table over folded arms.

"He's a little biased," Chase explained with a motion toward his brother. "Your uncle sends a lot of business my way, though. Ritter's was getting a new fleet of canoes in, so, I managed to get him a good deal on one of the used ones."

"And what do you do, Gregory?" Ashley made a point to steer the conversation back to Gregory and Lacey and Chase exchanged a knowing glance. He winked back at her with a nod.

"I'm a web designer."

"He's *the* web designer. He does all the work for the businesses around town, including this place."

"Why thank you little brother! You are too kind." They clinked glasses before Gregory added, "Well, it helps that I don't have much competition to contend with. There's not a lot of work this way, so, if you can figure out something to do that is home-based and can reach beyond the small towns around here, you're better off. It's turning into a good little business. Anyway, enough about us. What do you both do to pay the bills?"

Lacey and Ashley took turns answering and they told them about their lives in city and how refreshing it has been to experience a slower pace. They mentioned how they loved living in a coastal city and that Annapolis was a beautiful one with tons of charm, but the pace of living and working in any city had a way of catching up with you. It was easy to talk to Gregory and Chase and the four continued to make pleasant small talk as the buzz of the beers wore off and they prepared to end the night.

"Looks like it's about that time. We should go," Lacey announced in Ashley's direction

"Lacey, you better not stay away so long. Say 'hello' to your uncle and cousins for me. This was fun," Chase said as he and his brother stood to say goodbye.

"This *was* fun," Lacey said reflectively while grinning at him before bidding farewell to Gregory.

Gregory agreed and they all repeated their good-byes for good measure. Lacey started for the bar to pay her tab and collect her credit card. When Chase saw what she was doing he motioned for the bartender to give the bill to him and the haggard bartender advised Lacey the drinks were paid for before pouring a shot of whiskey for another patron.

Assuming Chase or Gregory were the benefactors of the paid tab, she began to walk back to the table and offered her appreciation. Chase stood and waved her off. A clumsy moment took place as if they were trying to think of more to say. Lacey simply smiled and waved goodnight before heading to join Ashley waiting at the door.

"Hey, you're not leaving tomorrow, are you?" Chase said

impulsively after her.

Looking back, Lacey shook her head. "No. We'll be around all week."

"Good to know. Drive carefully."

Chase stood for a moment and watched them leave. He wanted to at least follow them to make sure they arrived back safely, but knew that would just seem creepy. He noticed they had only a couple beers and nursed a glass of water along with the alcohol. Lacey seemed stone sober to him. He told himself they were fine and sat back down across from his brother.

"So, she seems nice," Gregory commented slyly.

"Yeah. They both are. It was a good time."

"Yep," Gregory added, waiting for more from his brother. When Chase played it cool, Gregory added, "Don't you think you should line something up before they leave? You were your old self with her. It was nice to see."

"I suppose you want to tag along to hang out with Ashley again?"

"Hey, that's up to you. I would be all for that, but, you, little brother, are clearly falling for Lacey. I think she's good for you."

"What?" Chase gave the best *'you're crazy'* look he could muster. It did not fool the one who knew him best.

"Yeah. That's what I thought. Here's what I'm thinking. It is clearly an Indian Summer week. Near seventy and sunny, they're saying for Thursday. You probably have a little free time this late in the year? Keep Thursday free and let's take a few kayaks down the river. I'll bring some lunch. It'd be a great way to spend the afternoon if nothing else."

"I guess. Don't know kayaking is their thing, though, you know? And, I don't have her number," he reasoned as he talked himself out of the budding idea.

"You know where she's staying. Just stop by. They're bored as hell and would probably jump at the chance to make some plans. If not, get her number or email and stay in touch. I like her and I think she likes you. It's a good thing, Chase. You

122

need someone in your life besides me. You know, I heard Lacey mention the 'good old days'. Well, It's time to start making some new memories."

"Oh, yeah?" Chase took obvious offense at his brother's well-intentioned assertiveness. "Sorry I've been too much for you. Guess you know what I need. "

Chase hunched his broad shoulders over the table as he pushed his empty beer glass away, apparently lost in thoughts only he could identify with at the moment. Frustrated, Gregory pushed his chair back from the same table and headed to the bar to pay the tab. He knew when his brother needed a little time to stew and chose not to push it any further. He had no regrets for saying what he did, though. He learned long ago how far he could take the standard conversation.

Returning to the table, Gregory took a seat across from his brother and waited with his hands stuffed in the pockets of his black leather jacket he now donned. Chase lifted his gaze to meet his brother's.

"So, how early do you think they'd be willing to meet us?"

CHAPTER NINETEEN
The Invitation

THE WARM, SUNNY DAY was one of the nicest of the year. The pleasant sky was a brilliant blue and October sun was soothing rather than hot. A gentle breeze worked to remove the last of the stubborn leaves from their branches. Lacey and Ashley took their now-regular morning seats on the porch of the cottage with their feet up on the rustic porch railing. The few resident crows cawed in the distant tree branches and broke the silence that the migrating birds left in their wake.

"So, I said it last night and I will say it again. You are certifiably nuts if you do not stay in touch with that so-called friend of yours. Wow. I need to find me a country boy. I haven't seen the likes of him anywhere near the city."

"Sounds like *you* need to stay in touch with him. Or maybe you are more interested in his brother," Lacey finally said. She had been hearing a version of this statement from Ashley since they left the tavern last night.

"Hey, either would be fine with me. Anyway, it all just seems different here. I swear time moves like a snail and I'm happier and more relaxed than I can remember being in a long time. I know it's because we're not working, but still. The surroundings and the open spaces just seem to remind you that there has to be more to life than the crazy ways we spend every minute of every day."

Ashley looked out across the yard and her gaze followed the tree trunks as they extended toward the billowy clouds.

"I love Annapolis. The harbor, the sailing and Naval community, the history. The problem is that I get a sinking feeling when I think of the work that waits for me when I return. My overbearing job has ruined home for me. Which client or deal will turn into the pain in the neck next week? I am so relaxed here and want to hold on to that feeling. It makes me sad to know it won't last past this weekend," Lacey ventured. "It's a little depressing."

"It's a lot depressing, Lace. You know, I feel the same as you. Plus, I love being a nurse, but the hospital I'm at is insanely busy all the time. It makes it hard to do my job and sometimes I'm afraid that the pace will cause me to make a mistake. It is pretty cheap here. We wouldn't need much to survive. I bet the local hospital is like a day spa compared to the hectic one I practically live in," Ashley continued as if she was seriously considering a move up north to this not only rural, but also mountainous terrain. "We could work half as much and sit on the porch and drink coffee more."

"True, but, we wouldn't get paid the way we do in the city, so, it would probably work out the same in the end? I imagine they would have less nurses covering shifts at a slower hospital? Listen to us and our crazy talk. Maybe we need to just appreciate the jobs we have. More coffee?"

Lacey took their cups inside for a refill and thought about their conversation. If a lifestyle change is in order, would either of them have the courage to make it happen? What would they do if so? In reality, it was highly unlikely they would make a move from their current reality. Lacey decided it was just fun to be on vacation and dream and that warranted a trip back as often as possible in order to contend with her reality. On the porch of the charming 1930's cabin in the forested mountains, they imagined all of the different lives they could start living. Life was simple again and they loved every minute of it. With the coffee pot reduced to half a cup full of grounds, Lacey dumped it and began to brew a fresh one. Once finished, she returned to the porch to let

Ashley know it would be a few minutes and to see if she wanted to come inside to warm up. She called out to her friend through the screen as she opened the interior pine door.

"Hey, more coffee brewing. Care to …"

She stopped mid-sentence when she looked out onto the porch and saw Chase leaning against the railing with arms crossed. He and Ashley abruptly stopped their conversation and he stood straight to greet Lacey. Even in wrinkled green cargo shorts and long sleeve t-shirt he was alluring.

"Hi, Lacey. Sorry for stopping by so early. Hope you don't mind."

He looked to the side for a second before looking back at her through the screen door. Feeling insecure in her sweats and tousled hair, she stayed slightly hidden behind the shadowy mesh screen.

"Oh, hi, Chase. No, no problem. Uh, how are you?"

"Good. You?"

"Good, good. Um, do you want a cup of coffee?"

Ashley watched the painful interaction from the sidelines and bit her lip to keep from laughing out loud.

"Yeah, Chase, have a cup of coffee with us," Ashley interjected spiritedly to help her friend, whether welcomed or not.

"No thanks. Have to get going. I just had a quick question for you two."

Lacey reached for the crocheted afghan lying on the sofa behind her and noticed a hair clip on the coffee table. In two swift movements she had her hair under control and clipped atop her head and the multi-colored blanket covering her. She stepped outside to join them. Although her cover-up choice was not fashionable, it did allow her to hide her frumpiness if only under more of the same.

Chase kicked a stone gently from the porch then smiled sweetly as he watched Lacey come from inside. In his mind he was in sixth grade all over and walking by to see if pretty Lacey happened to join her cousins on the trip to the

Williams' cottage. With that flood of youthful memories, Chase stood found his confidence once more.

"My brother and I were going to take a short kayak trip downriver tomorrow and wanted to see if you both were free to go. It'll be a real easy float. We'll have everything ready. The weather is supposed to be ..."

"Heck, yeah. That sounds awesome!" Ashley exclaimed. Lacey shot her a look. She continued despite her friend's warning glance. "Where and when should we meet?"

Chase perked up when he heard her answer, although, he hadn't heard 'yes' from Lacey yet.

"Do you know where Ritter's Landing is, Lacey?" he asked hesitantly.

"Uh, yeah. I think. Is it still that big, blue building by the bridge in Kline?"

"Still the one," Chase said as he looked at her with more focus. "Can you meet us there tomorrow morning around nine, nine thirty? Too early?"

Ashley watched Lacey mull it over for a second before puling her blanket more tightly around herself and nodding.

"Okay. Why not? We'll see you then. What can we bring?"

"Yeah? Great. That's great. Not a thing. Just dress warm for the morning, but in layers. It's gonna be a warm day." Chase rubbed his palms together in anticipation. "But you better not change your minds," he said with a wink and pointed towards them as he started walking back down off the porch. "My brother is a closet chef and probably planning the lunch menu now. Don't tell him I told you that, by the way," he added.

Chase waved as he got back into the old, but well cared for truck and closed the door with a thud that echoed in the forest. Ashley and Lacey stood at the railing and watched him back out of the drive and back onto the rural road.

"That was so nice of him," Ashley started after Chase was gone. "I can't wait."

"He seems like a good guy. You don't think he is a murderer who will dump our bodies in the river?" Lacey pondered as she stayed standing next to the door.

"No, I do not think that at all. You know him better, though! If you need some reassurance, it seems like your uncle knows him pretty well. Why not give him a call to let him know his canoe has arrived and see what he has to say about the guy? Plus, he can probably tell us what to wear. I have never even touched a kayak or canoe. You?"

"No. Well, we wanted to learn some new skills, right? Here it goes. That's a good idea. I'll call him now, but I have to drive a mile down the road to get a signal. Want to ride along?"

"Nah, I'll hang here if you don't mind. Maybe I'll jump in the shower and we can go somewhere to buy whatever we need for a day on the water?"

"Perfect," Lacey replied as she grabbed her keys from the hook next to the door.

CHAPTER TWENTY
Remembering Julia

CHASE WOKE ABRUPTLY IN the dead of night. As he came to his senses, he realized he was sitting straight up in his bed with one arm outstretched. He had been reaching for her again. His heart ached and raced and his breathing was still quick. Within seconds he remembered the dream and let his head fall back onto the soft pillow with a heavy sigh. Wiping his brow and rubbing his face, he was fully awake. Sleep was not an option and he wanted to prepare for the day ahead of him anyway.

With more vigor than normal, he did his usual morning push-ups and sit-ups on the floor next to his bed before moving on to the chin up bar in the doorway. The morning routine was a habit formed well over a decade ago and during a different stage in life. While he hated the memories the activity brought on, he knew it helped to clear his mind of the regular nightmares he endured, particularly the ones of late.

The coffee pot was full of strong grinds and water from Chase readying it the night before. He pressed the start button and leaned back against the butcher-block countertop. It was a chilly morning. He reached for the faded and worn gray high school sweatshirt that was strewn across the barstool and pulled it over his bare chest before checking the time. Three-thirty. This didn't surprise him as he had been waking at about the same time and in the same manner for years now. The usual dream had taken a different form over the past few months and was one that left his sister standing next to his bed muttering the same words over and over. Her words were not clear at first. Now, they were clearer than ever.

The smell of coffee filled the kitchen. Chase plopped down on the barstool and put his head in his hands. His rough elbows rested against the counter bar that jutted out into the middle of a kitchen that had been added in the early 1900's. An oversized cast iron sink that no one had the motivation to replace was the focal point and dark green beadboard framed the meager space. An inexpensive white refrigerator sat crookedly to the left and a small, mismatched stove to the right. The Mister Coffee coffee maker beeped a ready notice and Chase poured himself a heavy dose. He sipped the coffee until the caffeine helped to open his eyes and he thought about his reoccurring dream as he took a seat at the round table that separated the kitchen and living area. The dream. He had started to think of it as a welcomed nightmare. To have a chance to see his sister again is something he would do pretty much anything for. On the other hand, the painful memories that filled his gut after he wakes from her vision are pure torture.

Two cups of coffee later, he changed into his jeans and walked down to the storage area. Still dark out, he fumbled to find the right key to unlock and open the garage door. Inside, he set his coffee on the built-in workbench before selecting four kayaks from their perches and the paddles to go along with them. Going through a mental checklist that was second nature now, he had assembled the life jackets and put together his emergency dry bag in a matter of minutes. Placing everything by the garage door, he pulled the noisy door back down along its tracks and headed back up the rickety wooden stairs to his apartment for breakfast and more coffee.

By seven o'clock, Chase had the kayaks wiped down and sitting in a perfect line along the misty water's edge. He packed his own bag with any supplies and emergency gear he could think of. Not being too sure of Lacey and Ashley's paddling experience, he figured it better to be safe than sorry. He even brought an extra set of old clothes, a towel, and blanket in case anyone overturned their boat. An unlikely scenario, but one he wanted to prepare for all the same. The sound of crunching rocks and a muffled radio told him his brother had arrived. He turned to see Gregory parking his newer silver Chevy by the apartment steps.

"Looks like you're all ready to go! Need me to drag anything down from the garage?" Gregory yelled toward the river as he stepped down from the truck.

"No. All good. Just bring whatever you need to pack into your boat," he shouted up to him.

Gregory gave a wave of understanding and started to lug a soft cooler and backpack from the back seat. He slammed the door shut and walked down to meet Chase.

"Man, you're on top of things. Which one is mine?"

"The red one here next to mine."

"What the hell are you taking? I thought this was a short trip," Gregory asked in amazement as he looked at Chase's kayak that was stuffed to capacity.

"We are. Water's cold. I want to make sure everyone is safe. I have no idea if they've even been out on the water for something like this before."

"Alright. No need to get testy. You're the professional here," Gregory said gesturing with open palms to show he meant no harm. "You should have left something for me to do. What time did you get up?"

"Actually, pretty early," Chase muttered as he helped his brother place his items into the dry sack. "Well, well, well. What do we have here, Chef Gregory?" Chase teased as he unzipped the soft cooler to take a look inside.

"Nothing for you if don't loose the attitude," Gregory snapped as he grabbed the cooler. "Just some cans of beer I had in the fridge and some cheese and crackers. And I made some sandwiches, too. Nothing major."

"I see. That was real nice of you. Thanks."

"Yeah. You're welcome. Care for a morning ale to take care of the nerves? You seem a little on edge."

"Nah. You go ahead though. I'm just anxious to get out on the water."

"Suit yourself," Gregory said with a shrug as he opened the can of beer and took a long drink.

The two brothers looked out over the gently flowing river. The mist was starting to clear as the sun's rays reached the valley. They stood in silence as they listened to the water lapping the shore. Chase took a seat on a nearby rock and Gregory soon followed to rest in the classic Adirondack chair nearby. The water was calming and Chase slowly started to lose the disturbing effects that the vision of his sister had upon him. Gregory finished his beer and they made the short trek back up the gravel path to where their trucks were parked.

"So, you know where we're ending up, right?" Chase called out over the starting engines.

"Yep. I'll follow you, though."

The road wound along the river with evergreens leaning out over the road. The sunlight sparkled atop the water. In no time, they were parked at the boat launch located a few towns downriver.

"Do you want me to leave my truck?" Chase asked as he removed the keys from the ignition and stepped out into the morning sunshine.

"Uh, no. But, thanks for offering. One, we won't all fit in a two-door, and, two your truck is ancient and needs to be traded in for a newer model. I'll leave mine."

Gregory shook his head in frustration. He wanted Chase to make a good impression and forcing them all to squeeze into the worn and torn bench seat of a truck that could qualify for an antique plate was not going to impress anyone that day. He knew why Chase kept it around, but didn't know why he wasn't making more of an effort to impress Lacey.

"Whatever. That's fine," Chase retorted as he jumped back into his own vehicle and waited for his brother to get in.

Chase pushed an 8-track tape into the player and a Hank Williams tune blared out. He quickly turned down the volume as his brother got in. As expected, Gregory turned to his brother.

"You know this has been re-released on CD? You might even be able to have a CD player installed in this thing. Wow. Do you take girls out on dates in this thing?"

"I don't want to go out with anyone who'd demand a new truck. This gets me around just fine," he answered with slight bitterness as he pulled out onto the two-lane road.

"Uh-huh. You know you have a tail light out?"

"No, but thanks for letting me know. I can fix that myself this weekend," Chase said in an overly cheery voice complete with a wide grin.

"Hey, hey, hey. What do you know? I guess you would know how much room there is in this cab. Just who does this little thing belong to?"

Gregory was leaning back against the passenger door and dangling the gold bracelet Chase had recently found in the truck.

"Where'd you find that? I swear I took it inside with me when I found it."

"Well, it must've dropped out of your hand or pocket. It was lying right here on the floorboard. Looks familiar ..." Gregory trailed off as he held the piece of jewelry up to get a closer look at it.

"It should. It was Julia's."

Gregory was speechless as he took in the words and closed his palm tightly around the golden memory.

"She must've put it in the glove compartment for some reason before, you know. The door's latch is worn and its always swingin' open. I found it on the floor last week."

Gregory looked out the window in silence as he clenched his jaw to keep from shedding any tears. He strived to remain upbeat and keep a sense of humor ever since part of his family was taken away. Once in awhile, something caught him off guard. After a moment, he rubbed his face with his open palm.

"Shit," he cursed as though willing the pain away. Opening his hand, he looked back down at the shiny and dainty bracelet before he clasped his fist harder for safckeeping.

They drove on with an understanding of each other that made no words necessary. Finding courage to talk, Chase searched for the words he had needed to say for a while.

"Greg, do you ever, you know, sort of feel like she's with us? A presence or something? Like, even now, I swear I can smell that perfume she always wore. Crazy, huh?" Chase shook his head to try to clear it. He leaned his elbow up onto to door and rested the side of his face against his hand while concentrating on the road ahead.

Gregory looked back out at the passing scenes of water, trees, and little camps dotting the river. He took a deep breath for emotional strength.

"Honestly, I normally don't. I wish I did. Man, do I ever. But, right now, yeah. I smell that flowery perfume. It always made me carsick, but not anymore," he stopped as he began to choke up a little and his defense mechanism focused on the humor of the situation.

"I thought you had a date in here recently when I saw the bracelet. I was never going to let you live that one down," he continued with a chuckle as he wiped an errant tear from the corner of his eye. "I sure as hell wasn't expecting you to say this was Julia's."

They drove on in their dad's old truck that their little sister used to ride along in with them in and felt the absence of their family.

"You deserve to be happy, Chase. You're a good guy," Gregory asserted.

Chase gave a sober glance his brother's way before answering.

"She's always telling me, too."

PART THREE : CLARITY

CHAPTER TWENTY-ONE
The Girl She Used To Be

HOLDING HER HAND, HE steadied her as she stepped into the novel experience. Easing into the molded vessel, she sat down and Chase gave a gentle shove to send her and her little yellow boat glided into the water. Initially, the lack of control was panic inducing. The current was taking her against her and she saw the riverbed grasses passing swiftly below. To find a calmer state, she gazed directly ahead and it was immediately clear that this easy flowing stream was taking her nowhere fast. Giving in to it, Lacey leaned back against the seat and exhaled. This is what she was looking for. She gamely accompanied the water's pull.

It was an odd feeling to have a freely moving and partially submerged seat in the river. Nature's exquisitely lush flora enveloped her from that unique vantage point and she was in awe. Coniferous trees mightily extended upward and the deciduous types were sprinkled with brilliant oranges, yellows, and every shade of red imaginable. Lowly branches grazed the cool water as they caught diamond-like sparkles on the surface. It was otherworldly and she cherished the opportunity to be a part of it. As if not enough, the enchanting sights were enhanced by the gurgling and burbling riversong that resonated around them. It was the most contented feeling she had known, possibly in her entire life. She lifted her head up to the sky and felt the soft morning rays of the rising sun find her cheeks.

"You doing okay?"

Chase had appeared next to her with a concerned look. It was obvious he tried very hard to make sure everyone was content and safe.

"I'm fine," she said dreamily. "More than fine. You're lucky to do this as your job. Thank you for bringing us out here. It is beautiful."

"Very beautiful," he answered. His eyes rested on Lacey and she couldn't help but notice he seemed to be referring to more than the natural surroundings.

"I appreciate you taking time to explain everything. I know Ashley does, too. We were a little nervous."

"You two caught on quick. It will be an easy float today. Nothing to be worried about."

She didn't tell him that they were mostly nervous about meeting Chase and Gregory out here on the water alone. Her uncle had quickly alleviated any concerns, however. He confirmed Chase was upstanding and even predicted he would go above and beyond to ensure their safety. Lacey had been relieved to hear his words and at this point, as they floated silently alongside one another, she couldn't imagine having even one negative thought about him. She admired his life that was so detached from the world she knew.

"Now you look deep in thought. You know the rule out here is no thoughts of work or anything else stressful. I strictly enforce that."

"Just soaking in the moment," she said adding, "It's beyond peaceful. I can't even describe it. And, if you must know, I was thinking about how different a day in your life is from mine. I'm a little envious, I must say."

She returned his smile to let him know she meant the words in the utmost complimentary way.

"What? Envious? That's crazy. Just come visit me in

December and you'll change your tune. Winter paddling trips, if the ice doesn't prevent them, are different. A lot less people book those trips."

Chase paddled a bit to straighten his course. He left out the fact that he would like to have a career that kept him busy year around with steady benefits and paychecks. It wasn't in the cards, though.

"I know a thing or two about that. Winter is a little harder for me, too. Now and then I have a busy January or February, but that's rare and I can't count on it. Still, you should really appreciate all of this. From what I can see you have a charmed life."

They paddled in unison and in silence for a while. Lacey had no desire to go back to the life she knew. At that moment, life was perfectly simple and lovely.

"I guess I should appreciate it more," Chase replied contemplatively. "It's an alright life. I'm missing a few pieces of the puzzle, but I figure that will all come in time."

"Hey you two. Care if we join the party?" Gregory called out from behind.

Chase and Lacey had all but forgotten there were others around them as they casually chatted. Gregory and Ashley joined them in a row and Gregory mentioned now would be a good time for a break and some food. Chase cited an oversized rock outcropping a little further down that would be a good stopping point. He started to lead the way and soon enough he was helping the others beach their kayaks and step out onto the grassy bank dotted with smooth, round river rocks and bright purple asters with yellow centers.

"Chase, how is this thing floating? Could you have brought anything else with you?" Gregory called out over his shoulder as he dragged Chase's kayak further ashore. Chase was busy helping Ashley and Lacey.

"So, my brother may like to make fun of me for my dedication to my craft, but you have seen nothing until you taste Chef Gregory's gourmet cooking. It is a little over the top, if you ask me, but he insists you'll appreciate his efforts,"

Chase announced to the crew who were now climbing the gentle slope to gather upon the rocky ledge.

Eagle's Rock, as the locals knew it, did indeed look like the face of an eagle jutting out over the water. They climbed up onto the flat, dry surface and Gregory sat the cooler of goods down in front of him. Ignoring his brother's comments, he pulled out plastic containers of pre-assembled sandwiches and washed and cut fruits. A small, plastic cutting board was then placed in the middle of their circle and he began to arrange and assemble cheeses and crackers around some sort of cracker spread.

"Looks fantastic to me," Ashley eagerly commented. "I didn't realize how hungry I was until seeing all of this. Thank you!"

"Wow, Gregory. You really outdid yourself. Are these prosciutto-wrapped figs?" Taking a bite, Lacey added wide-eyed, "This is incredible!"

Gregory took a break from setting up lunch to calmly nod at his brother with an all-knowing look of '*I told you so*'.

"Stuffed with gorgonzola cheese and drizzled with Pear Balsamic Vinegar," he added to Chase's amusement.

The foursome ate and chattered non-stop over the next hour or so from their rocky perch. The sun was out full force by now and they began shedding their fleece layers and hats as the unseasonal temperature rose.

"Hey! Is that a Bald Eagle?" Ashley exclaimed as she shaded the sun from her eyes and pointed to a point over the river.

Sure enough, the powerful bird of prey glided along the water and gracefully lifted a fish with its talons before flapping massive wings to reach a safe tree branch to enjoy its freshly caught meal.

"Oh, yeah! That never gets old. Looks like that's Duke, as he's known around here. He has a nest nearby."

"You see that a lot, don't you?" Lacey asked Chase in amazement.

"Not often enough. It's an amazing sighting every time. It's actually one of the reasons I try to stop here. Not coincidentally, Eagle Rock is the best viewing spot for an eagle now and then."

They sat peacefully and let the birds and the river do the talking. Gregory pulled out a beer and offered more to the others. Each took a sip of ale and leaned back to soak in the last warm rays of the sun before gentle autumn gave itself to winter. Lying on their backs, they looked up at the enchanting trees towering above them.

"These are the tallest trees around, you know. This swatch of land was never timbered," they heard Chase say. "Must be nice to put down roots and grow such a proud, long life."

There was a shift in the atmosphere. Friendships were turning into something more. Trust was seeping in to fill the gaps of the tender and newly formed relationships. They could have sat on that rock all day, however, the excursion needed to move on. None of them wanting to move, they begrudgingly cleaned up and repacked themselves into the slim boats.

The water refused to be upstaged by the rock and led them past a show of poised heron, jumping fish, and dancing dragonflies. A group of young kids gathered at one point along the river and waved to the little fleet that floated by. Three boys fished along the shoreline while a girl about the same age soaked in the sun atop an oversized rock.

"Remind you of anything?" Chase asked Lacey over his shoulder as he back-paddled to let her catch up.

"Does it ever," Lacey answered fondly. "You and my cousins fishing and me not wanting to get anywhere near the worms or fishing hooks."

The welcomed memories slipped into her mind. They represented her being to the core and exactly what was missing from her life nowadays. She wondered how she could get back to being that girl in some way.

"You may not remember, but I tried and tried to get you to join us. I always told you I would bait the line for you. Still would if you ever wanted to try it."

"What? Fish? Oooh, no. No, that's not for me," she laughed.

"Guess I'll just have to keep trying," he said flirtatiously while proceeding to paddle slightly ahead of her. As if they were eleven and twelve again, she worked to catch up to the boy.

Once all four had caught up and resumed the same pace, the paddling stopped and each relaxed back in their seats to help lengthen time spent together. Lacey stretched her legs up onto the top of the boat and angled her face toward the bright sun before turning her attention back to the watery path.

Rounding the river bend, an enchanting building crept into view. It was in a state of decay that made it even more intriguing. Constructed with aged cut stone and built on a small knoll above the reach of the river's seasonal hazards, the imposing structure fought bravely against the wrath of time.

"Ashley, here's a place for us," Lacey joked. She pulled her feet back into the boat and sat forward as she shielded her eyes to get a better look.

Standing amid the overgrown shrubbery and trees, this two-story house sported an unexpected newer, red metal roof. A worn balcony with a ragged black awning jutted out from an over-sized wooden door on the second floor. Flower boxes and shutters hung unsteadily from random points around the building. Everything, except the roof, was in need of repair, but the vision was captivating.

"That would be the old General Store," Chase informed them Faded black paint revealed the name that was once painted on a simple wooden sign near the river's edge.

"That would also be Chase's dream home," Gregory called out as he and Ashley navigated past Chase and Lacey to reach the nearby boat launch where his truck was waiting.

"It was built in the 1920's by a German immigrant who modeled it after the buildings in the Black Forest villages he knew best. He used river rock and cut stone from the land he cleared to have it built and it was a successful business until the 1980's. I guess a descendant owns it and planned on doing something with it until it was finally put on the market about a year ago," Chase explained.

Lacey was enamored. The building had a magical storybook quality to it and she wanted to know more. Once a regal abode, it was now shamefully pathetic.

Chase glanced up ahead and noticed Gregory and Ashley were gliding onto the paved launch.

"It's really cool on the inside. Lots of carved woodwork and an amazing two-story stone fireplace," he said to Lacey before adding with a mischievous grin, "And I happen to know a way in, if you're interested."

CHAPTER TWENTY-TWO
All Good Things Must End

"HERE, LET ME GET that for you," Gregory said as he carefully took the kayak pull handle from Ashley's hand. The trip was over and Gregory and Ashley were pulling their boats from the water and gaining their balance back on land. Gregory dumped the water and started to drag the kayak back towards the bed of his truck. She began picking up some of the dry bags and followed him.

"I didn't realize there was so much stuff packed in your kayaks. What is all of it, anyway?" Ashley inquired.

"My brother's overkill planning for every possible situation to be found on the river."

"What a great day. Lunch was terrific, too. You went all out!"

Gregory took the bags from Ashley as they chatted and he tossed the gear into the kayak he already had loaded in the back of his pick-up truck. He started to walk back to grab the next one when he realized Lacey and Chase were nowhere to be seen. Knowing his brother as well as he did, he was concerned for no more than a second or two. Ashley made the same observation.

"Where are the lovebirds?"

"Ha! I know! He won't admit it, but it *is* pretty obvious, right?"

"Oh, yeah. Same with her. They make a good pair, don't you think? Lacey could use some real companionship. All she does is work and talk to her clients at home. It's kind of pathetic."

"They *are* really good together. Lacey seems great. Chase was clearly enjoying himself and so did I. Glad you could make it."

Gregory glanced at Ashley as he pulled another kayak from the water to dry it off and carry it away. Returning his interested gaze, Ashley walked over to help.

"Would be nice to have some help from them, though. They certainly know the right time to take off," Gregory quipped, although, secretly, he was glad to have some alone time with Ashley.

"That's for sure. Maybe we should look for them?" Ashley shielded her eyes from the sunshine and looked along the riverbank for her friend.

"I know exactly where they are. Chase is infatuated with that old building we passed and looks around, or should I say trespasses, every chance he gets. I'd bet a thousand bucks they're in there. Nothing to worry about. The place is abandoned, but solid."

Ashley and Gregory sat down along the shoreline. She looked up at the section of the shabby building that was still within view. It was a wreck. Ashley's better judgment suggested she check on her friend. Her imagination took off and she felt a little nervous as her mind flashed various images of distress. Before she could fret any longer, Chase and Lacey paddled into sight.

"Ah, there they are. I was a little worried," Ashley admitted.

"No need to worry about her if she's with him," Gregory assured her. He stood and extended a hand to help her up from their resting spot.

"Why doesn't he try to buy it? It can't be that much. Maybe an investor would partner with him?"

"I don't think he could swing it, you know? It would take a lot to fix up. I don't know, I guess he's put some serious thought into it. I'm thinking there are a few things getting in the way."

Ashley sensed he was leaving something out. He chose his

words carefully and turned his head as if wanting to turn the subject. Relief was obvious when Chase and Lacey were within close range and he yelled out to them.

"Hey, we were just wondering where our trusted river guide went to. Do you always leave the heavy lifting your group to do the heavy lifting?"

"You're on to me I see," he yelled back with his trademark-dimpled grin. "Nice of you to make Ashley haul everything since I know your scrawny self couldn't do it."

"Okay. Okay. So, who has time for some post-trip beers? Penn Tavern? I'd say we earned them," Gregory asked once they were together on shore. Once again, before Lacey could think of a reason to say no, Ashley agreed they would be there. Lacey happily gave in, but said she needed to stop back at the cabin first. Chase mentioned he had to put the gear away anyway so they agreed to meet in an hour or two once the guys dropped them off at their car.

They had one more night before they would head back to the city and it was shaping up to end perfectly. Although the beginning of the week had Lacey pining away for the comforts of home, she was now settling into an altogether different life. She hoped re-entry wouldn't be as rough as she expected it to be.

Once all four of the kayaks and the remaining gear were stowed away in the bed of the truck, they hopped in for the ride back. Ashley sat up front with Gregory while Chase and Lacey nestled themselves into the back seat. Ashley and Lacey were amazed that the trip by vehicle was so short. A twenty-minute drive compared to a three-hour trip by water. Safely back, they made a sincere offer to help with putting everything back in place. Chase and Gregory would have none of it. Chase insisted he had a system and would be done in no time. Instead, they said their good-byes and headed back to the cabin to freshen up before meeting later.

Left alone with his brother to do the grunt work, Gregory heaved the last kayak up to Chase who was standing on a stepladder and ready to stack the boat in its cradle.

"You and Lacey were in the General Store a long time," Gregory grunted as he lifted the bulky boat. No answer. Chase positioned the kayak with little effort.

"What were you two doing in there?"

"Talking. Hand me those dry bags, please."

"Hmmmm. Sure, here you go."

Silence filled the cement garage as Chase positioned the equipment just so.

"Just talking, huh?"

"That's right."

Chase hopped down and folded the ladder against the wall.

"You need to go home first? If so, I can pick you up."

"Yeah, I'd like to change. I'm not sure I want to be subjected to the ride in your old truck, though. Maybe I'll just pick you up on my way back through town."

Gregory could tell his brother was annoyed and let up on him.

"Hey, you alright? Something happen between you and Lacey?"

Chase walked to the garage door. He waited for his brother to walk out before pressing the button and ducking under the closing door.

"Not a thing. There's nothing going on between us, you know. Don't make more of it than it is."

Gregory held up his hands in defense. "Alright. Got it. You just seem off. Seems like we all had a great day and now there's this dark cloud hangin' over us. Over you."

Chase stopped next to his brother's truck. Hands in his pockets, he shrugged his shoulders and looked out onto the water and the trees swaying in the breeze. Some clouds had moved in to block the sun's generous warmth.

"Lacey's great. What's not to like? Yeah, It's been real nice seeing her again after all these years and hanging out, but where's it going? Nowhere. She's going back to her successful life in Annapolis and I'm staying here in this shack along the river. You and I both know I can't be anything more than this," he said pointblank with open palms out to his sides.

"I think she likes who you are."

They stood in awkward silence before Chase turned to his brother.

"She doesn't know who I am."

"You need to ease up on yourself," Gregory looked his brother in the eyes. "You *are* a good guy. What's in the past is in the past. Let yourself move on."

"I'd like to. I really would. I don't know how. I've tried. Between background checks and these damn … nightmares, I'm realizing this is it for me."

Chase continued to look downriver with a wide stance and crossed arms. Gregory leaned against the truck as he awkwardly inspected his keys.

"Do you have the nightmares a lot?"

Chase shrugged his shoulders while keeping the riparian view in sight.

"More and more." Breathing deep, he exhaled heavily. "Always the same. I'm standing in a cell alone when … she … Julia … appears and opens the door. She tells me I'm a good person and to go. She tells me to move on. I walk out, stand next to her and then wake up."

Gregory took a step forward to stand directly next to his brother.

"You know, she's trying to tell you something. Maybe you should listen," he said quietly.

"Yeah. Well, no one's going to give a felon a chance."

Gregory watched his brother walk away. He knew Chase was a decent, moral person who had a bad thing happen to him eighteen years ago. He also knows he would have done the same thing in his shoes, if he had the guts.

"Chase. Come on. Don't leave like this."

"I'm okay, really. Don't worry about it. How about I pick you up in thirty minutes?" Chase said from the landing at his apartment door with a forced smile. To ease his brother's concern, he referenced the out of date stereo system in his decades-old truck in jest.

146

"I'll let you pick the 8-Track."

"Sounds good, little brother. See you soon," he called out with a wave as he opened the driver's side door to the flashy, new vehicle that was parked next to the timeworn Ford. Chase disappeared into his humble apartment along the water.

Inside, the dwelling was dated and rustic. Chase liked it that way. It had been a living quarter since the early 1900's when the building operated as a mill and had a long list of boarder tenants. Besides updated utilities, a little bit of added insulation and newer appliances, not much has changed since then. When Barney Ritter bought the place in the 1990's and turned it into a canoe and kayak rental operation, the apartment sat empty until he hired Chase to help with setting up the paddlers with the gear they needed for their trips and to help with scheduling and shuttling. Once the business grew and more tentative customers asked for a guide, he volunteered a glad-to-help Chase. Soon, Chase was on site daily and Barney was looking to take more and more time off as he neared retirement age. Knowing Chase needed a hand in a fresh start, he offered Chase the apartment in exchange for handy work and watching over the building. It was a symbiotic relationship built on trust.

Chase grabbed a beer from the fridge on the way to the shower. He thought about the day as steam began to fill the small space and knew that Gregory was right. It *had* been a good day. Hands down, the best he had in the last twenty years and he knew the reason for that was Lacey. Shutting the water off and grabbing a towel, he walked to the adjacent bedroom and pulled some clean clothes from the basket on the floor. Jeans with a grey, cotton quarter zip pullover and he was on his way back out the door.

The old truck rumbled to life and smiling, he rummaged through the glove compartment for the most dated and uncool music selection he could find. Gregory wanted everything to be modern and high tech. Chase was fine with things as long as he could fix them. He would never get rid of their dad's truck and knew Gregory was thankful for that regardless of his teasing. Now, with it just being Chase and Gregory left in the family, any ties to the past were good to have around. His thoughts ventured back in time. Back when he hung out with Lacey and her cousins in their younger years. He had never let his little sister tag along and he felt a pang of guilt. Lacey would have liked having her around back then. She probably would have liked her today, too, he thought. He felt his eyes sting from the tears that tried to escape and quickly pushed the thoughts away. With a shake of his head and a deep breath, he cleared his mind. Gregory was right. It *was* time to move on.

CHAPTER TWENTY-THREE
Back To Reality

"HEY, LACEY. HOW WAS your time away?" Terrance answered on the second ring. She had gotten back into town that day and was still not accustomed to the quicker pace of things. She quickly gathered her thoughts.

"Hi, Terrance. Thanks for asking and thanks for covering for me. How did everything go?"

"Fine, I think. We did close early on that deal I told you about. No issues there. Two clients called wanting to meet with you when you get back about listing their homes. I will email that info to you. Other than that, I did some showings and put out a few fires. Nothing major."

"Oh, good. I'm glad it wasn't too much of a hassle for you. I will pay you for your time, of course."

"Don't worry about it. Just cover for me sometime?"

"Absolutely. I'm happy to return the favor."

"Oh, one other thing. Some guy named Stuart called three times wanting to know if you were back yet. He seemed a little strange. I confirmed you weren't and asked if I could help him. He finally told me he wanted to set up some showings, but he didn't have any specifics. Just vague descriptions of the properties. I tried to help, but he couldn't provide any useful information. I asked him for his email and told him I would see what I could find and email him some available properties matching his descriptions. He hung up on me, though. I'm sorry, I ..."

"Please don't apologize. It's not you, trust me."

Lacey suddenly felt nauseous. She thought Stuart Benson was out of the picture for good. If her vacation taught her one thing, it was that she would take a new approach to work. Clients like Stuart Benson were not a part of this approach.

"You know, Stuart is a little, uh, high maintenance, but he is looking in a very high price point. If you want to work with him, I'll refer him to you for a twenty percent referral fee?"

"He did mention some list prices. That *is* enticing."

"How about I email you his contact info and set it all up with him so that the transition goes smoothly. What do you think?"

"Why not? Thank you!"

"Thank you," Lacey said with a little too much conviction. "Well, my other line is beeping. Gotta go. Thanks, again, Terrance. Really."

"Anytime. Talk later, sweetie."

Lacey clicked over to answer the other call without checking the caller ID. To her surprise, it was Sam.

"Well, hello stranger. Are you back in action and well rested?" Sam greeted.

Lacey had forgotten about their plans to meet for dinner. After the kayak trip and drinks with Chase, she was having a hard time assimilating back into this life she knew best. She knew Chase was a big reason for that. There was no reason to not meet up with Sam, though, and she tried to hide her sudden lack of interest in their dinner date plans.

"Hello. Actually, I am, thank you very much," she said pleasantly. "How have you been?"

"Up to my elbows in lawsuits and petty details, to tell the truth. I need a break. Care to join me for dinner this Friday night or sooner?"

"I would love to," she lied as she wondered what was going on with her rollercoaster emotions these days. Last week at this time she would have been more enthusiastic about another date with Sam. "Friday is fine with me."

"Fantastic. Meet me at The Creek House at eight? How

about a drink at the bar first?" Sam had an upbeat and confident demeanor about him that came through loud and clear even over the phone.

"Love that place. Yes. Friday. Seven o'clock at the bar. I will see you then."

Hair in a bun and still in pink yoga pants and a long-sleeve tee from the long drive home, she tossed the phone on the coffee table and sank deeply into the plush sofa while plopping her slippered feet next to the phone. She had calls to make, paperwork to file, updates to receive and appointments to schedule and could not muster the motivation to do any of it. That mountain air certainly did do something to her and it was a chilly and overcast October day in Annapolis. She justified her laziness on the weather as she got up to turn on the furnace for the first time that year. She listened for it to start and breathed a sigh of relief when she heard the click and low rumble of it firing up. As nice a convenience it was, she thought it would have been better to curl up in front of the fireplace at the cabin. As the imagined scene developed in her mind's eye, it barely registered with her that Chase was very much a part of that picture.

Grabbing her phone off the table, she headed upstairs to continue to unpack. Work could wait until the morning, she told herself. She filled the laundry basket with clothes needing to be washed and thought about the General Store Chase had shown her at the end of the kayak trip. It was an interesting building. It would be perfect for as an outfitting and rental shop for the plethora of outdoor enthusiasts that flock to the region year around, just as Chase had said. He had a great vision for the place and she could see the finished product through his eyes. The building was surprisingly solid despite being vacant for so long. It was dripping with character inside and the heavily varnished woodwork had somehow withstood the wrath of neglect. A large stone fireplace was the hallmark of the open first floor and Lacey had been astonished to discover the stunning design element extended to the second floor. She had encouraged Chase to buy it and turn it into what he envisioned, but he seemed reluctant. Lack of funds, she assumed. It would, of course, take a lot to make that dream a reality. She knew she was not in the position to take on such an endeavor.

In spite of her practicality, she picked up her laptop and in seconds had the listing pulled up through a real estate website. She was inclined to waste a little time daydreaming. She blinked and squinted when she noted the unbelievably low price. Fifty thousand dollars. There had to be a missing number somewhere in that listing entry or something significantly wrong with it. She was curious.

Without thinking, she picked up her phone and began dialing the listing agent's number. Call it second nature. The listing agent not only answered the call, he was a wealth of information. No, there were no structural issues as far as he knew. The seller was finally serious about selling after initially listing it way too high about two years ago and refusing to negotiate with interested buyers. Yes, there sure was a lot of potential and he could not imagine a well-run business *not* succeeding as long as it was a good fit for the building and location. He wasn't sure why it hadn't sold yet, to be honest. He imagined it would sit on the market over the winter and probably sell in the spring.

After disconnecting the call, she sat in a dumbfounded state at the foot of her bed. What was she thinking? Why was she even considering the thoughts that began to tumble around in her head? Still on autopilot, she pulled up her online mortgage account and the pay-off was right where she thought it was. What fun she had imagining the possibilities and, if nothing else, she was realizing she could take steps to make a major lifestyle transformation. Making herself her own client, her fingers moved at a lightning pace as she quickly pulled up recently sold properties comparative to her own duplex. Having had the units deeded separately, she could easily sell her side and put the equity into something else keeping the other side as a rental for regular income. A plan was shaping up in her mind. A plan that was from out in left field and unlike her conservative self. A creative escape plan that made her feel alive again.

For the remainder of the evening, she explored random thoughts and discovered new horizons. The Internet became her secret confidant for endless insights as she perused blogs and websites featuring alternative lifestyles and housing. She read about people who traveled the country while living in recreational vehicles and people who traveled the world while living on sailboats. Start-up business success stories of those who followed their passions in life and claimed to be happy and then there were visions of extremists who sold everything to reside within a peaceful Buddhist temple, native tribe, or commune. In the end, she realized she was far more mainstream than she would like to admit, however, this short study in how other humans lived was enough to prove any change she might strive for would be doable and dull in comparison.

When she had arrived home earlier in the day, she had noticed Bryce's car parked out front along the road. She decided to send her a text.

"Wine on the deck?"

"Yes," came the reply before Lacey heard her doorbell chime.

She opened the door and found her neighbor dressed in similar attire, holding a bottle wine and already standing in the Victorian tiled vestibule. "It's mid-afternoon and you're not in a suit," Bryce stated dryly.

"Hi. You look nice, too. Come on in," Lacey invited sarcastically as she stepped aside. "I have plenty of wine on hand, by the way. How were your flights?"

"Just add the bottle to the collection, then. I'm sure I'll end up drinking it here at some point. Flights were good. No issues. Most people in society are miserable. Blah, blah, blah. Glad to be home."

In the kitchen, Lacey pulled two wine glasses from the cupboard, opened a bottle of merlot and filled the glasses to an obnoxious amount.

"Woah. Heavy pour you got there," Bryce exclaimed.

"Are you complaining? I have a lot to fill you in on."

"I'll bring the bottle with us, then. Lead the way, my friend."

They filed out to the back deck. The grey clouds were thick and sat low in the sky. Lacey pulled two rolled blankets from a large antique crock she kept by the back door. It was a decorating and lifestyle tip she had learned from her grandmother and one that had always been on-hand at the cabin. Taking their seats at the wrought iron table, they wrapped themselves in the warmth of plaid flannels and Lacey dove into everything that had happened since the last time she saw Bryce at the crab shack.

"Two romantic interests, dinner on a boat, dinner with friends, a trip to a cabin in the mountains, ridding yourself of a pain-in-the-ass client, drinks at a random bar, and a kayak trip down a river in upstate New York. You sure as hell throw yourself into things whole heartedly," Bryce noted in amusement.

"Because of you. Your words kept ringing in my head every time I agreed to do something new. I really broke through some kind of barrier and am not going to be one of these miserable humans you see all the time. Life is so much more than work. I am ready to make some changes, but land on my feet, of course."

"I see I've created a monster. You're not going on tour as a motivational speaker, are you?" Bryce tucked a lock of hair behind her ear and looked at Lacey with sheer delight. "Because I don't think you have the credentials to do that, yet."

"Yet. I will, though. And, no, I have other plans," Lacey revealed.

"Go on. I'm intrigued."

CHAPTER TWENTY-FOUR
A Metamorphosis

LACEY WAS IN THE full swing of things by mid-week. While there were no major problems to speak of, she was still finding it hard to stay motivated. It was a scary feeling for someone like herself. Like anyone, she had tired of work before, but this was different. One minute, she was on cloud nine with dreams of a new future and the next she was in fear of the impracticality of it all and all but resigned to keep everything the same.

She knew of other agents who got to this point and knew many of them took a few months or a year off. She couldn't afford to take a considerable amount of time off without relieving herself of some financial pressure. Something had to give. She simply wasn't the same since she returned from New York and that scared her.

"Am I suddenly lazy and unmotivated?" She gave the notion that popped into her swimming mind some serious consideration and decided she was far from either of those characteristics.

If these feelings persisted, she owed it to herself and her clients to find a new path. She thought about the fact that she, like most people, had committed to a career when she was youthfully green. Eager, but green. Now, this once vibrant and spirited woman needed to face the fact that a little quality time with herself had revealed a different side to her personality.

Recognizing her distinct split personality, she liked the other Lacey way more than the Lacey she had been pretending to be for so long. The Lacey Williams she had foolishly convinced herself she was.

Farmer Jim's words echoed in her head: *life doesn't have to be so hard*. She now not only knew what he meant, she had a vision of a new life. A life that was full of more fulfilling days and less grind. She was tired of just getting through the day only to start it all over the next. Life was more than that. It *had* to be more

On that note, she went full tilt as she began to mildly research her many varied options for a new business and way of life from the privacy of a home some three hundred miles from where she wanted to be. It was a place that had molded her more youthful self and its pull on her today her suggested she was an unfinished project.

She poured over websites and reviews and prices and offerings from the Kline, New York area and beyond and grabbed a notebook from her desk as she began to jot down ideas and crunched numbers while scrutinizing every detailed satellite map view. Next, she scoured the tourism and town sites for demographic, business, and visitor statistics. The more she thought about the possibilities, the more excited she became. If the General Store was any indication, she had more than enough equity in her side of the duplex to seriously consider a new venture.

There was a reliable plan somewhere in the chaos of her awakening mind. The mere thought of selling her house and moving to a more remote location was affording her an odd sense of relief. She would sell her car and buy something that went better in the snow and could haul supplies. A used pick-up truck perhaps. The thought made her smile then laugh out loud when she realized she really was capable of trading in her Lexus in on a used pick-up truck. She wanted to sell everything and start fresh. Who knew she needed a change this badly? She was amazed at how invigorated she became at the realization she could be knee deep in a simpler way of life within a year.

Lacey continued this way the rest of the day. She vowed to keep all the particulars under wraps until she figured out what she wanted. Anyone in his or her right mind would tell her she was crazy. Maybe she was, but it was a good kind of crazy. For now, it was something to sink her teeth into and keep her spirits up.

By Friday, she was elated with the idea of a new life. That was also the day of her date with Sam. She was looking forward to it, but was way more into her covert plan. On occasions, she had doubted her ability or the realistic nature of the idea, however, on that day, she would have none of it and she forcibly cast any doubt aside and continued to live blissfully in her naivetés. As she prepared for her date, she saw a new version of herself in the mirror. Bright-eyed, spirited and in charge of her destiny. She plucked a bright red cocktail dress from her closet and stepped out of the house with a new kind of confidence.

Pulling into the parking lot of the restaurant, she parked farther away than necessary and, after stepping out of the car; she walked to the edge of the lot and looked out onto the harbor. The boats rose and dipped on the surface and some were decorated with white lights as they welcomed a darker and colder time of year when more time would be spent at the dock. Lacey leaned against the railing, closed her eyes and breathed the salty air.

"Beautiful sight, ain't it?"

Lacey abruptly stood straight up as Sam leaned in next to her.

"Yes. You caught me loitering."

Seeing his relaxed pose, she leaned back against the railing with her chin resting on her fist. They looked out onto the dark horizon in silence for a few seconds before Sam went on.

"Doing a little daydreaming, are we? Well, I just hope one day you decide to share that dream with me. For now, though, it's a pretty clear night and you should take a moment to make a wish on that big bright star above you. I'm telling you it works."

Lacey looked at him and smiled.

"Go on now. Trust me on this one."

Sam looked back out onto the water while he waited for her to comply. He glanced back at her then motioned toward the stars as a feeble prompting.

"If you say so. What do I have to lose?"

She looked up at the twinkling sky. As she did she made the most sincere plea in her head and gazed intently at the stars beginning to shine overhead.

"Wait! I just saw a shooting star. No lie! I've never seen one before!"

"You haven't? You don't do nearly enough star gazing then," Sam said calmly with a kind look her way and still keeping a relaxed lean into the railing. "Well, I sure do hope you made that wish a good one because," he paused as he pointed to the sky, "it is being granted." He stood from his bowed position then toward his date he offered a bent elbow.

"Shall we?"

She was charmed and accepted his invitation by placing her hand on the inside crook of his arm. Sam exuded exquisite southern charm and was ever so polished from years spent in the finest schools and among a well-to-do family.

It did not take long before Lacey remembered what she liked about him in the first place. They walked in the direction of the bustling restaurant and he placed her hand in his with a chivalrously firm hold. His romantic intentions did not let up as held the door, helped her with her coat and checked it for her before they headed to the bar for a cocktail. Holding her seat for her he asked what she was in the mood for and before long two icy vodka martinis with twists of lemon were served. They raised their glasses to commence the evening. Lacey was glad she had decided to dress up a bit since Sam was looking dapper in his fitted grey suit with a sapphire tie which matched his eyes. The way Lacey had been this past week, it was surprising she found the time or desire to dress up at all. She had been in a mountain-state-of-mind. It all seemed silly to her now as she sat in this fine restaurant by the harbor in a city she really did adore and next to a captivating man who seemed to adore her.

"Maybe I had gone a little crazy this week," she thought.

The conversation between them continued with no ends in sight. Sam brought up their last meeting and apologized for seeming distant. He explained what happened and Lacey mentioned Stuart Benson's involvement in that whole situation.

"I have no doubt the fellow put you through the ringer. I actually used to be a lawyer in his dad's firm and could tell you more than a few unflattering stories about him. Come to think of it, that firm is probably the main reason I decided to start my own practice."

That comment opened the floodgates and they continued to trade war stories without naming the innocent. In the process it became painfully obvious they led very much the same life.

Time was flying and after the pre-dinner cocktail, they followed the smartly dressed hostess to their reserved table. More than a few diners turned to watch this handsome couple stride along. Together, they had the makings of a power couple with incredible confidence and good looks to boot. They ordered a second cocktail at their table and barely took time to open the menu. Lacey decided quickly on the vegetable risotto and Sam ordered the lamb chops and a few appetizers to share. The appetizers were served efficiently along with an unordered bottle of wine.

"Compliments of the couple at the table to your left, sir," the waiter said as he offered the bottle for tasting. Lacey followed Sam's glance and noticed the same man and woman who Sam had dined with at lunch the day they formally met. They waved a greeting and Sam waved them over.

"Len and Tara Miles, Lacey Williams," Sam introduced as the couple ducked over for a quick hello. "I worked for Len for fifteen years and he taught me everything I know. I should be buying him wine. Thank you, by the way," Sam said to his elder associate.

They were mismatched to say the least. He being a squat, messy fellow and she a tall, thin platinum blonde with pizazz who appeared to be about half his age.

"Hi, Lacey. Forgive us for intruding," Tara said meekly.

"Oh, they don't mind, right Sam?" Len nearly shouted as he slapped Sam on the shoulder.

"Not at all," Sam concurred.

"We're heading out anyway. Just wanted to say hi and tell you to enjoy your evening. Nice to see you with some companionship, Sam. Gotta step away from the office once in awhile."

Lacey glanced at Sam who appeared visibly and uncharacteristically uncomfortable. Bidding farewells all around, Len and Tara left and Sam seemed to be in deep reflection for a second or two before bouncing back.

"Oh, I meant to tell you. Gus and Vern are all over me about having you back to the dock," Sam said with a gulp of wine.

"They are so sweet. I forgot to mention him to my dad. I'll have to call him tomorrow."

"If you can make the time, I could host a dinner on my boat for the four of us?"

"I'd love that. I could help out with dinner," Lacey proposed.

Before they could discuss it any further, dinner was served, wines were topped off, and conversations ramped up again. As the restaurant quieted around them, Lacey and Sam ended up being one of the last tables left. They ordered a coffee when they couldn't finish the bottle of wine.

"The waiter would be happy to help us out with what's left in the bottle, don't you think?" Sam asked when Lacey insisted she was finished.

By the time the second cup of coffee was filled and the check was dropped off, exhaustion was setting in from a long week for both of them.

"So, do you have any plans for the weekend or will you be

working?" she asked Sam.

"Ha, lawyers never work on weekends, right? Okay, actually, always. Unfortunately. I have a hard time not working. I am trying to remedy that problem, but I am realizing more and more I am a lost cause. I'll pop into my office and catch up on some research and do a little work at home, I suppose. Maybe get some things done on the boat to prepare for winter. I guess weekends are always pretty busy for you?"

"Oh, yes. I can't say no to work either. I'm kind of tired of it though. The constant stress, that is. How do you find balance and get a break now and then?"

"Now that I opened my own firm, I don't. Funny, I made this move to have more control over my time and I work more than ever. I have employees, so, that is an added stress. I can't say I dislike it. I kind of thrive on the business and challenge of it all."

Lacey slowly stirred cream into her coffee as she thought about his words.

"Don't you get caught up in the thrill of it all? The deals fall apart, but, then come back together. New business is always just around the corner. Closings, of course, are big motivators I'm sure," Sam contemplated. He was energized by the discussion.

"I used to," Lacey started slowly. She didn't want to tell Sam exactly how unmotivated she was since returning from vacation. "I think I just need to work in some more time off now and then. I've gone years without taking a break until last week and I'm coming off of a few stressful deals. Nothing that I can't get over. Just a little more me time is needed, you know?"

"I sure do. I was like that all of last year, I think. You're right. A little time off and you'll start to get your mojo back. We've all been there."

What if you don't want to get it back? Lacey thought as she unceremoniously nodded her agreement.

Sam paid the bill and Lacey thanked him for a wonderful

evening. He walked her to her car and gave her an embrace and a soft kiss on the cheek before suggesting dinner at his place next. Lacey agreed sincerely. Before they could experience any awkward hesitations, she said to give her a call and maybe they could even grab a cup of coffee or lunch mid-week as she started to open her door.

"I'd like that, Lacey. This was a real good time, I must say."

Sam held the door open for her and waited while she started the car and pulled away. He placed his hands in his coat pocket and watched the car leave the lot before looking up at the stars to make his own wish.

CHAPTER TWENTY-FIVE
The Real World's Not So Bad?

LACEY WOKE TO A picturesque sunny day. She instantly thought about what she could do outside to enjoy the weather before the snow and ice arrived in the upcoming weeks then quickly realized she had some morning appointments to get ready for. Two listing appointments and six showings. She could be back by one and if the weather stayed pleasant, she planned on getting out of town to do a little hiking to satisfy her other side she was now choosing to recognize.

She was still a little groggy from the night before and realized mixing the wine with the martinis was probably not the best idea. First things first: Excedrin, water, a hot shower and some strong coffee with breakfast. Maybe it was the slight headache she had, but the glitz of the evening had already worn off.

Sam had kept the conversation going non-stop. Non-stop conversation about work. Lacey was scared of turning into a version of him. Whether or not she and Sam started seeing each other, she was still confident that a life with less pressure and sweeter moments was imperative. Her head was pounding harder now and she was tired of thinking about anything and everything. She wanted to crawl back into bed. In the end, she pulled herself together and was pulling out of her drive ahead of schedule.

The Carter residence was a late 1800's townhome just a few blocks from her own home. She had sold the property to the couple about five years earlier and they were out growing out of the tiny row house now that they were expecting their second child. Using the lion's head doorknocker, she announced her arrival. Ben Carter answered the door quickly and Lacey stepped inside.

Melissa Carter was waiting at the kitchen table for them as their two year-old ran to her legs for cover. Lacey gently greeted the child so not to frighten her any more than she already was and Melissa rubbed her hand through the little girl's adorable ringlets. They were a picture-perfect family in a picture-perfect home that was neat-as-a-pin. This would be an easy sale. Lacey felt a pang of sadness as she sat down. Her home was neat and pretty, too, but, lonely.

Ben explained that they had already spoken with their lender and were pre-approved. They would like to sell as quickly as possibly to avoid paying two mortgages and to be settled in before the baby arrived. Melissa rubbed her protruding belly as an unconscious comparison to a ticking time bomb that was propelling their lives forward. Lacey pulled the file and was ready to get down to business after getting a quick tour of the house to check the condition and see if they had done any significant upgrades. She carried the file with her as Ben gave her the tour.

The cozy home featured soothing shades of tans and greys, and blue accents provided an aesthetic background to framed black and white photos showing off the Carters' travels around the globe before they started a family. While nothing was over-the-top, the fixtures were new and everything was well maintained. Not a chip of paint was missing and the ancient pine floors were well oiled and as smooth as butter. A faint scent of cinnamon filled the air. They stepped into Lilly's room.

"Oh, this is sweet," Lacey declared.

An over-stuffed upholstered rocking chair sat in the corner next to a small nightstand with a little pink lamp. A short stack of books on the table gave insight into a serene bedtime routine and a light lavender aroma drifted throughout the pastel room with the tiny toddler bed. Lacey felt some form of homesickness and had no idea why.

"Thanks. This is our life," Ben quietly stated before they turned to leave and head back downstairs.

Lacey was sold on the home and the little piece of heaven the Carter's had presented. She knew the home would sell quickly and for top dollar and she was excited about helping them move to a new home that could potentially be the one their grandchildren visited them in someday.

"Lilly, can you play with your blocks while mommy and daddy talk to Lacey?" Melissa pleaded sweetly with the little girl. Lilly sat down at her mother's feet and began to play on a sage blanket. "We should get about, oh, thirty seconds of peace," Melissa warned as the three adults sat down to begin their discussion.

"Well, I will get straight to the important details, then," Lacey said keenly with a grin for little Lilly. "Your house is beautiful and will show wonderfully. We will have no problem selling for top dollar as long as you can accommodate the rush of showings we will get initially. I have a feeling we will receive plenty of requests the minute I enter the listing."

"No problem. We will do what we have to do," Melissa stated with Ben nodding his agreement. He sat on the edge of his seat and Lacey knew he was eager to talk numbers. She normally kept that for a follow-up visit, but, in this case, she could easily pinpoint exactly what this house would sell for.

"Since I sold the house to you and I live a few blocks from here in the same market vicinity, I went ahead and pulled some recently sold comps to give us an objective idea of what we can expect the home to sell for. Experience has shown me you will want to list it very close to the expected sale price if you want a quick sale. Doing so will elicit multiple offers and a sale price at or above list price with little in the way of contingencies that could cause a deal to fall through. Listing it too high only causes the house to sit on the market longer than necessary."

Lacey passed out the copies of the Market Analysis she had brought along and gave Ben and Melissa time to look over the information before she went on to discuss the data. She could see Ben's face fall as he looked over the information, which, was common since sellers typically thought they could get a higher, and unrealistic, sale price.

"All of these comps are low," Ben stated.

"They are all within a realistic range and will be what potential buyers and appraisers will look at, which is very important to keep in mind. Regardless, my professional experience and knowledge of this exact area tells me to expect a sale price of around three hundred fifty thousand. I would advise you to price the home just under three hundred sixty if you want to sell well within thirty days."

"No. We need to be in the four hundreds. I know similar houses have sold in the four hundreds." Ben was clearly annoyed.

"The homes that have sold in the four's have at least three bedrooms and off-street parking. Keep in mind, as I told you when you purchased the house, it is an unusually small two bedroom with on-street parking. If you price this house in the four hundred range, you will be competing with listings that offer more and the house will stay on the market until you reduce it closer to market value. There are other comps out there selling well below three fifty. I think you can get just over that, though, due to the condition and the décor of the house."

Silence. Lilly began to fuss and Melissa picked her up. Lacey noticed a glance between them that she couldn't decipher. She let Ben take more time to digest the information she just provided and waited for his response while Melissa took Lilly into the kitchen for a snack. Ben was putting his family in a bad spot if wanted to list this little home so high, regardless of how nice it was. Lacey was tired of this song and dance on virtually every listing appointment with younger sellers. The homes always sold for what she predicted in the end and only after months on the market and multiple reductions. She didn't want to see that happen to this family. She decided to move forward with the next piece of information.

"Here is a net return sheet based on a sale of three hundred fifty thousand with a standard six percent commission and the average settlement costs and taxes the seller is responsible for."

Lacey passed the sheet to Ben and left a copy for Melissa. Lacey hoped they had not taken out equity loans above what the home is worth. They got a fantastic deal on the house five years ago at just under three hundred thousand due to the massive amounts of dated wallpaper throughout the home. Now that they had remedied that and some other cosmetic items, they were poised to sell at the top of the anticipated range. They were sitting pretty and should be happy to move on. It was clear Ben was not. Lacey waited for him to respond.

"Well, I don't know. I think we may have to just try to sell on our own," he stated.

"That's fine. Remember, price and exposure sell homes and we are heading into the slower months of winter. I want what is best for you and will sell this house quickly for you. I just don't want to see you play around with a overpriced listing, Ben."

"I really wanted to net a hundred grand in the end and the numbers you are showing me aren't getting that done."

"It is what it is. I can't make it sell for fifty grand more than what it's worth. Five to ten, maybe. The market data proves that to be true every time. Well, why don't you and Melissa talk about all of this and we can get together again in few days. Would that be helpful?"

"Uh, yeah. That's good. Let us talk tonight after Lilly goes to bed. Thanks for coming over, Lacey."

Ben was shuffling to the door before she had even collected her items.

Once back in her car and onto her next appointment, Lacey was emotionally exhausted. She really didn't care if she got the listing or not. If they were in a bad position, she would have advised them to try to sell it on their own. Unlike many other agents, she didn't take overpriced listings simply for the sake of having her name on a sign in the yard.

Her next appointments of the day took much the same course. She, a true professional with real-world experience and skill, was now competing with vague information gleaned from Google searches and cable real estate shows.

By two o'clock she arrived home. Sitting in the car and emotionally exhausted, the buzzing of her phone caught her attention.

"Hello, this is Lacey," she snapped back at the device that she resented more and more.

"Um. Hi, Lacey. It's Chase. Did I catch you at a bad time?"

CHAPTER TWENTY-SIX
A Friendly Voice

"CHASE. I'M SO SORRY. I must've sounded so rude. How are you? It's really nice to hear from you."

"I'm fine. I can call back if it's not a good time."

His voice was relaxed and calm and Lacey felt the tension in her body diminish by just listening to him.

"No, no. Yes, I do need a break and now is a perfect time."

"I hope you don't mind. Your uncle called me yesterday about that canoe and I asked him for your number. I wanted to make sure you got back to Annapolis okay."

Lacey could tell he sounded nervous and felt bad. What a contrast in personalities it must have been at that moment.

"I don't mind at all! I'm glad you called. Really. I'm here and back to the grind," she laughed.

Thinking about the cabin and Chase's hometown she unwound instantly. Their breezy conversation turned from one laidback topic to another and for the time being, Lacey was transported to an altered state. Without realizing how much time had passed, the beep of her phone announced the battery was dying. She had been sitting in the car talking to Chase for almost an hour.

"Argh. This phone is going to be the death of me," she stated abruptly. "It's dying and I don't have a charger with me. The other line is beeping, too. Can I call you back?"

"Sure! I have to go pick up my brother anyway. It's a Penn Tavern night."

"Ahh. I wish I was there."

"So do I."

His words melted her. He lacked even a trace of posturing.

"Well, tell your brother I said 'hello' and how about I give you a call tomorrow?"

"Sounds good to me. Looking forward to it. Take care, Lacey."

"You, too, Chase."

Suddenly, the day's lackluster events faded to a distant part of her mind as she walked in the front door. At that moment, Lacey Williams realized that she alone was responsible for creating her happiness and she would not spend another day wallowing in frustration, pity, or resentment due to an unbalanced or mismatched life.

Plugging in her BlackBerry and firing up her laptop, she pulled up the website her office used for downloading the state-required documents needed for listing and selling properties. She found the e-files she needed and started typing to fill in the blank spaces. She was a woman on a mission and taking charge.

On the listing address line she took a deep breath and typed her own address. On the listing price line, she placed a price that was five thousand less than what the data showed it would sell for. She was effervescent with the idea of not knowing exactly where this journey would take her.

Within minutes the forms were completed. She grabbed her camera and walked through the home. No husband, kids nor pets combined with a homeowner who was barely living in it allowed for an easily maintained neat home. She snapped well-lit and well-staged photos instantly and was back at her laptop reviewing them in no time. She smiled. At least she earned one listing today. Printing the documents, she created a file for the sale of her own home in a bright pink file just for the fun of it and another set in a standard manila file to hand in at her office. She would complete a deep clean and quick organization of the house before she officially put it on the market.

Sitting back, she looked at the time up on the corner of the laptop. Almost five o'clock. If there was ever a time for a glass of wine in recent months, this was it. She got up to head down to the kitchen and heard her phone buzz back to life and the three dings letting her know she had three voicemails waiting for her.

"Whatever I do next, I'd rather you not be a part of it," she said aloud as she entered the passcode to retrieve the messages.

"Lacey, it's Sam. Give me a call when you get a chance? Thanks."

Lacey deleted the message, but not without having her interest piqued. He sounded unusually subdued.

"Hi, Lacey. It's Kristen. Josh and I were driving around and saw a property on West Street in the five hundred block and we are dying to see it tonight. Please call us back right away. Thanks!" Lacey knew which house they meant. It was actually under contract and about a hundred thousand dollars over their budget.

"Yes. Lacey. Ben Carter here. Thanks for stopping over today. Just wanted to let you know we are going to list the house with Rupert Snodgrass. We appreciate your input, but, he thinks we can get something in the four's. We are hoping you could sell it, though, so please bring your buyers by? Thanks."

It was known as 'buying the listing'. Pricing a house for whatever the sellers want just to get another listing. She knew Rupert and didn't care for his slimy tactics. Taking a big gulp of wine, she returned the calls.

"I don't know, Lacey. The sign is still up, though," Kristen smugly pointed out after Lacey confirmed the property she called about was under contract.

"Yes, the sign stays up until after the property closes. Anyway, that house is definitely under contract and currently off the market."

"Can you make sure?"

"I already did and it is. I will let you know if that changes. Are you considering upping your desired price range?" Lacey said a little more dryly than she intended.

"Well, maybe they would take less."

"Not one hundred thousand dollars less and certainly not in this case. I will email you similar properties that are currently available and in your price range. Okay?"

Kristen went on and on about how much she liked the property that was too much for her and her fiancé and not even on the market. Lacey drowned her out as she downed her wine.

Up next, Sam and then the couch and a movie as far as Lacey was concerned.

"Lacey. Thanks for calling back."

"Sure, what's up?"

"James, uh Farmer Jim, passed away today. I was wondering if you would join me at his funeral on Monday?"

CHAPTER TWENTY-SEVEN
A Little Less Character In the World

SITTING IN THE BACK of the funeral parlor, Lacey watched Sam speak to Jim's family. Jim had meant a lot to Sam. He had elaborated on their relationship when he picked her up and they were on their way to the funeral.

"When Esther, his wife, had passed a few years ago, I had handled the legal details for Jim. That's how I got to know him," he had explained. "She was everything to him and it wasn't long before I noticed he liked to talk about her and relive the memories. I liked to listen to the stories. It sure was different back when he and Esther were in their prime and raising their family. I was in awe of his character and the life they created entirely on their own. They held on to a different set of values than people do today. "

Lacey listened from the passenger seat and memories of her grandparents came to mind as he talked.

"I would meet him at his farmhouse to go over things and he would make a pot of coffee. He would always start off by telling me how Esther made the best coffee. To be invited to sit at his kitchen table and talk all evening like we did was something I just didn't tire of. Time slowed down and life seemed doable. Uncomplicated."

Lacey nodded her understanding and thought about her morning coffees at the cabin. Sitting at that wobbly table, even without company, had been restorative.

Sam told her that he looked forward to seeing Jim every week at the Farmer's Market not only for the friendly banter and conversation, but also because the old man always imparted sage wisdom on him. His view of life had been different from the rest of society and Jim just shook his head at the perceived craziness that swirled around him.

"'Life doesn't have to be that hard' he had said the first time I met him," she revealed.

"Right. Exactly!" Sam exclaimed as he shot Lacey a knowing glance. "But we sure as heck all make it hard, don't we? He just always knew a little more than the rest of us, in my opinion," Sam reflected.

"I guess that's what eighty-some years of life gets you," Lacey said softly as they had pulled into the parking lot.

"I'm not so sure that everyone ascertains so much wisdom from life's lessons like he did."

James Eustice Miller had lived his life on his own terms, as far as anyone could tell. He did what he had to do to modernize farm life to make a living while maintaining a belief in going back to basics when life got too complicated. At least that's what his son had stated in the eulogy.

Lacey looked down at the In Memoriam she held in her hand. She gazed at the photo on the pamphlet. Mr. Miller's pleasant eyes looked at her from a face full of patina and gumption. It reminded her of her grandparents. They had worked hard to keep a tidy and well-run home with home cooked meals for their children. They worked hard, but always had time to relax with a cup of coffee or a game of cards. They made the children feel loved and special and lived a rich life on a meager income. What did they know that today's society doesn't seem to get? A haggard society that would be on full display the moment Lacey and Sam walked out of the funeral parlor doors. Traffic jams, long lines for over priced groceries, unreasonable commutes, and sixty-hour weeks left little time for the important things in life.

She looked back down at the pamphlet and read the epitaph that would adorn Mr. Miller's final resting place. The popular quote by an unknown source resonated with her:

"Focus on what matters and let go of what doesn't."

"Sorry to keep you waiting, Lacey," Sam said glumly as he stood before her. "Are you ready?"

"Yes. I am."

CHAPTER TWENTY-EIGHT
Startling Details

THANKSGIVING WEEKEND WAS A fine time to officially list her house and Lacey made sure everything was ready before leaving for her parents' house on that Wednesday afternoon. She left a few lights on in the house and spritzed some high-end floral air freshener in every little corner. Placing an agent lockbox on the front door with a spare key, she was ready. She left the front porch and vestibule lights on, stepped out onto the porch and locked the door behind her.

"It's official," she whispered.

She would drop off the listing file at her office on the way out of town and, hopefully, set up some showings as she drove to her childhood home about an hour outside of the city. She would also need to call Bryce to alert her in case she arrived home early and noticed the showing activity or a sign up in front of the duplex. She felt strangely calm and told herself that must mean she was doing the right thing. She also felt a tinge of excitement as she backed out onto the street.

Thirty minutes into the drive, the first call came in.

"Lacey. Alexis Dixon here. Want to show your Cathedral Street listing this Friday if possible. Say, between 10 and 11?"

"Hi, Alexis. That's fine. It's my house and I'll be gone until Monday morning. There's a lockbox on the front door so go anytime."

"Perfect. Thanks."

From there, the calls kept coming. By the time Lacey pulled into a gas station for a cup of coffee and to refuel, she had scheduled five showings for Friday through Saturday. If her instincts were correct, the list price would create a showing frenzy and the house to be under contract by Monday. Then what? Only time would tell. As she slid back into the driver's seat and out of the November chill, her phone rang again. This time, she recognized the number as belonging to Chase.

"Why, hello there," she answered and pulled the car to a nearby parking spot to talk before hitting the road again.

"Hey. I'm glad I caught you. I figured you would be on your way to your parents."

"I was. Just pulled over to get gas. Your timing is impeccable."

"Good. I was just sitting here thinking of you and wanted to wish you a Happy Thanksgiving. I missed talking to you the past couple days."

"Aw. That's sweet. Happy Thanksgiving to you. I know. I'm getting way too accustomed to our end-of-the day chats. You help diffuse the craziness of the day. Are you going to your parents' place for the holiday?"

There was a noticeable pause before he answered.

"Uh, no. Gregory actually cooks a meal for ten people, even though it is just me and him, so, we make gluttons of ourselves then watch some football. I actually, uh, volunteer at a soup kitchen nearby; so, I'll do that before heading over to his place. Too bad you can't join us. It would be nice to have you here."

"I can only imagine the meal he cooks if his picnic-atop-a-rock menu is any indication. I wish I could be there! Really, I do. So, soup kitchen, huh? Model citizen you are."

"Hardly. I had to, um, I started going few years ago and kind of got attached to it. It feels good to do what you can, you know? Well, I don't want to hold you up. You need to get back on the road. I'll call you over the weekend if you'll be around?"

"Sounds perfect. I'll talk to you then. Enjoy your holiday, Chase. Tell Gregory 'hello' for me, okay?"

"I will. Thanks. Have a good Thanksgiving."

Disconnecting the call, Lacey felt a yearning for a place she hardly knew anymore and a person she knew even less.

Thirty minutes later, she arrived and her mother was at the front door of the brick colonial waiting to greet her only child. Her chin length ginger hair was perfectly coiffed as usual and she held her cashmere olive green shrug tightly around her as she waited for her daughter. Pulling her suitcase from the trunk, Lacey rushed over to get out of the cold and to give her mother a warm hug.

"Come in, come in. It is too cold. We are supposed to get some sleet mixed with snow tonight, you know. I'm glad you left when you did."

"Hi, mom. Me, too. The traffic was starting to get a little wild. I made pretty good time by leaving early."

She entered the foyer and the familiar smell of home wafted around her like a warm embrace. What it was, she would never know. It was pleasing. Like cotton, soap, and spice mixed together for a signature scent. Decades of putting down roots and creating family memories seemed to conjure a distinct and pleasant atmosphere in any family home.

"Lacey," her father bellowed. "Give your dad a hug."

He stood in the door of the kitchen with a yellow Williams-Sonoma apron and a matching kitchen towel in hand. A look that was a divergence to his Naval Officer's uniform Lacey knew him for. At over six feet, top physical shape, and salt and pepper hair, he may have seemed out of place in his own home at the moment, but he was familiar as ever to his loving daughter.

"Hi, dad!" Lacey hurried over for a hug. All was right in her world at the moment. "What are you cooking?"

"Oh, just putting together the Green Bean Casserole and cleaning the Brussels sprouts. The only tasks your mother will let me help with."

Carol Williams gave her husband an amused sideways glance as she hung Lacey's coat up in the foyer coat closet.

"Well, finish whatever you are doing in there, George, and pour a glass of wine for Lacey. She must be exhausted. Pour one for me, too, while you're at it, please."

"Yes, ma'am," Lacey's dad called out and Lacey heard the pop of a wine cork having been removed against its will.

Lacey's mother smiled at her daughter and motioned to follow her into the living room. It was a room filled with quality furniture delivered from a local shop in 1985. The faux Queen Anne accents and upholstery were dated although held up well.

"Oh, this is so nice," Lacey uttered as she sunk down into the same sofa she collapsed on as a teenager after a long day at school. Soon, all three had a drink in hand as they filled each other in on the week's events. Lacey mentioned Sam and the funeral and her mother showed interest in hearing more.

"Oh, he's just a friend. Really. In fact, I haven't talked to him since Monday at the funeral. He's very busy with a trial he's prepping for. We do have a lot in common on the work front, I must say."

"You really need to work less, Lacey. This Sam fellow sounds nice. You should bring him by for dinner some time."

"Maybe I will."

"And your week at Grandma's cabin. I never got to hear about it all the details. You girls enjoyed yourselves, I'm sure?" Carol inquired.

"Yes, it was great. Thanks for suggesting it. Just what the doctor ordered. The first night was a little scary because Ashley got tied up at the hospital. In fact, I planned on coming home, but Ashley called just as I was leaving and encouraged me to stay. We had a terrific week and it was so relaxing."

"That's good. What did you two do?"

"Not much. Drank some wine, sat in front of the fire, drove into town a couple of times. Just enjoyed the scenery. The weather was summer-like during the day."

"Glad you used it," her father proclaimed as he broke into the conversation. "I keep telling Grandma she should think about selling it. Prices are really going up and there seems to be a real interest in the area right now."

"You don't say," Lacey thought.

She found herself withholding her own interest in the area, along with her interest in a certain someone. Her mother and father ran a tight ship at home and cared deeply about their only daughter. She knew they would not react well to any thoughts she had about selling her place and running off to rural America to do who-knows-what. Not to mention her sudden attraction to a random guy who lives in a rundown apartment along the river. When she put it that way, even she began to second-guess herself. It was nice getting to know Chase, though. They had settled into a rhythm of talking almost daily since he had called last Saturday. The old-fashioned way, she supposed. No texts, no Facebook, no emails. Just good, old conversation over the phone. More than one occasion found them talking well past midnight and their talks were weightless and pleasant. Often, Lacey felt guilty about not divulging her plans to Chase. He never brought up personal or heavy topics, though, and this made for satisfying conversation. Lacey didn't want to ruin a good thing.

"Uncle Tim will be here tomorrow with the boys and they are bringing grandmother, did I tell you that?" Carol mentioned as she broke Lacey's train of thought.

"No, you didn't. Wow, I haven't seen them forever," she said of her cousins.

The three of them chatted and watched TV late into the evening. Lacey told her father about meeting Gus Stover and her dad got a kick out of hearing about their meeting. Her mother got a kick out of hearing about another interaction between her daughter and the potential suitor that she saw Sam as being.

Throughout the conversation, Lacey's phone buzzed away and she periodically excused herself to answer the calls and confirm appointments. She, of course, failed to mention to her parents that the appointments were for her own house.

Thanksgiving dinner was one of the best Lacey could

remember.   Having Tim, Jamie, Chris and Lacey's grandmother there made it all the more festive. Tim and his wife had been divorced since the boys were in grade school and Lacey was glad her cousins decided to spend the holiday with their dad's side of the family. Everyone was in good spirits and Carol had gone all out with one spectacularly good meal. Grumbling about over-eating ensued and they were all ready to succumb to the living room for some rest.

"Coffee, anyone?" Lacey's mother asked. "And we have plenty of pie, too, if any of you have room."

"Yes, please! Let me help," Lacey started to rise from her chair as she laid the almond linen napkin next to her mostly-empty plate.

"No, no, no," her father ordered. "You just stay where you are. You, too, Carol. I can fill the carafe and bring everything out. It's the least I can do after this fantastic meal."

Lacey sat back down and watched her father plant a sweet kiss on her mother's forehead. How lucky they were to have found such a deep love that was still intact after almost forty years. Carol patted his hand as he rested it on her shoulder.

"I'll help, Uncle George," Jamie insisted as he rose from the table.

"So, Lacey. How was the kayak trip with Chase? I hear you two have been talking. In fact, if I didn't know better, I might say he has a little crush on you."

Tim let the cat out of the bag and Lacey felt her face heat up.

"Why does that name sound so familiar? Who is Chase, Lacey? Fill us in!" Carol asked. She was all too excited about hearing the news that her daughter may have not one, but two romantic interests. It was no secret she wanted nothing more than to hear that Lacey was on her way to marriage and a baby.

Lacey could only roll her eyes and hope for the conversation to take a new course. Unfortunately for her, it did.

"As a matter of fact, he did call me, after *you* gave him my number, Uncle Tim," Lacey stated. "And, yes, we have been talking now and then over the phone. Nothing more, mom."

"Lacey has a boyfriend," Chris teased.

"Who might that be?" Jamie asked as he re-entered the dining room with George and a couple of homemade pies.

"Chase Robbins, you remember him?" Chris replied.

Lacey continued to blush as she lost control of the conversation swirling around and about her.

"Oh, yeah. Man, those were the days. We all had some great times way back when. I never thought he and my little cousin would be an item all these years later," Jamie said as he looked at Lacey accusingly. He sat down across from her and smiled to let her know he was simply teasing and offered her a plate of pie that Carol was passing out.

Lacey motioned she wasn't interested. She had lost her appetite in the midst of the sudden commotion. She wanted to crawl under the table as it were and things only got worse from there.

"Oh, the Robbins boy. He was a sweet fellow," the elder Mrs. Williams said tenderly from her perch at the end of the table. "What happened to that family was such a shame. Such wonderful people."

Lacey's grandmother's words took her by surprise.

"What happened to his family?" she pondered silently as the conversation around her continued.

"Chase. Haven't seen him forever. As far as I knew, he was still in jail."

As soon as Jamie uttered the words, he regretted it. Looking across the table at his cousin, he could see her confusion mixed with agony.

"What ... did you say ... jail?" Lacey quietly muttered.

Silence came over the table as forks and spoons clanked to a resting position.

"I'm sorry Lacey. I thought you knew," Jamie kindly explained.

"Who is this Chase guy and why was he in jail? Better yet,

why are you spending time with him, Lacey?" George sternly questioned as he returned to his seat.

"I … I had no idea," Lacey stammered. "I'm not hanging out with him. There's really nothing going on. Let's just drop the conversation, okay? Really. I don't even know the guy."

"Obviously, dear," Carol said as she patted Lacey's hand. "I'm sure there is a misunderstanding. Lacey would never …"

"Hey, I don't know the story, but Chase is not a bad guy. There was an incident that happened a long time ago and he was in the wrong place at the wrong time. Something like that," Tim said as he tried to steer the conversation in a lighter direction for the sake of his niece and the river guide he knew fairly well and, frankly, thought highly of. He offered a look of compassion to Lacey over his rectangular black glasses and Jamie and Chris looked down at their plates.

The family went back to their deserts and coffee amid the thick tension. Lacey was far more distraught than she revealed and felt like a fool. That feeling intensified as she remembered her impressive home she was selling for no specific reason. As if on cue, her phone buzzed from it's place on the buffet table behind her and she excused herself to take the call in the kitchen.

"Hi, Lacey. I was expecting to leave a message. This is Alexis again. Sorry to bother you on a holiday, but my clients ended up looking at your place last night since you said it would be vacant. I am emailing an offer to you that I think you will be very pleased with, to say the least. They would like a response by five o'clock tomorrow evening."

Lacey thanked her and fibbed when she claimed to be looking forward to seeing it. Head spinning and short of breath, she walked upstairs to the bedroom that was still decorated as it had been in her teens. Sitting on the edge of the pink ruffled bedspread, she cradled her head in her hands and questioned her motives for selling and for wanting a change of pace in the first place. She needed to talk to someone who would help her regain composure and sensibility.

After a few rings, the only person she could relate to answered her impromptu call.

"Hi, Sam. I was just calling to wish you a Happy Thanksgiving.

CHAPTER TWENTY-NINE
Clear Ambitions

"MOM, I AM NOT doing drugs. Seriously, will you relax?" Lacey pleaded.

"Well, what do you expect us to think, Lacey?" her father asked unsympathetically. "You've been rather detached over the past year or so and then we find out you're planning on selling your home for the equity with no real reason or immediate plans? On top of that, we find out you have been hanging out with some loser who spent time in jail?"

His face reddened as the pulse in his neck became visible to Lacey from her seat across the room from him.

Carol patted George's knee from her seat in the winged back chair next to her husband. He reacted to her touch quickly and the veins in his neck stopped throbbing. He took a breath and leaned back into the couch with his head now resting against his fist.

"I understand and appreciate your concern, mom and dad, but, believe me when I say I have not lost my mind. Would you just listen to my explanation?"

Lacey watched them with pleading eyes as she wringed her hands in nervousness. Calling Sam the night before had given her unexpected clarity of her ambitions. The conversation, as it always did, turned to talk of work. Even on Thanksgiving, he had spent half of the day in his office and the other half with strangers at a local restaurant serving a holiday dinner option. His life was career, nothing else, and he was fine with that. In fact, he seemed proud of it. In the end, the conversation only confirmed to Lacey that she wanted more out of life than he. She confided in him that she was selling her house and he was happy for her. Happy that she would cash out on so much equity and could transfer it into an even more impressive address in town. She had not revealed her true intentions that focused on transforming that equity into a different life for herself rather than something to impress the masses. She had called him thinking he would remind her of the good life she had. Instead, she found it hard to open up to him and became certain that she still desired a more genuine existence.

The emailed offer had come in from Alexis and it was, indeed, an offer she couldn't refuse. Ten thousand dollars over list price and 'as-is'. After a good night's sleep, she decided to come clean with her parents for her own sake. She thought they might even support her. As they sat in the living room with their morning coffee, she knew any expectations of support from them was premature. Her grandmother had stayed over and was in the corner knitting with a slight grin as she took in the dialogue around her.

"Might I interject for a moment?"

The threesome looked up at the frail and elderly woman.

"Yes, mother. Please do. Maybe you can talk a little bit of sense into her," George sighed.

The granddaughter respectfully turned to her grandmother and waited patiently for her input.

"Lacey, dear. You are right that your parents just want the best for you. They mean no harm. George, do you remember when you decided to join the Navy?"

"Yes. What does that have to do with anything?"

"Well, you were going through a bit of a rebellious time, if I remember correctly. Trying to find yourself, I think."

"Like any teenager."

Gloria Williams rested the knitted yarn and needles on her lap now as she evenly addressed them.

"Perhaps. Lacey has, I think it is safe to say, never done anything remotely rebellious. George, you found the life that was right for you by going against the grain for awhile, would you agree?"

"I am grateful for what the Navy has done for me and my family," her son retorted curtly as he leaned forward in his seat with elbows on knees.

"Now, I don't think this is a rebellious phase, dear," she said as she looked lovingly at her granddaughter, "however, I think you are trying to find yourself. You were fortunate that your parents gave you the chance to attend a fine university. You came out of the gates running and built a business out of dedication and hard work."

"We don't want to see you throw that all away," Carol gently offered.

"I know, mom. I'm not throwing it away. I'm putting it toward something else."

Lacey smiled graciously at her grandmother who had gone back to her knitting.

"I fell into a career that, while it has treated me well, just isn't a good fit anymore. When I think of spending the rest of my days as I am now, I get a little depressed. Dad, you say I've been detached. Well, I don't have time for anyone other than my clients. I don't have time for myself. You taught me that if something's not working, change it. I just want to make money doing something else while making a little more time for things that matter to me."

Her words began to nudge her parents' views toward her own perspective.

"Well said, Lacey," he grandmother verbally applauded without looking up from her task. "So, maybe we just need to offer you our support now," she added with a raised eye toward her overly disciplined son whom she loved with all her heart and showed the same patience with years ago.

CHAPTER THIRTY
A Fresh Start

AUTUMN CAME TO AN end and winter settled in with a bitter cold vengeance. After the Thanksgiving dinner fiasco, Lacey came back to a whirlwind of activity that kept her mind off the intimidating aspect of her so-called plan. It was poorly thought out since she would be homeless in thirty days. In spite of it all, it was exhilarating and within a week her grandmother came to the rescue. She encouraged Lacey to settle in at the family's cabin until she was ready to make her next move.

Gloria Williams had shared a story with her granddaughter. Years ago, she and Lacey's Grandfather had lived in the wooden cottage for a year when their own home had needed a major renovation. Being of a different era, her grandmother thought the cabin was aptly suited to serve as a fine, safe and reliable shelter. In the end, Lacey couldn't agree more, as long as she could increase her tolerance for nights spent alone there, and she was eager to move in for a spell if only for solitude and reflection. Uncle Tim went on a firewood-cutting frenzy and her parents promised to visit as much as possible to check on her. Although, Lacey suspected their motive related more to making sure their daughter was not fraternizing with Chase Robbins.

After arranging for most of her belongings to go into storage, she traded her luxury sedan in on a rugged Subaru. Bryce had accompanied her for the test drive.

"You know, crazy lady, when I told you to change your life a little, I didn't expect all of this."

Lacey came to a stop at a red light and turned to Bryce

seated in the passenger seat.

"If you even try to persuade me to give up on what I've started, I will be certifiably crazy. Too late to turn back now."

"Not really," Bryce shrugged as she looked out the window at the traffic streaming through the busy intersection.

"Yes, really. It's ok, though. I'm excited to see what the future holds."

"What about Sam? Seems like things were going well with you and him."

Lacey contemplated her question while she moved forward with the green light.

"He can visit me. I can visit him. I don't know. He's really wrapped up in his career and I get the feeling he really doesn't have time for much else. We'll see where it goes. I'm not counting anything out right now."

"Except Chase."

Lacey took a deep breath inadvertently. The thought of him stung.

"Except Chase. There's a good chance I'll run into him. That'll be awkward, but it's not like we had any real relationship to break off. He obviously hid a lot from me," she reasoned. "Plus, I don't care. I'm making these changes for me and not with any guy in mind. I'm confident that if I do what's right for me, a better life will follow. Maybe it means I'll find someone to share that life with, maybe it doesn't. It's not part of the scheme."

"Do you have a formal scheme laid out for yourself?" Bryce inquired with a smile.

"Yes. No. Kind of. Will you visit me?"

"You bet. I'm proud of you and I can't wait to meet the real Lacey."

That test-drive-slash-therapy-session led to the purchase of the All Wheel Drive station wagon and it was in this red car she drove to meet Sam for what would be a farewell dinner date. He was not aware of the finality aspect. While they were initially supposed to meet at his boat for dinner with the Stovers, he had gotten held up with a client meeting and suggested they meet at restaurant near his office instead.

On the way to the restaurant, her phone buzzed and she instantly recognized it as being a call from Chase. She had spent the bulk of the past month ignoring Chase's calls. Hard to do at first, but eventually it led to less calls from him. Although still concerned about bumping into him in the near future, she knew she would move from the cabin and onto the next phase of her life shortly. Anyway, she thought of the area as her childhood home, too. She stubbornly refused to give up on her new ambition simply because he lived in that vicinity. She hit ignore on the phone. He never left a voicemail.

Walking into the bar of the restaurant, Lacey immediately spotted Sam. He was seated at the far corner with a cocktail straw clenched between his teeth and looking at his phone. His crisp white button down shirt was now unbuttoned at top and his green tie loosened. His silver cufflinks caught the overhead lights as he pulled the phone closer to type a message. He was caught up in whatever he was doing and barely noticed Lacey as she took the seat next to him.

"Is this seat taken," she asked coyly.

"Why, hello there beautiful," Sam greeted her with a peck on her cheek as he sat his phone down on the bar.

"You seemed deep in thought over here by yourself."

"Oh, you know. Work, work, work. Is there ever anything else?"

"I'm beginning to wonder," she said quietly as she asked the bartender for a glass of Sauvignon Blanc.

"So, what's new in Lacey William's world since we last spoke? How was the rest of your stay at your parents' place for Thanksgiving?"

Sam turned his barstool slightly toward her.

"Well, it was interesting, to say the least," she began as she took a sip of the crisp white wine.

"How so?"

"Like I mentioned to you, I am thinking about making some changes in my life. I told my parents about it and they weren't too happy, to say the least. A little more than just selling my house."

"This does sound interesting. I think I'd better order another drink."

Sam held up his empty glass to the bartender who, in return, signaled another was on its way.

"Yes, well, for starts, I'm closing on my place in a few days and will live in my family's cabin in New York for a bit until I figure out my next move," she said deliberately.

"You're kidding me? Why would you do that?"

The harshness of Sam's response caught Lacey off-guard. The bartender brought him another bourbon on the rocks and he took a sip before looking at Lacey intently. His disappointment in this new development was obvious and a little odd. Maybe he was just disappointed to see her go? They had been getting along well despite the fact that their relationship had not gone past dinner. How could it? They were far too consumed with work for a solid relationship to develop. Taking another sip of her wine, Lacey continued.

"You know, I've been at this real estate thing for a long time now. I started before I even graduated from college. I'm thinking it's time for a change. That's all. I think there's a life out there that's better suited for me."

"So what are you going to do?" he asked as he took another sip of bourbon.

"I have an idea or two, but nothing concrete yet."

"So, you are selling your place in a prime location in the city and walking away from a career you spent over a decade building to sit alone in the woods?"

Sam was clearly unimpressed. Lacey was offended. Having to defend herself to her parents was one thing. This was uncalled for.

"I won't be all alone," she said defensively before realizing the truth of the situation. "I'll move on to new accomplishments. I just need to make sure whatever I do next is a good fit for me. In that respect, yes, I'm taking a little alone time. What's wrong with that?"

He shook his head and turned toward the bar as he took another long sip and glanced at his smartphone.

Lacey couldn't hide her amusement. She set her glass down pointedly and looked directly at Sam.

"What? You don't approve?" she asked sarcastically expecting him to realize and rebuff his patronizing ways.

"No, sweetie. It's not that," Sam said as he turned to her.

Lacey was even more bristled with his word choice. She needed not read between the lines to see she wasn't living up to his expectations of her. He went on in shameless fashion as he pushed himself away from the bar and rested his ankle atop his knee.

"You have such a good thing going here, that's all. You don't want to throw it all away. You need to take all that money and put it into something that will gain appreciation. I don't have to tell you that. I'm sure you know it. I'm sure your parents told you the same thing."

"I can't believe you," Lacey uttered. "Are you seriously trying to tell me what to do with my life? *My* life?"

She shook her head slightly with an incredulous laugh. He was no longer amused.

"Sorry. Didn't mean to offend you, Lacey. Let's change the subject."

She thought for a second before continuing. Straightening her hunched shoulders, she changed the subject per his request.

"So, how's the planning going for your sail to Florida."

She struck a nerve. His lips pursed.

"I've been too busy for that lately."

"Hmmm," she responded casually while continuing to hold her gaze on him.

"Too bad winter's coming. Did you get a lot of sailing in over the summer and into the fall?"

"A little. Like I said, I've been busy. The trials I have pending are big cases," he answered boastfully. Sam was re-engaged with the conversation now that his date was taking the verbal upper hand. That kind of exchange was a rarity for him.

"Too bad. A gorgeous boat like that. She's meant to be taken out on open seas," Lacey continued coolly.

He nodded thoughtfully.

"Yes, she does. If you stick around, you should join me for a day out on the water next spring."

"Someday when you have time?"

"Yeah, when I have time."

"Sam, do think you'd want to visit me sometime in New York? This move I'm making is important to me."

"If I can make the time. Yeah, maybe I could swing that," Sam said as he adjusted his cuff link and glanced at his phone again. "You ready for dinner? I'll grab the hostess."

"Sam. You know, I hate to say this, but I don't think I have time."

She walked out into the crisp December night leaving Sam alone at the bar with his bourbon, phone, and expensive cuff links. Snow had held off so far, but winter's icy clutch was in full effect. Lacey wrapped her wide, knitted black scarf closely around her. It had been a going-away gift from her grandmother and the gift was comforting in so many ways at that moment. The sight of her newly acquired car was a reminder of what was in store for her and her heartbeat quickened. The frosty air was wholesome and full of promise. She looked up at the clear sky. There were no shooting stars to be seen. She had already made her wish and it was starting to come true.

CHAPTER THIRTY-ONE
Moving On

FOR THE BETTER PART of Christmas week, Lacey had stayed with her parents before moving into her new home. Because of this, she was stocked with food and winter clothing for her fresh start. Collectively, her Christmas presents from her parents would make her closet double as a miniature L.L. Bean pop-up store. It became comical after opening the fourth or fifth box of fleece-wear, gloves, or some other type of outerwear. After seeing her parents bury their fear and doubt and instead show her the unconditional love and support she needed, she was determined to regroup and make something of herself once again to ease their concerns. Her grandmother insisting she stay at the cabin and her uncle making preparations there for her made Lacey even more grateful for her family.

She was also grateful for Richard Lyndhurst. She waited until her move from Annapolis was definite before making any official announcements. When the time came to speak to her boss, he was initially quiet. She quickly became wary, just as she had when Sam tried to change her mind. Instead, he related her decision to his own past regret, much to her surprise.

He relayed a story of being engaged in his thirties to a person he referred to as his soul mate. He wistfully spoke of being so wrapped up in his career and clients that he lost sight of this person's needs. He lost sight of his own needs. The relationship ended, he threw himself into work even more. It became all he knew how to do.

"Lacey," he had said sincerely, "Life is a journey. You need to get out there and live it. Fully. If this is what you think you need to do in your heart, then do it. You'll have no regrets."

With those being the last words received before leaving, she was full of hope and confidence as she drove north. While one would think this would have been a drive time filled with momentous reflection, emotional anticipation and maybe even some tears, Lacey was calm. It seemed more natural than anything she had done in her post-college life. She suddenly had no reservations. As she drove out of Maryland and through Pennsylvania her old life became more and more distant. She waited for fear to set in. It never did. She crossed the New York state line and soon the cities and suburbs gave way to dense forest and mountain ranges. A comfortable and at-ease feeling set in and she knew that she was heading to the place she was meant to be.

Once settled into her new home, she couldn't believe how quickly she was able to turn her life around. All it took was commitment and a vague plan. It was now the twenty-ninth of December and she had been in her new home for a little over forty-eight hours. Lacey sat in front of a roaring fire in the middle of the forest with a cup of hot chocolate and a book. She thought back to her first night at this same spot in October and how terrified she had been to sit here alone. Not this time. She was at peace. She was now comfortable with the sounds of the world around her.

Already, the life she led just a month or so ago was a distant memory and she was ecstatic when she realized she would never have to go back to that pressurized world unless she decided to. She craved a kind and gentle life. For now, she was in total control of the minutes and hours of her days and that was more than could be said for most of the population. She needed so little and, as far as she could tell, she had all that she needed for a happy and peaceful existence.

Lacey was particularly excited that Ashley would be arriving the next day for a New Year's Eve celebration. It would be just the two of them, toasting a new year full of endless possibilities. Besides Bryce, Ashley had been her biggest supporter once Lacey filled her in on what she had planned on doing. She had even helped her move her furniture into storage and for that Lacey was eternally grateful.

The night was a cold one and Lacey threw another log on the fire before turning on a few space heaters and readying for bed. She was sure the convenience of a thermostat-controlled furnace would be on the top of her list once this little adventure was over. For now, she was proud of herself that she could do without some modern conveniences.

Life doesn't have to be that hard.

The dreamlike voice echoed in her head as she drifted off to sleep in the vintage pine bed. The mantra continued softly.

Focus on what matters and let go of what doesn't.

"You got that right, Mr. James Miller. May you rest in peace," she whispered as she fell asleep to the crackling sounds of the fire.

CHAPTER THIRTY-TWO
Ringing In a New Year

"GOTTA HAND IT TO you, Lace. You walked away from the crazy pace of life we all secretly despise and never do anything about."

Ashley and her bubbly personality, along with some snow flurries, had rushed in the door as Lacey greeted her earlier in the day. The friends had exchanged hugs and Lacey helped her with her bags as she quickly closed the door behind her to keep the warmth inside. An almost-continuous fire and an electric heater kept the cabin toasty warm all afternoon as they caught up with each other. Now sitting comfortably in front of the blazing fire, they were contentedly tucked in for the evening for the quietest New Year's Eve celebration ever.

"I know!" Lacey squealed in excitement. "I try not to think about it too much. If I do, I start to think I might be crazy."

"I'll drink to that. You *are* crazy and I love it! And actually inspiring me, I have to admit. I just might make some changes of my own this year. You know, it feels so good to be back here."

"Glad you could make it. Stay as long as you want," Lacey urged.

"Don't tempt me. So, what have you been doing with your time now that you are unemployed and camped out in the backwoods?"

"Oh, that sounds so bad," Lacey groaned with an open palm to her forehead as she tucked her feet under her sideways in the large recliner. "Not much. A little bit of planning for the future, I guess you could say, and a lot of nothing, really. I'm letting myself enjoy the silence. I think that's the first step in all of this."

"Good for you. I bet whatever you do next will be extraordinary."

"Thanks, Ashley. I needed to hear that. Really."

The friends talked and laughed non-stop and it was turning out to be one of the best New Year's. No expectations, crowds, expensive drinks or holiday packages. Just two good friends, a fire, wine some snacks and champagne for a midnight toast.

"Oh no. I never brought in extra firewood. I have a feeling we'll want to keep this fire going for awhile and I'm still too scared to go outside alone late at night," Lacey announced.

"Here, let me help," Ashley said as she started to get up.

"No. Please. I'll just be a second. I could use some fresh air anyway!"

Lacey rushed to put on her toggle coat, big red mittens, and boots and slipped outside. Seconds later, Ashley heard a few logs being dumped on the porch and the crunch of the snow as her friend made a couple of trips to the nearby woodpile. After a second thud of firewood being deposited near the front door, she was surprised to see Lacey hurrying in without anything in hand. Slamming the door shut and with her back against it, Lacey seemed flustered and upset.

Ashley jumped up from her seat and stood facing Lacey who was breathing heavy and still leaning against the door.

"What's the matter, Lacey? Are you okay?"

"No. I think Chase just pulled up."

"So?" Ashley asked with a confused grin as she crossed her arms in front of her.

"I didn't invite him. I don't want to see him and I don't know what to do. I don't even have cell reception. What if something happens?"

"Wait a second. What happened? I thought things were going well between you?"

"How did you…" she started until she realized. Ashley had kept in touch with Gregory.

"Okay. Listen, I'm sorry. I had no idea," Ashley sincerely

offered. "I, um. I told Greg they should stop by. I am so sorry, Lacey. I thought … it's just… we all, you know, had such a good time. I never made any real invitations. Just a casual mention."

One slam of a truck door then another announced the duo's immanent arrival. The sound of heavy tread in the snow got closer.

"Here. You go back in the back room. I'll take care of this. Do you want me to get rid of them?" Ashley asked.

"Yes. Please. I really don't want to see him. I'll explain later, okay?"

Still dressed in her winter wear from gathering logs, Lacey crawled on the floor to avoid being seen through the front porch window and headed to the bedroom. Her heart was beating so loudly in her head she swore it was audible to anyone in close range. She was scared that he wouldn't go away peacefully and maybe start trouble. She imagined him being drunk from an early New Year's Eve celebration and thoughts of a potentially bad situation continued in her head as she sat alone on the floor of the dark room.

After a few muffled exchanges of voices, she heard the main door open wide with a creak. Through the slightly opened bedroom door, she saw Ashley step out onto the porch as she pulled the door shut behind her. Lacey waited in the darkness and Ashley stayed outside. Not knowing what else to do, she decided to try to at least peek out to check on her friend. She had a sinking feeling and needed to make sure Ashley was all right. Lacey began to crawl back into the living and was a pitiful sight in her grey coat and red knitted cap with matching mittens. Ashley walked back inside and looked down at Lacey whose desperate and pathetic position kept her from laughing at her friend on the floor.

"Are they gone?" Lacey hoarsely whispered.

"They will leave," Ashley started to slowly and quietly explain, "but I really think you need to talk to Chase. I don't think you know his story and you need to. Will you trust me on this and talk to him? He's outside. I told him to wait on the porch until I talked to you. Just trust me, okay?"

Ashley was pleading and something resonated with Lacey. She knew more that Lacey had cared to find out.

"He was in jail, you know, Ashley."

Ashley crouched down to face Lacey on the wooden floor.

"I know. I thought you knew, too. Greg filled me in on that a few weeks ago," Ashley sweetly confided.

Lacey noticed the familiarity Ashley used when talking about the older brother.

Sighing and slowly rising from her crouched position, she agreed as she walked slowly toward the door while brushing herself off. Out of habit, Lacey peeked out the window closest to the fireplace before opening the door to see Chase. She noticed movement in the light of the full moon. Stepping back to look again, she saw the exact sight as before. A girl in blue stood among the snow-covered hemlocks and looked directly back at her. Lacey gasped. No mist clouded her view this time. In fact, the full moon cast a spotlight on the girl. Her features were accented in the lunar glow. Frosty disheveled hair, pale thin lips, and cat-like green eyes.

"What is it?" Ashley whispered hoarsely.

"I think I see something … someone. Look. Do you see?"

Ashley huddled in next to her at the side window that looked out onto the expansive property.

"No. Where?"

"There," Lacey pointed. Now seeing nothing unusual, she slowly lowered her pointing hand and took a step back. "Strange. Must've been a deer or something," Lacey calmly added.

"So, will you talk to him? He's waiting on the porch," Ashley whispered.

"If you insist. I'm trusting you on this one," she said with her mitten-covered hand resting on the doorknob. Hesitating, she turned to face Ashley to read her expression. Ashley nodded confidently.

Lacey stepped out onto the porch. Her eyes instantly met his. Feathery snowflakes swirled slowly and sparkled while suspended in the frozen air. The precipitation glistened in the light of the bright and clear moon. He quickly stood from his leaning position on the porch rail. His red and black-checkered wool coat was now lightly covered with the glistening snow as was his hair. He kept Lacey in his sight without making a move. Seeing him again made Lacey weak in the knees. Chills that were unrelated to the winter night extended from head to toe despite her body temperature beginning to rise.

They continued to stare at each other with their feet frozen in position. Lacey crossed her arms indignantly and an unnoticed Gregory uttered a greeting to Lacey that she didn't hear. He slinked past her and into the cabin to join Ashley. Without delay, Chase began the overdue conversation.

"You haven't been taking my calls and I don't blame you. Can I tell you my story? Please. Just give me that. If you never want to see me again, I'll respect that decision."

The yellow glow from the lamp inside the window shone on his face and Lacey could see the pleading in his hazel eyes. His was an innocent face and Lacey felt nothing but trust for him now that she stood by him again. She wanted to run into his arms, but couldn't. She needed to know the events his past held.

"Okay," she heard herself say in a voice that didn't sound like her own.

"It's really cold out here. I don't mind, but you must be freezing. We can talk in my truck, if that's okay with you. Please know I would never do anything to hurt you. I don't want to hurt anyone."

He took a step toward her and put out his hand. Against her better judgment Lacey placed her hand in his and let him lead her toward the truck that was coated with a fresh layer of powder. He opened the passenger door for her and she stepped up and in and watched him go around the front. He brushed the snow from his broad shoulders then rubbed his hands together as he blew warm air from his mouth. Once inside the vehicle, he turned the key and the twang of some classic country tune came on the radio rather loudly. He quickly reached for the vintage stereo and ejected, to Lacey's surprise, an 8-track.

"Is that what I think it is?" she asked awe.

"Yes. And that will also make sense when I have had a chance to explain everything to you."

The sweet dimpled smile that Lacey adored since she met him as a boy one summer so long ago melted the chip on her shoulder. She was ready to give him a chance. She turned toward him and nodded for him to begin. A little sign of encouragement to let him know she was not there to judge or be angry. Chase took a deep breath and looked at Lacey before glancing out at the snowfall that was light and steady.

"About twenty years ago, my parents were on their way home from a shopping trip with my little sister, Julia. There was some kind of school dance coming up and they took her to find a dress. She was so excited," he began. He looked down as he revisited the agonizing details.

"Greg and I stayed home. It got late. We fell asleep in the living room watching TV and waited for them to get back. We had gotten kind of worried they were taking so long, but, didn't let on."

He took a deep breath and looked away from Lacey. She placed her mitten-covered hand on his. Looking down at her hand on top of his own, he went on.

"There was a knock on the door. A State Trooper. He said they never felt a thing. I guess that was supposed to make us feel better. Our grandparents came and got us. The worst part … the worst part was that Greg and I had gotten detention for being late to school one too many times that week. Then, I wanted to stop by a buddy's place after we left school. My parents had waited for us and they left later than they had wanted to. They left later because of me and because of that timing the accident happened. I will never forgive myself."

Chase could not hold back the tears and neither could Lacey. His emotions were out of character and more than she could handle, not to mention the story itself. Even without the specifics, she knew the tragic outcome. She wiped her tears away and placed her hand back with his.

Lacey gently moved closer while facing him on the saddle-covered bench seat. Without words, and she wrapped her arms around him with a caring embrace. He held her tightly and buried his face in her hair. His sobs became heavy and she got the impression he may have never allowed himself to let go until now.

"Uh. I feel like a fool," he started as he looked up and softly butted the back of his head against the cab and rubbed his face with open palms.

"You shouldn't," she whispered. She wiped a stray tear from his cheek and he managed a smile for her.

"Alright. Here it goes. So, a little time goes by. Greg's home from college for the summer. I had recently graduated and somehow managed a full scholarship to join him in the fall. My whole life ahead of me. I was ready to leave this town and get a fresh start. I had big plans. We were still living with my grandparents at that time. Things were starting to get a little easier, I guess. My grandma kept that damn dress in the house until she died. I have no idea why. It just killed me every time I happened to see it hanging in the closet where she kept it. I don't even know where it is now, thank God."

He rambled a bit and took another shaky breath before continuing.

"So, Greg and I, we run into town to grab a pizza. A little joint with a bar and a separate restaurant area. We sat down at a table, put in our order. He gets up to use the restroom and, when he comes back out, he's acting real weird. He suggests we get the food to go and walks over to tell the waitress we changed our mind. All of the sudden, this guy comes over to the table. It takes me a second before I realize who it is. I can still see Greg's face as he looks back and sees what's going on. This guy," he stops for a second and the tears are gone. His face is flush with anger. "This guy, RJ, he's called, starts telling me how sorry he is about the accident and how … how he never meant … well, I stand up and, without even knowing what I'm doing, I deck him. Hard. Greg grabs me. This loser falls fast onto the floor. I guess his head hit the concrete in a way … a way … that killed him."

Lacey sees the anger in Chase's face and she's frightened. His hand still under hers, but now clenched in a fist. The story doesn't make sense yet to her and she's not sure what to make of it all.

"RJ killed my parents and sister, Lacey."

Looking deeply into her eyes, he desperately wanted her to empathize with him as he went on.

"He was hardcore into drugs. Everyone knew it. He was leaving a party and, from what we found out later, was high as a kite when the friend's car he was driving slammed into my parents'. He left the scene and somehow, I don't know, a rookie mistake or something, he got off with no more than a few fines and citations. When I hit him that night, I had no idea he was dead. I just kept thinking at least he wouldn't be leaving the bar any time soon and putting anyone else in danger."

Chase stopped to maintain his composure.

"He *apologized for killing my family*. He was slurring and acting like he was my friend. Can you imagine?" Chase said while looking back at Lacey. "The owner told me to go, Greg dragged me out, and the next thing I know, another police officer is standing on my doorstep again. This time, taking me away for manslaughter."

Lacey swallowed hard. His hurt and anger was palpable.

"So, that's it. I'm grateful you let me explain. I hate that any of it happened," he said hoarsely before sitting in silence. He slouched in the seat and uncomfortably gripped the steering wheel. He had expended all energy and, as far as he knew, it may have been for nothing.

"I hate that any of it happened to you," she said softly before looking in his eyes for some sign of comfort and taking his hands in hers. "Can we start again?"

A look of relief washed over him.

"There's nothing I want more right now than to have you

in my life, Lacey."

"Can I ask you something, though?"

"Anything."

"The dress. Your sister, Julia's, dress. Was it blue?"

Chase searched Lacey's eyes for some clue as to why she would ask.

"Yeah, it was. Why?"

"I swear I've seen a vision of her here. I'm sorry. I shouldn't have said that, it's just ..." she stammered while looking out the windshield nervously.

"No. I know," he watched Lacey warmly. "I think I have, too."

Looking at the clock on the dash, Chase happened to notice the time showed 11:59 PM.

"Happy New Year, Lacey. Let's make it a good one?"

Leaning in toward her, he caressed her hair as he memorized every inch of her face. She leaned in at the same time as he reached around her waist to pull her closer. Gingerly, then more urgently, they shared a passionate New Year's kiss that was raw with emotion and trust and arose from a spark of true love that may have been planted long ago. They may have been searching for the other ever since.

PART FOUR : FOUND

CHAPTER THIRTY-THREE
State of Grace

JULIA'S PERPETUAL BODY FORM emanated a soft glow in the billows of snow she lay in. She looked up at the tall evergreens above her and watched the snow and ice drip from their branches to her forest floor. The deer began to stir from their resting spots and shook the wetness from their soft fur. The gentle soul smiled and reached out to stroke the one nearest to her. It bowed its head toward her hand, enjoying the soft caress it received. Other than the dripping snow and the deer quietly gnawing at the bark and buried grasses, the winter morning was silent. Julia slowly rose from her wintry cushion and began to move effortlessly toward the forest's edge. Surprised at her own lightness, it was apparent she was less attached to the ground than ever and more weightless than before.

Gracefully, she moved. Through the hemlocks limbs she glided. Dusty snow brushed off and puffed in the air. Soon, the gray wood of the Williams' tiny dwelling came into view along with the three vehicles that were snow-covered and situated in the drive. She recognized one.

Peering through the pines, she was struck with a strong inclination to approach the cabin so she moved out from the shadows and into the gray light of morning. The peaceful herd looked on. The cabin was more rustic than the ones occupied by year-round residents, but it was loved and welcoming. The elongated front face of the roof created a hideaway porch. She quickly found herself at the dark stained door and rapped upon its thick planes.

She tried again and again with no response to her knocks. By the forth time, she was filled with determination to have her call answered. She felt drawn to whoever it may be. The door swung open and Gregory peered out at her through the screen. She had not laid eyes this brother for so long. His face was still kind and tolerant. In the process of being startled by his sight, her vigor knocked a nearby broom onto the porch floor. It fell with a dull thud. The deer scampered.

She murmured his name, but he couldn't hear her. Although accustomed to that by now, she still ached with yearning to have him acknowledge her. She retreated to the pines once more and, from their cover, she watched the scene unfold. Gregory stepped out onto porch, pulled the broom upright and stood tall as he peered out from his vantage point. Soon after, a female with short, curly blonde hair joined him on the porch before they went back inside.

The sight of her oldest brother comforted her and she could tell he was happy by the aura around him. She was charged from this discovery. Julia sat next to a younger deer that had found refuge behind a Mountain Laurel and gently ran her small hand along its back. It leaned against her. Together, they watched and eagerly waited to see who else might appear. Her excitement grew and the snowflakes crystallized around them in their little green fortress.

A curtain moved aside and smoke soon came billowing out of the tall, stone chimney. The smoky puffs appeared white against the grey sky. Another face appeared before his tall frame came fully into view. The sight of Chase brought more joy and comfort until suddenly struck with the notion that her brothers might still be angry with her for causing them to lose their parents. Thinking of her mother and father, she longed to be peacefully with them again.

He looked in her direction then exited the porch as he began walking toward the firewood pile. He stopped. His head slowly turned toward her and he followed his gaze. His heavy, unlaced boots trudged along through the snow. Could he see her? She stood and in the excitement of it all the bright green Mountain Laurel branches recoiled.

The siblings approached one another. Chase was as alive as ever and his magnetic energy pulled the little sister toward him. Standing still and facing each other, Julia spoke to him over the whistling winter airstreams.

"I miss you, Chase, and I'm sorry. I miss our family. I'm so sorry," she sobbed softly. "Please tell Greg I'm sorry. I didn't mean for any of it to happen. I just want you both to be happy. We'll all be together again when the time is right."

He looked around with his feet seemingly frozen to the tundra. Clasping his bare hands atop his head and with a look of confusion, he looked up at the treetops then placed his hands in his coat pocket with a forward stare. He finally addressed her.

"Julia? We miss you. We love you."

A flock of bright crimson cardinals flew from the Mountain Laurels and a family of deer leapt from its resting spot. Meanwhile, a young, lost soul was filled with peace and free to return to her heavenly home. Her toil was finished.

Little did she know, she would be returning to them in the near future, as misfortune would strike.

CHAPTER THIRTY-FOUR
Finding Her Footing

ON THE SECOND DAY of January, the sun shone brightly on the white surroundings as it welcomed a new year. Lacey ran out to her car to warm it up for a venture into the nearby town of Elliot. There, she would be able to find wireless access for her laptop and arrange for a phone line at the cabin. The freezing temperature of icy metal radiated through the thick mittens as she tugged the driver's side door open. Turning the ignition, the car reluctantly chugged to life and the dash read five degrees. She turned the heat and defrosters on full blast and ran back into her tiny home as her boots scattered the powdery snow before cracking the icy lower depths.

Entering the cabin, she quickly shut the door behind her to trap the heat indoors and immediately pulled her tote bag out from the corner where it had been stashed; she verified her laptop and charger were there. They were, along with a landslide of papers that were no longer needed. In a move that was more meaningful than just being tidy, she tossed every last one of them into the embers where they flared up and were quickly reduced to ashes. She was moving on with her life there and had a long list of tasks to complete before she could begin the next chapter.

The small town of Elliott had a population of less than two thousand and, like most in the vicinity, had a river running through it. This little gem was also a stop along one of the largest bike trail routes in upstate New York. Its main street was full of interesting shops and cafes. A corner brick building caught her attention with a mural featuring a steaming cup of coffee. Better yet, a sign in the front window indicated free wireless access so she pulled into a parking spot located conveniently out front.

"Hi, there. Just grab a seat anywhere. I'll be with you shortly," a middle-aged woman called out from the back before disappearing through swinging double doors.

Lacey muttered a thank you and hung her heavy wool coat on the hook outside of her chosen wooden booth. The establishment appeared to have been solely an ice cream and malt shop at one point and, according to the hanging sign, they were still serving Hershey's ice cream at the gunmetal grey, gleaming serving station. There were two men sitting in a nearby booth and the salt and peppered haired gentleman facing Lacey bid a hello in her direction as she slid into to an oil-soaped seat.

She found a laminated menu tucked between the ketchup and sugar and began to look through it. Her stomach grumbled as she perused the traditionally American selections. It was only nine o'clock and near zero degrees. A hearty breakfast was in order.

"You decided?" the waitress asked as she looked sternly down at Lacey with one hand on her aproned hip. Lacey looked up and smiled.

"May I have a coffee and the Sunrise Breakfast plate, please?"

"Sure can. Anything else?"

"I think I saw you offer free wireless? Is there a code to enter?"

"Oh, yeah. Password is COFFEE. Be right back *with* your coffee."

Before Lacey had a chance to pull her laptop from her still-dreaded work tote, the waitress was sliding a fresh cup of coffee in a retro white diner cup with maroon rings at the rim atop a matching saucer. It looked much like the one painted on the outside of the building.

"You visiting town? Haven't seen you in here before?" She stated more than asked.

"Well, kind of. I just made a temporary move to the area a few weeks ago," Lacey felt her cheeks flush for no real reason as she admitted her recent life change.

"Ahh. Glad to see you. Welcome to Elliott. My name's Karen."

She held out her hand for a welcoming shake. Lacey obliged.

"Hi, Karen. I'm Lacey."

"Just let me know what you're looking for before you leave and I'll point you in the right direction. We have a little bit of everything."

"I appreciate that. Seems like a great little town."

"It is," she answered matter-of-factly. "Moved here myself from Pittsburgh twenty years ago. Love it."

"Really? I moved from a larger city, too. My family has had a cabin here for generations and I'm making it a home until I decide my next move."

Lacey's cheeks reddened even more so and she looked down as she stirred her coffee to try to hide it. Insecurity set in as she admitted to being a run-away. As if Karen could relate, she went on.

"Yeah, before this I commuted and hour each way five days a week and sometimes on Saturday to a big fancy office on the fiftieth floor of a fancy skyscraper. Nice views of rivers that tempted me to float away. Eventually, I decided to change course and here I am. Upriver instead of an easy float down.

She smiled as a tiny laugh escaped her hardened face. Pushing an errant brown lock behind her ear, Karen seemed humanly relatable all of the sudden.

"No way?" Lacey hugged her cup closer as she sat up straight. "I just left Annapolis. I was a real estate agent there. Are you happy here? Have you been waitressing here since the move?"

Karen let out a hearty laugh and threw her head back.

"Yeah, you could say I waitress here day and night. Even in my dreams, right boys?" She glanced at the two amicable men and they, too, found a little comedy in her words. "I bought this place when I moved here because of the apartment upstairs. I guess I could hire more help, but it's my baby, you know? Plus, this is our slow season so I tend to take the reins a bit more to save money. Yeah, I'm happy. You will be too once you allow yourself to relax and enjoy your new life. It takes awhile to get that city work pace out of your veins. You couldn't pay me enough to go back to the work I knew, though. The thought of spending my days in that cubicle and on that highway every day sends shivers up my spine."

She mimicked a chill going through her gave a little wink before tapping the table with her glossy, red nails and heading to a table in the front of the restaurant where she was doing some bookkeeping.

Lacey thought about her words and instantly felt better. Karen knew what it was like to try to retrain your brain, and subsequently your nerves, to accept a different way of living.

Getting down to business, she returned a few emails for a few straggling real estate deals that she had a hand in. Karen approached with a fresh pot of coffee for a refill.

"Thanks, Karen."

"No problem. You need any help finding anything today?"

"Well, since you asked, I need to set up a landline. What's the local phone company around here? They don't, by chance, have a satellite office nearby?"

Karen let out an easy laugh and with hand on hip replied, "Now why would you want a thing like that? Ha!"

Lacey laughed, too, at her kindred spirit's response.

"You are so right! I know! But, I've been here about three weeks without one and there is no cell reception, so I guess for emergencies, right?"

"I guess," she replied half-heartedly as she shook here head. "ComTech is the local company. I think the nearest office is an hour away, but, here. I have the right number for you. Save you from looking it up."

Karen walked briskly to the front counter and jotted down a number from a notecard attached to the wall with dried-out masking tape and brought it back to the table. Lacey downed the last sip of coffee from her cup.

"Hey, thanks!"

"Sure. You stay in touch and just take care of yourself. You won't regret what you did. Trust me. Just find out what you really like and go be you."

"I will. I'll be sure to stop back soon."

After setting up the appointment with the phone company, she stepped back out into the frigid air. Lacey reached for her car door handle as she looked across the street and The Mason Hardware Store caught her attention. The storefront windows were adorned with the store's name arranged in an arc and written with mustard shades outlined in gold. A matching awning covered half oak barrels and window boxes that were all filled with evergreen swatches tied with red ribbons designed to disguise the unplanted planters. She decided to stop in. A dainty bell chimed to signal her arrival and she was delighted by her surroundings.

A faint smell of sawdust, metal, plastic and old wood mixed with the air. The floors had once been painted brown and were now worn mostly to their natural shade. A penny candy station sat to the right in front of the cash register area and was filled with dozens of selections. Some were a little more than a penny, but Lacey was flabbergasted at how much truth remained tied to the vintage "One Cent" sign displayed above the counter. To her left were rows and rows of unique toys that she had not seen much since she was a little girl. Balsa wood planes, kites, Silly Putty, gooey slime packets, and such. Walking back further, her boots sounded muffled thuds along the aged floorboards. More typical hardwood store finds were abundant all around her. PVC pipefittings, nails, tools, pegboard and the like.

Slowly making her way to a back corner, she located a sewing and yarn section. The yarns were wound into small balls and were of the most unique colors she had ever seen. She felt compelled to touch them and before she knew it, she was balancing six in her clutches.

"Looks like you have your hands full. Can I help you with that?"

Startled, Lacey looked up to find a young man matching in age. He stood with arms crossed and a slight grin. His olive green shirt was tucked neatly into his ironed khaki pants with a brown leather belt polishing off his look.

"I guess I should have grabbed a basket. Do you have one handy?"

"Sure, I do," he replied in a friendly and helpful tone before reaching for a plastic shopping basked from a nearby corner. "Here you go. Let me help you with those."

He took the yarn from Lacey and handed her the basket with her selections.

"Thanks so much. These are beautiful," she complimented.

"Aren't they? They are spun and dyed by a woman who owns an Alpaca and sheep farm an hour or so out of town. She is very skilled at her craft and ships her yarn all over the country."

"Wow. You know," Lacey started with a chuckle, "I don't even know what to do with them, but I need to buy some. I crocheted with my grandmother when I was little. Maybe it would come back to me."

"Well, my wife loves to crochet, so, if you live around here and need help, stop back in and she'll get you started."

"That is so kind." Lacey graciously accepted the kind offer and tossed an instruction book and crochet needle into the basket.

Meeting him back at the front counter, Lacey noticed a Help Wanted sign. While the man rang her up, she found herself spontaneously making an inquiry.

"I just noticed the Help Wanted sign. I was looking for some part-time work. Can I fill out an application?"

"Absolutely. My wife is pregnant and won't be able to help around here soon. I figured I better get the word out. Do you live close and have reliable transportation?"

"Yes and yes. I'm about fifteen minutes away near Kline."

"All right. Are there any days or times you can't work?"

"No."

"Want to come by this Sunday to get acquainted with the store and register and fill out paperwork?"

"Sure, you mean …"

"The job is yours if you want it. Just come back here on Sunday at one. We pay $9.50 an hour we'll need you maybe ten to fifteen hours a week. Deal?"

"Deal!"

Lacey walked back out to her car with her paper bag of yarn in hand and was feeling fantastic. A small job would be good for her. To get out among people and make some extra spending money is just what she needed.

She pulled into the gravel drive at home shortly after two and put the car in park. She was ready to waste away the afternoon by diving into her new craft. Her thoughts veered to the hardware store owner's description of the woman who perfected her craft of spinning and dying yarn. Lacey wanted to be good at something besides calling customers back and snuffing out contractual problems. She would settle into her cozy cabin for a day all to herself and let her mind wander freely.

Walking up to the door, she noticed a torn piece of tablet paper sticking out of the closed screen door. Chase's name was easily visible where it was scrawled at the end of a short note. Gently pulling the white notebook paper from between door and frame, she read the note that invited her to dinner at his place the following evening.

CHAPTER THIRTY-FIVE
Let the Show Begin

THE SMOKE ALARM HAD sounded more than once and Chase fanned the choking fumes away from the device. His invitation for a home-cooked meal was turning out to be a less-than-stellar idea. Standing back against the cast iron sink, he rubbed his flushed face in exasperation as he considered his options. Lacey would be arriving in a few hours and the air in his apartment was filled with charred mist. He thought about ordering pizza or dinner in. In the end, he refused the idea of total defeat. He wanted the night to be special and a stack of Styrofoam boxes hidden in the garbage or dishing out slices of a casual weekend treat just did not sit well with him. He reached for the phone.

"So, I need you help and I don't want you to give me a hard time."

Gregory agreed and, for once, waited in silence to hear his brother's dilemma.

"Lacey will be here at seven. The eggplant Parmesan I attempted to make is now a charred heap in the skillet. The place reeks of burnt food and there is a haze I can't get rid of. I promised to make dinner for her and I want to deliver. I know she likes eggplant Parmesan. She mentioned it in a story on New Year's Eve. Suggestions?"

The lack of an answer on the end of the line told Chase his brother was holding back any sarcastic comments while stifling his laugh. Chase patiently waited.

"Hmm. Okay. So, do you have some appetizers ready to

go?"

"Cheese, crackers, and grapes. And, I bought some of the wine I noticed she had around on New Year's."

"Good. Just have that ready to go. Can you make a salad?"

Chase wasn't sure if he was being sarcastic or not. He chose to give him the benefit of the doubt.

"Yeah," he answered through a twitching, clenched jaw.

"Okay. So get that all ready, open the windows and I'll bring over some eggplant Parmesan already prepared and ready to bake."

"You bake it? I thought you fry it. The recipe I found …"

"Are you seriously going to argue with me on this now?"

"No. I guess not."

"Trust me. She'll like this better than that the oily and greasy mess you tried to prepare. I'll have it there by six. Good?"

"Yeah. Thanks," Chase grumbled as he looked around at the mess he had to clean up.

Opening the windows, the fresh air rushed in and replaced the scorched atmosphere. He cleaned and prepped non-stop and by five thirty, things were looking up. Leaving the door unlocked for his brother to come in, he headed to the shower with a beer to calm his nerves. He told himself this was all still better than sitting in a stuffy restaurant trying to make stiff conversation. He just hoped Lacey felt the same.

Knowing she was into the finer things in life than he, Chase suddenly believed this to be very bad plan. Berating his home cooked dinner idea, he deemed himself to be the second-rate citizen he thought of himself as. He stopped his and instead thought of Lacey's easy-going smile and upbeat personality. She had agreed to his invitation and he told himself that her acceptance did, in fact, mean something. Now, it was up to him to show her a nice evening. She deserved it. He thought about the life that she walked away from and her current living conditions. He admired her. He knew of no other females who would leave the creature comforts of the city to live like a creature in the forest and something about all of it told him they were more alike than he realized. He wanted to get to know her better and wanted her to like him.

As if on cue, his late sister's words echoed in his head again. As always, they assured him that he was a good person and deserved to be happy. His dreams of Julia had subsided in recent days, but her words still played over and over in his mind whenever he was feeling down. He had begun to give in to the advice, if only out of respect for her memory.

Looking through his closet, he was defeated. He certainly did not have a plethora of choices. Choosing the cleanest tee, flannel, and jeans he could find, dressed, he looked at himself in the full-length mirror attached to the inside of the closet door and winced. He was clean-shaven and his short, brown hair framed his face all right. Not much he could do with that anyway, he resolved. He was freshly showered and clean, so, that was a start, his mind added. The dark blue flannel shirt over a dark blue t-shirt matched and his jeans *were* newer. He shut the door before he could criticize himself further. He was who he was and, although his wardrobe could stand a little updating, it couldn't be done in time for his date with Lacey. Hearing his brother's knock coincide with his entrance, he quickly gathered the clothes that were lying on the bedroom floor and made his bed look presentable before leaving the room. Finding a half-used and decades decades-old bottle of Calvin Klein cologne, he gave a few spritzes to his shirt.

His brother stood inside with a rolled up paper bag in hand. Not bothering to shed his wintery layers, he handed the bag to Chase with an outstretched arm.

"Directions in there. If you can operate the microwave for the sauce and heat up the oven to the right temp, you can't mess it up," he stated dryly. "Call me if you have questions, but I will doubt your level of intelligence if you can't figure this out."

"Thanks, Greg. Really. I owe you."

"Nah, I'm doing this for Lacey. The poor girl would've

starved."

He folded his arms in front of his chest and laughed at the thought of the meal Chase would have served without his help.

"The place looks nice. Real nice," he added as he looked around. "The little candles on the table are a nice touch. Romantic. Not over the top. Need me to open that bottle of wine for you?"

"Are you serious? I can handle it."

"Okay, okay. No offense. Have a good time," Gregory said with a wink. Chase thanked him again and give him a little shove out the door as he shut it.

Pulling the casserole dish from the bag, he was more thankful than ever for his brother. The breaded slices of eggplant looked amazing and, as promised, the directions were simple. Chase felt more upbeat as he realized he would be able to pull this dinner off. The salad was ready to go and he had some good balsamic vinegar and oil to dress the greens. The wine and appetizers were set out on the kitchen table and the candles were lit. Standing in the kitchen, he took a moment to survey the scene and he was downright proud of his effort.

Finishing the last swig of the beer bottle, he rinsed it out and tossed it into the recycling bin on the adjacent deck. Shuffling through the drawer, he located a corkscrew and glanced at the microwave's digital clock. His nerves kicked up a notch when he realized she would arrive any minute. He hoped she had a habit of running late. From what he knew of her so far, he doubted that.

After guzzling a long drink of pilsner, he grabbed the wine bottle by the neck and removed the foil wrapping. Turn by turn, the corkscrew attached firmly and he gave it a tug followed by another. The dry cork came out in pieces with half still tucked in place. He tried to wind the screw back in and the remaining chunk was pushed into the dark red liquid.

"*Shit,*" he muttered. He threw away what evidence remained of the botched attempt just as a knock at the door sounded Lacey's arrival. Chase left the opened bottle on the kitchen counter next to the refrigerator and out of view as he wiped his palms on his jeans and headed to the door.

"Hey, you," she greeted in her usual happy tone.

"Hey, yourself. Come on in."

Stepping back from the doorway, he held the door open for her.

"Let me help you with you coat."

Standing there with coat, mittens, hat, and scarf in hand, he now wondered where he should go with it. Tossing it on the doorknob wouldn't do. Taking it all to his bedroom seemed suggestive. He opted for the recliner in the corner by the television.

"Here, uh, have a seat," he said as he nodded toward the couch. "Wanna glass of wine?"

"Sure. Thanks so much for having me over."

She sat casually with one elbow on the armrest of the couch. Her tall, brown leather boots were worn over black leggings and her flowing black top found a way to flatter her thin frame. A dainty gold chain rested over her collarbone and her shiny, long hair with a reddish hue cascaded over her shoulders. Chase glanced at her, unable to help himself. She was beautifully at ease. In comparison, his anxieties were in overdrive.

Back in the kitchen, he poured the wine. Glancing to make sure she wasn't watching, he used the corner of a paper towel to fish out a few small pieces of cork that had ended up in his glass.

"Here you go," he offered and handed over the half-full glass of merlot.

"Thank you," she smiled as her graceful hand reached for the glass. Chase noticed her nails were painted a light shade that sparkled like the rest of her in his meager abode. She seemed out of place in the sparse surroundings. He sat down in the opposite corner of the couch with a half-finished bottle of beer.

"I'm really glad you could make it, Lacey." After a slight

pause he added sincerely, "You look beautiful."

"You are too sweet. I'm glad to be here. This wine is excellent, by the way. Nice choice."

"Glad you like it. So, what've you been doing with yourself since New Year's?" he asked in an attempt to get some conversation going.

Lacey looked at him for a few seconds and smiled as if lost in her thoughts. New Year's Eve had been special and she had not been able to get Chase off her mind ever since. After the talk in his truck and a few marvelous kisses, they had spent the night laughing and modestly celebrating with Gregory and Ashley who were obviously in tune with one another. He had stayed over and as she had lain in his arms, she could hardly sleep from the thrill of all that had been said and the magnetic attraction between them. Blinking her way back to the present, she energetically began to fill him in on everything.

"Oh, wow. Lots, actually," she started while taking another sip of wine. She sat up a little straighter and Chase felt himself finally begin to relax in her presence. "First of all, if all goes as planned, I should have a real phone line by tomorrow."

"Good. When I dropped your note off I was kind of thinking you needed that."

"Aww. Were you worrying about me, Chase Robbins?" she asked flirtatiously.

Chase smiled at her accusing tone and thoughtful expression. She had a way of making him feel better about himself.

"Well, I know you can take care of yourself and all, but, yeah. You need a way to call for help if you need it. Like I said, you know you can call me anytime you need anything. Winter around here can be brutal. Not that you need help, but you know."

He stopped himself before he said anything that might be offensive.

"That's nice of you to offer. I feel a little better about living up here alone knowing I have someone nearby to call."

Lacey gave a warm smile to let him know she appreciated his kind words. She could tell he was nervous and thought it was sweet since he wasn't a nervous person normally. Lacey got the impression he spent more time alone and probably by choice. She thought it was a shame.

"So, a phone line. That's good. What else?"

Chase relaxed more and more as he watched her go into the details of her week and thought about how he could get used to sitting around in the evenings like this with her.

"Don't screw this up," he thought as he watched her hand and fingers flail while as she spoke. As he admired her, he consequently stopped listening.

"So, are you familiar with that place?"

Silently, he cursed himself out.

"Wait, what's the name of it again?" he asked in an attempt to make her believe he missed only a word or two of her conversation.

"Mason Hardware."

"Oh, yeah. I know it well, actually. It's been around forever. I went to high school with Dean Mason. I think he took over things there now that his dad has retired. Dean's grandfather actually started the business."

Chase leaned forward to convince her he was a good listener.

"Well, I start working there Sunday. It is such a cute place and I think it'll be good for me to get out a bit while I decide what my next move is. I guess Dean is who hired me, then. He said his wife was pregnant. Is he nice?"

"She is? Good for them." He took the last sip of his beer. "He was always a good guy. Quiet. We didn't really run in the same circles, but liked him."

"So, what circles, did *you* run in?" she asked with laughing eyes. It was hard to get him to open up about his past and she had started to take advantage of any and all opportunities.

"What, in *high school?* You don't care about all that."

He leaned forward with elbows on his knees and set the

empty bottle on the coffee table as he gave her a sideways glance. His crooked smile appeared and her butterflies ensued with the sight of his dimples that contradicted his broad shoulders and more masculine appearance overall.

"Sure I do. Let me grab another beer for you while you tell me."

Chase quickly stood as she did and gently motioned for her to sit back down.

"You have a seat and relax. I can get it myself," he said kindheartedly.

She obliged and he was back with a fresh bottle along with the cheese plate and the bottle of wine.

"My high school was pretty small, so, you knew everyone."

"What type of things were you involved in?" she pressed.

"Sports. Football, track. Nothing special. Although, football was what earned me a scholarship until, you know. Anyway, same as a kid in any small town."

"What about you? Cheerleader, I bet? Homecoming queen? Most popular girl in school who broke the hearts of guys like me?" he teased as he leaned back into the corner of the broken-in sofa.

"No, no, no. Not at all," she blurted out as she waved her hands in front of her and set her glass of wine down. "I also played sports. Track and soccer. I had a couple close friends, but mostly kept to myself. Hey, what are those?" she asked pointing to the corner of the room.

"Lanterns. We sell them here. People like to let them go along the river."

"Lanterns? I don't think I've ever seen one."

"You don't say? Well, I will just have to show you later."

"How about now?"

"Sure, I guess. You just got in here and warmed up, though. It's freezing out there."

He stopped as he had an idea.

"Tell you what. I'll set a few off and you take this blanket. I'll get your coat."

He got up and helped her put her coat back on before

holding the wool blanket out in front of her. She cautiously turned and with her back towards Chase, she closed her eyes and felt his strong arms brush against her. The feeling of being so close to him was distracting.

"I'll get you set up on the deck," he exclaimed.

With his hand on the small of her back, he led her toward the kitchen with her glass of wine in his other hand.

"Have a seat out here. Wait, let me get your hat and gloves."

She stood at the doorway leading to the deck as she watched him fetch her belongings. He was always so concerned about making sure she was comfortable and those characteristics made her adore him even more.

"Okay. You should be warm. Feel free to step back inside. I'll make it quick."

He held the thick glass door open while she stepped out onto the wooden balcony. The ice on the river shuffled by with quiet crunches. It was a clear night and the vast array of stars was beginning to twinkle in full force. She took a seat on the unpainted Adirondack chair to the right and waited for the show to begin.

CHAPTER THIRTY-SIX
Meant to Be

ONE BY ONE, THE illuminated paper orbs brightened and lifted from ground level. In a minute or two, they were collectively floating upward. Lacey watched Chase standing along the riverbank and his gaze followed each lantern as the air carried them upward. Once he was seemingly satisfied that each would take flight successfully, he glanced up at Lacey and noticed her leaning forward in her seat with eyes locked on the golden orbs. He rushed back up to join her.

Situated along the railing, he soon noticed she was standing alongside him. He placed his arm around her shoulders and pulled her in closer in an attempt to keep her warm. Silently, they stood as one and watched the glowing globes of fire ascend higher and higher against the backdrop of the blackened sky.

"Its the most beautiful sight ever," she exclaimed in a hushed tone.

He gently kissed the top of her head and his arm encircled her while pulling her closer.

Chase had somehow managed to illuminate ten lanterns and set them free almost simultaneously. Now, they floated faster and higher together into the thinner atmosphere. Lacey simply couldn't pull her gaze away as they rose above the tall ridgeline on the opposite side of the river. The bright orange glow distinguished them from the dazzling white stars in the background. The glow of each lantern eventually diminished and Chase and Lacey were left together under a canopy of wintry stars.

Lacey leaned her head against his strong chest and sighed. This was where she wanted to be. Where she was meant to be. He placed his hands on her shoulders and turned her toward him. Placing a finger under her chin, he gently tilted her face upward until their eyes met. His fingertip ran along her cheek then brushed the tips of her thick bangs from her eyes. Only the silent winter night bore witness to the earnest kiss with tender beginnings. Becoming more fervent, she gamely partook.

Chase took a few steps toward the door and opened it with a hearty push. Forcing himself to pull away, he led her back inside with a steady handhold. Locked in an amorous gaze, he removed her hat and gloves and she followed him to the sofa. Only a few tea lights and a tiny lamp in some unknown corner illuminated the apartment. Lacey's head buzzed with anticipation for him as he sat down in the center of the sofa and encouraged her along with him. Their lips quickly found the others' once more while hands explored each other for the first time. The potency of blossoming love took the reins.

"I'm falling in love with you, Lacey," Chase uttered.

"I've already fallen," she whispered back.

There was no denying their feelings now. As they gave in to their primal urges, he stood once more to guide her to his bed. Words were no longer needed.

Chase was finding contentment and love in a companionship with Lacey and knew he could never let her go. He breathed her in until he was overcome by a deep sleep that was now completely devoid of restlessness.

226

CHAPTER THIRTY-SEVEN
Aftermath

IT WAS STILL DARK when Lacey began to stir. She waited for a moment of sleepy confusion to pass until she gained orientation. She lay still next to Chase, afraid to breath, as she decided her next move. Remembering that she needed to be home somewhat early for the cabin phone line installation, she gradually eased out of the queen bed. Bare feet touched the cold pine floors and she gathered her clothes while feeling a tad bit mortified. She headed to the bathroom to get dressed. Splashing cold water on her face, she had a *'what have I done?'* moment with her reflection in the mirror. Was it regret she was feeling or simply awkwardness?

Tip-toing into the living room, she found her purse, coat, and other effects. The floorboards announced her every move and caused her to wince with every step. The century-old floors were intent on divulging her escape. She sat down on the couch and searched her purse for a pen and paper. An old receipt was as close as she could come to a note pad and she began to write politely.

She placed the note in the center of the kitchen table where Chase would see it when he woke and snuck out into the blue light of dawn. She felt a sense of relief to be in her car - a place of her own - then slightly panicked to see a layer of ice covering the windshield. It would only cause delay and risk of being discovered. The car dutifully started to life and an icy chill seeped into every crevice. She quickly realized she did not have an ice scraper. Remaining hidden in the car, she put the defroster on high and used the antifreeze in excess until the windshield wipers could remove some of the iced glaze. Afraid Chase would discover her sorry attempt of leaving the morning after, Lacey quickly pulled from the drive and glanced at the building in her rearview mirror. The back wheels slipped a bit and she slowed to a safe crawl as she started home. The events of the past night came back to her. She cherished the recollections as she replayed every detail over and over. The heater had not kicked in yet, but warmth blanketed her. His initial awkwardness was sweet, however that had morphed into confidence. The lanterns were mystical and his embrace was strong and gentle all at once. Getting over him would be arduous. She hoped it wouldn't come to that. She now knew the feeling of utter solace and contentment. As Lacey drove on through her crystallized surroundings, she pondered if she had made a mistake in staying over. It wasn't like her she was amazed at how she had given in to her feelings with him. Her brain had, for once, instinctively taken a backseat to her heart and her heart showed her what her lovely soul was truly made of. Her spirit was uplifted.

After the cautious and reflective drive back, she arrived safely at her temporary home. Exiting the little red station wagon, she crunched through the frosty groundcover. The porch steps and sleeping rose bushes were covered with a light coating of ice. Upon entering, her breath showed in the cold interior and she quickly plugged in the space heaters before getting the fire going. Fingers numb, they fumbled with the newspaper and kindling before dropping the matches. The bitter cold was unbearable. Her mind veered to thoughts of Chase in his warm bed and how she wanted to be there instead.

A hot shower was desperately needed to clear her mind and make her presentable before the representative from the phone company arrived. Still clad in coat and hat, she reached for the faucet and gave the hot dial and strong turn. Nothing happened. She tried again. Still nothing. She assumed the pipes were frozen and had no idea what consequences that might lead to other than a lack of running water for the time being. The bitter cold temperatures were here to stay for a while and this wasn't a dilemma she would be able to contend with day after day. She needed to cope with this setback and the phone installer would be arriving in as little as two hours. Her mind raced with thoughts in all directions and she became light-headed. Slumping to the floor, shivering, she pondered her next move and what she was even doing here in the first place.

She had slept in the bed of a man she was just getting to know well and who spent his post-jail time floating in a kayak downriver, she mused. Who was she? Was he really who she believed him to be? What did he think of her in that moment as he lay in his bed that he had to himself once more? What would her parents, Sam, Bryce, or Ashley think of her cold and pathetic self huddled on the floor of this meager bathroom? Her clients would lose all respect to see her like this.

She shook the nagging thoughts from her head and tried to look at the big picture. This was a minor issue and finding a way to deal with it would only show her what she was made of. She was getting caught up in the details and it did not matter what anyone else thought, she reminded herself. Thinking again of Chase, she knew he would only want to help her and instantly felt remorse for thinking of him in such drab and negative light. He was more than that. She found the strength she was looking for when she realized she, too, was more than this weak version of herself helplessly crumpled on the floor succumbing to the negative side of her mind. Even as she sat in a heap on the floor in this primitive cabin that was drastically different from the beautiful home she just walked away from, she knew the best was yet to come.

Taking a shaky breath, she emerged from the tiny bathroom and the sight of the cozy living room and glowing fireplace warmed her heart. Outside, the sun had finally risen well above the horizon and a beautiful winter scene was on display. Hardships abound in any lifestyle and this was nothing she couldn't handle. There were people dealing with much worse. The clock told her she had an hour and thirty minutes until the phone installer arrived and, with any luck, he wouldn't arrive at the beginning of the timeframe. She walked to the kitchen and tried the faucet. It, too, was malfunctioning.

A sign at the truck stop a few miles away advertising hot showers popped into her mind. It would be entirely out of her comfort zone, but a shower and a hot coffee to go was calling her.

Moments later, she was standing at her bed with a duffle bag packed with fresh clothes, a towel, and sneakers to use in the shower in place of flip flops. Passing the bathroom, she tossed in additional shower necessities and made her way back out to the car. Still warmed up, she was thankful for the hot air that rushed into the interior once she turned the controls and she drove toward the highway exit before she could change her mind. She had to do what she had to do and knew she would feel better in as little as an hour. Why not?

The parking lot was half full with travelers stopping for breakfast at the diner and Lacey walked in with her head held high in spite of herself. Walking past the hostess stand, she found the adjacent store and an attendant sitting at the counter reading a Motor Trend magazine.

"Hi, excuse me," she started as she cleared her throat of nervousness.

"Hi." The clerk was barely in his twenties and looked up from his stool as he gave the monotone greeting.

"The pipes have frozen at my house and I have an appointment soon. Do you have showers here?"

She stopped herself from divulging more unnecessary details.

"Yeah. Down that hall," he said. "Need quarters?"

"Oh, I don't have any cash on me," Lacey realized aloud.

"ATM over there." The unmotivated employee pointed to a spot behind Lacey. She turned to follow his directions. "Come back and I can give you some change."

Returning, she waited for him to slowly hand over the change for a twenty and she made her way to the public showers. She was relieved to find the restroom area vacant and two clean, private shower stalls. She had not been sure what to expect, but it wasn't that bad. Blue tiled walls gave an aroma of bleach and other chemicals. Lugging the duffle bag behind the curtain, she modestly undressed. Precious hot water streamed out. Steam began to billow and Lacey would have gladly spent a small fortune on what was currently a minor luxury to her. A feel-good shiver coursed over her body. Pungent lilac-scented shower gel added to the unlikely spa created in a drab truck stop along the interstate highway. The soapy and shampoo suds gathered around her shoes and Lacey was no longer in a rush to shower and dash. Instead, she soaked up every ounce of the reassuring hot spray of water until the metered timer signaled the shut-off.

After drying off and getting dressed behind the privacy of the vinyl curtain, she emerged. In little time, her long hair was combed and dried and she was no worse for the wear.

Walking out into the store, she thought about how insecure she had felt about an experience that made no difference to anyone around her. She had never thought of herself as being self-absorbed, but she mentally scolded herself for thinking she was above this scene. The clerk never noticed her walk out and it made her realize even more at how insignificant we are in so many ways.

She still had thirty minutes to spare. Some pre-made breakfast sandwiches where assembled, wrapped in foil and enclosed in a heated Plexiglas case in a convenience store area of the complex. Lacey requested one to go. A few jugs of water and a large coffee completed the order. A burly truck diver held the door for her with a warm smile that seemed to welcome a humbled and improved Lacey back into the world.

CHAPTER THIRTY-EIGHT
Inspired By Downtime

BY NOON THE TEMPERATURE was still hovering well below freezing. It was toasty warm inside the cabin and Lacey sat on the couch looking through her crochet book and trying to make sense of instructions with a muddled lump of yarn on her lap. Frustration set in. She vowed to keep at it anyway if only to make a useless crocheted chain of red yarn. That would at least be something. Her concentration on the task at hand took her mind off everything until the phone installer announced he was finished working.

"Okay, miss. You're all set. The line's working and your phone in the kitchen has a dial tone. You said that's the only one, right?" the uniformed employee asked.

"Yes, that's the only one. Thank you for coming out in this weather," she said sympathetically.

"All part of the job. That fire looks good, though. Enjoy it for me," he laughed as he left a pile of phone company papers for her and went out into the frigid temperatures.

Lacey bid him good-bye without moving from her seat. Rubbing her sock-covered toes together for additional warmth, she set her useless crochet needle down on her lap and laid her head back. Sitting up then, she arose with a stretch and went to the kitchen phone to test it out and check her cellphone voicemail. Still no call from Chase. She figured it didn't really mean anything that he hadn't called her yet, but needed some kind of assurance from him that things were good between them. She was nervous of a rift setting in after getting too close too quickly. She thought about calling him and in the end decided to give things a little time to develop. It was making her crazy. The thoughts swimming laps in her head refused to take a break.

A cup of tea appealed to her and she pulled a handmade clay mug from the cupboard. The kettle was still full of water and she turned a dial on the small electric stove to high. A tea bag and a dollop of honey in the little mug awaited the scalding water as it sat poised next to the stove. When the kettle whistled its tune, Lacey let the water sputter and splash angrily into the little mug. After a quick stir, she took it back to her seat. Picking up the crochet instruction booklet with more determination than before, she was still irked that this timeless and simple skill was evading her.

Again, she held the bright red yarn between her thumbs and forefingers and made what the book called a slipknot. Inserting the cold, metallic blue crochet needle through this little loop, she began to hook and pull the soft yarn. Tiny and coarse fibers slid along the fingers that steadied the long strand in place. She continued the process again and again until she started to see the pattern shown in the book. Her confidence grew and the rote rhythm of it all demanded her attention while slowing her mind. It was therapeutic. She was creating something and it felt wholesome and satisfying. Over and over she repeated looping and pulling and suddenly she found a disk of crocheted yarn in her hand. She continued for another twenty minutes until it was about the diameter of her hand and stopped. Knotting and cutting the end, she admired her masterpiece and placed it under her mug of tea. It was only a coaster, however it was full of significance to someone like Lacey who, up to this point, rarely had time to do anything other than work, eat, and sleep.

Inspired by her downtime, she decided to drive into Elliot to her favorite cafe. From there, she could use her laptop to connect with the outside world and get her mind off him. She would also need to to give attention to a few real estate deals that she remained involved with. A little web browsing and Facebooking would help pass the time. She readied herself and the cabin for her exit, however, not before calling to check her voicemails once more. Disappointment set in with the recorded voice telling her she had no new messages on her cellphone.

Arriving at the coffee shop, she was happy to see Karen behind the register. After exchanging friendly 'Hello's' and a little casual banter Lacey ordered a coffee and a turkey club before finding a seat. The shop had a spattering of locals and they provided enough conversation around her to make her feel a part of a warm and welcoming while winter continued its attack outside. Sliding into an empty booth, she immediately checked her phone again. Still nothing. It struck her as funny that four months ago she would have been thrilled with that. Opening her laptop, she perused her Twitter and Facebook accounts. The postings annoyed more than inspired and after the fifth unflattering photo of food atop a dinner plate, she logged off. She pulled up her emails and returned the handful that sat in her inbox. Minutes later, she was staring off into space with nothing to do except deal with a restless and insecure mind that was accustomed to being engaged nonstop. A vision of Bryce filled her mind and she pulled out her phone to call her real friend.

"Lacey! How are you?" Her buoyant voice was a joy to hear.

"Fine. I'm glad you were able to answer. Are you home?"

"I am. It is freezing here. How are you coping with this blast of freezing weather?"

Lacey didn't care to go into how she was feeling in the moment.

"I'm coping. It's a balmy two degrees here. Feels like negative fifty."

"Ouch. I won't complain about the twenty-degree heat wave, in that case. So, the new neighbors moved in to your place. They seem nice. Not as nice as having you here."

The words created a scene in Lacey's mind that made her

uncomfortable. The thought of the unfamiliar married couple entering the varnished front door, walking up and down stairs she had sanded herself and having their morning coffee in *her* kitchen was odd to think about. It *did* still feel like *her* house and although she had not wanted it anymore, she really didn't want anyone else to have it either.

"Glad they are getting settled in. How long are you home for?"

"Another week. Hey, that British pilot I mentioned?"

"Yes?" Lacey acknowledged Bryce while smiling up at Karen who brought her coffee.

"He has a layover in DC this weekend. We're having dinner at the Creek House."

The restaurant brought back the memories of Lacey's last dinner there with Sam and she started to feel foolish for thinking this whole thing was a smart move. She gave up so much on a whim.

"You better call me with every detail and I mean *every*," Lacey instructed. "I miss you."

"I miss you, too, friend! I really do. I feel like I should be making a pot of coffee or opening a bottle of wine with you here. I'll plan a trip up to visit you soon, if that's alright?"

"Are you kidding? Come up whenever. Oh, I had a phone line installed. I'll text the number to you. It's the only way to reach me at the cabin."

"It must be nice to live somewhere without all these instant tech distractions," Bryce considered.

"It is, but it's something you have to get used to. I'm working on it." Karen quietly slipped Lacey's lunch onto the table and topped off her coffee and Lacey mouthed a thank-you in return. "Well, my lunch just arrived. I'd better go. I'll be waiting for your call updating me on your fabulous date."

"Don't worry. I kiss and tell. Talk soon!"

Her words brought on a chuckle from Lacey and they said their good-byes.

Lacey finished her lunch while pulling up her Pinterest site when she had nothing more to look at or do. In impromptu fashion, she deleted most of her previous boards that she had occasionally created and began to tailor new ones that catered to her new life. She felt a spark of energy. Seeing the visions of summer gardens, beginner crochet projects, woodsy decorating ideas, outdoor fire pits and summer cook-outs reminded her of the life she was indeed living, or, at least would be when she acquired some friends and winter released its aggressive grip on the region. She shut the computer down when a pang of sadness accompanied a view of a kayak sitting along a private and wooded stretch of river.

"Coffee?" Karen stood next to the booth with a steamy fresh pot.

"Yes, please. Thanks, Karen," Lacey answered.

"So, what are you up to today?" Karen inquired.

"Oh, not much. I had some emails to return and a deal to handle that I am still involved with. I'm all wrapped up, though, and not sure what to do next. Guess I shouldn't complain, huh?"

"No you shouldn't. You need to enjoy it. You'll be back into something in no time and will be longing for this peace and quiet. If you're looking for something to do, though, have you ever been to the ice carving festival in town? The carvers are working on their displays now and the crowds won't build until this evening and over the weekend. You should check it out. It is only a few blocks from here in McHenry Park."

"Sounds like fun. I'll take a walk over there."

"I'll bring you a to-go cup of java to keep you warm."

"Sounds perfect."

Bundling up to brave the elements again, Lacey briskly walked to cover the three short blocks to the park. The fresh air invigorated her and her blood coursed to her extremities. The carvers were all hard at work as they readied their displays for the throngs of visitors who would descend on the event over the weekend. Ice chips and water streamed into the air from the chain saws as they concentrated on their craft under the abundant snow-covered oak trees. The sun came out to battle the glacial temperatures and the ice sculptures came to life in its light.

Lacey was amazed that such detailed and exquisite works of art could come from harsh machinery. She walked the perimeter of the park as she sipped her coffee. A swan, bear, and castle shaped up before her eyes and the sculptors were mostly unaware of her presence as she watched from a distance. One enormous, finished exhibit stood alone. Now standing before it, she was in awe. Most of the pieces were barely as tall as she. This striking piece loomed slightly above her. The block had been carved into the shape of a tree that had lost its leaves. Its twisted and pointed branches stretched from a thick trunk with a heart carved deeply into it. A bird was designed to perch upon one of the limbs.

Admiring the glistening artwork, she was delighted furthermore by three live cardinals that landed for a rest atop the ice sapling. Two were a rusty brown color with orange beaks and the third was the brightest crimson she had ever laid eyes on. They twitched their tiny heads toward Lacey then flew away as quickly as they had appeared. Lacey smiled at the sweetness of the scene.

Just then, her phone rang and she quickly retrieved it from her coat pocket. It was Chase. Lacey's heart quickened and her mouth went dry as she nervously answered his call.

"Hi, Chase."

"Lacey. I'm glad you answered."

He sounded breathless and Lacey was confused by his terse tone.

"Of course I would. So, hey, I got my phone line installed."

She winced at her lame conversation starter.

"Can you meet me at Memorial Hospital? Do you know where it's at?"

Chase did not sound like himself.

"Yes. Yes, I do. Are you okay? What's wrong?"

"I'm okay. It's Greg. He was in a pretty bad accident this morning. I've been here since about ten. I just … uh. It would be nice to have you here if you can make it."

Lacey would have run to him if had been the only way.

"I'm in Elliot and will be there as soon as I can. Have you eaten? Should I pick something up? Does Gregory need anything?"

"No. I don't need anything and he's in surgery now. Just drive careful, alright?"

"I will. Don't worry and I'll see you soon. Everything will be alright."

"Thanks, Lacey. I mean it."

It crushed her to hear his sad and desperate voice. She had no idea if it would be all right, but she was going to do whatever she could to comfort him. She tossed the coffee cup into a trash receptacle as she ran to her car and reached it in record time. Everything around her was a blur and her mind was focused only on helping Chase.

CHAPTER THIRTY-NINE
You Have Me

THE HOSPITAL STOOD IN the middle of what was once a farmer's field. The old building that Lacey was familiar with from riding past it in her parents' car when she was a young girl was now long gone and a brand new facility stood in what was once a nearby field. The parking lot was half full. She found a parking spot near the main entrance and entered the building with much trepidation.

A woman sat at the front desk handling the incoming phone calls and visitor requests as Lacey approached the oversized reception desk. She looked up with a worn out expression. Her dark blonde hair was lackluster and pulled back with a plastic headband.

"How may I help you?" she said to Lacey as she entered. A security guard watched as she passed.

"I just received a call that a friend of mine has been admitted. I believe he is in surgery now, but I need to meet with his brother who is here somewhere," she rambled breathlessly.

"His name?" she asked in a matter-of-fact tone.

"Gregory Robbins. I need to meet with Chase Robbins."

With little fanfare, the reception employee pushed one of the many buttons on the black office phone. She made her inquiries. Lacey shuffled nervously and looked at a pastel print of pink and blue flowers hanging on the wall behind the desk. The thin, plastic gold frame was outdated. Lacey wondered if it made it out of the old place before the rubble.

After a few *'hmmm's'*, *'okay's'*, and *'uh-huh's'*, Lacey was relieved to hear *'I'll send her right up'*.

"Okay, dear." Lacey was irrationally irked by the way the receptionist addressed her. "You need to follow the signs to 'Surgery'. It's on the third floor and there's a waiting room outside the elevators. If you don't find who you are looking for, the receptionist there can page him."

"Third floor, surgery waiting room," Lacey repeated in a slight daze. "Okay. Thank you."

She found her way to the elevator and depressed the button. It marked with a three. As she ascended in the hushed environment, she thought about what Ashley would think about working here. It would certainly be a different environment than the busy city hospital she worked in now. The halls were quiet other than the few visitors who shuffled around.

The elevator sounded its arrival at the proper floor and Lacey stepped out with some hesitation. She looked to her right and noticed a long waiting room with a glass front wall and large opening. About half a dozen people sat in the area. All seemed casual and slightly uncomfortable. Some looked blankly at the TV hanging from the upper corner of the room. A talk show could be heard with escalated voices coming from the screen. Some flipped through a magazine. None appeared overly concerned. None except one.

Lacey's eyes scanned the room until she found him in a seat that was positioned as far back in the corner as it could possibly be. His feet were spread apart on the floor and his elbows rested on his knees. His head cradled in his open palms. His athletic and strong body appeared weakened and beaten. She walked to him and rested a hand on his shoulder as she softly took the seat to his left. He looked at her with reddened eyes and managed a smile. Turning toward her, he pulled her in for a long and silent embrace before finally speaking.

"I'm so glad you're here."

His voice was raspy and desperate and gave her a sense of

the seriousness of the situation. She rested her hand on his closest knee. He sat back and placed his hand on hers.

"I can't lose him Lacey. He's all I have left. This can't happen."

He looked away and at the blank wall before he could show any more emotion.

"Hey, look at me," she pleaded softly. "You haven't lost him. He's here. It's going to be fine and you're not alone. You have me, too."

He continued to stare at the wall before taking a deep breath and looking in her eyes.

"I can't tell you how much I needed to see you."

His words struck and recharged her heart. She wished she were hearing them under different circumstances.

"Can you tell me what happened? Do you know much?" her gentle and quiet voice urged.

He rubbed his face with open palms. He cleared his throat as he leaned forward again with elbows to knees. He clasped his strong hands in front of him while his jaw clenched.

"All I know is he was out this morning for some reason. Driving home, I guess, he took a turn too fast and hit a decent patch of black ice." He continued to look ahead with a steely gaze. "His truck flipped off the road and down the ravine. Landed upside down at the edge of the river. The idiot wasn't wearing his seatbelt."

Pain turned to anger as he recalled what little he knew. She waited, not knowing what to say.

"Some guy happened to be doing some winter fishing in front of his nearby camp and saw it happen. I guess he called the police who got to my place around nine. I've been here ever since."

She took a breath of stale hospital air. She was tense. He was angry and sad and surely scared. They sat together quietly before she reached to hold him tightly. She felt his tension release as he leaned into her and returned her hold. He sat back up and pulled her to him and held her with a one armed embrace as though she was the one who needed comforting.

He kissed the top of her head and rested against her for a second before tilting his head back against the wall.

"They had to remove a section on his skull. God, Lacey. I didn't even know that possible. He's in an induced coma until the brain swelling goes down, they said."

"When did you last speak to anyone?"

"About an hour ago when they told me they were starting the surgery," Chase answered flatly before adding with a choked up voice, "They asked about his religion and if I wanted to contact his priest."

He looked at her and she had never seen so much anguish in someone's expression. She ached just witnessing it.

"I should call Ashley. She has worked in the ER forever and has seen some crazy stuff. I'm sure she could shed some light on the situation for us?" Lacey looked at Chase tentatively. She had no idea what he would think of the suggestion.

To her surprise, he agreed.

"Yeah. That's a good idea. I felt pretty stupid when the surgeon rushed into all of the medical crap and descriptions. I'm just putting my trust in them to save the only family I have left."

He put his head back into his hands. He was clearly holding a lot of emotion in. She wanted to tell him to let it out.

"Okay. Also, you need some nourishment, Chase. You have to have a clear head with all of this. I'm going to make a run to the cafeteria. I'll put a call in to Ashley first."

He did not answer. His blank stare told Lacey all she needed to know and chose not to press the conversation. She dialed Ashley and to her surprise she picked up.

"Ash, it's Lacey. Chase and I are at the hospital. Gregory has been in a pretty bad accident and we don't know what to think or do. Chase is, understandably, upset and worried," she added to make sure her sometimes over-the-top friend was sensitive in her conversation, "Would you mind talking to him? Gregory is in surgery now. We don't have anyone to talk to."

Ashley went silent. Her usually bubbly personality subsided and her serious but calm ER instincts kicked in.

"That's why he didn't call this morning. He was supposed to call me when I finished my shift," she said in a raspy and hardly audible tone. "Let me talk to him."

Lacey handed the phone to Chase before running off to the cafeteria. She heard Chase mumble a greeting to Ashley before he began to tell her what he knew. That description included much more than what he had revealed to Lacey. As if the brain and skull injuries were not enough, she overheard mentions of multiple rib fractures, femur fracture, facial lacerations, glass removal, collapsed lung and unknown prognosis. Lacey couldn't stand to hear any more of it. It was too much. Her heart ached with every word he painfully uttered. She feared the thought of what would happen to Chase if his brother did not make it. She refused to believe that the dire outcome was even a possibility.

CHAPTER FORTY
Struggling to Make It

"MR. ROBBINS? CHASE ROBBINS? I'M Doctor Simmons."

The surgeon stood before them in his scrubs and mask around his neck. He was pulling a chair up to sit closer. Lacey woke from light slumber and jerked her head from Chase's shoulder. With a sore neck, she rubbed a muscle kink as she sat up. Startled by his greeting, Chase sat up abruptly.

"Yeah, how is he? How did it go?" Chase blurted out.

"We won't know exactly how well it went for another twenty-four hours. He is stable. Critical, but, stable," the doctor calmly began. "He pulled through the surgery with no complications or unexpected issues, but the swelling is still a concern. We hope to see an improvement with that aspect within the next twenty-four hours."

"Okay. That's good. That's good, right?" Chase looked at Lacey with a naïve expression before giving his attention back to the doctor. It was obvious he was frantic to receive any kind of good news in regards to his brother.

"As good as we can possibly hope for at this point. He has a long way to go, Chase, but I am confident we have the best team assembled to give him the care that he needs."

"Can I, can we, see him?" Chase asked hopefully with a quick look at Lacey.

The surgeon turned his attention to Lacey who was hanging on his every word.

"Are you Julia?" he asked and Lacey felt a shudder run up her spine. "Who is Julia?" He now directed his question at Chase as Lacey shook her head.

"Our little sister," he diligently answered with downcast eyes. He continued to look at the dark maroon and blue patterned carpeting as the surgeon looked for more information.

"As you know, Gregory was in and out of consciousness when he first arrived and he has since been placed in an induced coma. I'll explain more on that topic," he quipped when he saw the look of concern on the brother's face. "We could not decipher his words initially, but a nurse on our team insists he is having what seems to be a conversation in his mind with someone named Julia. It very well could help his recovery to have that person present at some point. Would you be in agreement?"

Exhausted, Chase leaned to the side in his chair with his elbow resting on the armrest and head resting on fist. He was no doubt beyond ability to feel. What more could be thrown his way?

"She was, is, our little sister. She passed away about twenty years ago in, in a car accident along with our parents."

Lacey felt the sting of tears well up into her eyes. Chase was numb. She instinctively rubbed his back lightly while holding his hand in hers. She could only imagine the tortuous memories this experience was conjuring.

"I see. I am very sorry, Chase," the surgeon said sincerely. He was gaining a glimpse into the full scale of pain Chase had to be suffering from today. "You know, it is not the first time I have experienced a similar situation. It makes even a scientific and objective person like me wonder."

The surgeon shook his head and leaned back in his chair with clasped hands as though he was contemplating this amazing thing called life and what wonders the universe may hold.

"Alright. So here is the plan to get your brother back on his feet and back to himself."

His confidence was contagious and Lacey was grateful for his brilliancy. She believed in him and knew he was committed to his patient's health. Chase seemed to be feeling the same and he came back to life a little with a deep inhale. Two sets of tired, red, watery eyes were fixed on the face of Dr. Simmons.

"First off, yes, you can see him. Like I've already mentioned, he is in an induced coma. It is necessary to slow his system down a bit while the swelling in his brain subsides. That is the biggest issue we are dealing with. We will not know the extent of the brain trauma for a while and we are monitoring him closely. When the swelling goes down and his brain is able to function better we will bring him out of the coma."

"When will that be?" Chase asked.

"Could be tomorrow, could be next week. I don't want to give any false hopes. Let's take this day by day, or, better yet, hour by hour and we will work to help him recover little by little while we hope for the best."

"Okay. I understand," Chase said flatly.

"He is in a recovery room now. Please be prepared. He is hooked up to many devices and is virtually covered with bandages and casts. Try to be strong for him. He may be able to hear you. Help him by being positive and encouraging. Can you do that?"

The surgeon looked at them both in turn. Lacey was glad she would be able to accompany Chase despite being nervous about the scene that awaited them.

"Yes," they answered in unison before Chase added, "I'm just relieved to be able to see him alive."

Like two zombies on a mission, Chase and Lacey walked down the long hall. The florescent bulbs cast gloomy light. The floors shined and their shoes announced their arrival with muffled echoes. Quiet conversations between loved ones and hospital staff occurred outside of some of the rooms. A colleague passed them and gave a smile and a nod to the doctor before doing the same to Lacey and Chase. A woman pushed a cart of sustenance to people in various stages of getting better. The doctor stopped in front of room 331 and asked them if they were ready. They whispered yes and the three of them entered the buzzing and beeping room. The doctor stepped aside to allow them to enter first. A nurse looked up from the machine she was tinkering with then walked out of the room with an encouraging expression as she passed.

Gregory was alive, but far from well. It was a blessing he was covered from head to toe in some form of bandage, tape or other medical masking to keep the initial vision of his condition from being more of a shock to Lacey and Chase than it already was. Much of his face was exposed, however, and it did not tell a good tale. Bloody and lacerated, there was a network of stitched trails across it. The swelling was so bad that his eye sockets were barely visible. An oxygen machine pumped away to keep him somewhat present in this world.

Chase approached the bed and Lacey stood back to give him space. He reached out for his brother then immediately jerked back and turned to face the window. One hand came to rest on his hip while the other covered his mouth to remain silent. He stood for a few seconds before he mustered the courage to face his potentially dying brother.

"Hey big brother. You really gave me a scare," he began kindly.

The doctor brought a chair over for Chase and motioned for him to sit. He then brought one over for Lacey. She quietly thanked him.

"You're gonna be okay. I need you to be okay. Summer's coming and we need to get back out on that water. My groups will be disappointed if they don't have that gourmet lunch from Greg, right?"

An endearing and slightly nervous chuckle came from the little brother and he reached out to touch the uncovered arm lying limp beside him.

"Lacey's here with me, too," he continued with an affectionate glance her way, "and, oh, I talked to Ashley. She said none of this is anything you can't overcome and she's gonna get here as soon as she can to be with you. I thought you'd like to hear that."

Chase looked at the doctor who was watching the computer screens on the other side of the bed. With arms crossed, he looked at Chase and nodded for him to continue. Lacey speculated whether the doctor was seeing anything good on the monitors. The steady beeping sped up. Lacey watched the doctor intently as another nurse calmly entered the room to join him. Chase was oblivious, though, and cleared his throat as he thought of what to say next.

"Also, you really rescued me yesterday. Thanks for that. That dinner was incredible," Chase glanced at Lacey again and she blushed. Confused, she gave a questioning look back to him. "I think Lacey liked it, too."

She thought back to not having dinner. She made a mental note to follow up on this conversation at a more appropriate time.

Suddenly, the beeping got louder and faster. Chase and Lacey looked at each other nervously and watched the doctor and nurse. The nurse adjusted the drip and the doctor looked into Gregory's deep-set eyes. Chase asked the doctor to tell him what was happening. The surgeon made an urgent and quiet request to the nurse while ignoring Chase's question.

"Hey, man. Relax," Chase pleaded, "You'll be alright. You're okay," he choked quietly as he rubbed his brother's forearm.

The beeping turned from a staccato rhythm to a steady and high-pitched scream. Chase stood up and backed away from the bed. Additional staff quickly entered the room and began to swiftly address their individual tasks around the lifeless body around them. A nurse pushed in front of Chase to get closer to Gregory's head bandages. Everyone in the room was becoming more and more frantic within a matter of seconds.

"Greg, what the hell! You can't do this to me, man! Get a hold of yourself," he yelled over what was now a building chaos in the room. "I need you. Don't you dare …"

He stopped before the rest of the sentence could form on his lips.

"Carl, please escort Mr. Robbins out."

The surgeon made the firm request to the orderly before announcing a string of demands to those around him.

Chase shoved the orderly's hand from his arm.

"I'm not leaving my brother. I'm staying right here," he said determinedly with clenched jaw and fists. Lacey wiped tears from her own cheeks. She didn't know what to do and was frightened that Chase was going to lose control. The orderly approached Chase and Chase stepped away from him as he watched the scene unfold. The team of doctors ignored Chase and the orderly spoke to him in a serious and exact voice.

"We are only in the way here. We need to let them do their job if you want what's best for him."

Carl was matched with Chase in size and strength and his tone suggested he was losing his patience. Lacey worried about how Chase would react with this stranger trying to push him from his only brother who was losing a battle.

"Chase," she calmly started. "Please look at me."

She had no idea how this would go, but she knew they needed to get out of the way of these efficiently working doctors and nurses. By now, a line of medical professionals were coming and going as they shoved past Chase, Lacey, and Carl.

"Get him out of here. Call security if you need to," Doctor Simmons bellowed as he continued to focus on Gregory.

Chase looked at her with more hurt in his eyes than she had ever witnessed in another human being.

"We'll stay close, okay? Let's just give them some room. We aren't helping."

Her voice was thin and weak and she held on to his hand with a tight grip and squeezed it. He did the same, looked down at her pleading expression and nodded in a sign of defeat. They slowly walked out into the hallway as a nurse rushed out behind them. Chase took a dozen or so steps before leaning against the wall and sliding down onto the floor. Carl walked over to the nearby nurse's station to keep watch while Lacey knelt down in front of him and wrapped her arms tightly around his shoulders and head. He had no tears left at this point in his life. She felt his body shaking and held him tighter to try to make it stop.

Eventually, they moved to a set of chairs near the station where a few nurses were typing and filling in charts. Carl brought them each a coffee.

"Doctor Simmons is one of the best trauma physicians you can get, you know. He moved here to be close to family and we all considered that move to be pretty lucky for our area. Your brother's in good hands. I thought you might like to know that," the orderly said as he moved on to help another patient. Chase acknowledged him and took the coffee from his hands.

She glanced at the clock on the wall. It had only been fifteen minutes since they were ushered out of Gregory's room, which was still in sight. The stream of staff coming and going from the room had slowed. Not sure what to think of that, they chose not to mention the observation and, instead, sat together in silence.

"You are amazing, you know that?"

Lacey was startled to hear the words.

"What? What are you talking about?" she asked.

"It seems like I've known you forever," he began as he rolled the empty Styrofoam cup between his open hands. "I guess, in a way, I have." He managed a defenseless smile. "You don't owe me a thing and this is, I'm sure, the last way you want to be spending an entire day and evening. It's just, well, I don't know what I would have done without you today."

Choosing not to hide her true feelings, she looked directly into his hazel eyes and admitted, "There is nowhere else I want to be than with you. Really. Anyway, I'm not doing anything. I feel pretty helpless. I wish I could do more."

"You are all that is holding me together right now."

He leaned forward to let his lips meet hers. She caressed his now scratchy face and noted his fatigue.

"Once we get the confirmation from the surgeon that Gregory is doing better," she said as she gave a convincing and knowing look that told him not to question her confidence, "we should get out of here for a little bit. You need to clear your mind a little. We can grab some take-out or something. We'll come right back."

"I can't leave him, Lacey. You should take a break, though. I'll be fine here. You may have been able to keep me from losing it with that Carl guy," he said with an embarrassed sideways glance, "but I'm not leaving."

After some time, his hoarse voice spoke again.

"I don't think he'll make it. I think I need to face it."

His statement did not suggest he was looking for reassurance. He sounded strangely normal for the first time since arriving at this dreaded institution. A *'been there once, can do it again'* attitude.

Lacey was speechless as she looked to follow the sound of approaching footfall. Chase followed her gaze and they watched Doctor Simmons walk toward them. Lacey searched his face for a clue as to what type of news he would bestow upon. The doctor looked exhausted as well and, with hands in his white jacket, his eyes followed the floor.

CHAPTER FORTY-ONE
Necessary Relief

"HE IS STABLE AGAIN," the doctor announced before reaching them.

They breathed a heavy sigh of relief and stood to greet the surgeon.

"What happened? Did I cause something to happen?" Chase respectfully asked while allowing relief to flood him.

"No, no. Nothing you did. Personally, I think it is good for him to hear you, Chase. Like I said, stay calm and talk about pleasant things. Just as you did. We can't predict what his recovery will be like and he is going to take a step back now and then as he moves forward."

"You think he's going to make it?" Chase asked in a concerned voice.

"He's made it this far, right? That's more than I can say for others who have been in his shoes. Let's be positive and, like I said, we will monitor him closely. I need your cooperation in order to do my job, though. I'll keep you informed of everything."

Chase looked down with his hands in his pockets as he rocked to and fro a bit while giving a few thoughtful nods. He resembled a teenager who was being scolded by a parent.

"Yeah, I get it. No problem." Looking up he added, "Thank you Doctor Simmons. It's just he's all the family I have. Please take good care of him."

"I can assure you I will. We all will. Now, you two really need to get out of here for a bit. Now is a good time. We'll watch Gregory closely."

"Yeah, Lacey suggested that, too. I guess you're both right. Can you or someone please call me if anything changes? It would make me feel better about leaving. I won't be long."

"Sure, we can do that. Tell you what. Give me your number. I'm here until tomorrow morning, at least. I will personally make sure you get a call if there's anything to report."

The doctor leaned over the nurse's station to retrieve a notepad and pen. He dutifully etched Chase's cell number before tucking the sheet safely in his pocket and returning the pen and pad. Lacey and Chase headed to the elevator. Soon they were walking out into the bitter cold night.

"Where is your coat? Did you leave it back there?" Lacey inquired as she rubbed her arms to generate more warmth.

"Didn't wear one. I ran out of my place as soon as the cops left."

He started to walk toward his truck as they passed it.

"No, no, no. I don't think so, mister. I'm driving. Come on," Lacey instructed sternly.

"I can drive. You've done enough. Anyway, it's late. You should get back and get some sleep. You can stay at my place if you want. That way you don't have to worry about heating up the cabin. Or, I'll start a fire there for you. Whatever you want," he went on as he stood next to the bed of the two-toned truck.

"I'm staying with you. Unless you need some alone time?"

She didn't want to push herself on him when he had so much on his mind. Then again, she worried about him being alone and driving while he was u so distracted.

"I want you with me. I do. Okay, you drive if it makes you feel better, but you stay at my place tonight? Even if I stay at the hospital. You need some sleep, Lacey."

"Okay. Let's go now," she said trying to remain upbeat to keep his spirits up.

Getting into her car she immediately turned on the heater. The cold air spewed out and Chase rubbed his hands together as he warmed them up.

"I'll let you drive, but I'm buying you dinner," he announced.

"If you insist, but that's not necessary. We can just grab something to go. I'm sure you don't want to sit down in a restaurant right now."

Lacey pulled out of the parking lot and headed toward the highway that would take them back toward their homes. Chase snuck a look at his phone to make sure it had a signal and battery life. No calls yet. He placed it in the cup holder between them. It reminded Lacey of her former, albeit recent, life and relished the fact that she was not chained to her phone anymore. His action was also a reminder of what is truly important.

"Nah, I'm feeling a little better now that I know he snapped back from whatever happened in there. Getting out might do me good. I need to stay in the right frame of mind for him and I want to spend some time with you. On that note, what were you doing sneaking out earlier this morning? I didn't even hear you leave."

"You were fast asleep. I didn't want to wake you," she admitted.

"Well, next time, wake me."

"Next time?" Lacey inquired sweetly.

"If I'm lucky."

She couldn't resist a quick look his way and his sly smile spread across his handsome face made her susceptible to his flirtations.

"You're some kind of trouble," she laughed. "Anyway, where do you want to have dinner? I don't even know what would be open this time of night."

"That's true. There is one place, but nah. You wouldn't want to go there."

"Where?"

"It's nothing special but its open twenty-four hours and they do have surprisingly decent food."

"Wherever. I am starving now that we're talking about

eating."

"The restaurant attached to the truck stop on Route 79. It's at the exit above ..."

Lacey cut him off.

"I actually know the place well," she said guardedly before she broke into a fit of laughter. Chase gave her a confused expression and she told him all about her morning.

"Oh, wow. You know, I think I love you even more after hearing that story. But hearing that makes me insist even more on you staying at my place tonight. You shouldn't have to deal with that. It's far from upscale, but I can generally rely on heat and running water."

"Okay, as cold as I am right now, I don't have the energy to argue with those selling points."

They drove on into the night before Chase eventually broke into a fit of laughter. He laughed so hard and so uncontrollably that Lacey thought he was going a little insane after the events of the day.

"What? What are you laughing at?" she asked.

"Nothing."

He tried to quell it, but the laughter continued to burst out of him.

"Chase, tell me what is so funny. I'm serious."

"Okay, okay," he said between laughing sobs. "It's just, you know, I never thought I'd be dating a girl who freshens up at the truck stop."

After trying to be serious and looking at her with pursed lips that were holding in another fit of laughter, they both laughed until they cried. It was just the release they needed.

CHAPTER FORTY-TWO
Critically Stable

LACEY HAD KEPT HER word and stayed at Chase's apartment. After dinner they had made their way there and he got her settled in. She had picked up a toothbrush at the truck stop that brought on more teasing from her boyfriend. There was no denying they were closer than ever now. No call had come from the hospital and he agreed that no news was good news at this stage. The place was littered with traces of the evening they had shared only a night ago and Chase had run in ahead of her while trying to pick up on the go. She, of course, had not cared and urged him to lie with her for a moment to rest. He had insisted on returning to the hospital until he realized she would be left here without a vehicle. It was the realization he needed to agree to stay and they both succumbed to sleep's powerful appeal within seconds.

Morning brought new perspectives along with anxiety. This time, it was Chase who had awoken first. He had cleaned up the clutter from the apartment while she slept and brewed a pot of coffee. The aroma wafted back the hall and gently nudged Lacey awake.

"Good morning," she greeted while still wearing the sweater and black corduroy pants she had put on the day before.

"Morning. Here, have a seat. I'll get you a cup of coffee. Milk and sugar, right?"

The wooden chair scraped against the floorboards as he got

up from the table. He was freshly showered and had changed into a dark blue pullover with jeans. She groggily took a seat across from him.

"Thanks. Yeah. That sounds great."

"I needed that sleep. Sure you did, too," Chase said as he stirred her coffee before setting the cup down in front of her.

"I didn't realize how tired I was until my head hit the pillow. How are you doing?" she asked while taking a sip of the strong brew.

"Better than yesterday, thanks to you. No call from the hospital still, so, I'm guessing nothing has changed."

"Well, I'm sure you're anxious to get back there. Let me splash some water on my face and break in my truck stop toothbrush."

"Wow. I forgot about that," he chuckled.

"Yeah, well, don't judge."

"No judging going on here," he exclaimed with hands up in defense.

"Uh-huh. I hear ya. Whatever."

"Sounds like someone's not a morning person," he said as got up to refill his mug.

"Sounds like someone *is*. I used to be one. This mountain air, and lack of a job, has gotten me used to sleeping in. Shoot. A job," she exclaimed suddenly with a slap of her palm on her forehead. "I forgot I'm supposed to show up for my first day tomorrow. I think I'll call and try to postpone that."

"Not on my account you won't. Your life doesn't have to be put on hold because my brother drove too fast and flipped his truck. I can take care of myself and I don't want you to lose out on a job over all of this."

He set the coffee pot back in its place and returned to the table.

"I know. I know you don't expect me to be there, but I'm worried about him, too. Like I said last night, I want to stick with you through all of this. It's rough. You shouldn't have to deal with all of it on your own. I have money coming in from my rental back in Annapolis. If the Masons can't understand and need someone sooner, well, so be it."

"Suit yourself," he shrugged. "It's your decision. I'm happy to take you with me wherever I go."

Lacey finished her coffee and was off to freshen up now that the caffeine had kicked in. Her hair was up in a ponytail, face freshly washed, and she returned smiling with sparkling clean teeth.

"Ready?" she asked as she walked toward him.

"How can you possibly look so darn good when you just wake up?"

Chase pulled her close and kissed her forehead before pulling her in for a long hold. She leaned into him and they stood together gathering strength to get through whatever this day might have in store for them.

"Alright, Casanova. We should head out."

"Agreed. Thanks again for driving. Do you need to check on things at home? Want to stop on the way?"

"No, but I might head over there later this morning if everything's going okay."

"Absolutely. Give me your keys. I'll warm up the car while you finish your coffee," he stated as he grabbed his coat from the coat rack near the door.

"Really? Sure. Here you go."

She eagerly tossed the keys to him, which he easily caught.

"Hey," she called as he stopped with his hand on the door handle and turned toward her. "How did I get so lucky to find you?"

"I can assure you it's the other way around."

With a wink, he quickly shut the door behind him.

The hospital was much busier upon their return. After checking with reception, they were instructed to return to the waiting room they had spent the prior day in. The receptionist at that desk assured them she would have the doctor paged to give them an updated report. They took a seat and stared blankly at the television show that was airing from the opposite corner of the room. An unfamiliar doctor entered the room shortly after and called out Chase's full name. He abruptly stood and raised his hand as if in a classroom and not his current situation. With long strides, the doctor approached and extended his right hand to make his introductions.

"Hello, Mr. Robbins. I'm Steve Blake. I assisted with your brother's operation yesterday."

"Hi," Chase greeted.

"So, the swelling is beginning to go down and that is a very positive sign. We are keeping him in a coma state for now to allow for that to continue. Other than that, his vitals are stable, which, is really all we can hope for at this point. But, we are encouraged that this day should bring more progress."

"That's great. I'm so glad to hear that," Chase smiled broadly at Lacey. "Can I see him, or do you think that could cause problems?" he asked hesitantly.

"Sure. It can only do Gregory some good. Follow me."

Chase and Lacey exchange hopeful glances as they followed the doctor to the room. The initial alarm of seeing Gregory in the state he was in had worn off and they each pulled up a chair to the side of the hospital bed. Chase began to make pleasant conversation once more. This time, the beeping machines sounded steadily and normally with nothing to cause alarm. The doctor excused himself to tend to another patient. Lacey and Chase sat in the quiet room with the buzzing hums and hushed swooshes of monitoring devices creating a mechanical background melody. Gregory's eyes were starting to show more as the swelling receded, although he still showed no movement or signs of acknowledgement.

They chatted quietly beside him and spoke to him intermittently, not knowing if he was hearing any of what they said. They kept the atmosphere calm and agreeable. Lacey made a run to the cafeteria to pick up some snacks for their bedside vigil.

Later on, Lacey decided to run home to check on the cabin and call the Masons about delaying her start date. She knew it would also give Chase some time alone with his brother. After spending a considerable amount of time with Gregory that day, she was starting to become more concerned about his recovery. It made her uncomfortable and she didn't want Chase to recognize her doubts. Whether sincere or not, he acted blissfully unaware of Gregory's still grave condition. While she couldn't let it show, she was beginning to loose faith in Gregory's ability to bounce back from his extreme injuries.

CHAPTER FORTY-THREE
Simple Life's Not That Simple

BY THE TIME LACEY reached the front door, she heard the running water. In a panic, she unlocked the door and ran in as quickly as she could. It sounded bad and once more, she had come home to find a minor catastrophe awaiting her. The temperature had warmed up enough to unfreeze the pipes and, apparently, she had neglected to turn the shower faucet off the morning before. Water flowed from the showerhead and had spilled out onto the bathroom floor and hallway. Fortunately, it was the hot water faucet she had left on and that initial blast of water probably kept a partial ice rink from forming.

Wearing her boots, she ran into the bathroom and turned the now-cold water off. It was a mess. She grabbed as many towels as she could find and began to sop up the water before ringing out the saturated cotton into the sink and shower tub. Her clothes were quickly soaked as well, but she only stopped to find a mop. Her teeth chattered and her fingers were numb. She kept working until the last drop was dried up. Stepping back to admire her work, she realized how clean the floors were and it was this thought that made her laugh out loud in the face of adversity.

She moved on from this hardship easily and her only remaining concern was that the water hadn't done any damage to the floorboards. Choosing not to worry about the unknown, she changed into one of the comfortable and warm fleece outfits she had gotten for Christmas and turned on all available space heaters. At the same time, her new landline began to ring and the new and obnoxious ring caused her to jump.

"Hello," she greeted.

"Hi, Lacey. It's mom. I got your message and wanted to try out your phone line to make sure it works."

It was wonderful to hear her mother's voice.

"Mom! You are my first call! Yep, it works. How are you?"

"I'm fine. How are you? You sound out of breath."

"Oh, yeah. Sorry. I just got done cleaning the floor."

"So, I haven't talked to you in over a week. Is everything okay? What have you been doing with yourself up there? Your dad and I were worried about you with the cold weather and all."

"I've been great. It's been cold, but the fire and electric space heaters do the trick. No major issues to report."

She left out the minor details about the pipes freezing, having to use the truck stop shower and flooding the place. She had only been there a month. What else would she need to contend with?

"Good, well, I bet it is pretty there with the snow."

Lacey let her mother go on while she moved to stand next to the heater positioned in the kitchen. She also wanted to tell her about Chase and Gregory, but she wasn't sure how to approach the subject since they knew only that Chase had spent time in jail. Not an attribute, to say the least.

"Oh, I was watching the news the other night and there was a story about a major lawsuit that was settled. They mentioned Samuel Hinkley was the defendant's attorney. Is that the Sam you were seeing?"

"Well, I wouldn't say we were *seeing* one another, but yes. That's him."

"Hmmm."

"What?"

"Do you still speak to him?"

"I saw him before leaving town. Not since."

"He is rather dashing. And successful," her mother hinted.

"Yes, and your point?" Lacey asked with a laugh.

"Well, maybe you should stay in touch with him. That's all."

"Okay. I'll think about it, mom. Who says he wants to talk to me anyway? He was kind of a jerk last time I met him out."

"You don't say? Humph. Well, you don't deserve that, so, forget I said anything. Have you made any friends up there? I hate to think of you all alone."

"Mom, I'm not a child in need of friends. I have made a few acquaintances, though. There is the owner of a coffee shop I go to and she made a similar move as I did. She moved here from a corporate job in Pittsburgh to open her own business. And, I'm going to start working part time for a really nice family who owns a little hardware store in Elliott."

"What? A hardware store? Why would you want to work there?"

"I know," Lacey agreed. "It is an old fashioned one with all sorts of things. Toys, crafts, stuff like that. It's cute. I don't know. I guess I figure it's a way to get out and meet people and decide what I'm going to do next. Actually, I'm supposed to start tomorrow, but I have to call them to see if I can start next week instead." Lacey couldn't stop the words before they flowed from her mouth.

"Why do you want to postpone it? What are you busy with?"

Lacey took a deep breath and figured it was now or never.

"Well," she began slowly, "Do you remember me mentioning Chase Robbins at Thanksgiving?"

"The one who was in jail?" she snorted.

"Yes. There *is* more to the story."

She filled her mother in on everything and tried to make her understand what a good person Chase was. Then she told her about Gregory and the accident.

"Lacey. I don't know about all this. I mean, I'm sorry to hear about the accident and all, but this Chase character doesn't seem like a good fit for you. You know what I mean?"

263

Lacey heard her father in the background and braced for a conversation with him. Fortunately, her mother stayed in control of the conversation.

"I know if you meet him, you would gain a better understanding. Or, talk to Uncle Tim. He knows him pretty well."

"Yes, he mentioned that he knew him over Thanksgiving. I don't know, though. Please, just use your better judgment."

Her mother sighed as she tried to keep from meddling then shared an idea. "Hey, we should drive up for a visit soon. If you and Chase are still seeing one another, we could meet him then?"

"Sure! I'd like that. Or, maybe I'll plan a trip home and bring him along? Would that be okay?"

"Of course. Let's get together one way or another in couple weeks. I'm looking at the calendar now. Looks like the weekend before Valentine's Day would work? Yes? Your father says yes."

"That's fine with me. I can't wait. We'll talk later this week and decide what to do."

Lacey just knew her parents would like Chase once they met him. If they, didn't, well, there wasn't much she could do about that. She was happier than she could remember being in a long time and he was a big reason for that. His companionship made her life better. Combined with a fresh handle on her future, she was feeling more content than ever.

Before she forgot, she decided to call the Mason's in hopes of delaying her employment. Debra Mason answered on the second ring. Lacey introduced herself and she confirmed that her husband had mentioned her. Lacey explained the situation in a nutshell.

"Your friend isn't Gregory Robbins by chance?" Debra politely asked.

"Yes, actually it is. Chase, his brother, mentioned he knew your husband in high school."

"And me. We were so upset to here the news of the accident. How is Chase holding up?"

Lacey was struck by how sincere Debra sounded.

"He is upset, of course, but doing well. Gregory is stable, but critical and we are waiting for some additional signs of improvement before we can relax a little."

"Oh, of course. I just can't imagine this happening again. It's heart wrenching. They are such great guys and they've both been through so much. I'm glad to hear you're there for them. Please don't even think of coming in until you are ready. This baby isn't coming for a while. We have plenty of time. You're still interested in the job, though, right?"

"I sure am. I'll be able to make it in next Sunday if that's okay."

"Let's just plan on that, then. Call if you need anything. Tell Chase we are thinking of them and praying for Gregory's recovery."

After the call, Lacey was anxious to meet Debra. She might have been the nicest person she had ever encountered, at least over the phone. By now, it was one o'clock. She called Chase.

"Hey, I was just thinking of you," he answered.

"Hi. Any improvements?"

"Not really. Less swelling, which they keep telling me is a good thing. I just came down to the cafeteria to grab some lunch. Everything alright at the cabin?"

"Yeah, no issues to report at this time. I'm going to get a quick shower and come see you, okay?"

"Heading to the truck stop, are you?"

Lacey could see this joke was going to be slow to die.

"Glad your sense of humor is back," she stated dryly. "No. The water is now in working order here."

"Good. Remember where the hidden key is at my place. Feel free to use it if you need to. No more truck stop showering for you, got it?"

"I got it, I got it. I'll see you around three. Call me if there are any developments of if you need me to pick anything up on the way."

She decided to make one more call before hitting the

shower and figured a little more time to allow the hot water tank to fill would be good. She left a message when voicemail answered.

"Hi, Ash. It's Lacey. Just wanted to let you know I have a phone at the cabin now and to thank you for talking to Chase yesterday. Call me when you can."

By the time she started the water for a shower, the hot water tank had been replenished and the preheated water shot out from the small showerhead. She was overjoyed. To have a steaming, hot shower in the comfort of her home was truly an indulgence. She wondered what homeowners thought of this treat once it became mainstream in society. If she had a to choose, this feature would be a necessity over the convenience of a furnace any day. The tank was not a full as needed, however, and the water soon cooled to her disappointment.

She dressed comfortably in black tights and a long sweater to leave the house, but decided to leave her hair down and flat ironed it. A little bit of pink lip gloss made her feel better about herself before packing a bag with some snacks, magazines, and a new crossword puzzle book she had been working on since moving to the woods. She still couldn't believe she was somebody who had time for crossword puzzles. Before heading out she turned on a few space heaters and left the faucets to drip. While situating everything just so to prevent any disasters, the phone rang and she hurried to answer it before the last ring.

"Lacey, it's me. He's awake."

CHAPTER FORTY-FOUR
A New Lease On Life

"I CAN GET THE next two weeks off if I needed to take that much time. Could I at least stay with you for a few days if I make the trip?" Ashley's concerned voice asked. She had called as Lacey pulled back into the hospital's visitor lot.

"Of course. You can stay as long as you want. I can't wait to see you," Lacey said excitedly.

"I have a confession. Greg and I have been talking or emailing on a daily basis since before New Year's. I had no idea where things were heading, but this little scare really put things in perspective for me. I don't want to barge in on him for an extended period, but I figured if you don't mind putting up with me for a long weekend I would really appreciate it. I want to see him and I want to catch up with you, too."

"I had no idea," Lacey admitted while she sat in the parking lot. "You two make a great couple. I'm glad you kept in touch. And, in thinking about it, the only reason Chase and I are together is because of your relationship with his brother."

"That's true. Well, I'll let you go. Please keep me posted on him?"

"I will."

"Thanks. I'll call you later."

"Sounds good. Talk soon."

Lacey found Chase positioned next to Gregory's bed and in the same spot she had left him earlier. She knocked softly to announce her arrival. He looked up and with his hand, motioned for her to join him. Gregory's eyes were now open and visible and, although immensely dazed, he was communicating slightly.

"Hi, Gregory. It's nice to see you," Lacey gently greeted from his bedside. She was afraid of saying something wrong.

"Lacey has stayed with us this whole time, Greg. Ashley is asking about you, too."

A wiry smile emerged on Gregory's lips as he expressed an inaudible word with a whispery and scratchy voice. He followed Lacey with his eyes as she sat down next to Chase. A nurse came in quietly to check his morphine drip briefly before leaving the room.

Lacey mentioned that she just got off the phone with Ashley. She omitted the fact that Ashley wanted to visit in case that was something that might upset Gregory at this point. She told him that Ashley was concerned about him.

Gregory's smile returned and was an encouraging sign that his brain and memory were functioning better than expected.

Things got better from there as Gregory seemed to try to communicate with them more and more. After about an hour, it occurred to them that he may need rest, but hated to leave him alone. With perfect timing, Doctor Blake arrived to check on his patient. He ran Gregory through a short course of instructions and Gregory was, to their surprise, up to the task of each small request. The doctor was visibly impressed.

"This is all wonderful. Really wonderful. Now, Gregory, you've been working hard and you need to rest. I'm going to escort your visitors out for a bit, but they'll be back. Do you understand? It's okay to blink if speaking is too much."

"Yes," he managed to whisper.

"Get some rest brother. I'm real proud of you," Chase said as he held his brother's hand.

The doctor joined them in the hallway and repeated his feelings of a good prognosis. They were relieved to hear that Gregory was giving indications of making a full physical recovery. The doctor reminded them that they have no way of knowing how the brain will function after head trauma, though. The fact that he, so far, did not seem confused was a very good sign. Chase mentioned Gregory's smile at the mention of Ashley and the doctor was glad to hear that as well. It was then that Lacey told them of Ashley's plans for a visit.

"If they have a positive relationship, then, yes. A visit from her would be a good," the doctor stated.

"He was calling her every day up until the accident," Chase said sheepishly.

"So I've heard. Thanks for telling me!" Lacey exclaimed as if o

Laughing at the exchange, the doctor agreed, in that case, Gregory would very much like some attention from his female friend and Chase and Lacey headed to the cafeteria for a celebratory dinner and to call Ashley.

Two days went by and Gregory continued to improve. He was drowsy and did not always make sense although he was becoming more and more lucid. Ashley announced she would be on her way first thing Tuesday morning.

On that Tuesday morning, Lacey had a fire going strong, a bottle of wine and a crockpot of stew with a fresh baguette waiting for her good friend's lunchtime arrival. She had an hour or two to kill before that time and decided to get a few calls out of the way.

She called her mother to let her know all was still well and she let her know that Ashley was coming for a visit. She spilled the beans about Ashley and Gregory supposedly being an item and her mother was becoming more interested in the soap opera that was unfolding in upstate New York. She found it comical and was glad to hear Lacey would have company for at least the better part of the week. After a little more small talk, they promised to call one another again soon.

She then placed a call to an agent she had been working with on one last lingering deal that was taking a little longer to close than they had anticipated. Some title issues were being resolved. She was anxious to wrap up this final deal.

"Lance here," the agent barked.

"Hi, Lance. Lacey Williams."

"Hi, Lacey. I think we got the bugs worked out on this deal. Talked with settlement first thing this morning and they sad they just got what they needed from the title insurance company to remove the lien."

"That's great news," she conceded.

"Sure is. So, we should be able to close on this on Friday at the latest."

"Great. And I verified that the funds were wired. I'll check with settlement to verify the amount needed to close is the same, but we should be good to go. Other than the settlement sheet, all the necessary paperwork has been signed and notarized."

"Good deal. Well, call if you hear of any problems and I'll do the same. Otherwise, I'll be talking to you before the end of the week."

Lacey headed to the couch with a cup of coffee and a feeling of immense accomplishment. Chase confirmed Gregory was communicating more than ever and was increasingly showing signs of his regular self. It was the first day Lacey hadn't joined Chase at the hospital, however, she figured it was good for the brothers to have some time before Ashley arrived. She flipped though a new magazine she had purchased at the hospital and put her wool sock-covered feet up for a spell.

Shortly after noon, the sound of a car signaled Ashley's arrival. She ran to the porch to greet her. Once inside, the normally vivacious Ashley became emotional and Lacey was completely caught off guard by her friend's sudden outburst. Through tears, she began to laugh a little.

"*Oh* my. Look at me. What is going on here?" she asked Lacey.

"Uh, you tell me. Come in and sit down. What's the problem?"

"It's all too good. That's the problem. I like it here too much. I like *him* too much. Please tell me he is still improving."

Lacey rubbed Ashley's shoulder and provided a sympathetic look.

"He is getting better and better every minute and every hour. Even his doctors are surprised."

"Thank goodness."

Ashley leaned into Lacey for a friendly hug.

"We'll head to the hospital soon. First, some food to get your emotions back under control. I can't take you there like this."

"I know. You are so right. Thanks."

Ashley wiped her eyes and blew her nose with a tissue from her coat pocket before hanging the coat on a hook by the door.

"Glass of wine or do you want to abstain?"

"Yes, please. I need to get these nerves settled. What the heck has happened to us over the past three months? Living in a beautiful city, good jobs, fiercely independent females and now all this. You live in a cabin in the woods and are working at a hardware store and I'm rushing away from my perfectly fine life to see a man I hardly know and who has some degree of brain trauma."

Ashley had the most perplexed expression on her face as she stared at Lacey for some explanations. Lacey could not even pour the wine due to the cackle that took hold of her.

"Well, when you put it like that," Lacey blurted out as she bent over laughing and tried to catch her breath. "Ash! What a way to describe it all!"

"I know! Why in the world do you think I showed up crying? I was trying to figure it out the whole way here and since leaving at four o'clock this morning. The thought even crossed my mind to turn around and just head home," Ashley confessed as she shook her head and took the glass of wine from Lacey.

Lacey sat down next to her and wiped the tears from her own eyes as her laughter subsided. Ashley continued by justifying her feelings.

"Look at this, though. I think of you sitting by this fire all the time when I'm at work or sitting in my sadly furnished townhouse. This is the life. I don't mind my job, but I'm starting to feel like you did, I think. Just, a little unfulfilled. I work, sleep, and eat. And drink too much wine when I'm able to stay awake. That's it."

"I know. I keep saying it, but stuff like this accident puts it all in perspective. It makes you want to stop playing silly games and be honest with each other and yourself. It's nice to recognize who you actually want to be."

"Amen to that, sister," Ashley said as they clinked glasses and giggled.

"Well, let's have some food then head off to the hospital," Lacey declared.

"Sounds like a plan. Two pretty special guys are waiting. Mine's pretty banged up from the sounds of it, but, I know I can nurse him back to health in no time."

"Oh, geesh. I'm sure you will. That poor guy has no idea what's store for him."

CHAPTER FORTY-FIVE
Better Every Day

ONCE GREGORY REGAINED CONSCIOUSNESS, a week went by quickly. Ashley's presence was a boon for everyone. She was able to keep Chase and Lacey better informed and positive as she provided more explanations and details on what the doctors were saying. Though not an expert, she had experience with helping patients with head and brain trauma and prepared them for what could come. Most importantly, Gregory was more responsive when she was around.

In a few short days, he was speaking coherently and able to move the unbroken arm. He had a few more surgeries which he recovered nicely from and the doctors were even beginning to discuss a plan that would see him be able to go home within a couple of weeks so long as his insurance would cover some in-home medical equipment and a visiting nurse. The other caveat was that the doctors, of course, preferred him not to return to an empty home any time soon regardless. Chase volunteered to stay with him when that time came and Lacey could see Ashley's wheels turning during that particular discussion. Time would tell how it all played out. Gregory was out of the woods, though, and with therapy and solid care; his doctors predicted a full recovery was possible in a matter of time.

They all agreed that Ashley should stay as long as possible and she did, indeed, take that second week off from work.

Chase had checked on Gregory's apartment and Ashley settled in with Lacey. It was nice having help with keeping the cabin toasty and having company around. The threesome worked well together and the ordeal brought them closer in record time. Lacey now knew that companionship was something she had been missing tremendously and she treasured the deeper bonds she was forming.

Lacey made it to her new part-time job on Sunday and relished having something of her own to focus on. She arrived about fifteen minutes early and found Debra standing at the cash register finishing up with a customer. She acknowledged Lacey who stood off to the side and out of the way. A group of men were picking up some supplies for an ice-fishing excursion on a local pond, according to the bits and pieces of conversation Lacey picked up, and once they exited, Lacey stepped up to the counter to greet her new boss.

"Lacey, so nice to meet you. Let's go back to the office to get some paperwork out of the way. I'll watch over the store from there until Dean gets here."

Following the petite woman's lead, Lacey fell in line behind her. Debra had thick, dark blonde hair that fell in waves just past her shoulders. Her pregnant belly appeared to be getting to the uncomfortable stage as she waddled to the back room.

"Here, please pull up a chair. I'll leave this open to listen for the front door," she said as she moved a doorstopper wedge in place. Taking a seat at the desk, she exhibited perfect posture and had all of Lacey's paperwork in small piles. She began removing paperclips and pulling pens from the drawer.

"Thanks for waiting for me. We really need to stock more fishing and outdoor sporting gear. We had only half of what those guys had asked for. While I'm thinking of it, let me know what kind of inventory you receive requests for once you are up and running? I've been telling Dean he needs to focus more on outdoor recreational needs."

Lacey found that interesting. She had been thinking about

some type of outfitting business being sorely needed in the immediate vicinity.

"I sure will. I'm anxious to get started. Thank you for the opportunity."

"Believe me, I am grateful for you. My feet are too swollen for standing around here all day. First things first, how is Gregory doing?" Debra leaned into the old office desk with hands clasped that showed off a pretty pink manicure.

"Every day gets better. I actually can't believe how swiftly he's improving. He's able to hold normal conversations again with no signs of any major memory loss and also beginning physical therapy now."

Debra looked down at her clasped hands and shook her head.

"When I heard the news, well, my heart just sank. As if those two haven't been through enough."

She sighed as if unable to comprehend the recent turn of as she continued.

"When their parents had that horrific accident, the whole town came together for Chase and Gregory and when that judge handed out such a severe sentence, you wouldn't believe the amount of push-back he received from the community. I heard he had letters and phone calls a mile long in support of Chase. Well, that's all in the past. Right? We just need to focus on helping Gregory. Please let us know if you can think of anything we can do?"

Lacey was touched not only by her sincerity, but also how she regarded Chase.

"I will, absolutely. I'll pass your words on to them. I know it would mean a lot."

"How could you not care about either of them? Right? Okay. So, let's get down to business before I get called out front."

The previous communal goodwill that Debra spoke of that day was seen first-hand as news continued to spread about the accident. Flowers and notes of well-wishes began pouring in to Gregory's room and a donation fund was even set up by a local church congregation to off-set the medical expenses and bills Gregory would certainly incur during his time spent in the hospital. He and Chase were against the idea of using it, but the Pastor would hear nothing of it when he visited and said the money was in safe keeping for Gregory's needs, case closed. They agreed to table the discussion for another time.

The only problem they were having was how to handle Gregory's business. He was self-employed and they wanted to make sure he didn't lose business due to his injuries. Chase was able to get a handle on his current contacts with Gregory's limited help and reached out to them while monitoring his brother's emails. Gregory informed Chase of a business card on his desk that included the information of another web designer that he trusted to help out. Regardless, they didn't want Gregory to fret about it and it was a minor distraction to them after all that they just went through. Making a full recovery was of the utmost importance.

And, then there was the issue of plans of a visit from Lacey's parents. She had been thinking about it a lot. The cabin was small for the three of them, four if Ashley stuck around or revisited, and Lacey really wanted to treat Chase to a couple days away, just the two of them. Apparently, Chase had similar thoughts in mind.

One particular Wednesday afternoon found Lacey home alone when the phone rang. The caller ID showed Chase's number as she reached for the wireless phone from her comfortable position on the sofa.

"Hi, everything okay?"

"More than okay."

"That's a good report."

"It is. Ashley is in the room with Gregory. He is obviously loving her company and I'm feeling like a third wheel and missing you."

"Is that so? What are you going to do?"

"I can't discuss my plans over the phone. Not appropriate. There are people nearby."

"You planning to rob a bank or something?" she deadpanned.

"Nothing of the sort. I'd rather not go back to the slammer."

Lacey was pleased to hear him joke about something he was normally so guarded about.

"So, you want to meet up somewhere?" she asked trying to think of what they could do.

"I want you to stay right where you are. I'm coming over. I need to thank you properly for all you have done for me."

Two hours later, Lacey and Chase were still lying together. Entwined in sheets and enjoying the comfort of one another, neither wanted to move.

"Question for you," Lacey started.

"I just may have an answer for you," he quipped.

"So, what would you think about going to Annapolis with me this Friday and Saturday? I will have you back on Sunday and it seems as though Gregory will be fine. He may even get a little more rest with us gone for forty-eight hours."

Her request was initially met with silence.

"It's okay. I guess the timing is bad. Stupid idea and forget I mentioned it."

"Sure. Let's go."

His answer surprised her. She leaned up on her elbow to look at him.

"Really? Are you sure?"

"Yeah. We've been tied to that hospital and I know it's not fair to you. He'll be fine and Ashley will still be here to keep him company. Might as well go while he's under the care of doctors. Once he gets home, I'll have to stick around to help him."

She kissed him before revealing the other part of her plan.

"Are you still willing to go if I admit we would be staying at my parents' place the first night? Saturday night we could head into the city and get a hotel."

"What? Meet the parents? No way. Deal's off."

Thinking he was serious, her hopes were dashed. That is,

until she caught a glimpse of his expression. His poker face gave way to a grin.

"Are you sure you want them to meet me? If I recall, the Williams family was cut from a different cloth than the Robbinses. I'll go if you want, though, and I'll do my best to make a good impression."

"They will love you. Not as much as I do, though."

Taking advantage of the privacy and having nowhere to go, he pulled her close and made up for the quality time lost over the past week.

CHAPTER FORTY-SIX
Meet the Parents

PULLING INTO THE DRIVE, Chase took in the view of the stately and grand brick colonial that was situated on the cul-de-sac. It was intimidating to him. He had reached a level of comfort and security with Lacey. As he sat in the passenger seat of her car in the paved drive of the ambitious home, he started to unravel. He vowed to ignore these inner feelings of inadequacy and put on a brave face. Her family was important to her and she was important to him.

"I love you."

Lacey broke the silence not knowing how much he needed to hear those words from her.

"I love you more. And I am pretty certain your parents are not going to care for me. I wouldn't like me if I were them," he waged as he peered out the windshield at the impressive Colonial in front of them.

"Oh, stop it. What's not to like? Just be yourself and if they don't like you then, well, that's their problem."

As though he was the bellhop instead of the highly anticipated guest, he went around to the trunk to fetch their bags and followed Lacey to the portico. After a quick rat-a-tat-tat on the crimson door, Lacey opened it with little fanfare and Carol Williams met them in the foyer as she stepped from the last step on the center stairway. Lacey gave her mother a big hug. Chase watched from behind as he saw the loving expression on her mother's face. He shut the heavy door and set the luggage down. To his surprise, the petite woman extended a big bear hug to him next.

"You must be Chase," she greeted warmly with a pat on his back. Taken aback, he gave a one-arm hug in return.

"And you must be Mrs. Williams. It's nice to finally meet you."

"Please, call me Carol. George," she yelled over her shoulders and up the center staircase, "They're here."

"Just leave the bags there for now. Come on into the living room. I have some drinks and appetizers for us there."

Lacey gave Chase's hand a quick squeeze of encouragement and they followed Carol into the living room where they sat together on the love seat. Carol sat on the wingback chair with her tiny ankles crossed and perfect posture. Her red sweater and white collared shirt were crisp and presentable and her red lipstick was perfectly applied. Lacey wondered where her father was. She was reminded of some awkward high school moments when he would show up in full Naval regalia to meet her dates. She told herself he would never do such a thing to his thirty-five year-old daughter. She desperately hoped he would do no such thing, anyway.

"So, how was the trip?" Carol asked.

"Fine. No traffic. Clear weather," Lacey answered as she poured herself a glass of wine. "Do we have any beer, mom? I sure Chase would prefer ..."

"Wine is fine for me," Chase quickly said.

"If you're sure. Here you go," Lacey handed him the glass. As he took the glass from her hand, her father entered the room.

"Lacey. Glad you made it safely," he boomed.

"Hi, Dad." Lacey enthusiastically walked toward her father to give him an embrace as she extended her arms on tiptoes.

"Dad, this is Chase. Chase, this is my father, George."

"Mr. Williams. Nice to meet you, sir," Chase stood and offered his hand. George obliged with a strong shake to let Chase know who was in charge.

280

"Hello, Chase. Put that wine down and follow me. Do you like bourbon, son?" Lacey rolled her eyes and gave her mother a desperate look. Her mother shrugged and took a sip of wine. George had his arm around Chase, but Lacey knew it was for show. She looked at her watch and told herself to check on him sooner versus later.

She and her mother made small talk until they returned twenty minutes later. Chase was flush and Lacey was concerned.

"Where were you two?" She questioned more so to her father.

"Just having a chat. You never told me Chase here was an ROTC student.

"It never came up," she answered dryly with arms crossed.

"You also never told me that Chase has quite a business going for himself."

"That also never came up, dad," she said not knowing where this conversation was going. If the evening continued this way, they would be checking into the hotel early.

"Did you know, in one tourism poll he was rated the number one river guide in the Adirondack region? Sorry to put you on the spot, son. I did a little research on you," he quietly added.

"Are you?" she asked him as she leaned toward him. He was seated next to her on the loveseat once more.

"I don't really pay attention to those polls," he admitted modestly. He was obviously uncomfortable with being the conversation topic.

"So, mom. How is the fundraiser going for the shelter?"

"Wonderful. Thank you for asking dear. We are close to hitting our goal and preparing to open another safe house."

Chase's interest was piqued.

"Do you do charity work for domestic violence shelters?" he asked. Lacey was confused by his sudden interest in the topic.

"Yes, I do. I have for, oh, about ten years now. It is very rewarding."

"My mother did, too. She volunteered at a safe house when I was in high school."

Lacey had never heard Chase willingly bring up his family on his own. She listened as he held steady conversation with her mother. Her father seemed content to allow others to hold the conversation now that he had his chance to grill him. She tried to read his face on whether he approved or not, but, it was no use.

"I hope you two are hungry. I have lasagna ready and heating in the oven."

"I'm famished. I'll help you, mom," Lacey offered. Then, knowing her father was ready to jump on the opportunity to question Chase alone again, she added, "Come on Chase. I'll show you the kitchen."

"I'll be right there."

Lacey couldn't believe it. He was purposely staying back with her father. Her dad smiled and offered him a beer.

The next morning, Lacey found Chase dressed and in the kitchen making coffee. He greeted her and mentioned her parents told him where the coffee was in case he got up first.

"So, last night went well? Right?" Lacey asked. She knew her father could be intimidating, however, they seemed to have unexpectedly hit it off.

"Yeah. I had a great time. Your dad is really interesting to talk to. We actually have a lot in common."

"You do?" she stated in disbelief.

"Yes, we do. And your mother is really sweet AND a terrific cook. That was the best lasagna I ever had."

Their conversation was cut short by her parents entering the kitchen. Thankful that the coffee was already made, each helped themselves to a cup and sat down at the large kitchen table. The light morning discussions flowed easily between the protective parents and Chase. In fact, Lacey was starting to feel like the odd one out in most of the discussions. She wasn't going to complain, though. She was happy they seemed to genuinely like Chase.

By mid-morning, Lacey announced that they needed to

head out. Chase retrieved their bags and set them at the front door to prepare to say good-bye.

"Thanks for everything, Mr. and Mrs. Williams. I had a great time getting to know you."

"Chase, thank you for taking care of our Lacey up there while she is doing whatever she is doing," Carol gushed as she gave him a hug.

George approached with an outstretched hand and Chase extended his own for a healthy handshake.

"Please give Gregory our best. We wish him a speedy recovery."

Chase held the door for Lacey placed the bags in the trunk before getting in the passenger seat. Seatbelts on, she backed out of the drive while Chase returned the wave to her parents who were standing in the doorway.

"Your parents are really great."

"Yeah, they are. I'm glad you think so. They really seemed to like you."

"You think?"

"It was pretty obvious."

"That's good to hear."

"I mean, I knew they would like you, but, not *that* much."

"Thanks, I think," Chase retorted light-heartedly.

After a blissful afternoon nap at the downtown hotel she had booked, they were ready to head out for dinner. Lacey had made reservations at one of the city's better restaurants. Chase was glad he had raided Gregory's closest for more appropriate attire for the evening.

"Wow, look at you," she said with a low whistle as he appeared in his collared shirt and dark slacks. She was stunning in a cobalt blue dress that fit her snugly in all the right places.

"Me, how about you? Hello, gorgeous," he teased as he began to overzealously kiss her neck.

"We need to get going if we want to have a drink before our reservation," she reprimanded while hitting his arm with her clutch.

"After you," Chase held the door for her after helping her into her long, black wool coat.

They arrived at the restaurant a half hour before their reservation and Lacey cursed under her breath when she noticed Sam Hinkley sitting at the bar. Beautiful people surrounded him and the atmosphere had a plastic vibe to it that Lacey had never picked up on when she had frequented the place in the past. The lighting was adjusted just so to highlight the sparkling people and décor. Tiny candles were situated the length of the bar and on the tables to cast a warm glow upon the faces. Faces of people desperately trying to be noticed and many believing they were a little more than they were under the intoxicating effects of over-priced martinis.

"You have to be kidding me," she muttered as she noticed Sam Hinkley seated at the crowded bar.

"Did you say something?" Chase asked.

"No. You know, the bar is kind of full, do you want to …"

It was too late. She had been spotted. Once Sam glanced her way, his eyes took hold and would not let go. He had a renewed interest in this certain someone who was once more-than-a-friend. Their eyes met and Lacey's mind went into overdrive on how to steer them towards a table and not into a court the vibrant and charming attorney now held. He waved her over. Her heels clicked towards him with Chase in tow.

"Lacey, so great to see you again."

He stood to offer a friendly embrace with open arms. He was still clad in an expensive suit despite it being Saturday. She figured he must have had a wedding or some similar function. She obliged his request politely. Even when trying to avoid him, his charm was difficult to resist.

"Hello, Sam. We were, oh, let me introduce you both. Sam Hinkley, Chase Robbins."

She stepped aside in the sea of people around them to allow them to shake hands and give manly greetings. Sam appeared to puff up and barely give Chase the time of day as

284

he turned back to Lacey.

"Here, please have a seat with me. Let me grab that other stool."

"I got it," Chase offered as he pulled the lone, empty seat toward him and slid in next to Lacey. She took her seat between Sam and Chase after Chase helped her with her coat. Sam remained standing, leaning into the bar with his cocktail straw held between his fingertips and teeth. It brought back the memories she had of the last time she saw him.

"Well, well, well. Lacey's back in town. This calls for something special."

He signaled for the bartender who was there in an instant.

"Joe, Champagne cocktail for my friend here, and, her friend will have ..."

"Just a draft. How about a Saranac."

"A lot of people have been missing you around here, Lacey."

"Stop it. Like who?"

"I keep hearing your name, that's all. Your clients respected you. You made a name for yourself."

"Thank you," Lacey said to the bartender as she took a sip of the fizzy concoction. "There are plenty of other agents in this city. I think everyone will be fine," she laughed.

Chase hunched over his beer and appeared to down half the glass in one swoop.

"So what have you been doing up there? The fresh air seems to have done you good."

He looked her up and down and it did not take much to read between the lines.

"Well, we've been staying busy, right Chase?" she stated in an attempt to bring him back into the conversation.

"Yeah, yeah we have."

He turned slightly to face them and leaned his forearm onto the bar.

"What do you do, Chase?"

"I'm a river guide. I do kayak tours, mostly."

"What do you do in the winter, then?"

Turning in his seat to fully address Sam, Chase answered him matter-of-factly. "People still go out. You have to have a wet or dry suit, but winter paddling makes for some good trips."

"Chase here is one of the best guides in the Adirondacks," Lacey beamed.

"Is that so? Well, maybe I'll have to make a trip up there. I do mostly sea kayaking, but I'm sure I could catch on to your scene."

Chase turned back toward the bar. "Sure, I'll take care of you." The loaded words were shot out before he finished his beer nonchalantly. He signaled for another, jaw twitching. Lacey swallowed uncomfortably.

"Thanks for the drinks, Sam. It was nice running into you, but we still need to see the hostess. We have a reservation."

"No worries. Hey, Joe?"

The polished bartender walked their way as he simultaneously hung a dried wine glass on the rack above them.

"Yes, Sammy."

"My friend, Lacey, here has a reservation. It's under your name, right?"

Sam looked at Lacey and she nodded.

"That's what I thought. A table under Lacey Williams. Can you let the hostess know they're here and finishing their drinks?"

"Sure thing." Joe smiled politely at Lacey before walking over to the nearby hostess stand. The young hostess with long, brown hair appeared to be in high school. She looked back at them before making a note in her book.

Sam adjusted his cuff links and sat down as he reached between his legs to pull the seat forward. He took a slow sip of something dark on the rocks. Lacey took an uncomfortable drink from her champagne glass.

"Excuse me," Chase announced and stood abruptly. Sam appeared amused. Lacey was concerned.

"Where are you going?" she asked him as she reached out

to steady his bar stool.

"Restroom break," he smiled as he leaned in to kiss her cheek.

His answer satisfied her and she nodded before turning back toward the bar. Sam turned his full attention on Lacey as Chase sauntered away and before she could make another excuse to see the hostess, he had her deep in conversation.

She never noticed Chase bypass them on the way out of the restroom, walk past the hostess podium and straight out the front doors. Meanwhile, Lacey continued to keep up with Sam's conversation. He was turning the charm on heavily and some of his powerful and aggressive colleagues and acquaintances showed up from time to time with non-speaking trophy wives, or dates, beside them. She was sitting in a sea of egomaniacs. Finally she had enough and told Sam she needed to get to her table. She left him to the others whom had arrived to spill attention on one another.

"Have you seen the gentleman I was sitting with at the bar?" Lacey held her coat as she addressed the pretty hostess. It occurred to Lacey that Chase should have returned by now.

"Yes. He left," she answered sweetly as she pointed to the main entrance.

CHAPTER FORTY-SEVEN
It's What You Make It

LACEY RUSHED OUTSIDE AFTER escaping the clutches of Sam Hinkley. Desperately looking around, she finally spotted Chase leaning against the rails by the adjacent marina and looking out at the sea of sailboats and motor yachts gently bobbing in port.

"Hey, what are you doing out here?" she asked briskly while pulling her coat tighter.

"Just needed some fresh air."

"Thanks for leaving me with Sam. Sorry about him. Not sure what was going on. He must have had one too many."

"You seemed to be holding your own with him."

Chase continued to stare out over the harbor.

"What's that supposed to mean?" she fired back.

Chase shrugged his shoulders in a sign of casual defiance, his chin resting on his closed fist and foot up on the bottom rail.

"What's wrong, Chase? Come on. Our table's ready."

She held out her hand to him then dropped it to her side when he failed to oblige. He retained his silence as he slowly turned toward her.

"I can't give you any of this, you know," he warned as he motioned a long arc with his arm that spanned the parking lot filled with high-end SUV's, a fine dining restaurant, and the salty sea that cradled dozens of sailboats that were salty in an altogether other sense. She looked at him, unsure of what to say. She shifted her weight uncomfortably as she waited for him to say more. "That's your world, Lacey. It was nice of you to give me a glimpse into it and all, but I don't belong there. I don't fit in."

She stepped closer and placed her arm on his. "I love you for you. What's going on here?"

He shook his head and uttered a raspy chuckle.

"What's going on here? I'm holding you back. That's all. Your new life, me, your little part-time job. It's all a novelty that you'll get tired of. You will. Your parents want more for you, you want more." His voice was strained as he continued. "You will want more and I can't give it to you."

"Did my dad say something?"

"No," he cut her off. "Your father's a great man. He's done well for himself. Better than I will and I'm okay with that. I am. But you won't be happy. I see how most of the women in our town live and that's not you."

She felt tears well up in her eyes as she felt the sting of having a budding relationship cut short. Soon enough, though, her sadness turned to anger.

"What the hell do you know about what I want or need?" she hissed as she turned to face him more squarely. "If I wanted '*all of this*', as you put it, I could have it. I know that and I don't need you or anyone else to get it for me. In many ways I had it and I didn't fit in there, either."

She was short of breath and her head lacked the oxygen it needed to think clearly. She continued anyway as she spit out the words that were tinged with deep-rooted frustration.

"What do you expect from me? Yeah, I like a fine wine now and then, but I also like to kick back with some beers and good friends. We all have two sides. You, of all people, should know that."

She immediately regretted her words. Chase looked over at her with wounded and anxious eyes as she continued to hurl her thoughts at him.

"Sam was an idiot tonight and it wasn't the first time I saw that side of him. He didn't *approve* of me ditching this way of life. Now, you don't *approve* of where I came from. My parents don't particularly approve of me right now, either. Oh, and Sam says my past clients and colleagues don't even understand me."

She took a deep breath and looked up at the star filled sky. Chase remained silent as he took in the words she slung at him.

"I don't care about that anymore, Chase. I really don't. I don't need any of you to give me the life I want. I can do it perfectly fine on my own. I don't need *you* to give me the life *you* think I deserve."

He firmly gripped her shoulders in his hands and turned her toward him.

"But, I want to," he said calmly and purposely.

As far as Lacey was concerned, it was, without a doubt, the most loving and tender thing any man had said to her and she crumbled into a sobbing mess against him. She cried until she knew he was not going to leave her again and they held each other tight before joining in a long, passionate kiss.

"Let's get out of here. I know a better place," Lacey urged as she pulled him toward her car.

"The hotel room?" he asked snidely.

"Later."

In reality, Mike's Seafood and Crab Shack *was* her favorite little spot in town and she told Chase she was taking him there for some real Chesapeake civilization. Having had stood in the same cove since the late 1800's, its tarnish proved it had weathered storm after storm while standing the test of time. Coincidentally, Lacey and Chase were seemingly set on course to do the same.

Laughter filled the air as they walked past the vibrant and diverse patrons who filled the bar area. A hostess kindly showed them to a table with a darkened view of the bay. They shed their coats and piled them in one of the two empty chairs at their table. Chase held the captain's chair as Lacey took her seat before he took the seat across from her.

"This place is really cool," Chase said as he relaxed in his chair with one hand resting on the armrest while he took in the nautical gear that graced the dark paneled walls.

"It's one of my favorite places. Funny to think last time I was here I was fresh off a mild breakdown in my driveway. This time followed a little breakdown in a parking lot."

Lacey laughed and leaned back in her seat as a waitress arrived and took their drink orders.

"What happened?" He asked while leaning in to the table and giving her his full attention.

Lacey sighed heavily. "Not even worth talking about, really." She waved off the idea of rehashing the past. "I think it was the moment when I realized I had had enough of pretending to be someone I wasn't. Bryce found me crying in my car and we came here from some beers. She has a way of finding my voice of reason when I've lost it. Ashley's that way, too."

"Bryce? Who's he now?" Chase asked in an exhausted manner. His smile told Lacey he was slightly joking.

"Calm down. Bryce is a *she* and I can't believe I've never mentioned her. She was my good friend and was my neighbor here in Annapolis. She is actually still my tenant as well. We had a tendency to frequently solve the worlds', or our own, problems over wine or coffee. I miss her. I mentioned we might try to meet up with her before heading back, but the weekend is flying by. I'm not sure ..."

"You should. Why not? I'd like to meet her."

"Really? Maybe I'll text her to meet for breakfast tomorrow?"

"Sure. Sounds good to me. I'm up for whatever."

Lacey retrieved her phone from her purse and sent a text to Bryce before setting the phone on the table. The waitress dropped off two frosty mugs of light beer and took their order for massive amounts of boiled shellfish seasoned with Old Bay. A minute later she was back with brown paper cut from a roll to cover the table along with the necessary tools to dig into the specialty crabs that would be delivered shortly.

In the meantime, the couple tucked away in the back

corner of the eatery made an effort to turn their date night around. They discussed Gregory's improvement and how happy they were that he would be all right. They talked about life at the cabin and how Lacey was looking forward to un-thawing. Then, inadvertently, they forged new territory by talking about the future.

"I was surprised my mother didn't ask me about what I'm going to do with myself now. Thankfully, you being there may have stopped that *'where-do-you-see yourself-in-five-years'* discussion from starting," she chuckled.

Chase leaned in and crossed his forearms on the paper-covered table. He looked at Lacey thoughtfully. "Where *do* you see yourself in five years?"

She breathed in deeply before exhaling while looking out over the water. "I have some plans."

Chase wanted to ask if they involved him. He held back.

"Care to share?" he instead asked.

She paused before starting, then glanced sideways at him. "Before I left here, I had a vision of a new business and new personal life. On the business side of things, I saw that some type of outdoor outfitting business was really lacking around our area. I think you made some mention of that as well at some point?"

"Oh, yeah. I have a lot of ideas in that department. I could go on and on. I'll just say you are definitely on to something there."

"At Mason's the other day, I noticed some ice fisherman were looking to pick up some gear. What they needed wasn't there. That got Debra talking about the fact that outdoor gear was sorely lacking in their inventory and she was looking for input on what specifics they should stock. My mind's been running with the whole idea. Your input, of course, would be crucial."

Chase sat back and grinned. "You know I'd love to help you with that idea. You're talking my language now."

"That's what I thought. There's a concept I keep mulling over. I've come to realize that life is what you make it. I suppose this is also true for adventure in the great outdoors. Some people want raging rapids while others, like me, are perfectly content with floating down a calm river and that might be all the adventure they are looking for. Some people want a camping excursion to be a part of the weekend, others, might want a spa package with a hotel room once their adventure is done. What if I, we," she said cleverly as Chase's grin doubled, "specialized in tailoring individual outdoor experiences to the individual?"

Chase nodded as he shared her vision.

"I like it. Whether you want to float down the river on a tube with a six pack or kayak the gorge in the spring when the waters are raging, we could put them with the right guides and with the right equipment and even partner with the area's retreats to offer lodging and spa packages."

"Right. And Gregory could create meals and menus 'till his gourmet heart's content. That is, if he wants to."

"He'll want to, trust me. We'll have to set some boundaries for him," Chase said with mock aversion.

They were trading ideas and getting more and more motivated by the minute. Lacey mentioned seeing a For Lease sign in Elliott. Chase pointed out that riverfront property would be ideal and that Barney Ritter might be into this idea since Ritter's Landings would be a perfect location. They were deep in thought complete with cocktail napkin lists and drawings when their dinner arrived. The waitress poured the shellfish onto the table and Lacey and Chase went to work on cracking dinner open while they continued to plan the business side of their future. Then, Chase remembered the other half of Lacey's initial musings.

"One question you haven't answered," he started while using a hinged claw cracker on a heavily seasoned, boiled red crab. "You told me about your plans for the 'business side of things'. What about the 'life side' of things?"

"I suppose that remains to be seen," she stated plainly with a coy smile.

CHAPTER FORTY-EIGHT
Looking Beyond the Past

SUNDAY MORNING BROUGHT SUNSHINE and blue skies to the port city. Chase had slept longer than he had in years and found a note from Lacey on the nightstand when he woke shortly before nine-thirty. She had decided to fit in a morning run before they met Bryce for brunch and the long drive home to New York that would follow.

Home. The word suddenly had new meaning to him. The small town he lived in was now shared with a woman he had fallen deeply in love with. There was no denying that emotion. As the mug of in-room coffee brewed, he instinctively began his morning push-up and sit-up routine which had been started during a bleaker time in his life. His thoughts turned to Lacey and the new outlook on life she had unexpectedly given him. With her, he saw himself differently. He was no longer just a guy with a past. He now believed in a future. The single-brew coffee maker sizzled as it spewed out the last bit of hot coffee into the mug and the alluring smell of the fresh brew called to him. Chase aborted his efforts and took a seat by the window with coffee in hand.

The view from the tenth floor hotel room was inspiring. He gazed out over the port and onto the watery horizon. The sun cast a blazing white shine over the sea. Chase couldn't take his eyes off the glare. To him, it represented the beginning of a life worth living and he vowed to never waste the gift of a new day.

As he finished the rather bland cup of coffee, he thought

more about all of the opportunities that lie before him. Lacey took life by the reigns and was not short on big plans. The night before, her side of the conversation all but dared him to join her. He was ready to. The business ideas she mentioned were spot-on, from his perspective, with what the immediate area needed and he knew she, they, would find a level of success that would only enhance the seasons of their lives. He decided to approach Barney upon their return to talk to him about incorporating her ideas into his business. The location was perfect.

He also thought about how he needed to step up to the plate in terms of being who Lacey thought he was. The man he knew he was. It was time to let go of the past and evolve with her by his side. He was who he was, there was no changing that. He had lost his parents and sister and felt largely responsible for that. He had also killed a man and spent time in jail for that crime. Those are not events one can easily sweep under a rug. Still, Chase knew he was more than those events and needed to find a new perspective to look beyond them. With an open mind and a positive outlook, it would come to him.

His coffee now gone, Chase decided to get a shower and dress before Lacey returned. His suitcase was neatly half packed and he pulled out one of his brother's V-neck sweaters to wear with jeans. He chuckled to himself when he thought about what Gregory would say if he knew some of his clothes were borrowed. He would let him know later just to hear his reaction.

Twenty minutes later, Chase was showered, dressed, packed, and enjoying his second cup of coffee when Lacey returned. The atmosphere instantly perked up with her entrance.

"Hi! I hope you don't mind I went for a run. It was too nice of a morning not to," she said hastily as she rushed inside and let the door slam shut behind her.

"Good morning. Not at all. I got myself ready so you could have the shower to yourself."

She smiled a devilish smile as she downed the rest of her water and, now closer to him, leaned against the wall.

"That's a shame."

He smiled back at her, enthralled with her suggestive words.

"In that case," she said as she pulled an outfit from her overflowing leather duffel, "I will be ready in a jiffy and we can head out to meet Bryce at her place. Good?"

She stopped and looked back at him just for the fun of it.

"Way better than good," he retorted with certainty.

Bryce had suggested a homemade brunch at her place and Lacey parked in front of her old home right on time.

"So this is it," Lacey announced as she turned the car off.

Chase looked out of the windshield to see the neat duplex tucked between two ancient sycamore trees. The Victorian property was tidy and dignified and the street was clearly one comprised of devoted homeowners.

"Very nice," he offered sincerely. "Do you miss it? Seems like a great place to live."

"Surprisingly, no. I mean, I'm sure I'll feel a little nostalgic once we get inside," she said slowly while looking out the driver's side window, "but I know where I belong now." She looked at Chase and reached for his hand to give it a squeeze. "Let's go. I can't wait to see Bryce."

They exited the car and Lacey stole a few glances at what had been her side of the duplex. The blinds were drawn and, despite the Audi on the gravel parking pad, she couldn't catch any signs of life. She led Chase up the steps to Bryce's decorated porch and knocked upon the door. Within seconds, they were greeted enthusiastically.

"My goodness, get in here!" Bryce held open the inside door and they walked through the vestibule and into the foyer that was a spitting image of what was Lacey's previous home. "How are you?" she exclaimed as she wrapped her arms warmly around Lacey.

Stepping back, she tucked her dark hair behind her ear and

wrapped her oversized, olive sweater shrug around her as the blast of cold air rushed in along with her guests.

Lacey looked around the gleaming wooden foyer that smelled faintly of oil soap. Her mind drifted back to a time years ago when she had tediously stripped and stained the staircase and removed layers of dingy wallpaper prior to painting the plaster walls with the creamy ivory paint that now coated them. She had put so much work into the property to prepare it for a little much-needed cash flow. It was still paying off.

"Good. Great actually. Bryce, meet Chase. Chase," she said while stepping aside to allow introductions, "this is my dear, dear friend, Bryce Gathers."

Bryce held her arms wide open to allow for a friendly hug.

"Chase. Great to meet you. I trust you are taking care of this girl?" Bryce gave a wink and a smile at Lacey.

"I would like to, but this is one girl who does not need taken care of."

He shook his head slightly and looked at the floor before glancing up at Bryce then Lacey to flash his charismatic smile.

"Yes. You have your hands full, I'm sure," Bryce stated emphatically with arms crossed.

"Excuse me?" Lacey stated with dismay.

"Come on in. Let me take your coats," Bryce offered with a chuckle. "I have a smorgasbord waiting for us in the dining room. Lacey, you know the way. Help yourselves while I hang up these coats. Oh, and there's an envelope on the buffet for the rent. Don't forget to take it," she called out.

Chase followed Lacey into the dining room, which featured high ceilings and thick, decorative crown moldings. The oversized round table commanded attention with its hand-hewn thick planks of wood that appeared to be reclaimed from another life. Rather than formal dining chairs, the table was surrounded by vintage club chairs upholstered with grey velvet and featured invitingly rounded backs. Upon the table was a feast of sorts presented in uniquely mismatched platters, bowls, and glassware.

"Bryce, you are amazing. This all looks spectacular. Thank you. Did you cook all of this this morning?" Lacey gushed while pouring three Bloody Mary's into blue rimmed, hand blown Mexican rocks glasses and garnishing them with prepared skewers of shrimp, olives, and pickles.

"I'll second that," Chase added while accepting the drink from Lacey. "Thanks for having us. Everything looks incredible."

Bryce waved them off and motioned for them to have a seat around the table. "You know I love to entertain when I have the chance and I was too excited about seeing you both. I couldn't help myself. I can't lie, though. Some of it's from Berkshire's. I hope you're hungry, though. I leave for Paris this week and hate to waste all of this food."

"I'm starving, so, I won't be shy," Lacey announced while loading up a small plate of fresh biscuits, deviled eggs, and slices of London Broil to accompany a hot bowl of crab bisque.

"Berkshire's Deli. Boy, do I miss that place. Hey, you have a few new pieces?" Lacey asked as she gestured toward the alabaster tureen holding the bisque. Painted blue sparrows decorated the lid and sides. She placed the ladle back before gently lowering the lid back in place.

"You noticed? Isn't that beautiful?" Bryce asked while reaching for the butter for a biscuit. "My French lessons paid off and I was finally selected to start the non-stop to Paris a few months ago. I made sure to fit in a really quick window-shopping excursion that turned into a really quick purchase. I found that little darling in a boutique and it was surprisingly inexpensive. I had it shipped home as a present for myself."

"I can see why. Chase, you will find that Bryce's home is a menagerie of purchases from around the globe. I think I mentioned she's a flight attendant?"

"You did and I've noticed that," he said while looking around at the multitude of paintings, masks, and other wall hangings that adorned the walls. "You have quite a collection, Bryce. That must be a great job. To see the world, meet a lot of interesting people," Chase said while placing a blue linen napkin across his lap and turning his full attention to her.

"It is. Most people immediately ask me if I get tired of the schedule, the rude people and the travel, but I don't and I actually like st of the passengers I get to interact with. Sometimes I end up with a flight where bad moods are contagious, but they aren't the norm. Maybe I'll tire of it all someday? For now, it still suits me. I got into it for the travel perks and I just keep sight of that when mundane aspects of the job take the spotlight. I didn't go to college and I started this career right out of high school. I can't see myself doing anything else." Bryce tucked her feet under her while settling back into the dining chair. She hugged her shins with one arm and rested her head against her free hand with an elbow casually resting on the curved armrest.

"One of my favorite possessions is that bowl with the biscuits," Bryce added while pointing to the stark mahogany bowl.

"You know, I was just going to ask about it. It caught my eye right away," Chase said.

"About five years ago, I took a trip to Africa with a few other flight attendants. It had been a dream of ours to go, so, we booked the flight on a whim, and as if that's not crazy enough, went on the most affordable safari we could find without much investigation. It turned out to be the best experience of my life. We also wanted to visit a peaceful tribal community and our American contact in Africa set up a visit for us. That was incredible. Please stop me if I'm boring you," Bryce said while looking at the two sets of eyes hanging on her every word.

"Boring? You? Never in a million years. Go on," Lacey encouraged while Chase nodded his agreement.

"So, we are escorted to this little village of huts situated along a muddy river and there are kids running up to us from all directions and barely dressed adults squatting and standing a safe distance from us as we exit the dugout boat and begin to cautiously walk toward the elders of the community to pay our respects. I begin to have second thoughts. It was right out of National Geographic and really very incredible, but I was suddenly way out of my comfort zone and had no idea what to expect. Plus, and I don't mean this disrespectfully," she paused while searching for the right words, "but it was, well, dirty and just plain deplorable to someone who lives a more civilized life. I felt really bad for these people in the conditions they lived in."

Lacey and Chase had stopped eating and were waiting for her to continue. Bryce poured a glass of sweet tea from a large glass pitcher and took a gulp.

"That, however, was where my pity ended and I soon saw the beauty of their existence. Once our translator and guide helped us to make the proper introductions, there was a noticeable ease to the interactions and activities amongst everyone. There was so much love showered upon the children from the parents and laughter was constant. They were so proud to show us their meager, neat huts and they served us some type of root tea with little green leaves that was actually really good. We couldn't speak the other's language, but amazingly we had no problem communicating. Smiling, laughter, and gracious gestures were all that were needed to enjoy the company of each other. They had this sweet and simple existence that I often think of to this day. Before we left, the head of one of the families presented each of us with a carved bowl. I learned later that this is what this tribe was known for. It was their craft - their work - and I was honored to receive this gift. I tried to pay them, but they would have none of it and our guide explained they didn't really use money anyway. I found a way to donate goods instead."

Bryce stared at the handcrafted bowl longingly before looking back to her guests.

"You never told me about that trip," Lacey pointed out. "What a fantastic experience."

"It was," she agreed. "You were always so busy, Lacey. We never got the chance to talk about a lot of things. I'm happy for you. You look really well. Content."

"That's true," Lacey blushed. "I am. Content, that is," she added, perking up.

"Anyway, dig in. That little tribe would not know what to make of this obscene amount of food for the three of us," Bryce wagered. "They wouldn't know what to make of our society in general," she added with a friendly chuckle.

Chase watched the interaction between the two friends and could tell there was a solid bond between them. There was a raw level of honesty and trust that seemed to benefit Lacey more than Bryce. Bryce obviously went her own way in life and it served her well. Lacey was obviously influenced positively by her friend's freewheeling outlook. He helped himself to some sweet tea and a spoonful of baked French toast from a mustard-colored baking dish. It had a few chips in it and one of the handles was broken off completely. There was something familiar about the rectangular dish.

"Now, don't ask me why I still use that old thing. The story is not as intriguing," Bryce stated as though picking up on Chase's inspection of the worn cookware.

"Looks a little familiar to me," Chase pondered aloud.

"I think every mother had one in her kitchen in the seventies?" Bryce concluded. "I know I sound a little too philosophical now, but let me tell you why I keep that thing around. No only because it works, I swear it cooks more evenly and better than anything else I bake in, but because it is has character. Patina. A few chips and missing pieces don't make it any less. It has done its time and became stronger for it in my eyes. I suppose time has worn us all down a little in one way or another, but we're better for it. We're all just a product of our experiences in the end. Wouldn't you say?"

The profound words resonated with Chase on a deeper level. He was speechless and suddenly lost in thought. Fortunately, upon Bryce's prompting, Lacey began to update Bryce on all that had happened since they last saw one another and he was free to preoccupy himself with the thoughts swirling in his head. In an instant he had more clarity and understanding of himself and his potential future than ever before. Who would have thought a few comments about an old cracked baking dish would provide the insight and perspective he had been looking for?

CHAPTER FORTY-NINE
Nursing Him Back

MARCH LEFT LIKE A lamb that year and the last of the ice was swiftly melting from the riverbanks where throngs of umbrella plants began to emerge from the mud. April brought morning birdsong back to the mountains and that glorious sound took the place of an alarm clock for Lacey. She stretched with a sleepy smile as she awoke from her peaceful slumber. The sun's encouraging rays drew her out of bed with thoughts of a trail run and, after digging her jogging clothes from the depths of a bottom drawer; she swiftly dressed and pulled her hair up in a taut ponytail before pulling an ear warmer headband into position. The sun continued to stream in through the slightly dirty panes of glass as she laced her running shoes into a swift bow. A light windbreaker was all she needed.

Into the woods she headed to run along the smooth trail worn out by decades of use. As she ran, her thoughts churned about the future. She had so many ideas. Details and optimistic plans rolled around in her mind as he pace quickened. She would find a new kind of success soon enough, of that she was certain. Her lungs burned and her leg muscles ached from a decreased stamina. She had neglected her morning runs for too long on account of the weather and she was paying for it. Hands on bent knees, she leaned forward to catch her breath until she gathered her strength to continue. Finally, she reached the bottom where the river met the rocky bank. The torrential spring waters raged and gushed through the riverbed that was suddenly too narrow. She stood and closed her eyes as the sound of rushing water filled her ears and silenced her thoughts. The smell of mud, water, and grass replaced the frosty unsoiled scent of winter. She had pulled through one of the coldest winters on record virtually unscathed and virtually alone and for that she was proud.

Later that morning she headed into Elliott to check her work schedule and transfer some funds from her savings account to checking. She could finally get down to business and was anxious to talk to Chase about their business plans again. They had not had much time to talk about it since returning from Annapolis and she hoped he was still interested in working with her on it. After a quick lunch at the coffee shop, she decided to call Ashley to check on her progress.

"Lacey. Nice to hear from you."

"Likewise. So are you ready?"

"I am. I really am. Human resources just emailed my confirmation of employment and I start the second week of June. That will give me about two weeks to get settled in at Gregory's place," Ashley excitedly reported.

"Well, I can tell you Greg's doing really well. I had to work yesterday, but I saw him the day before and couldn't believe the improvement. Chase told me he's walking with crutches in therapy and he seems sharp, as far as I can tell. Other than the accident itself, no memory loss or depression, which was a relief. And, he's back to work." She paused amid the details as she remembered whom she was talking to. "I guess you know all that, though."

"Ha! Yes. I've been keeping close tabs on him. We Skyped the other day and I was able to watch a snippet of his therapy. He grumbled about it, but his therapist and I have a friendly agreement."

"Oh, I wanted to tell you. Chase couldn't believe how much Gregory improved by the time we got back from Annapolis and after you started spending time with him."

"I'm determined to take special care of him. He's a pretty special guy. I have to say, I was a little worried about telling him I was taking a position at Memorial. I was relieved to find he was as happy as I was about that decision. Suggesting I move in with him floored me, but I think it's going to work out. Time will tell, right?"

Lacey knew exactly what she meant.

"So when are you getting here?"

"Leaving tomorrow morning! Thanks for setting me up with that agent. He's done a heck of a job and it looks like I will even end up with a little money in my pocket. We in two days."

"Nice. Well, call me tomorrow when you get close. Chase and I will both be there waiting to help you move in. He's been busy with the spring groups, but was able to keep his schedule clear since it was mid-week."

"You have no idea how much I appreciate the help. Plus, you can help me make it look like I don't have too much stuff. I swear I sold and donated everything, which felt terrific, but my SUV is still loaded. I rented a little trailer, but don't tell them."

"Your secret's safe with me. Drive carefully and see you tomorrow!"

As it turned out, Ashley wasn't kidding about still having a lot of personal belongings. Upon her arrival at Gregory's three-bedroom brick ranch, Chase and Lacey immediately started to unload her possessions. They hauled in box after box and didn't seem to make a dent in the pile. They started to stack some of the boxes in the finished basement.

"Ash, what is in all of these square boxes? They're the same size and weight and I swear it is the tenth one I've carried."

"Shoes," she sheepishly admitted as she took the box from Lacey at the front door. Gregory was positioned in the recliner in the corner as he watched the madness unfold. He smiled as Ashley carried the box to the corner he sat in and she planted a smooch on his healed cheek. He was returning to a true vision of himself.

"I owe you all big time. I feel really guilty about sitting here while you work. How about I treat you all to dinner at the Penn tonight?"

"You aren't paying for a thing," Chase grumbled as he dropped a particularly heavy box and rubbed his lower back. "You have medical bills from here to eternity."

"What do you know? Not that it's any of your business, but I don't. Insurance came through and I had a little in savings that took care of the extra. What do you say?"

They agreed a night out would be fun even if Gregory would have to abstain from his beloved ale at his favorite place. Ashley offered to be his designated driver and it was decided they would meet at five.

With the last of the boxes and bags unloaded, Chase and Lacey left and he told her he would pick her up at four thirty. She was ready and waiting when he arrived and jumped into the passenger seat as soon as he pulled into the drive.

"No music today?" she inquired.

"No one seems to appreciate it, so, I keep my eight-tracks to myself nowadays."

"They've grown on me. Kind of like you," she teased.

"Oh yeah? Is that so? Well go on right ahead and take your pick. Ladies' choice."

A dated chart topper began to fill the cabin.

"Dwight Yoakam fan, are you?" he asked in a serious tone.

"Just thought the name sounded interesting. This song's pretty good, though."

"At least you're honest."

They pulled into the parking lot and waited for Ashley and Gregory to arrive so they could help him to a table. Once they got him to the door and off the gravel, he became steady in his crutches and they stood by closely as he took a nearby seat. The slight crowd that filled the place turned in their seats and in no time at all each began to shout greetings and words of congratulations. Gregory blushed and took his seat as he tried to ignore the fanfare. One by one, the patrons arrived at the table to offer well wishes and see how he was doing. Everyone was glad he would make a full recovery.

A man with long hair and an abundance of facial hair made his way over after the crowd at the table had thinned. He asked Gregory how he was feeling and told him he was glad to see him. He asked if he remembered him.

"Um. I'm sorry. I don't," Gregory stumbled in disappointment. He'd been thankful that he was able remember everything before and after the accident until this point.

"My name's Don Mack. I have a little place a ways down from where you had your accident. I'm there mostly in the summer, but I just happened to be up there and doing some rare winter fishing when you took your little tumble down that ravine."

Gregory was overcome with gratitude.

"Don, I'm glad I get the chance to thank you in person. I think it's safe to say you saved my life by being at the right place at the right time and calling 911. Who knows how long it would have been until someone else spotted me."

Gregory's words drew the blood from his brother's face. Chase stood and approached Don.

"Don, thank you for saving my brother. Have a seat. Let me buy you a beer. It's the least I can do," Chase insisted as he pulled another chair up to the table.

Chase walked over the bar and was back in an instant with a Pabst Blue Ribbon, which he handed to the slightly familiar man. He had seen him in the Penn Tavern before and was fairly certain he had even met him at some point.

"Thanks, I appreciate that," he said as he lifted the can in a salute. "I didn't do anything out of the ordinary. How's your recovery going?"

Gregory and Don talked a little bit about the accident and Gregory's therapy while Chase tried to place the man. It wasn't long before it dawned on him. Don Baker was the current owner of the Robbins' family house. He had bought it to use primarily as a getaway for hunting and fishing trips and had a permanent residence in Albany where he had a welding business. The estate lawyer had handled all of the details of the sale of the house and Chase never knew the new owner's name, but he remembered his grandparents talking about it and had seen Don around the house as he had driven by over the years. The coincidence of it all was unreal.

"Hey, I had a question for you, if you don't mind," Don addressed Gregory.

"Yeah, sure. Anything," Gregory encouraged.

"How is that girl doing that was with you? Was that your daughter? She's the one who handed me your phone and she sure wasn't prepared for the weather in that dress."

What could they say? It wasn't important, anyway. Julia had been there for her brothers all along and always would be. No one could deny it now. That reassurance elicited eternal bliss to the newly formed family seated around the table that evening.

CHAPTER FIFTY
All That Matters

LACEY HAD BEEN BUSY with her plans. Plans she had kept to herself and was, by now, bursting at the seams to share. Chase spent all of his free time with her and the two were rarely apart. The same could be said for Ashley and Gregory who were getting along remarkably well, especially under the conditions. Ashley was doing whatever she could to help him make a full recovery and by June he walking with only a cane and any and all cosmetic traces of the accident were barely visible. As summer temperatures warmed the waters and the spring winds and rains slowed to a stop, Lacey was accompanying Chase downriver and around the nearby shallow lakes every chance they got. She couldn't get enough of this placid and serene life she had sought out for herself. Chase just couldn't get enough of her.

One sunny day, Chase had made sure his schedule was free to kayak with Lacey. He had decided to recreate their first trip downriver for a celebration of sorts. That fateful day had occurred a little less than a year ago and the bond they had formed since then was monumental. He was readying their boats at the edge of the water when she arrived. Stopping what he was doing to watch her walk toward him, his heart skipped a beat as it had when he was just a boy.

"Excuse me, yoo-hoo," she called out in a high, obnoxious voice as she waved her hands in the air. "Is this where that handsome river guide works that I hear so much about in these parts? I'd like him to guide me."

She began to laugh as she stood before him on the tips of her toes and wrapped her arms around his neck.

"I'll guide you, all right. Why don't you just come along with me," Chase said into her ear as he playfully nibbled the lobe and began to pull her toward his apartment.

"No, no, no. You are taking me out on this beautiful water. No time off for you. Let's go," she laughed.

"Yeah? Okay. You're one demanding customer. I'll take you downriver, all right. It just might take us awhile to reach our destination," he warned friskily.

Helping her into the boat, he gently pushed it from its rocky beach and out into the deeper water. Grasses swayed below and Lacey waited patiently for Chase to join her.

Soon he was paddling next to the one he had not only found true love with, but the one who saved him from himself. Giving in to the current, they relinquished control to a force of nature and found a bubble of tranquility amidst a mostly chaotic world. They were living in the moment and discovering the secret of what life was really all about. To her relief, Lacey was realizing that the real world was not so daunting as long as you remembered who you were. It really *wasn't* that hard. Much to the surprise of these independent beings, the companionship of the right partner made it even easier to find a sweeter way of life.

Silence is golden and that was particularly true when the natural world had so much to say. The babbling river's current pulled them past the signs that summer was near. White trillium grew in pleasant bunches in the shade of flowering dogwoods. Lazy ferns stood their ground beyond the muddy banks. As if on cue, the Bald Eagle's shriek called out above them and they watched in awe as it sublimely soared higher and higher. Just as it had on their first kayak trip together, the eagle made its appearance in the vicinity of Eagle Rock. Using the eagle's call as a cue, Chase suggested they break for lunch.

As they steered to shore, he held her hand as they climbed up to the rock and spread the contents of his backpack out onto the granite surface. Two beers and two waters were included.

"This has Gregory written all over it," she deduced.

"Right you are. He's been making lunches for more and more of my regulars, too. They're starting to request it. I think he has at least a side job in it."

"Did you tell him about any of our plans and how he could be involved?" Lacey opened her water and took a long, cool guzzle. It tasted good as they sat under the warm sun. Setting the water back down, she unwrapped a perfectly toasted Panini with roasted red peppers. "Okay. I think we *need* him to be a part of our plans."

Chase chuckled as he imagined the exuberance his brother would surely show upon hearing their ideas for him.

"No. I figured I'd wait to talk to you more about it. While we're on the subject, Barney's getting back in town next week. I thought of setting up a time for you and me to meet with him and discuss using Ritter's Landing as the base for the business. If you want to?"

"Yeah, sure. Next week? That'd be great. I'm really serious about doing this," Lacey looked at Chase to gauge his level of interest in her new business venture. By now, she realized he was a big part of it being successful regardless of where their relationship ended up.

Chase looked at her directly. "I'm serious about it, too. I've actually been jotting down some more ideas. Maybe we could go over them later since you're not working tonight?"

"I'd love that," she gushed before taking a bite of Panini. "Wow. He really is good. I don't even know what makes it so delicious. You know, I hear he makes one mean eggplant Parmesan. In fact, he told me he'll make it for dinner for me sometime."

Struggling to keep a straight face, she looked out at the sparkling ripples on the water.

"What did that loser tell you, exactly?"

Chase put his can of beer down with irritation.

"Just what I said," she said casually while taking another

scrumptious bite of sandwich and wiping her lips with a napkin.

"And?" Chase prodded.

"Just that he worked so hard making a dinner for you to *pass off as your own* and you ended up not even sharing it with me."

"He can be a real jerk, you know? I would have gladly served his precious dinner to you the following day if he hadn't decided to roll his truck into the river like a fool."

"Hey, that fool is your brother," she reminded him as she continued to enjoy the lunch in that setting which was more beautiful than the finest restaurant. She listened to the breeze rustle the treetops while Chase tried to avoid the infamous dinner topic.

"Yeah, well, he's caused me a lot of trouble lately. I can't believe he told you about that," he added with a honeyed smile that was impossible to start trouble with.

"I thought the whole story was really sweet. Don't be mad at him."

After lunch, Lacey kicked her river shoes off and laid back on the warm rock. Closing her eyes, she soaked up the hot, mid-day rays of the June sun before sitting up on her elbows. She thought about how quiet her mind was on this random Tuesday afternoon.

"Who does this on a Tuesday?" she pondered aloud.

"Apparently we do."

"We're pretty lucky."

"Yes, I am," he said with a glance her way.

"I know exactly what I was doing last year at this time," she continued as they relaxed side by side. Chase's visor cast a shadow eyes that scanned the tall trees lining the river. Lacey kept her own eyes closed while lying in the sun and reminiscing.

"What's that?"

"Today is June twentieth and I had a closing that I was banking on to pay some bills. I represented the sellers. The nicest couple with four adorable children. We were sitting at the closing table when I received a call. The mother was keeping the kids occupied with crayons and coloring books in the corner of the meeting room. They had a rented moving truck waiting for them in the parking lot, which the dad planned on driving to closing on their new home. A home that they were to move into that evening. The buyer's agent called to tell me that the buyer was backing out of the deal. For no reason other than finding a house he liked a little more at the last minute."

"What kind of creep does that to a family?" Chase asked in disgust.

"The worst part, like I said, was that the sellers were to close on their new home that same day, so, we had this horrible chain reaction to contend with. I still get sick to my stomach thinking about it. If I never have to live a work day like that June twentieth again, I think I will like whatever job I end up."

"Sounds like I need to make sure the twentieth of June takes on new memories for you."

Pulling his visor backward, he leaned over and eclipsed the sunshine from her face. The giant trees loomed above before a blue backdrop. Tenderly, he kissed the old memories away.

After their riverside picnic, they paddled gently in unison. There was not another person in sight while the sunlight flickered atop the water. Occasionally a fish jumped with a quick splash. Ducks gathered along the riverbank and glided out to their kayaks to beg for a handout. Taking in the spring-to-summer scene frame by frame as it unfolded, they eventually began the turn that approached the battered and timeworn stone building with which Chase was enamored.

"I saw someone's been working on the General Store when I took a group out last week. I meant to tell you. For Sale sign's down. That's one missed opportunity," Chase said wistfully.

"Oh, yeah?" Lacey glanced at him as she tried to think of what to say next. She knew how much that building meant to him and he would be crushed to know someone bought it.

"Looks that way. Oh, well. There will be other opportunities for me. For us," he said as he looked at Lacey.

"You said it. Today is just too beautiful to think about missed opportunities."

"You're right. How about we pull over and take advantage of a little opportunity?"

His crafty tone told Lacey he had other things in mind, but so did she and right now she wanted to keep on paddling.

"Hmmm. Very tempting, but we must continue on. You are not a very professional river guide, I must say."

"Never claimed to be, Miss Williams."

Lacey looked over at the stone structure and noticed a contractor looking up at the balcony. He walked back around the side of the building and out of sight. She noticed most of the weeds and overgrown shrubbery had been removed and the building was looking less forlorn. "You're right. There is some activity over there. Let's go talk to them and see what's going on with it," Lacey suggested.

"I don't know. I'm not really sure I want to know."

"Come on. Maybe there'll be a business opening up again. You're gonna want to know about it, right?"

She looked at him hopefully.

"How can I ever say no to you? All right. You win. Let's see what we can find out."

Swiftly, they moved in for a closer look. Not only had the weeds and shrubbery been cleared and trimmed, but also the balcony had been re-supported and the original flower boxes and shutters had been restored and painted black again. Some new windows were put in place and the little building was once again inviting. The workers were placing the last of their tools in their trucks and started to pull away as Lacey and Chase beached their boats on a sandy portion of the shoreline.

"Looks like they just left. Maybe we should head back out on the water?" Chase said as Lacey exited her kayak. She motioned for him to follow her and he obliged.

"No harm in looking around. Maybe the owner's here,"

Lacey called out over her shoulder and in no time at all, Chase was following her.

She got to the main door and knocked. With no answer she looked at Chase and shrugged her shoulders. He looked around a little bit and turned to leave.

"Well, whoever bought is doing a great job with it. That's nice to see," Chase reasoned as he started to walk away.

"I think she is, too. Want to take a look inside?"

Chase stopped and turned to see what Lacey was up to. In her hand was a key the she dangled in front of her.

"What do you mean?"

"What I mean is, *I* am the owner and *I* have been working with the contractor to restore this beautiful building which will soon be a new home and business."

Chase began to walk toward her shaking his head, his face a vision of pure amazement.

"Our new home if you care to join me in this little adventure," she added as he stood before her.

"You're kidding me? How? When?"

"For awhile now. Let's go in and I'll tell you all about it."

"Well, just wait one second. I'm anxious to hear about your scheming ways, but if you think I'm going to shack up with you and live in sin, well, you just don't know me very well," Chase said in a mocking tone.

Lacey wrapped her arms around his waist and leaned in for a kiss. He obliged before pulling away and kneeling before her.

"You see, you're not the only one who has been keeping a secret," Chase revealed as he reached into his pocket to pull out a little black box. Opening it, a diamond ring flashed wildly.

"Lacey Williams, I now realize I've been in love with you since I was about twelve years old. Will you marry me?"

Hands covered a sentimental heart before tears of joy began flowing from her eyes. Unable to speak, she nodded tenderly as she extended her shaking left hand. Chase placed the age-old sign of mutual commitment and love on her slender finger. Standing, he pulled her close and up into his arms to share an amorous embrace and kiss that represented hope and new beginnings. Lifting her up and into his arms, he opened the door and prematurely carried his bride-to-be over the threshold. Neither knew what the future had in store for them. Regardless, together they would carve out a life based on appreciation, simple pleasures and loving companionship.

They had met during an innocent stage of life. As tendency would have it, complications and strife had seeped in and eroded that innocence while pushing them along different paths. They were suddenly back on course and had every intention of keeping it that way. Shielding their lives from the potential ravages of time would be a full time job and they were up to the challenge. Distractions that threatened hard-earned joy would not be tolerated.

From the nearby thickets and unseen, a girl with a beaming angelic face and a pretty blue dress drifted gloriously to her heavenly resting place. For now, the ones she cared about most were happy and that was all that mattered.

Acknowledgments

Thank you to Laura Thomas, Lawrence Thomas and Frances Munko for showing me the meaning and joy of simple pleasures and unconditional love. Simple pleasures such as the hours spent reading to me as a child. I cherish those memories. Over time, that fostered a love of reading and writing that simply could not be quelled.

For taking time to provide invaluable and critical feedback: Laura Thomas, Jennifer Hartle, Heather Thomas, Branden Weber and Elizabeth Redhead Kriston. I am appreciative beyond words.

Lauren and Hannah Weber - I live for you and you inspire me to live to the fullest every day. xoxo

Branden Weber - you are truly an amazing person and I am humbled and grateful to be able to share my life with you. Why you consistently and whole-heartedly believe in and encourage me is something I will never understand. I love you for that among so many other reasons.

About the Author

Dana Thomas Weber resides in a small Pennsylvania town along the Allegheny River with her husband, two young daughters, and their Portuguese Water Dog, Pepper. She documents their simple life on the tourism and lifestyle blog, **www.Emlenton.org**.

Ms. Weber's official author website can be found at
www.DanaThomasWeber.com

Holland Press

www.HollandPress.co

Made in the USA
Charleston, SC
07 August 2016